VERITY

Center Point
Large Print

Also by Lisa T. Bergren and available from Center Point Large Print:

Keturah

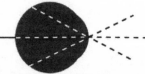

This Large Print Book carries the Seal of Approval of N.A.V.H.

The Sugar Baron's Daughters • TWO

VERITY

Lisa T. Bergren

CENTER POINT LARGE PRINT
THORNDIKE, MAINE

This Center Point Large Print edition
is published in the year 2019 by arrangement with
Bethany House Publishers,
a division of Baker Publishing Group.

This is a work of historical reconstruction; the appearances of certain historical figures are therefore inevitable. All other characters, however, are products of the author's imagination, and any resemblance to actual persons, living or dead, is coincidental.

The text of this Large Print edition is unabridged.
In other aspects, this book may vary
from the original edition.
Printed in the United States of America
on permanent paper.
Set in 16-point Times New Roman type.

ISBN: 978-1-64358-191-0

Library of Congress Cataloging-in-Publication Data

Names: Bergren, Lisa Tawn, author.
Title: Verity / Lisa T. Bergren.
Description: Center Point Large Print edition. | Thorndike, Maine :
    Center Point Large Print, 2019. | Series: The Sugar Baron's daughters
Identifiers: LCCN 2019009285 | ISBN 9781643581910 (hardcover :
    alk. paper)
Subjects: LCSH: Large type books.
Classification: LCC PS3552.E71938 V47 2019b | DDC 813/.54—dc23
LC record available at https://lccn.loc.gov/2019009285

For Emma,
Learning to follow where God leads,
and trust him as you wait.
I love you.
—Mama

VERITY

CHAPTER ONE

Spring, 1775
Nevis, West Indies

There was nothing for it. Verity had to set aside her misgivings and do what she felt she ought. She dug her booted heels into Fiona's flanks, and the big chestnut mare resumed their climb up the steep, rocky path. She wished her resolve could be as steady and sure as her mount's gait. Because what was to come . . . well, the mere thought of it left her feeling quite ill.

Verity found her sister where she knew she would, this time in the morn, on the promontory high above the top field of what once had been called Tabletop, but now, combined with Teller's Landing, was called the Double T. The view was marvelous up here, where one could see all of the Covingtons' land and out across the blue-green waters of the Caribbean and Atlantic, stretching toward St. Kitts and Saba. It was Ket's favorite place to think and pray.

Keturah glanced over her shoulder and smiled as her sister came into view. Ket's mare's ears twitched, and she tossed her mane and whinnied a greeting to Fiona. Ver's horse snorted a dismissive response. "Do not be rude," she chided her.

Ket giggled. "So uppity, your Fiona!" She leaned forward to pat the mare's neck as if to soothe any hurt feelings.

Primus sat on a svelte brown gelding beyond Ket, keeping silent watch. He gave Verity a nod in greeting, smiling along with them over their horses' antics. Her own guardian, Gideon, reached the clearing and sidled up beside Primus to wait. This was Gray Covington's only requirement of the Banning women: They could go where they wished, when they wished, but never alone.

High above them, Brutus circled and screeched. Ket gestured upward. "I knew you must be somewhere about."

"I should send him with you each morn," Verity said, shielding her eyes to watch the falcon ride the trade winds. "He loves it up here." She pulled Fiona in a tight circle so she could come alongside Ket and look out. Down below, acres of sugarcane waved in the wind. "It appears as if it shall be another winning crop for the Double T."

"If God smiles on us again, we shall be harvesting come late summer or early fall."

"He did last time. What should make Him frown now?"

Ket took a long, deep breath. Her hand traced

her round belly. "I do not know. 'Tis only that now—with a babe on the way—I find myself wanting security more than ever."

Verity reached out and took her hand. "All of this—" she paused to look outward—"is lovely, tempting in her abundance. But you've been on-island long enough, Ket, and heard enough stories to know that what can be given can also be easily taken away. We have to trust that God will see us through the years of plenty as well as the years of lean. You've done all you could; you must trust in God to see it through."

" 'Tis a good reminder," Ket said, giving her hand a squeeze and casting her a grateful look. "I do not know what I would do without you, Ver."

Verity swallowed hard and gently pulled her hand away. Of all the things to say right at this moment . . .

Keturah frowned. "Ver?"

She sighed, inwardly reminding herself of her decision. "You always were a planter at heart, Ket, just as Father was. But my blood flows fastest when I am with the horses. Or at market. I love it here on the Double T, but . . . of late I have been thinking of other options—other places I might be called to live and work."

"Other places?" Ket said, blinking slowly. "Such as?"

"Other islands. Or even America," she said, grinning with excitement.

Keturah's frown deepened, and she sat more erect in her saddle. "So 'tis it, then?" she said stiffly. "You intend to leave us?"

"Do not say it that way," Verity said, slowly shaking her head and reaching out to rest a hand on her sister's knee. "You know I shall never leave you. Not for long, anyway. I am thinking of visiting other places but building something of my own in Charlestown."

"Charlestown," Ket repeated, as if it were a foreign city and not the town only half an hour distant.

"Come now, Ket. You have Gray and a babe on the way now. Selah. The plantation, our people. I must . . . I must be free to find my own way too. Please do not treat me as a prodigal asking for her inheritance in advance. I merely want what you did—a chance to prove myself, to follow a path that God seems to be pointing out to me."

Keturah considered that for a long moment. "How much has Captain McKintrick's silence influenced this decision?"

"Not at all," Verity said. Then, "Or some. Oh, I do not know." She glanced over at Gideon and Primus and then waved them down the path, wanting more space, more privacy for her and Ket. Even here, here on this blessed mountain, she was feeling trapped. Confined. As if she could not breathe freely. Again came the urge from deep within. The pull to leave. The desire to find out what had become of Duncan McKintrick. To discover something new.

"I ran across Mr. Jobel in town. He informed me that the funds from the sale of Hartwick have arrived. I intend to take my portion and set sail for the American colonies," Verity said, forcing herself to level a gaze at Keturah. "At my first opportunity."

"You might not like what you find there, Verity," Ket warned. "Perhaps there the captain has found . . . other distractions. Perhaps that is the reason for his silence."

Verity shifted in her saddle, refusing to rise to the bait. "If the captain simply suffered a change in his affections, I have no doubt that he would have written to me and explained. 'Tis not like him to simply be silent. Not after . . ."

Not after all they had shared. Not after his sweet, fervent declarations to her. Not after he'd promised her that he would return in all haste. No, a man did not look at a woman like Duncan McKintrick had her and then simply never return to the Indies. It was not in his making. Verity was certain of it.

"You should never have given a sea captain your heart, Ver," Keturah said, shaking her head in both sorrow and reproof. "Did I not warn you of the danger of it?"

Verity laughed under her breath. "And who

13

are you, Sissy, to lecture me about how others might disappoint you? Of how it is dangerous to follow your heart? Was it not you who led us to this wild, wonderful isle? Are we not continually in danger here? From disease? From uprisings? From drought? Can you not feel it, Ket? The winds of change? Anywhere might be considered dangerous."

Keturah looked out and surveyed their land, the sea, and closed her eyes as the trade winds wafted her hair. When she opened them, she turned to Verity and said, " 'Tis true. There are no promises in tomorrow, only the hope in today."

"Indeed. And my hope, today, leads me to this. I want my share of what remains of our Hartwick fortune because I want to build something new. For me. Perhaps for all of us."

Ket's mare, sensing her tension, pranced and shifted a bit, but her sister resolutely stared outward, jaw clenched. After a long moment she said, "What would you build?"

"A mercantile, in town. I want to sail to the colonies and bring back horses and more to trade, Ket. If I become a merchant, perhaps it shall prove a boon to you too. My trade might benefit the Double T, allow me to discover new import and export options for you and Gray. Ways to maneuver around those who would rather see you give up and move home to England."

She let that settle a bit with her sister. She could

see Ket was working through the concept of it, as well as the idea of letting her go.

"I need the truth, Ket. Of what has become of Duncan. And to find out if I could be a successful merchant at all. Right now, there are only two islands regularly importing horses—Hispaniola and Jamaica. The Leewards need a source too. I have gained word about some good potential breeders, both in North Carolina as well as New York."

Keturah's eyes rounded and Verity laughed under her breath. "Come now, Ket. I am not a silly twit with a dream, giving no thought as to how I might accomplish it. Tell me, how do you spend your time at every soiree on-island when your handsome husband is not insisting you join him for a dance?"

Ket's brow wrinkled as she considered the question. "Learning more of what might benefit our plantation and her people."

Verity nodded once. "As do I, though from a different direction. Over the year past, I have made inroads with men who do significant trade in the colonies. You taught me well, Sister. The Double T—seeing it come to this—has taught me well."

Together they stared down at the verdant fields, at the long lines of men and women entering the western side to work along the trenches, Gray and Matthew and Philip among them. Inspired by their relationship with their emancipated overseer, Matthew, Ket and Gray were gradually employing freed men and women rather than purchasing new slaves. With the proceeds of Hartwick's sale, they had offered the rest the chance to earn their freedom too, but it would take years to transition to a fully paid staff. Word of their plans had made them even more the pariahs among the other planters, who wished to brook no conversation on the matter. The Covingtons' decision was widely considered a direct threat to the planters' traditional way of life. They had received few social invitations of late, and just last week Gray had been refused supplies at two of the four importers of goods.

Keturah took a deep breath, then reached out to take her sister's hand again. "You know I do not wish to hold you back, Verity. Never would I wish that." She shot her a glance, her amber eyes full of tears. "But the idea of you going from me . . . from us . . . never to return . . ." She shook her head fiercely and rubbed a gloved hand under her nose, sniffed, straightened her shoulders. "Well, I could never countenance that."

"Nor could I," Verity replied. "So I shall see to it that it does not transpire."

"Promise?" Keturah asked. And in that moment, Ket did not seem the older sister, a grown woman, a wife and mother-to-be, the lady of this plantation. She seemed more a small girl.

Verity remembered being children on Oak Hill, running barefoot through the bramble and grass, hunkering down beneath the roots of a giant tree in a makeshift cave. And the three of them—Keturah, Verity, and Selah—making solemn pledges to forever be together. To never part.

It had been a girl's naïve promise, not a woman's. Before they'd faced potential financial calamity, the depravity of men, or known the world outside of England.

"I can only promise to return to Nevis as fast as I might," Verity said, squeezing her hand. "You know I would miss you and Selah far too much to do anything else."

"I know," Keturah said, her mouth twisting in concern.

She tried to pull her hand from Verity's then, but Ver held on. "Ket. Please do not send me away without your blessing."

"Oh, my dear sister, do you not see? I cannot bless our separation. 'Tis not within me. You yourself insisted you come with me to Nevis. Do you not remember how it felt to be the one who might be left behind?" They shared a long glance, her heart, her pain in her eyes. Ket squeezed her hand and then pulled away; this time, Verity allowed it.

It was enough, that. More than she expected, really. "I shall return, Ket."

But Keturah only nodded sadly, lifted her reins

and turned her mare down the path, her usually straight, proud shoulders slightly hunched and shaking. And Verity knew she wept.

Her breath caught. They had seen many people depart the island, never to return. Some lost to a storm, others to illness. Had not Duncan himself promised to return to her, then disappeared? What made her think that she was any less vulnerable to fail at fulfilling her own promise?

Please, Lord, she prayed, looking back to the northern waters, as if she could see all the way to the American colonies. *Please keep me safe, and those dear to my heart safe here on-island too.*

She waited a moment, paused to see if her heavenly Father might direct her differently, but this path seemed to only swiftly solidify before her. 'Twas what He desired for her.

She was certain of it.

Captain Ian McKintrick strode down Broadway in New York, coat flapping behind him. He was reasonably aware that his grim face and demeanor made the tide of people he faced part for him but found himself unable to care. He was here for one reason and one reason alone—to settle his brother's affairs. See to his belongings. Empty his small apartment. Close his accounts.

He refused to weep again. Not only was he out in public, but he had wept more for his older brother in the weeks past than he had ever wept for his parents and grandparents. Perhaps it drew down to the fact that he had never imagined anything could kill his beloved brother. From the time he was but a wee lad, he'd seen Duncan— three years his elder—as invincible.

A glimpse of red brought his head up, slowed his step, but it was only a lady of ill repute on the corner, not one of the redcoats who so easily drew his ire these days. He turned around, remembering his sister Marjorie begging him not to pick any fights with the English. "It shall do you no good, Ian, nor Duncan," she had enjoined, urgently grabbing his lapels to make him stand still and meet her gaze. "What's done is done. Duncan would not want ye in prison on his account. Agreed?"

"Aye, agreed, lass," he'd slowly replied. But his agreement had not taken away the hate-filled fire that burned in his belly. It was the cursed English who had pressed Duncan into service, forcing him to accept a shipment bound for the Barbary Coast. It was the cursed English who had oppressed his kin for generations. The cursed English who had stolen their lands. The cursed English who had forced his grandfather to pledge his fealty after Culloden.

He and Duncan had spent many a night dis-cussing it. Was his Jacobite grandfather's pledge one that he must honor? It was a Scotsman's way to hold to such things, yet there was talk in every tavern he visited here in the colonies, some whispered, some shouted. Even in New York, where the Loyalists still clung to power. Talk about taxation without representation, separation, independence, freedom . . . and by the heavens, that talk only seemed to fan the flames of rage that burned in his belly.

Duncan was gone. Stolen from the clan forever. Pressed to fetch a shipment of spices that the king's cook had insisted he must have straight from the Dark Continent. It had been a stroke of ill luck that Duncan had arrived in the Liverpool magistrate's office directly after the man had received the orders from London. He'd been there solely to file his plans with the harbormaster to set sail in two weeks. Marjorie did not know why he had been in such a rush. "Why, he'd been home but two days when he set to establishing his next cargo for a return trip."

"To where?"

"New York, o' course," she said. "But I think he had plans to go by way of the Indies again." She'd given Ian a sad smile, wringing her hands. "Something about him made me think he had an eye on a lass there. I'd never seen him in such a state."

She hadn't known the girl's name, nor where she lived exactly. 'Twas odd, that. Duncan was— had been, he corrected himself with an inward wince—as open with his mind and heart as Ian

20

was cautious. The man had rarely encountered a secret he could keep; it had been a family joke since they were but lads. It had been with Ian that Marjorie shared any of her true secrets; she only told Duncan when she had not a care who knew.

Oh, my brother, he thought, feeling a familiar lump form in his throat at the thought of the man sharing one of his many stories. Had he not told of outrunning—or outgunning—several pirates in years past? He had not even made it to the coast of Africa, this time waylaid by a Spaniard privateer named Santiago. Why had the Spaniard not imprisoned and ransomed his brother, rather than kill him? Ian looked up to the slate gray skies. *Where were you, Lord? Why did you not intervene on his behalf?*

He shook his head in disgust and turned the corner, dodging a lad selling dried mackerel and a woman selling jugs of grog. The harbor edged nearer again, the smell of brine and tar briefly overcoming the foul stench of the city—spoiled food, human waste, and unwashed bodies. Ian disliked spending much time within the confines of stone and mortar. Like his brother and their father before them, he'd been born for the sea. He loved the water whether it was raging, tall and fearsome, or dancing with tidy whitecaps or even resting in glistening, flat doldrums. He loved reading what was ahead by studying the horizon, feeling the moisture on his skin, in his nostrils.

From the start, he'd been a better sailor than Duncan. He'd made first mate and captained his own ship a year before Duncan had managed to do so. He'd purchased his first vessel a year before him too.

That made him smile, the first in a while. But then he'd reached the old boardinghouse in which Duncan had rented a room. And thinking of seeing his belongings, the last things he'd touched before leaving American soil . . .

Soberly, Ian removed his tricorn, brought it to his chest and banged the iron knocker against the huge mahogany door, waiting for the building's mistress or master to come to him. *Oh, Duncan, lad,* he thought again, swallowing hard. *How could ye have up and died? How is it that I shall not find ye here waiting on me?*

It seemed impossible that Duncan was gone— even now, eight weeks after learning the truth of it. He was gone, gone forever.

And it was all the fault of the cursed English.

CHAPTER TWO

Verity sat down at the table for her final breakfast at the Double T, politely acknowledging the four British soldiers the Covingtons had been forced to house. The Nevis Assembly had not come to an agreement yet on building the defensive forces a proper garrison, and so the planters who had so vociferously demanded military support had been asked to each quarter a portion of the hundred men stationed there. Those nearest Charlestown, of course, were looked to first.

Verity usually felt sorry for the poor men; they clearly felt ill at ease over the Bannings' forced hospitality. Yet there was simply nowhere else for them to go, and since the Nevisians' agents lobbying in Parliament on their behalf had demanded it, there was nothing to do but accept it. But today . . . of all days, she wished it was only family present.

Selah sniffed, took a dainty bite of eggs, and refused to look her way. Ever since she had told her younger sister she was to set sail, she'd acted as if Verity had stabbed her in the heart. Honestly, the only thing to do was to get on with it and return; 'twould be the only thing that would ease the tension between all three of them.

The men shared surreptitious glances and sipped their tea, well aware by now of the difficulty between the sisters. Captain Howard, ever the gentleman, fished a handkerchief from inside his coat when Selah again sniffed and hurriedly brushed the corner of her eye.

"Please do not cry, Miss Selah," he said. "Your sister shall return to us in but a hop, skip, and a jump."

"I shall," Verity said, purposefully ignoring the captain's own sorrowful, longing glance. She took a warm bun from a basket that the rather rotund Lieutenant Angersoll passed her, then helped herself to a thick dollop of butter. It irritated her, the captain's words *return to us.* Who were they to so thoroughly insert themselves in private family business? This all would be so much easier if they were not at their table this morn!

"And we shall do our best to keep you company in her absence," Second Lieutenant Cesley added, casting Selah a long look.

Of course you shall, Verity thought darkly. He and Angersoll followed their every move each time they were in proximity. While Angersoll seemed innocently curious—as if he'd never been about women of stature—Cesley and the middle-aged Major Woodget gave her an unpleasant feeling. Not the foreboding she felt every time

24

they'd neared their neighbor's former overseer, Angus Shubert, but something akin to it.

It was untenable really. There was a reason that soldiers were generally stationed in separate quarters; to put them in genteel homes was to ask for mischief, or worse. Had not Esmerelda Weland turned up pregnant just last month and then hurriedly rushed into a marriage with a soldier far beneath her station? Verity narrowed a glance at Selah. Had all her warnings—and Keturah's—been enough to keep the bighearted girl from doing something foolish?

It comforted her that the soldiers—to a man—chafed at how Selah spent so much time with the field workers. Clearly, Major Woodget thought it unseemly, while Captain Howard found it distasteful, and the two lieutenants might very well consider it her sole shortcoming. Happily, her duties of seeing to the sick and teaching the children kept her from the house most evenings. By day the soldiers went to report to Charlestown, leaving only mornings for these odd meetings between them all.

Keturah arrived, muttering her apologies for her tardiness while still folding a letter newly come from London. To preoccupy her so, it was likely from their father's attorney, Clement Abercrombie. Mitilda approached with a steaming bowl of porridge and gracefully served one man after another.

Second Lieutenant Cesley let his eyes linger on the pretty black woman's hip and rear as she bent. Verity pointedly stared at him until he felt the heat of her gaze, and a blush rose at his jawline. She didn't grin back when he attempted to send her an innocent shrug and the blush grew deeper. Over the last year and a half, the girls had come to care for Mitilda and their half brother, Abraham. Not a one of them would allow a guest of their home to make any inappropriate overtures with Mitilda—or any other servant on the premises. While other families on-island might look the other way, the Covingtons and Bannings refused to do so.

Gray and Philip were last, as usual. The conch shell called the field hands to rise and report before sunrise; the men accompanied Matthew and the rest to the field, consulted on what was to be done that day, began to work for a time, and then returned to break their fast. They washed their hands and faces in the kitchen, toweled off, and rolled down their sleeves before joining the others—since the arrival of the soldiers, donning coats too.

Gray bent and kissed Keturah on the cheek while still straightening his coat. He knew that she cared not if he wore it or not, but he did so as a sign of respect for her and their shared household. Inwardly, Verity sighed. There wasn't much about her brother-in-law she didn't adore, and day by day she thought her sister's love deepened for her husband too. The promise of the pregnancy—a surprise after her barren years with Lord Tomlinson, Keturah's first husband—had only seemed to cement their devotion to each other.

He greeted the men and Selah, then winked at Verity as he took his seat and unfolded a napkin. "Your last full day with us, is it?"

Well he knew it. But he was the first to openly speak of it and neither frown nor weep.

She nodded, unable to keep an impish grin from spreading.

He cast a furtive glance to her sisters, but observing that Ket still perused her letter and Selah spoke with Philip, he covertly returned her smile, reached out and touched her hand. "All will be well," he whispered. "Your father would be most proud of you."

"You think so?" she whispered back.

"I do," he said, taking a spoonful of steaming porridge when Mitilda stopped beside him. "After he was done throttling you, of course. But it would go against a Banning female's nature to not go where she was forbidden."

Verity stabbed several slices of mango with her two-pronged fork and set them on her plate before passing it to Gray. "Am I forbidden to go?"

"Not in so many words, no."

27

"Truly it feels less daunting than setting sail for Nevis. I assume New York shall remind me of London or Liverpool."

"I daresay. Still, it would please your father, as it does your sister and me, that Philip will accompany you."

She turned her smile to the older man. "It is most kind of you, Philip, to agree to it."

"Speak no more of it," he said, bending his head in consternation in the face of her gratitude. " 'Tis far less hardship to be your guardian than it is his," he said, ribbing Gray.

Gray lifted a brow. "Doubtless, the man speaks the truth. Were I not an expectant father, I'd have volunteered for the task myself. I'd give an eyetooth to see New York or the Carolinas for myself."

"Not without me would you go," Keturah said, setting aside her letter. "Perhaps if Verity succeeds in her business ventures, there shall be cause for us all to go in the years to come."

"If?" Verity asked, pretending to be dismayed at any portion of doubt. "You meant to say when, of course."

Keturah smiled. "Pardon, Sissy. I meant to say when you succeed in your business ventures, there shall undoubtedly be cause. Shall we visit you in your new home on Wall Street? Or Long Island? Or along the Carolina shore?"

"If I am not in my tidy shop apartment in

Charlestown, visiting you every other day," she added firmly, catching Selah's eye, "then I shall expect you to come and enjoy a cooler summer with me among the American colonies."

"And you shall come to celebrate Christmas and the winter here," Selah said.

"Far better to winter in the tropics than 'tis in New York," put in Lieutenant Angersoll. He shivered, causing his jowls to tremble. "Only takes one foul season in those miserable clapboard barracks to make one long for England. Even England is more temperate than New York. And here we have mangoes!" he added gleefully, sliding his own slices of fruit off the serving plate.

Verity nodded toward the affable young man, yet she couldn't help but feel as if he'd intruded on a private family moment. What he'd said was appropriate and relevant, but it had broken the momentum of her banter with Gray and Keturah, even a bit with Selah, and all abruptly fell silent.

"You leave on the morrow, then, Miss Verity?" Major Woodget asked, wiping his mouth and beard with the napkin.

"We sail midmorning," she affirmed.

"Do you have Loyalist kin up in New York?" His graying brows furrowed in concern. "The rebels grow thick in New England."

"I do," she said. "A cousin in New York and his wife shall be glad to greet me."

"Good. They shall see to your safety then, just as we shall see to the rest of your family here."

What sweet relief, she thought sourly as she sipped her tea to keep from retorting aloud. *As if Gray and Matthew and the others could not see to themselves . . .*

Ian spent the night in Duncan's room, drinking the remains of a bottle of whiskey and listening to the sounds of bickering, laughter, and an amorous young couple in neighboring rooms. His brother had been as accustomed to the close quarters of a ship as Ian was himself; he found comfort in the sensation of being alone, surrounded by a few of his brother's possessions and yet not isolated. It reminded him that he wasn't adrift upon a sea of his own grief; there were islands of humanity that pointed him in the direction of home.

He felt less content with it come morn. Waking to the sound of a slamming door and the wail of a baby's cry, he groaned and turned over, blinking until his blurry eyes cleared. Duncan had left little behind. The bottle with three fingers of whiskey; a threadbare coat and torn trousers; stockings that needed mending; a washbasin and pitcher. But atop the small writing desk was a finely wrought silver inkstand, several quills, a new bottle of India ink, and ten sheets of linen paper. At the top his brother had written, *10 September 1774,* and the words *My Dearest*

Verity, then nothing more. Had he been called away? Disrupted, never to return to it? Had he been reluctant to go on with the letter, puzzling over how to . . . what? Profess his undying love in some new manner? Or perhaps to let the poor girl know that his heart had led him to another? Was this the lass whom Marjorie had suspected drove Duncan to return in such haste?

Ian sighed heavily and turned onto his back. Above him, a young mother was crooning to the wailing baby, walking back and forth in their attic bedroom. Bits of dust filtered between the boards, drifting down to the floor and chair and bed and desk of the spare room, across the clothing that would never be repaired, over stockings that would never be darned, over a bottle that would never yield another drink for either brother again. " 'Tis like watching a burial in layers," Ian muttered, casting his legs over the edge of the bed, then forcing himself to rise. He vigorously rubbed his face and ran his fingers through his unruly hair. For the first time he realized Duncan had not a looking glass in his small apartment.

He padded over to the pitcher and bowl in the corner, took up the vessel, and peeked outside. As expected, a servant had left a fresh one filled with water by the door, as well as an empty chamber pot. Ian sighed in relief. While the establishment was clearly meant for tenants who needed to stretch their last ha'penny, it was at least clean.

He traded the chamber pots and an empty pitcher for the full one and then closed the door. He went to the washstand, poured half in the bowl, then set to washing his face, neck, chest, and arms. Then he went to his bag and fished out a reasonably clean shirt—he'd need to leave the rest with a local laundress. After all, he intended to set sail in a couple of days, and he never left port without all his clothing in fine order. The voyage oft became unbearable without the promise of fresh linen to greet him every other morning. Some of the men teased him about his "fine ways," but he always saw a quick end to such ribbing—and a better-smelling crew on the whole—by assigning them mid-voyage laundry duty.

Ian went to the writing desk and took the sheet of paper—perhaps the last his brother had ever written to anyone—folded it, and slid it into his jacket pocket. The inkstand and quill would be given to the lady who ran this boardinghouse in trade for the rent she was owed. The clothing she could give to the workhouse. Ian wanted none of it.

With a last look around the room—as if making certain he wasn't missing anything that would help him remember his brother—he closed the door and went downstairs to knock on Mrs. Eplett's door.

A moment later, the short, squat woman opened the door. She patted her apron straps and cap as though still wondering if all was in order. "Ah, Captain McKintrick. I take it you are to be on your way?"

"Indeed," he said, shifting his tricorn in his hands. "Would ye kindly accept my brother's fine inkstand and quills as any payment yet owed ye?"

"Ach, the man owed me nothing. In fact, he paid me for six months' rent, two of them yet outstanding."

"Then do me a favor. Accept the inkstand and quills as payment to allow some other poor soul rest for a couple of months after I leave. Perhaps someone down on his luck, looking for a job? That would please my brother greatly, to aid an unmet friend in need."

She squinted up at him as if puzzled by the request. "Aye, that I can do. But do you not wish to hold on to the place in case you return in the coming months?"

"I've sold my ship but aim to purchase another and set sail in posthaste. In a month's time I ought to be gone for good. There is nothing more for me here. Not now . . ." His voice cracked, and he hurriedly looked away, coughed and blinked back tears. "Nay, I was only here to set the last of my brother's affairs in order. I might spend a few more nights. But no more."

She nodded, tears now in her own small eyes. "He was a fine man, your brother. Spread

33

kindness and glad tidings where'er he went."

"That he did." Ian turned to go and then remembered just as the mistress of the house was shutting the door. "Mrs. Eplett?"

She opened the door again. "Yes?"

"Do you perhaps know a woman named Verity? Someone my brother might have . . . fancied? I found a letter begun to her but never finished. He had not mentioned a woman to me, and I thought . . . well, I thought I might seek her out. To inform her of Duncan's passing."

"Verity, you say?" She squinted, crossed her rounded arms, giving it some thought. "Nay, the only Verity I know is an old dowager across the East River."

"I see," he said, swallowing a sigh. "Thank you." He set his tricorn firmly atop his head. "Good day, Mrs. Eplett."

"Good day, lad. God be with you."

"And ye as well."

But as Ian joined the tide of shouting people, carriages and horses and mules and stray dogs, once again he wondered if God was within anyone's reach at all.

CHAPTER THREE

It took a week to reach New York from Nevis, and Verity enjoyed every moment. She spent her time discussing suppliers with two merchants from the Dutch-held St. Eustatius—a Jew named Mr. Loeb and an American named Statler—who both treated her as a precious amusement. She tolerated their patronizing ways and conversation, intent on finding out what she must, much like Keturah had always done with the planters of Nevis. "Grin and bear it and always be a lady," Keturah had told her as she pinned the last of her wavy hair into a knot, "then quietly beat them at their own game."

Philip had laughed at this, as had Gray. Only Selah remained consistently sober.

"I shall be back before you know it," Verity had promised her little sister again. "See to Ket, will you? Make certain she isn't out in the fields for more than a few hours and never overtaxes herself? After all, we must look out for our future little niece or nephew."

Selah nodded, gave her one last squeeze, and then tore herself away, tears dripping down her cheeks.

"She shall be all right, in time," Keturah said, taking Verity's arm and leading her toward the ship. "Trust me, in a day or two she'll be distracted and only suffer momentary moments of melancholy. And before you ask," she said, arching a brow, "I'll be sure to see that Abraham does as he promised to look after both Brutus and Fiona."

Verity smiled gratefully. And then with a pounding heart she strode up the gangplank with far more assurance than when she'd embarked on the *Restoration*. Both sisters had managed to wave and blow kisses her way as the ship's sails were unfurled and they headed out into the strong winds of the Atlantic. She'd watched the shore until she could no longer make them out, praying all the while that God would keep watch over them all.

Six days later, she spent most of each morning at the rail, watching as the ship skimmed along the coast of North America. In the afternoons she retired to her cabin to review her lists of potential supplies for her new mercantile . . . as well as ideas of how she might gain word of Captain McKintrick's whereabouts. Surely in a city as populated as New York, there would be a crewman or soldier or merchant who could point her in his direction.

She swallowed hard, the dark thought again haranguing her. Perhaps he was not ill or at sea.

Perhaps he had simply found another. After all, had not her own father found a way to assuage his longings for her mother by taking up with a mistress? If it was not out of bounds for him, what made her think it would be for Captain McKintrick, a man who had never formalized his intentions with her?

Nay. It simply was not his way. She remembered how he had defended Keturah on board the ship with the first mate. How he had risen to Selah's defense when attacked. How he had treated Verity with such tenderness at every turn. Nay, it was not his way. If he had had a change of heart, he would have come to tell her of it. Or at least written.

But what if he had written and the letter lost its way? What if he had written in haste and had not the time to send a copy, in case the first went astray?

That was it. He had tried, but somehow the letter had gone astray. He was somewhere at sea, longing for her as she had for him. And in time they would be reunited.

Or in New York she would discover the truth at last.

After a day spent closing his brother's bank account, visiting an attorney and establishing an agreement to see to any further issues that might arise when Ian was overseas, he wearily entered a tavern, intent on nothing but sipping a tankard of ale before returning to Mrs. Eplett's boarding-house. Yet the thought of seeing Duncan's belongings again made him feel sick to his stomach. Nay, he could not abide it, staying any longer than he must. It made him feel close to Duncan . . . and yet not close enough. As if his brother were but on another ship, slipping by his starboard edge but impossible to see through a dense fog.

The more Ian thought about it, the more he grew agitated. And one tankard of ale led to another and then another. Two men sat down beside him, then a third. They were American-born, and talk soon lapsed into how it wasn't right the way the Brits behaved. "Lordin' over us, acting as if they were but King Georgie themselves."

"Ought to cast them out, make them swim for home," muttered another.

"With their pockets loaded with all the gold they steal from us," enjoined the first, "we'd see how far they got across the Atlantic."

All three fell silent when eight soldiers entered, wearily taking off their hats. One gently but firmly gestured to a lone man to leave his table to make room for them.

"See there? A man can't even claim a table and chair without the lobsterbacks taking it from him too," groused Ian's companion under his breath. "Bottom-feeders, one and all."

Ian nodded, feeling unaccountable rage flood through him as the man moved from his table to the bar. Yes, he'd been alone at a table for eight. Yes, there were eight of them. But what right had they to demand he leave his spot? Was there no place sacred? No place where they honored a man who was not also adorned in red? The color of the setting sun, the color of the sky when storms were ahead, the color of blood . . .

He stood up abruptly. "Gentlemen!" he called, moving between crowded tables to reach the eight soldiers. All looked up at him, puzzled, wary. "Have you not the courtesy to honor those you claim to serve here in the colonies?" he asked loudly. "What right have you to displace a law-abiding citizen, a paying customer of this establishment?"

Murmurs sounded from all around, encouraging him.

One soldier, a captain, judging from his uniform, rose and lifted his hands. "We meant no harm, friend. Go back to your ale and leave us be. 'Tis been a trying day."

"A trying day?" Ian repeated, vaguely aware that he was trembling. "A trying day?" he said again through clenched teeth, leaning forward. "Have ye been lookin' after your dead brother's affairs, as I have? A brother sent on King George's own mission, despite his own wishes?

39

A man pressed into service he did not want? Did you have that sort of trying day?"

The captain's eyes narrowed, and he straightened as several of his companions rose behind him and around Ian. "Listen, sir. I am most sorry for your loss. I—"

But Ian did not wait for him to say more. He was not sorry. Nor was his commander sorry. Nor the king. To them, Duncan had been but a pawn to serve their idling needs. A means to the perfectly spiced pear . . . his life exchanged in the pursuit of saffron or cinnamon or pepper. His life.

His life his life his life were the words ringing through Ian's head as his fist smashed into the captain's cheek, as he drove his shoulder into the man's belly, as they both slid across the table and against a startled soldier on the far side. And as the soldiers set upon him, kicking and punching him senseless in retribution, Ian felt a quiet relief in it. As if the punishment somehow eased his pain, as if he could take a part of what Duncan had suffered at the hands of the pirates and give him some reprieve.

Dimly, he knew it was madness.

That his sister, Marjorie, would not understand.

Nor even Duncan himself.

But as darkness closed in, he welcomed it, feeling a portion of peace absent since the very moment he learned his brother had perished.

• • •

Philip quietly inquired about Captain McKintrick everywhere they went among the markets of New York. Even when Verity was in some of the establishments where she knew he had done business in seasons past, each proprietor returned a blank look to Philip's question, then a shake of the head and something on the order of, "Nay, I haven't seen the good captain in some time. When you do find him, greet him for me." To a man, they all seemed to genuinely like Duncan, and the mention of his name seemed to awaken some fond memory of him and the desire to see him again. It only made Verity's longing for him deepen.

To distract herself, she threw herself into her purchases, concentrating on items she knew were difficult to come by in Nevis or St. Kitts that would make day to day life more manageable on-island. Items such as sensible, pre-made dresses and wide-brimmed hats suitable for horsewomen, and seeds for gardens. She spent a great deal of time at a saddlery, ordering crates full of leatherworks—reins, bits, stirrups, children's and women's saddles. She knew that all of those were oft special-ordered from the colonies, whereas a proper man's saddle could be found on St. Eustatius—commonly called Statia—if not on St. Kitts or Nevis. She figured if one need not wait for a saddle to arrive, she

41

might corner that market. And if she had a fine horse to sell with it, all the better.

At another store she found portable, collapsible dovecotes, of which she ordered twelve, with another order to be delivered in two months' time. Next door she ordered henhouses. At the farrier she ordered crates and crates of horseshoes that might need only a quick heating and a bit of pounding to shape, protecting a Nevisian horse's hooves for a fraction of the price that the lone farrier charged there. She grinned to herself at the thought of it. The miserly blacksmith would be most displeased with her when he found out that she had discovered a way to capture a portion of his shillings.

Several days later, on Long Island now, with a letter of introduction from the Harringtons in hand, she and Philip toured one horse ranch after another, examining studs and mares, geldings and colts. Locating the finest breeders, she asked for recommendations of others in North Carolina, for she had heard she could purchase stock there for much less than what they asked in New York.

That would be the most challenging part of her return journey to Nevis—bringing the animals to the island. She'd arranged to build a corral on some rocky ground just above the small store and apartment she'd purchased. *Ah, there is all of that to obtain as well,* she thought, shifting her lists in her hands.

One list included items of furniture to outfit the apartment—a bed, washstand, armoire, chest, small cookstove. Another of items she'd need for the horses and mules—railing for the corral, wood to create a sunshield, hay and oats, troughs for water, basic medicines. Still another of items for the store—mannequins to display dresses and hats, wooden horses for the saddlery, pegboards for bridles and bits, bins for the seeds. She also needed to find replacement glass for the two cracked front windows, as well as copious amounts of vinegar to clean them. She intended to change the name of the store from the bland Mercantile sign that hung crookedly out front to Banning's Bridlery & More.

She was conferring with a sign maker, reviewing several of the signs he'd crafted and carved for other stores that were in the final stages of painting, when four British soldiers passed by. One had a black eye, and the others were teasing him . . . and she was certain one of them had mentioned the name McKintrick. She glanced at Philip. He, too, had heard the name. She ran after the fellows, ignoring Philip's call.

"Excuse me!" she called, hurrying after the men. "Gentlemen, please!"

One turned, saw her, and grabbed another. The front two took a couple of steps before noting their companions' pause and turned then too. Each took off their hats in deference to her, but it was the captain with the black eye who spoke.

"Miss? How may we be of service?"

"I could not help but overhear. Did one of you mention a man named McKintrick? Were you speaking of a Captain McKintrick, perchance?"

The man's face fell, and his companions stiffened. "We were indeed, miss. Do you have the misfortune of knowing the man?"

Verity could feel her face grow hot. Clearly, these men did not like Duncan.

As if sensing her uneasiness, Philip stepped forward. "We have been in search of Captain McKintrick for some time. Might you tell us where we may find him?"

"I must say it surprises me to find a lady in search of a drunkard and a brawler," said the captain stiffly.

A drunkard and a brawler? Verity thought in confusion. That did not describe her Duncan.

The man's description visibly surprised Philip too, but he pressed on. " 'Tis no concern of yours why we seek him," he said briskly. "Simply tell us—do you know where we might find him?"

The men shared a wry look, barely concealing their grins. "Aye, I can tell you. Captain McKintrick is in the county jail, serving a week's sentence for assaulting a royal officer. If you ask me, he got off easy."

"He'll pay in other ways too," said one of the

men. "He'll never get another royal commission or ship again."

"Jail?" Verity said, but no one heard her. Duncan was in jail? He'd given himself to drink and brawling? Was this why he'd ceased writing to her?

"Come, Miss Verity." Philip moved to take her arm. "Good day, gentlemen," he said over his shoulder.

"I would not take her with you to the jail," called one after them. "The only ladies who visit are those who reside on Holy Ground."

Verity started in surprise yet again. Holy Ground . . . the acres around Trinity Church where ladies of ill repute erected tents and entertained sailors and soldiers as well as men of fine standing, day or night. Duncan was in a jail frequented by prostitutes? The thought dizzied her.

"I shall go to the jail, Miss Verity," Philip said, "inquire after Captain McKintrick, and find out what has transpired. Let us get you back to the Harringtons' home, and then I shall go."

"No, Philip. I intend to go with you. Now."

He pulled up short and turned to gape at her, gesturing over his shoulder. "Did you not hear what the man said? 'Tis not the place for a fine lady."

"Nevertheless, I am going with you." She took a step toward him. "I have been waiting for

45

months to hear from Duncan. If he has landed himself in such dire circumstances, I want to hear directly from him how it transpired."

Philip hesitated, but she did not wait. Verity knew well enough where the jail called Bridewell was located. They had passed it several times while walking by the Commons on Broadway. The soldiers had been right—part of the reason it drew one's attention was because there were so many women of ill repute about. Waiting for beaus? Gathering money to pay for another's bail? She had no idea why they lingered. But she knew where it was. And if Duncan was inside, she couldn't get there fast enough.

CHAPTER FOUR

She knew her pace was rude; poor Philip had to lengthen his stride to keep up. It was unseemly to rush anywhere, but she didn't care. Duncan was near! At last they would be reunited . . . or she would find out why he had turned from her.

At the jailhouse, she only narrowly kept herself from pacing behind Philip as he spoke to the bearded middle-aged sergeant. The sergeant laboriously reviewed his ledgers as if he could not keep track of the names of his prisoners. *They could not number more than thirty,* she thought with irritation, *judging from the size of the building.* Verity knew he was stealing glances at her, curious as to what a woman of her breeding wanted with a prisoner, eager to gain a story to share with family or friends that night at the supper table.

"See here," Philip said, "we are friends of Captain McKintrick, and we have been searching for him for some time. We must see him at once."

Poor Philip probably feared that Verity would make a run for the cell block if he didn't make a way for her.

"Yes, yes," said the man. He pulled a sheet of

paper from a stack, perused it, and turned back to them. "Jailed for being drunk and disorderly. Struck a loyal soldier before his compatriots waylaid him. He's been in for four days and is scheduled to be released in another three, if all goes well. Or if you are as fine a friends as you say, a bail can be arranged."

"Let us see him and we shall consider that offer," Verity said, stepping up to the counter.

"Good then." He grabbed a ring of keys from a peg, waved a junior officer over, and the man led them down the hallway. They turned a corner, descended a flight of steps, where Verity paused. She hurriedly fished a handkerchief from her pocket. The stench down below was horrendous. Even the worst of the city streets had not rivaled this. Several oil lamps illuminated the passageway, and the junior officer called out, "Captain McKintrick! McKintrick! Ye have a visitor here to see ya."

Others lumbered to their feet in the shadows of cells they passed, but Verity's eyes remained on the officer, her heart pounding, her stomach roiling.

He stopped at the next-to-last cell. "McKintrick! Get up!"

Verity willed herself to take the last few steps and stand beside Philip at the iron bars. In the dim light and deep shadows, she could not see much of the man on a dingy cot, his back to them. He did not respond to the officer's shout, or the clatter of his baton against the bars, or his fellow prisoners' jeering. He was thinner than she remembered. Was he ill? Was this why he had ceased to write? Her breath caught, and her hand went to her throat.

The jailer sighed and turned the keys in his hands until he found the right one and slipped it into the lock. The metal latch sprung. The door creaked slowly open.

The sound seemed to at last rouse Duncan from his sleep. He was moving, turning. His actions were both familiar and yet different somehow, making Verity all the more certain he was ill. He swung his long legs over the side of the cot and put his head in his hands. His beard was so heavy, the shadows so deep, it was difficult to make him out . . .

Verity was moving before she knew what she was doing. Ignoring the jailer's outstretched hand, trying to catch her, as well as Philip's hissed warning. She crossed the last few steps and sank to her knees, ignoring the straw and filth that would likely cling to her skirts, her only thought . . . "Duncan," she breathed, taking his hands and pulling them from his face. " 'Tis I, Verity."

"Verity?" he said, and his voice was different. Lower. Strained. Perhaps from lack of water?

But as his hands came away from his face and

he looked upon her, Verity stared. He was like Duncan, so like him . . . and yet not.

"Ye are Verity?" he asked. He let out a humorless laugh and shook his head. "Leave it to Duncan to fall for so bonny a lass." His head again fell into his hands as if it ached.

Verity stood and stumbled backward on shaking legs.

Philip circled her waist with a strong arm, silently reminding her she was not alone. "Who are you, sir?" Philip asked and glanced to the jailer with consternation in his eyes. "We were told this was Captain McKintrick's cell."

" 'Tis," the prisoner said with another humorless laugh. He sighed and, with some effort, rose to his feet. "I am Captain Ian McKintrick," he said with a slight bow, "at your service."

"But . . . But . . ." Verity stammered. " 'Tis Captain Duncan McKintrick we seek. Is he a relation of yours?"

"Indeed, lass," the man said quietly, and his soft, tender tone made her want to back away, to run. Why the warning? The sorrow?

He brought a hand to his chest. " 'Tis with my deepest regret that I must tell ye that my brother, Captain Duncan McKintrick, was conscripted by the Royal Navy and sent on the king's own foolhardy errand. En route, he was captured by a privateer and in the melee suffered his bitter end."

His words ran through her mind as if repeated by a parrot. Captured by a privateer . . . bitter end. From a distance, it seemed, she considered the information. This was why he had ceased to write. Why he had not followed through to come and winter in the Indies. Why also the harbormaster had nothing in his ledger of late from Captain Duncan McKintrick, and why the merchants with whom he traded had not seen him.

Captured by a privateer . . . bitter end.

"I am most sorry for your loss, Captain," she managed to say to him, giving him a halfhearted bob of her head.

"As I am for yours, Miss Verity . . ." he led, lifting a brow.

"Banning," her man supplied when he saw she was too stunned to think clearly. "Miss Verity Banning of Nevis."

She turned to leave, her numb feelings rapidly turning to sharp barbs and prickles as she realized what Duncan would have her do. Look after his brother. Would he not have done the same for her were their situation reversed and her own sibling was in such a dire situation? She paused and glanced over her shoulder. "Why is it that you attacked that soldier, Captain? Why risk confinement?"

He sighed and shook his head. " 'Twas foolish of me." He looked to the jailer, then back to her. " 'Twas partly grief, partly fury toward the soldier's king—a king responsible for my brother's death. Clearly I was not in my right mind. But in the moment . . ." He rubbed the back of his neck and shrugged. "I have not my brother's even keel."

Their eyes locked then. So like Duncan's, only his turned down at the corners rather than up, giving him an intent, keen expression. It reminded her a bit of Brutus—how the bird took in everything, everywhere, in moments. "We shall see to your bail, Captain," Verity said. "Philip shall tell you where you can come to call on us on the morrow. I wish to know more of Duncan, if you care to share it."

Verity stepped out of the cell without a backward glance. Even as he called, "I can share what I know, but I warn you, 'tis precious little."

The man turned to him and crossed his arms. "I am Philip Schuyler. We are staying at the Harringtons' home, north of here. See to it that you have a proper bath and a change of clothes before you come to call. I'll not have the young miss seen with the likes of you in such a state. Do you have the coin to accomplish it?"

"Aye," Ian said, considering him. Who was this man to the girl? A servant? A friend? "I do. And I shall see Miss Banning repaid for her kindness."

"The only payment she seeks is information,"

Philip said, leaning forward. *A servant serving as her guardian,* Ian surmised. "Your brother was our captain two years past when we sailed from England to Nevis. He and the young miss had been courting." He moved back again and brushed his hands together. "Likely she needs to know more so she can put his memory to rest."

"Fair enough," Ian said. He knew the feeling. Even now he wished he knew more about the ill-begotten mission Duncan had been sent on, the Spanish privateer who had waylaid his ship, and why he took his brother's life rather than ransoming him. He knew it was futile, such wonderings. There was no one to ask, no way for him to learn more. And in the end, the result was the same—Duncan was dead and not returning. What else truly mattered?

The man named Philip turned on his heel and left, leaving the jailer to swiftly close the door with a clang and turn the key in the lock. "Fair stroke of luck, that," he said, casting him a cheeky grin and gesturing down the hall. "Granted both bail and a reason to call on a pretty girl."

My brother's girl, Ian thought, lying back down on his cot. *A lass he perhaps even loved . . . but can no longer.*

Verity held herself together until they reached her cousin's home. At the base of the front stairs, she felt the cry tear loose at last in her swollen throat; her attempt to hold it back was futile as she rushed up the stairs. Philip was right beside her, knocking on the door and fidgeting as they waited for a butler to allow them entrance. Inside, the man gave her an alarmed look and said to Philip, "Madame Harrington is out, I fear."

"Never mind," Philip said. "But Mistress Verity could well use a hot pot of tea."

The man set off, clearly glad for the errand.

Verity gasped for breath as he ushered her into the small front parlor and bowed his head. "Do you wish to be alone, Miss Verity?"

"No. No! Oh, Philip!" she cried, rushing to him. He wrapped her in his arms, and she leaned her cheek against his chest and gave sway to all the sorrow and grief that had been building in her chest all the way back to the house. "How can it be true, Philip?" she asked as he awkwardly patted her back. She looked up at him. "How can he have died and I not know it?"

The kindly man frowned down at her with knitted brows. "Sometimes, miss, we so care for a person that our memories of them carry even through an absence. Our heart remembers, even if the mind begs us to accept a change of course."

She nodded and gave into a fresh round of tears.

Again he patted her back and only pulled away to hand her a fresh handkerchief. She knew she was soaking through his vest and shirt, but she could not help herself. In this instant she felt lost, powerless to do anything but lean on the nearest friend she had. How dearly she missed her sisters in this moment! Never had she felt so alone, so lost. "I shall not ever care for another as I did for Duncan," she gasped forlornly, at last sniffing rather than sobbing.

" 'Tis special, the first time you give your heart to another. But mind me, you shall likely love again. And somehow your love for Captain McKintrick shall aid you when you do."

She leaned back from him, puzzled by his words. But he spoke with firm authority. "You have loved and lost, Philip?"

"Aye," he said gravely and turned to fetch another handkerchief from a pocket and hand it to her. He gently led her to a chair and folded his hands behind his back. "I have loved three women in my lifetime. Each claimed every portion of my heart available to her, and each continued to claim a portion after she was gone. But God worked through them all, for their good and mine. Trust me on this. It feels as if your life has shattered, but God can mend those pieces back together. And after a time your grief shan't feel so devilishly painful. After a time you shall remember Duncan with a tender smile and no longer have bitter tears rise with it."

"Truly?" she asked, her chest shuddering. "I cannot imagine it."

"Truly," he said confidently. He reached out and touched her shoulders. "Now, Lady Ket and Master Gray would have me tell you this. Head up to your room, wash your face, and take a rest before Captain Ian McKintrick comes to call. You've suffered a terrible blow today. Take your ease for a bit, yes? I shall ask Mrs. Harrington to look in on you when she returns."

"Yes," she said, sniffing. "Thank you, Philip." She allowed him to escort her up the stairs and to her room, then after a maid had delivered a tray of tea and biscuits she could not eat, she gently closed the door, at last alone. She turned back to the bed, pulled off her slippers and sank to her side, hands cradled beneath her head.

"Oh, Duncan," she said quietly. And impossibly, more tears slipped down the bridge of her nose and cheek, across her fingers and into the feather pillow. She had imagined the culmination of their romance in so many ways. But never this. Never this . . .

She cried for more than an hour before a soft knock sounded on her door. Verity rose, touched face and hair as if to put herself together, but then realized it was hopeless. She opened the door an inch.

Roberta, her cousin's tall, beautiful, pregnant wife stood there, her face awash in concern. "Oh, dear one," she said, wringing her hands. "Is there anything, anything I might do for you?"

56

The sisterly tone, the kind words—her stature and swelling belly, so like Ket's—was all it took. Verity opened the door wide and flung herself into Roberta's arms, sobbing again.

CHAPTER FIVE

The jailhouse had been darker than he thought, Ian decided. Because when Miss Verity Banning and her guardian, Philip, entered the Harringtons' parlor, she was even prettier than he remembered. It was clear she had been crying, but the slight dark circles only drew attention to her gold-green eyes, her wan complexion only making him see the curve of her round cheekbones, the dimples begging for a reason to form . . .

But he was not here to admire his brother's intended, he firmly reminded himself, resolutely turning to shake Mr. Albert Harrington's hand, then Philip's, and bow to Mrs. Roberta Harrington and Verity. He was here to serve her as best he could. *Treat her as a sister,* he told himself sternly, *as if this were Marjorie herself.* He owed Duncan that much.

Still, as she gracefully sank onto a settee and looked up to take a cup of tea from a maid, he could not help but admire the shine of her curly brown hair and the sweet curve of her long neck. Again he forced himself to look upon the maid, all the while thinking, *Duncan, brother, you always had an eye for the prettiest lass . . .*

"Captain," Philip said pointedly, and Ian realized he was staring blankly at the maid, who had clearly asked him a question.

He started and blinked. "For-Forgive me," he sputtered. "I am not . . . quite myself. A cup of tea, please."

"Or would you prefer something stronger?" Mr. Harrington asked, sitting down beside his wife in a pair of wing-back chairs. "I understand you have suffered quite a loss."

"No, thank you, sir. I think I shall stick with tea. The last time I imbibed, it did not turn out so well for me."

"I had not stopped . . ." Verity began, setting down her cup. If possible, she seemed to have grown even more wan than before. She swallowed hard. "Forgive me, Captain. Your news today so stunned me that I had not stopped to think about how dearly Duncan's loss has cost you too."

Ian gazed over at her, and in that moment their shared grief bound them. Bound them in a way that made Ian's heart seem to slow a moment, as if considering its next beat. "Thank you, Miss Banning," he said. "But I have borne this miserable news for more than two months now. While I keenly feel my brother's absence, I do not envy ye this fresh grief."

"And yet I did not have a lifetime to know him," she said, clearly trying to keep her composure. "He was your elder brother, I take it?"

"By three years. Our sister is between us."

"Marjorie," she murmured, picking up her tea-cup again.

The familiar use of his sister's first name surprised him, even as he nodded his assent. He gratefully turned to Mrs. Harrington as she offered him his own cup.

"Was it quite dreadful, for your sister too, to learn of it?"

"Quite." He leaned back in his chair to sip from the delicate china. "Our parents died when we were very young. A seafaring uncle—captain of his own ship—took us in."

"And taught you all a love of the sea?"

"Yes."

"What came of it for Marjorie, what with you two as captains?"

Ian gave her a small smile. "She married a sailor as well. It has pleased us—my brother and me—to tease our brother-in-law that he has yet to make captain. He's still but a first mate."

That elicited a quick smile from her too, her adorable deep dimples drawing attention to her nicely formed lips and fine, even teeth. "Duncan enjoys a good jest." Her smile faltered. "Did enjoy," she added in a whisper, her moss-green eyes drifting to the wall above him. Her dimples disappeared.

They sat in silence a moment, none of them aware of how this conversation was to progress.

Ian spoke next. "I came to settle my brother's affairs. In his apartment, I found this." He reached into his jacket pocket, fished out the folded paper, and handed it to her. " 'Tis likely not all ye wished it would contain, but I thought ye might like to see that he had been thinkin' of ye, lass, when last in the colonies."

Her wide eyes shifted over the short salutation, again and again, her thick lashes blinking rapidly. Slowly, she folded it at the creases, held it to her chest, eyes closed, then handed it to Philip, who tucked it inside his jacket for safekeeping. "Thank you for giving it to me, Captain."

"Ian. Please. If you pardon the informality, miss. Since you held Duncan dear and I did the same, does it not seem apt to use our Christian names?"

"Very well. Ian," she added with a gracious nod.

Mr. Harrington sat forward. "I think my cousin is eager to learn of any details you might know of, Captain. Might you tell us of Duncan's last moments in Liverpool, as well as his mission and the . . . privateer? Knowing more might aid her in some small way."

Ian did as he asked, telling Verity of Duncan's preparations to sail again to the Indies as he had promised, of soldiers arriving and giving him orders from the court to do as they bid. "There was naught he could do," Ian said, finishing the last of his tea. "The royals can press anyone they wish into service. Duncan knew it. Still, it rankled him, that errand. He tried going to the West Indies Company, which held the majority of shares in his vessel, but they were powerless to wrest him from the court's grip. A certain number of ships are always at the king's beck and call, and it was deemed Duncan's turn. There was nothing for him but to see it through. Marjorie said he was most bitter about it. Likely because he was eager to return to you, lass. For he dinnae mind traveling to Africa."

Verity nodded, lifted a biscuit partway to her lips, but then set it aside and elected to take a tiny sip of her tea instead. *Feeling a tad queasy,* Ian surmised. He was surprised at his own voracious hunger in the face of reviewing his brother's tragic end, but four days of the thin gruel served at the jail might make a man eat fish floating dead in the water, if it came to it. He hoped his hosts did not hear his stomach rumbling.

"And what do you know of the privateer who overtook his vessel?" she asked.

"Ahh, lass. Such things are not what a gentle-woman like yourself should contemplate," he said, eyeing her cousin, then Philip.

"I disagree. I would like to know."

He frowned and glanced again at Philip and back to her. "Such things are apt to ruin your slumber. Fill your head with night terrors."

Her eyes narrowed. "Ian McKintrick," she said with quiet authority, "you may not speak to me as if I were a child. I am a woman grown. My sisters and I traveled alone to Nevis to take over our father's plantation. I can assure you that in the two years hence, we've experienced sorrows and horrors that removed any remnants of a gentlewoman's naïveté. Your story shall not *ruin* my slumber. Instead, it will help me to put your brother's story into proper order in my head and heart as I mourn his passing."

With each word she uttered he knew his brows raised higher and higher, and yet he had never heard such passion from a woman of her standing. So forthright, so assured! He did not know whether he ought to fear her or admire her. What sort of woman had Duncan fallen for? *My dearest Verity* . . . The words were tender, he'd thought, meant for a girl, not a fiercely determined woman.

Mr. Harrington rose and went to a crystal decanter on a side table. He lifted it and cast him a wry grin. "Are you *certain* you would not like to join me?"

"I suppose I must," Ian said grimly. The man returned with two glasses and handed one to him. "Even as children, my cousins demanded their way," Albert said with a conspiratorial grin. "Best be out with it, then."

Ian took a sip of the fine amber liquid and with

a swift glance toward Philip again—who merely sat back, crossed his arms, and gave him a small shrug—he dared to meet the green-eyed lass's unwavering gaze once again. He sighed and leaned forward, turning the crystal glass between his palms. " 'Twas a privateer by the name of Alejandro Diego Santiago, one whom Duncan had encountered before. I know not why Duncan did not surrender when he was overtaken; 'tis common enough." *Was it pride? Or something Santiago did to offend Duncan or his crew?* "All I know is that I intend to find out from the man himself in the coming months. Rest assured, lass, I shall see retribution done when finally I come face-to-face with Captain Santiago of the *Juliana*. He shall pay for robbing us both."

Her mouth settled into a grim line. "Is that what you believe Duncan would have wanted? You seeking retribution?"

"Likely not," he said with a shrug, sitting back again. "But Duncan is no longer here. And I aim to make things right with that ol' King George, as well as that murderer." He was aware that the feel of kinship had loosed his tongue, that he ought not to speak so in public . . . in particular, in front of the Harringtons, what with Mr. Harrington being a prominent Loyalist. But sitting here with her, talking of Duncan, remembering all he had lost and why made his heart pound. He could feel a vein pulse in his temple, as well as the beginnings of a headache. *A fine situation,* he thought bitterly. *My first night free of the jailhouse, and I shall still suffer with the ache of it.*

He leaned forward again and asked quietly, urgently, "Do ye not long for a bit of retribution yourself, lass? Does it not rankle you that the king and his lackeys can pull our strings like puppets on the stage? Drop us at any time to the orchestra floor?"

Philip sat forward and put a hand on his arm. "I shall ask you to cease this line of discussion at once, Captain," he hissed, glancing nervously toward the Harringtons, then at a maid just entering to remove their tray. "Else I shall escort you to the door. I shall not see her endangered by treasonous talk."

But when Ian looked Verity's way again, she seemed unperturbed.

Nay, what he saw in the lass's eyes was fire. The same fire that burned within him.

After an initial shock, he felt yet another tendril of shared passion stretch out from him, wrap around her, and pull her closer. It was almost visceral. She actually leaned a bit toward him.

"What shall you do now, Ian?" she asked softly, breaking eye contact with him and fingering the fine edge of her teacup as if to gather herself.

"I sold my ship. I had my eye on another here, but that was before I . . ." He rubbed his still-bruised cheek, feeling the shame of it now in discussing it with this woman. He cleared his throat. "I may have trouble purchasing a vessel in this city, given my recent . . . accommodations. I shall need to head south, to territory—"

Philip leaned forward, his brow furrowed in warning.

"Ach, take your ease, man," Ian said, closing his eyes against the throbbing in his head. "All I intended to say was that I shall arrange to buy another ship, outfit her, reassemble my crew. Load her with cargo. And set sail for the Indies, in fact. I've done a good trade over the last years, running between New York and Jamaica. Some to Hispaniola too. And then . . ." *East. I'll head east and find that privateering scum. And I'll make him regret what he has done.* But she need not know all of that. He shrugged. "We shall see."

"You may not have as many difficulties as one might imagine," Mr. Harrington said, "purchasing a new vessel, even with your record against the Crown. This part of New York is firmly Loyalist, but I daresay there are many who would be eager to aid a man who has spent time in jail for striking a soldier. The city is rife with them."

Ian studied him. It was an odd thing to say, for a Loyalist. And yet perhaps he was but a realist, as aware of how the Sons of Liberty grew in number every day, as his wife was aware of the number of women wearing homespun on the streets, rather than the fine imported linens from Europe.

A butler came to the door of the parlor and summoned Mr. Harrington for a word. Mrs. Harrington rose and left by a separate door, perhaps to check on their supper.

Verity's warm green eyes returned to meet his. "Tell me, Captain. Have you ever transported horses?"

"Miss Verity," Philip said with a confused frown, "we already have transport arranged."

"We do. Likely on a ship the king's men might press into service as well, and at a moment's notice." She took a deep breath, then glanced over her shoulder. Lowering her voice, she added, "We're in the colonies now. I confess I may have caught a bit of their independent spirit, especially . . ."

Especially now, she'd meant to say. Now that she knew the English were partly to blame for Duncan's death.

She returned her keen gaze to Ian, who felt his lips turning up as much as Philip's were turning down. "So tell me. Have you transported horses, mules, other livestock?"

"I have. 'Tis its own kettle of fish, to be sure."

"And that livestock reached its destination?"

"Aye. Hale and hearty," Ian said, setting down his empty glass as if to emphasize the point. "I find it key not to embark until you know you have at least three days of fair sailing, to settle them into the soothing rhythm of the wind and waves before you might encounter anything more fierce. And while other captains ascribe to the practice of hobbling a horse and keeping them calm by confinement, I prefer the method of hiring extra crew to continuously walk the horses about the deck. 'Tis an added expense," he warned, "that I pass along to the customer, but I find it a far more pleasant journey for all involved."

"That is understandable," she said. "Tell me, would you be amenable to stopping in North Carolina to pick up horse stock en route to the Indies? As well as for other supplies? I have not had much luck in obtaining the basics—dried fish, corn, and the like. The locals have been reluctant to aid Loyalists in the Indies with their supplies—they seem more apt to allow them to starve. But if we sailed southward, under the sail of not the Union Jack but rather another—"

"You might fare better," he finished for her. Was she really intending to hire him?

Mrs. Harrington returned then. Clasping her hands she said, "Dinner is ready to be served."

Ian's once-rumbling belly was forgotten now. With Albert's encouragement to seek other means to secure a vessel, with Verity's interest in hiring him—and filling the majority of his hold—he could not fathom sitting at a table for a lengthy supper. "Mrs. Harrington, would ye consider it unforgivable if I declined your gracious invitation to sup? If I make haste, I might still gain word this eve of another vessel available for purchase. The faster I find her and outfit her, the faster I might serve Miss Banning."

"By all means, Captain," Mrs. Harrington said. "Be on your way with my blessing. I know Verity is eager to return home to the islands, and if you might aid her, my husband and I would be most grateful to you."

"Thank you." He edged around the settee and took his coat and tricorn from a waiting butler's hands, who had already anticipated his need. "And thank you for your kind hospitality."

"But of course," Roberta said.

Verity followed him out, Philip just behind her. "I would very much like to hear from you on the morrow. If you are able to purchase the ship you desire and outfit her within the week, I would fill a good portion of your cargo—as well as pay for modifications of the ship to best manage my stock."

Redirecting their conversation to points of business seemed to galvanize the girl. Her shoulders were straight, her head held high, making her seem quietly powerful. He leaned back, wondering what she'd been like when his brother first met her. Then he felt a piercing moment of shame the moment he found himself idly thankful that Duncan wasn't here to compete. *Of all the unthinking, callous . . . Forgive me, Lord. Saints above, forgive me for such shame. Forgive me, brother.*

" 'Twould be an honor to serve you, Verity," he said at last, resolving again to treat her with nothing but the respect he would give his own sister. "I think . . . I think Duncan would have approved of it."

"As do I," she said, and again there was that curious twining of their hearts, their shared affections for Duncan, though he was gone, drawing them together.

She offered her hand. He reached across, took it, and bowed briefly over it. "Until the morrow, then."

"Until the morrow," she repeated.

As he handed Philip the coin he owed Verity and left the house, there was something in the air that made him think that, had Duncan been here . . . aye, if he had been here, they would have smiled and together admired the steady, sure ways of the beautiful force that was Miss Verity Banning.

CHAPTER SIX

"What are you about, Miss Verity?" Philip asked sternly under his breath, turning toward her with a glower, arms folded.

She knew well enough of what he spoke. Felt a momentary flash of shame, but then an equally brilliant flash of justice. All her guardian need know was that she was safe. Quite in her right mind. "Ahh, Philip. Forgive me. I gave into a moment's foolishness. Not in hiring Captain McKintrick. But in . . ." She fell silent as the butler passed by them.

"You must guard yourself, Verity," he continued in a whisper. "There are as many Tories about as Loyalists here. Perhaps even in this very house. Captain McKintrick may wish to take such risks, but I shall not have you do so again. That man dared to attack an officer." He gestured furiously over his shoulder toward the door. "Perhaps they released him from jail solely to see whom he might meet, thinking they would uncover a network of Tories."

Verity managed to assume a proper frown over this, even as she felt another odd thrill deep within. "His attack was quite unwise," she said soberly. "But I think he shan't do such a thing again. 'Twas born out of misguided pain, grief, anger. Nothing more. And surely his visit here to my cousin's shall put any threat of treason to rest."

"Nothing more?" Philip whispered, cocking a brow and shaking his head. "I am not quite as assured. The man has a shorter fuse than Duncan ever did, and while Duncan had some leanings away from the Crown, Ian seems to have set himself firmly against the king."

It was true. But it did not put off Verity; instead, in the wake of the horrible news of Duncan's death, Ian's passion and direction seemed to toss her a sort of lifeline. Something to cling to, focus on, when the world had become awash with dark waves. Duncan would not have wished for her to wallow in her grief. The desire to pine was strong, but had she not been pining for him most of these last two years? He had come to Nevis two times since their arrival, yet she'd spent far more time missing him than with him.

She'd felt the odd startling pull toward Ian. The common traits he shared with his brother—his forthright ways, the keen awareness in his eyes—as well as their shared grief. She was certain he had felt it too. But while she had no intention of risking her heart to another man, particularly someone bent on tracking down the one who had killed his brother, there was an immediate trust felt between them. Kinship, she decided. *Almost kinship,* she corrected herself. And while she did not have what Philip deemed a "short fuse," she knew the fury that drove Ian. Understood him. And could not help but secretly cheer him on, whether it be to quietly move against the king who'd sent Duncan to his death, or to track down the murderer who'd done the deed.

"What would your sisters think of this new alliance with a McKintrick?" Philip asked her.

"I believe they'd prefer I work with someone close to another of whom they thought so highly," she returned.

"Even if they knew him to be a Patriot?" Philip growled under his breath.

"If they were here and saw for themselves how quickly the colonies divide between Patriot and Loyalist, they would see my conundrum," she sniffed. "Why, you heard what the captain today intended to charge me to sail to Nevis. At least with Ian I may assume a fair price."

"Are you so certain?" Philip asked, lifting his chin.

"I am," she said firmly. "Philip, he is Duncan's brother. Do you truly doubt him?"

"There are a fair number of reasons to doubt. And yet I understand the wisdom of your thought. Most ships are on the king's errand in this harbor. Perhaps if we venture closer to where you intend to secure your horses . . ." He heaved a sigh and put his hands on his hips. "I shall do my due diligence on the morrow. Ask about. Check his references, reputation."

"As will I," said Albert, joining them in the hall and overhearing that last bit. "But if you two would join us in the dining room, 'twould be most grand. Otherwise our cook might have a fit of apoplexy."

"Do what you must," Verity said, heading past Albert. "But I already take him at his word. He is as honest as Duncan. I can feel it."

"And if I discover unsettling things about him?" Albert asked. "Beyond his attack on the king's own men and time spent in jail?"

"Then I shall seek your wisdom on how we should proceed, as well as Philip's," she returned demurely over her shoulder. She was not at all sure that she would act on either man's wisdom, once considered. But the caring, fervently loyal Philip would toss and turn all night if she did not give him at least these assurances. There was a reason her brother-in-law had chosen him to accompany her, and this was it. He would do anything to protect her, on any front, just as Gray or Keturah might themselves.

Her quiet words seemed to mollify both men. "Good enough, miss," he said, the lines in his forehead easing as he took his seat across from her.

The Harringtons gently guided their conversation to neutral subjects, well aware of how taxing the day had been. And after their fine supper of roast venison, potatoes, and beans, Albert excused himself to attend a party on Long Island, despite the hour. "One must keep up appearances as a potential city alderman," her cousin said. He kissed his wife on the cheek and rested a hand on her shoulder.

"Thank goodness my advanced state of pregnancy allows me an excuse," Roberta said, waggling her eyebrows at Verity.

"Keturah is probably a couple months behind you in her own pregnancy," Verity said. "Most days Gray has to practically carry her up the stairs to bed, she's so weary."

"For a human so tiny," Roberta said, resting a hand on her belly, "they seem to take a full-grown man's portion of one's stamina. But I confess I do miss the chance to cavort and discuss and dance without thinking how dreadfully weary I am."

"Enjoy your rest, darling," Albert said. "Soon we shall have a nursemaid to hand the babe off to and you will be in my arms on a dance floor again." He turned to Verity and Philip, who had risen from his seat to shake their host's hand. "And I shall make inquiries of this Captain McKintrick."

Philip nodded. "Thank you, sir."

"Yes, thank you, Albert," Verity said with a sigh.

Roberta reached over and took her hand. " 'Tis been quite a day. You must feel as weary as I, what with all you've borne and considered, sweet girl. Please, retire at once. Rest well. We shall spend more time together tomorrow—no need for you to see to social niceties this eve."

"Bless you," Verity said, squeezing her hand. How was it that this one so easily assumed a sister's stance in her life, though they had so recently met? Perhaps it was because Roberta had three of her own . . .

She bid Philip good-night in the foyer, and a maid came up to help her undress and prepare for slumber. Verity felt as though her legs were water-soaked stumps as she moved toward the bed, the maid softly closing the door behind her. The day's tasks had not been at all laborious, but she felt as tired as she had those first days toiling in the Nevisian fields. Utterly spent. Empty. She sank onto the feather bed, turned to the candle and was about to blow it out, then thought the better of it. She lay down, hands cradled beneath her face, and watched the flame dance, glowing in hypnotic curves of indigo and crimson and gold.

It was her heart that made her body feel so weary, she decided. The constant effort of staving off grief—*Oh, Duncan*—in the midst of trying to move forward with her life. She knew she was doing exactly what he would have wanted her to do . . . moving on. Following through on her plans to outfit her mercantile and to sell horses. After all, they had not even reached a formal understanding, other than courtship. He had intimated a desire to move forward, hinted that he was saving funds to build an island home suitable for a bride, but that was all. The quiet hope of so many young ladies of society, she mused, a beau who would soon become a groom.

They had not reached a moment in which she might encourage him as Keturah had encouraged Gray, that it was not their thinking a man had to provide a home for his bride, regardless of how their set might consider it shameful to propose marriage without it. She sensed that Duncan would not have welcomed such a suggestion, that it might have offended him in some irreparable way. No, he was—had been, she corrected herself with a tear—a staunch traditionalist, in many ways. A man who embraced new thought as he might new sections of sea to explore, and yet he was also a man who leaned heavily on his traditionalist foundation.

That foundation had led him back to the promise his grandfather had made to remain loyal to the Crown. Had made him trust the Crown, obey their command to go wherever they sent him.

She silently cheered the fact that Ian now refused to do the same. That he had sold his very ship so he could be rid of the ties that might bind him as they had his brother. The same royal ties that forced Keturah and Gray to house soldiers in their home, even when one eyed sweet Selah as he might a girl on Holy Ground. And for what? They did not help toil in the fields. They left for town each day to perform their drills, then returned each night to drink the Covingtons' wine and eat their roast, to sleep in feather beds imported on the Bannings' account. And in the morning they downed breakfast gruel that Verity was finding nearly impossible to resupply.

More tears drifted down her nose and cheek and into her ear. She sniffed, sat up, grabbed a handkerchief and wiped both eyes and nose. She would not become bitter over all of this. No, Duncan would not have liked that. But she was a Banning woman. And Bannings did not accept ill treatment sitting down.

Ian was about to quietly strike back at those who thought they ruled their subjects' lives by taking a new path offered by those who refused to be ruled. The thought of it galvanized her, made her belly tighten and her fists round. This was far better than the vulnerable weakness of grief, she thought. Because vulnerabilities were always sought out by enemies, capitalized upon. Did she not see it, time and again with Brutus and among other animals? Both in prey and predator, as well as the more benign efforts of a male attempting to become alpha in any pride or herd?

No one, either Tory or Loyalist, male or female, shall see my vulnerabilities, she decided. *I will be strong. For myself, for my sisters, in honor of Duncan's memory.*

And with that she blew out the candle and at last gave way to sleep.

Three days later, Ian rose after a restless night's sleep. He was up before the sun and down on the wharf, waiting for the aging captain of the *Inverness* before the man had likely had his second cup of tea. But he could not help himself; for the first time since he'd been taken to his knees with news of Duncan's death, he felt as if he were on a divine path. Surely this was exactly what he was supposed to be doing— freeing himself of the bit that might choke him as it had his brother. Making his own way in the New World. There was something about it that seemed to awaken the Highlander in him. "*Nas fheàrr am bàs fhaighinn na bhith beò le cuing mu d'amhaich.*" That was what his grandfather would have said. *Better to die than to live with a yoke around your neck.*

Before Culloden. Before the English had taken down the heroic Jacobites. Before they had forced them to swear fealty and relinquish both land and sword. Until they had need of them, of course, to serve in their own forces. Against the French, the Spanish, or whomever the enemy of the day happened to be. *Perhaps Grandfather should have never sworn fealty,* Ian thought. *Perhaps he should have set sail for France or anywhere that was beyond the long reach of the English. Perhaps I am doing what he ought to have done two generations past.*

The longer he paced, the more certain he was. He'd spent enough time in New York now, purchasing goods from so many vendors that he had a fair idea of who tended toward Loyalist leanings and who might be rebels in the making. Many chafed under the weight of taxes the British demanded of their colonists, despite the fact that both the Stamp Act and the Currency Act had long been repealed. The British still chafed over war debts incurred during the French and Indian War, and clearly they intended to make the colonies pay. Those acts and others—the Townshend Acts most recently—still festered under the seemingly healed flesh of this young society, like broken bones that revealed themselves when the weather changed. That rheumatic feeling made the body uneasy, wary of further trauma, and in certain measure begged the mind to think about striking first next time, rather than waiting to get hit again.

Added to that was the oft-repeated gripe of

taxation without representation and this country had all the makings of a full-fledged war. And Ian knew if it came to that, he would fight against the Crown. If not before.

At last the old captain waddled down the buckling gray boards of the wharf, leaning hard on a silver-tipped cane. Ian turned back toward the ship, chin in hand, as if warily inspecting the twenty-year-old, three-masted sloop for the first time rather than the twentieth. It wouldn't do if the old codger caught wind of his eagerness.

"Young McKintrick!" greeted the captain, the grandfather of Michael McKay. Michael was Ian's first mate, currently on leave for two weeks.

"Old McKay!" he said back to him, shaking the smaller man's raw-boned hand. His skin was flecked with sun spots, the knuckles thick with age. Ian eased up on his grip, aware of how it might pain his older acquaintance. "So you're truly ready to sell the old girl, eh?" asked Ian.

"Aye. My days on the sea are done. I shall rest in my daughter's home now, over yonder in Bushwick. Leave the sea to the likes of you and young Michael. But what of your own sloop? What became of her?"

"I sold her," Ian said, crossing his arms and eyeing the man from the side. "Needed a smaller vessel, because I aim to focus my trade between the mainland and the Indies. Beyond the long reach of the Crown."

"Oh?" McKay said, lifting a grizzled brow. "What of the wee Marjorie? Dinnae she wish for ye to return home?"

"Wee Marjorie is a woman grown, married to a seaman herself, and with a couple of bairns. I hope to write them and convince them to emigrate as well." He lowered his tone. "I find it bracing for a Scotsman to have a bit of distance from England's shore."

McKay grinned at that. "Aye, lad." He quickly sobered. "Though there be a fair bit of English right here as well."

Ian pursed his lips. "But is it not reminiscent of Scotland herself, in certain measure? This land has her share of English influence, to be sure, but does she not have her own spirit too?"

The old man turned more fully toward him. "Do I read you right, laddie?" he asked under his breath. "Have ye a bit of the revolutionary in ye?"

"A bit," Ian chanced. He'd heard a few things from Michael that had made him think this was part of why old McKay was retiring from the sea, and why he might consider selling his vessel to Ian. He wearied of the English's hold on both the sea and the ports he frequented, yet he wasn't ready to sell to a staunch Loyalist. "Could be that if I had a good contact here in New York," Ian said, "I might aid others who had a bit of independent spirit in their souls as well."

McKay's droopy-lidded eyes shifted left and right, examining all who walked the dock. "Ye venture into risky territory, laddie. Mind yourself."

"So I shall."

The two turned back to the sloop. McKay lifted a gnarled hand and set it on Ian's shoulder. "Young Michael tells me ye are a fine captain and a good man." He gestured toward the sloop. "She would be a good ship for what ye have a mind to do. Trade, as you say, between the Indies and here. Twelve guns should the tides turn and ye have need of defending yourself. And between voyages, I would be here for ye, help ye along when ye are in port. To advise ye on the intricacies of the ship. Because as ye may have learned by now, ships are like women. Each one, her own magnificent creature."

Ian glanced back at the old man. Clearly he was speaking of more than the ship. The man had inroads to others, perhaps a whole network of those who chafed under British rule. He did his best to hide the thrill that sent his heart to pounding. " 'Tis good to know I might count on your counsel, McKay. A captain can always learn more about his ship. Or his woman," he added with a wink.

McKay laughed. "Indeed, lad. Tell me, what is to be your primary cargo?"

"Various sundries for the shops of Jamaica,

Hispaniola, and perhaps as far as Statia." He avoided mentioning Nevis for some reason. Because he felt protective of Verity? "Tobacco from the Carolinas," he hurriedly pressed on. "Of late I've considered horses too. Do ye have thoughts on that?"

"She's carried horses in her hold before," said the old captain. "As many as twenty at a time, though we did best with no more than a dozen. The horses tend to either be lulled by the dark of the hold or spooked by the confinement—and ye never know which 'twill be. Best to give them a mite more room."

Ian nodded. "And her capacity in the hold?"

"Five hundred hogsheads of rum or the equivalent in hay, give or take."

They continued to walk along the wharf, then boarded the ship, touring the captain's cabin, the hold, the deck. When finished, Ian asked, "What are ye asking for her, old friend?"

McKay considered him, chin in hand. "Weel, I'll tell ye, laddie. I think ye ken what I've advertised. But I'd consider a hundred less if ye commit to this trade of what ye mentioned, between St. Eustatius, Jamaica, and New York."

Ian studied him. He well knew what he was asking; he was offering a deal if Ian would provide consistent line of communication between the islands and the mainland. Ian was drawn to that, but . . . "Ye see, McKay, I have only just sold my ship to be free of the ties of anyone who might bind me. I'd very much like to see ye each time I come to New York. But I wish to remain my own man, keep my own schedule. There's a certain privateer I must hunt down, in time. Seek retribution for my brother's life. Ye ken?"

"I do, I do."

Ian named a sum, fifty less than McKay's asking price. "Would that keep ye in tea and crumpets while ye rest your weary bones in Brooklyn?" he asked. "If so, I'd be sure to come and share a cuppa those times I tie up along these shores."

McKay thought about it, a slow smile spreading across his face. He reached out a hand. " 'Tis a deal, laddie. But mind me, bring something stronger than tea when ye come a-visitin'."

Chapter Seven

Verity was taking tea with Albert and Roberta when she received word from Ian in the form of a brief note. He'd successfully purchased the *Inverness* and would have her outfitted and ready to set sail within the week. He asked her to confirm her interest in utilizing half his cargo space as well as the hold for up to twelve horses.

"Such a faraway look, Verity," Roberta said, leaning back with her tea fairly resting on her bulbous, pregnant belly. "What has you in such a state?"

Verity shouldn't have been surprised. Her sisters oft told her she wore her heart on her sleeve. If she were to protect herself, she'd have to get better at hiding her feelings. "Yes. Well. 'Tis from Captain McKintrick. Ian McKintrick," she added unnecessarily, given that the Harringtons had met him. "He has secured a new vessel."

"That is grand," said Albert. "Is it not what you hoped?"

"Yes, it is," she said, but she knew she did not sound at all certain. "He intends to establish a consistent trade between New England and the West Indies."

"Oh?" Roberta said, casting Albert a meaningful look. What was this? Did he have interest in such trade? She thought him merely a banker, a politician. Perhaps he had vested interest in a ship . . .

"It may be that his trade could prove a boon for me," Verity said with a wry grin. "Assuming that I am able to sell a thing in my new mercantile."

"Come now, cousin," Albert chided. "With your fine taste and beautiful form, men shall be knocking at your mercantile door before you unlock it each day."

"I hope so. Men do not take kindly to women doing such things on Nevis."

"Nor do some in New York. But look at Madame Trousseau, with her fine dress shop down on Queen Street."

"And Mrs. Taffon, with her candle shop on William Street," Albert said, lifting his cup as if in silent toast. "They have both found enough business, despite their naysayers."

"I fear that Americans are far more progressive than the Nevisians. They are still quite provincial in the islands."

Albert took a bite of a biscuit and chewed slowly, thinking. Swallowing, he said, "If you consider the origins of these people, it is logical, really. Early immigrants came to America's shores with a desire for more freedom, separation from Britain and other rulers. For many, they longed to make their own way. West Indians went to the islands merely to discover wealth and industry, not really as a means to make their way apart from England."

" 'Tis true," Verity said.

"And now England taxes us any which way they can," Roberta said.

"And sends us her prisoners." Albert cocked a brow at Verity and added, "Not the finest means to securing loyalty."

Verity paused, her cup halfway to her lips. Were they intimating some sort of commonality with the rebels? They, prominent Loyalists, who were again heading to yet another party this eve, hosted by other prominent Loyalists?

Surely not.

After finishing their tea, Verity paced her room for hours, considering a reply to Ian McKintrick. She did not know why she could not muster the capacity to do so. Time and again, she sat down at her small writing desk, dipped quill tip to ink and then hovered above the parchment, seemingly unable to write more than the date and *To Captain McKintrick,* before staring through the wavy glass of the far window. Slowly, she recognized it was because she had begun perhaps twenty other letters to a different Captain McKintrick over their year of courtship. And to address his brother in the same manner felt . . . odd. So it wasn't until she elected to take a different tack the next day that she was able to complete it. *To the captain of the Inverness,* she began. Within a minute she had finished the short missive, sanded it, and carefully folded and sealed it with hot wax. The butler sent a kitchen boy with the note out to the wharf.

"So 'tis done?" Philip asked, hat in his hand, looking after the boy. "We're to sail on Friday?"

"Indeed," she said "If all goes as planned, we shall reach North Carolina on Sunday, and as soon as our cargo is on board, we shall be off to Nevis, then on to St. Eustatius."

"Statia? Ian plans to go on to Statia?"

But she quickly turned and ascended the stairs. She well knew what Nevisians thought of the Dutch traders of St. Eustatius. They were indiscriminate, trading with one and all from around the world, and often thumbed their noses at the neighboring St. Kitts when trading with English enemies. Many spoke of the island as a hotbed of British traitors. But nearly all merchants of the Leeward Islands did their own trade there as well, obtaining goods they were unable to get elsewhere. On Statia, it was said, one could get anything from barber scissors to horse-hoof clippers.

And the thought of going there herself—for many reasons—thrilled Verity.

Ian went about his business all week, arranging for his other cargo to be delivered to the sloop on Albany Pier by Thursday at the latest. His last bit of business was seeing to an order on Long Island that Duncan had put in for two matched geldings at one of the region's most highly respected horse traders, which had been in the paper work left with his banker. Having spoken with Verity—and knowing she intended to stop in North Carolina to pick out her own horses at a far better price than what was offered in New York—Ian set out to cancel the order and see if he could negotiate an exit arrangement after the trader had held the pair for his brother.

It was odd, this. Although Ian had ventured into the transit of horses, he knew Duncan had never done so. Why had he placed this order? Most of his brother's voyages had been in the triangular route of England—West Indies—North America—England. And precious few captains wished to sign on to transport horses across the width of the Atlantic. While the transit was rather swift from the Indies to North America, riding the trade winds and favorable currents, it would take three times as long to tack against those winds and currents back to the islands. And yet with horses aboard, three weeks' voyage across the Caribbean was far preferable to six weeks across the Atlantic. Had that been his goal?

But when Ian reached the stables and was led to the corral where the pair was being held, he immediately knew why Duncan had intended to purchase them. The horses were magnificent. Beautiful lines, wide, brown eyes, burgundy hides. They were eighteen hands tall, perfect for pulling a fine carriage that could carry as many as six. A family, Ian thought with a pang.

Duncan had intended to purchase them for Verity, yes, but with a family in mind too.

He slammed his fist into the palm of his hand, teeth clenching as he watched the geldings nip and chase each other around the corral. It wasn't until the waiting breeder cleared his throat that Ian remembered himself and startled. "Do you not care for what you see?" asked the man with a fair amount of haughty consternation.

"No, on the contrary," Ian said. "They are exquisite," he admitted. Negotiation was not a factor in the face of such magnificence. "How much is left on the contract with my brother?"

The man fished a paper out of his pocket and handed it to him. Ian's eyes widened in surprise. They were no bargain, that was for certain. But eyeing the horses again, he knew he had to see through this purchase. His brother had clearly intended them as a gift to his intended. And if Verity did not want them, she might wish to sell them herself. Regardless, they would sell for twice as much on Nevis or St. Eustatius. Or they could unload them in Jamaica if Verity truly wanted to be rid of them, and even there be up fifty percent on the investment.

There was only one problem—with his other cargo, he'd only have room for ten more horses for Verity to select. Would she be angered by that? Feel as if he was not holding up his end of their agreement? Again, he looked to the two spirited horses and knew he had little choice in the matter. Duncan had clearly fallen for the horses for a reason . . . Verity would likely do the same.

Verity slowed her stride as she and Philip neared the *Inverness*. She looked back in confusion at the name of the ship to make certain this was Ian's. But yes, it was. And there was already a matched set of geldings being led aboard. A magnificent pair, to be certain, but not the horses she had chosen.

Ian glanced up, spied them, and hurried across the gangplank. He shook Philip's hand and then looked to Verity, then over his shoulder at the deck. "Forgive me, Verity. Ye see, I went to close the last bit of Duncan's business and found he'd chosen those two. They were too beautiful for me to say no. I hope I dinnae err in that choice. Take a look, lass. They are beauties."

"I believe I shall," she said, moving past him, knowing she was being rude but unable to stop herself. The geldings were stunningly beautiful, a matched pair like nothing she had seen since leaving England. Ian followed her into the hold, and they leaned over the central corral's railing. Verity stripped off her gloves, tossing them to the deck, clucked her tongue and lifted a hand, waiting for the nearest to notice her. At first he was too agitated, whinnying and ears rotating constantly, trying to take in his new surroundings. But then his brother came by and slowed, curious about her, so the first turned to pay attention as well. Verity spoke to them in a low voice, reaching up to stroke and scratch each one after they had accepted her.

Ian sidled up beside her, pretending to be completely focused on the horse beneath his hands while sneaking glances at Verity. She was so enrapt, so engaged, he might not even be present. And the horses . . . well, he'd had to fairly wrestle them aboard the ship, with the aid of three men. Verity appeared as if she was ready to ride them bareback and the horses willing to accommodate her. "So I take it that I made a good choice, Verity?"

"Oh, Ian. You did. They are"—she shook her head, still staring at the horses—"stunning."

"Aye. But it was Duncan who found them," he said hurriedly, feeling a flash of guilt. "Clearly he knew the way to your heart."

As soon as the words were out of his mouth

he regretted them, but she did not seem to. She only gave him a wistful smile, blinked her heavy lashes a few times, and then returned her attention to the horses. "What is their training to date?"

"To bit and harness but not to saddle."

She nodded in appreciation. "Good. Then I can see to the rest myself."

"Will you sell them with one of the fine carriages we brought aboard?" he asked.

Verity looked to the horses again. "Perhaps. Or perhaps I shall keep them. What did you pay for them?"

Ian pulled the receipt from his pocket and handed it to her. She whistled lowly, which made him want to laugh aloud. 'Twas a man's response, not a lady's. But from her, it seemed natural. She looked up, her brows knit in confusion, as if unaware that she'd uttered a sound. "What amuses you?"

"Ye, lass. A horse trader who might fall so in love with the horseflesh she intends to trade that she keeps them all for herself."

It was her turn to smile, a bit self-consciously. "Well, not all. But these?"

He turned to survey them again with her. "Aye, with these, I would well do the same. And I wager Duncan intended for ye to hold on to them." He paused, realizing what naturally followed. "Consider them a gift, if ye wish to keep them."

"Oh, Ian, I cannot!" she said, lifting a hand to her cheek. "Could not!"

"But these horses were meant for ye, lass." He reached up to stroke the nearest gelding's cheek. " 'Twas my brother who chose them, my brother who made the first payment. And 'twas out of his funds that I made the last. He meant them for ye. Consider it his last gift."

She blinked rapidly, clearly trying to hold back tears. " 'Tis . . . 'tis so extravagant a gift, Ian."

He smiled and nodded. "Indeed," he said, forcing the words beyond the swelling ball in his throat. "That is how my brother was with his affections." Then he left her to it, knowing she was but moments away from letting loose her tears and sensing she would not wish his company any longer.

He barked an order to his first mate, Michael, startling him. Then the second mate too, for good measure. The men had been gaping at Verity as if they had never seen a woman before. Both leapt into action and began shouting at the rest of the crew, preparing to make way, as Ian wearily opened the captain's door and closed it firmly behind him, before brushing away his own irritating tears.

CHAPTER EIGHT

They reached North Carolina in good time, where Verity made her selections over the course of five hours. He had expected two, perhaps three hours and would have complained had he not admired how she went about her business. First, she culled the herd of thirty potential animals down to eighteen. Next, she grilled not only the breeder but also demanded to see the groom and farrier, to whom she insisted on speaking with separately. After that she had four more horses removed. And she had the groom bring the rest to her in a side corral, one at a time.

Over the course of the next hour, one curious man after another drew closer, watching her take her time to settle each horse, at times absorbing half an hour, at times half a minute. She seemed to see none of her audience, only the horse, and each horse seemed mesmerized by her touch, her demeanor.

"She becalms them," muttered one man standing to Ian's left.

"Bewitches is more like it," said another. "Have you ever seen such a thing?"

"She has a way with all animals," Philip said.

"Always did, even as a child. You should see how she manages her falcon. Bested most of the men at the club back in England. And she even trained a little monkey as a pet for a boy on Nevis."

Ian blinked in surprise. The woman was a champion falconer? Her gift included training monkeys? He laughed under his breath. Clearly, there was much yet to discover about this girl.

She continued her work among the horses. Running her hands along flanks and legs, lifting up each hoof one at a time to examine it.

"What's she doin' now?" asked a boy to Ian's right as Verity grabbed hold of a mare's cheeks and stared into her eyes.

"I dunno," said the child's father. "Examining her sight?"

"Looks like she's talkin' to her, somehow. Silent-like."

"That's what I said," said the man on Ian's left. "Bewitching them!"

Ian shifted, wishing Verity would move on before that line of thinking took hold. Thankfully, she swayed to look at one side of the horse's jaw and then the other. Carefully she made a move, and the horse opened its mouth.

"Well, I'll be!" said a newcomer, joining the rest. " 'Tis as if he be presenting his teeth to the barber and not some woman!"

The others laughed. Still, Verity appeared aware of only the horse before her. In time, the fourteen were whittled down to twelve, then reluctantly to ten. At last she turned to the exasperated horse trader. "I want these ten, but I'd like you to hold those two in the side corral for me. The good captain there," she said, pointing to Ian, "will be back for them."

"Fine, fine," said the man, who seemed eager to be rid of her, his every action saying, *Just so long as you are not with him.* Apparently he was used to men doing cursory examinations and taking his word for it. Horses were in heavy demand on the mainland as well as the islands, and to be taxed so to make a sale might mean they would not be welcomed back, Ian feared. It irritated him, at first, Verity's assumption that he would do as she asked and return for the other two horses. But his irritation gave sway to gladness as he considered further business dealings with Verity Banning. And had he not himself said he intended to do nothing but trade between the mainland and the Indies? Perhaps running cargo for her and other merchants would give him all the rationale he needed to pick up critical information for revolutionaries as they made the necessary preparations to mobilize.

If that was what he was supposed to be doing. *Fine spy ye are, McKintrick,* he chided himself. *Ye are not even certain that McKay was saying what you thought he was saying, are ye?*

There was only one way to find out. Collect

valuable information, return to the American colonies, and meet with him again. Then he could determine if the old man was a conduit to the network he sought . . . or simply a man in need of a drinking partner. And in the meantime? His eyes again found Verity, who was brushing her hands together, her lacy sleeves pushed up to her elbows. Her skirts were covered in dust, and she laughed as one of the mares nudged her backside, as if already treating her like a beloved mistress.

No, in the meantime, he didn't mind sharing some of his days with this one at all.

Flush with the excitement over her fine selection of horses, Verity eagerly agreed to Ian's suggestion that they sup at the local tavern before heading back to the *Inverness*. It wasn't until they were in the rowdy gathering place—in which a group of men in one corner were singing while in the opposite corner another group debated loudly—that she realized how famished she was. The heavenly aroma of fresh-baked meat pie and the yeasty smell of ale made it all the worse.

Soon they were served both, the maid never asking if they cared for it. It was as if she had seen the hunger written in their wide, eager eyes. Together, Philip, Ian, and Verity dug in, the rich, brown crust crackling beneath their spoons, allowing steam to escape. Inside was a heavenly gravy covering thick chunks of beef and rounds of carrots and onions. In seconds, Verity had burned her tongue, unable to avoid the temptation to shovel in a spoonful before the food was properly cooled.

Philip and Ian shared stories of the men at the stables gawking at Verity in wonder, and she blushed under their collective appreciation. Philip, of course, had seen her with Brutus, as well as the horses at the Double T, but it was Ian's unabashed intrigue with her talent with animals that truly made her alternately fight off the urge to squirm or soak in his admiration. She liked that she had impressed him, she decided.

Why was that important to her? She dared to steal a glance at him as he turned to speak to a man he'd met at the stables. He was handsome, lithe, and strong. Not as tall as his brother had been but still formidable. His hair was a sable brown, long and straight, and tied neatly at the nape of his neck, his eyes an engaging green. He tended to show his emotions in quick fashion—a short laugh, a swift frown—yet his expression was constantly changing. And she liked how he smiled—the gentle curve of his lips, the crinkling at his eyes. He was largely a sober man, those keen eyes ever-searching, taking in all about him, as if cataloguing details and absorbing information everywhere.

Ian glanced over his shoulder to her and their eyes met. That curve of his lips widened a bit even as his eyes narrowed, silently expressing curiosity over her attention. Embarrassed at having been caught, she hurriedly turned her attention back to the bits of crust still clinging to her bowl, hoping he would think no more of it.

Philip was paying the maid for their supper when the door burst open and a man shouted for attention. " 'Tis begun, boys!" bellowed the man. Gradually, the room quieted as he waited. " 'Tis begun!" he yelled again.

All eyes turned to him, except for two very inebriated men who continued on in their song for another verse before lifting their dazed eyes to the door, clearly wondering who dared to interfere in their revelry.

"The men in Massachusetts have done it!" yelled the man, taking a few strides forward in order for all to hear. "Weary of the Intolerable Acts, and aware that King George intended to steal their supplies, the minutemen stood up to the lobsterbacks! Face-to-face, the redcoats dared to fire on our own, drawing first blood! Well, let me tell you," he said, lifting a finger to hush the crowd as gasps and shouts filled the room, "they did not let them get away with it! Both sides lost men, but our militias chased them all the way from Lexington and Concord back to Boston. It has begun, boys! Revolution has begun!"

The tavern erupted in pandemonium. Cheers, tears, hugs, and shouts. Eager direction for the local militia to gather this very night. Calls for more ale. The three serving maids were hugged and kissed by one man after another as if they belonged to all.

With one shared look of consternation, Ian grabbed Verity's hand and pulled her to her feet. Philip was right behind her, shoving aside one man who attempted to reach for her and then blocking her from another. Once outside, they paused, each taking a deep breath of the dewy dusk, but all along the street they saw similar rowdy celebrations taking place.

"What is it you fear?" Verity asked. "You do not sail under a Union Jack."

" 'Tis not fear of the rebels," he said, tucking her hand in the crook of his arm and setting a swift pace for the harbor, Philip on her other side. " 'Tis fear of the king's response. If what that man said is true . . . if blood has been shed and the Brits have been forced back to Boston, war is already upon us."

They walked the rest of the way in silence. Verity knew then what he wanted. The safety of the ship, a place apart from such heated emotions in which to think. And moreover, protection for her.

They had reached the harbor's edge when a woman in fine silks rushed over to them, a small girl clinging to her skirts, a bag in her other hand. "Pardon, but are you Captain McKintrick?"

"Aye," he said, turning to her. "How may I be of service?"

The woman, who appeared to be in her early thirties, glanced over her shoulder, then back to him. "I am the mayor's wife, Lady Channing. My husband has been arrested. Having gained word this noon, he sent me and my daughter to find the first ship out. I hear the *Inverness* is that ship. May we have passage?"

Ian paused. "But my lady, we embark for Nevis. Do you wish to travel so far?"

"I prefer South Carolina. Is it possible to make a stop there? My husband thought I might find passage to England from there. There is word of other Loyalists fleeing for home."

Behind her, the street was rife with tension. Fear and jubilation twining into one coiled rattlesnake. Three men in homespun advanced on one man in a fine coat, striking him to the ground and kicking him. One of them called, "Tar! Put some tar on the boil! And bring feathers!"

Five men carrying torches set fire to a print shop, screaming that "No more words shall be printed for the Loyalist cause!" In seconds, the shop was ablaze and threatening others around it.

The mayhem seemed to confirm Ian's decision. "Come with us, Lady Channing. We shall see to your safety," he said grimly.

Philip took Verity's arm, and they followed behind Ian, who had lifted the small girl to his hip and laid a gentle, protective hand on Lady Channing's lower back. Verity liked that he had given this woman aid—it showed honor in him, even though she knew rebellion was swiftly intensifying in his own heart. She also liked how he stole glances at the child, teasing a shy smile from her, as if he wished to alleviate her fears. When had he been about children before? Perhaps Marjorie had little ones . . . she could not remember what Duncan had said.

They reached the *Inverness*'s skiff onshore. Two crewmen stood guard. "Is it true, Captain?" asked one. "Has war begun?"

"Perhaps," Ian allowed. "This is Lady Channing and her daughter," he said, setting the girl into the skiff and pointing to the seat in back, then turning to help the lady step into it next. "We shall be seeing them to safety in South Carolina before embarking for Nevis. Are the horses and all the cargo safely aboard?"

"Aye, Captain," said one sailor. "All is in order."

"Good, then," Ian said.

Philip helped Verity into the front of the skiff. Ian climbed in the opposite side and went to sit in the back beside Lady Channing.

Verity wondered briefly about the pang of jealousy this caused her. She chastised herself. What was this? Was she so spoiled by the attentions and guardianship of two men that she could not do without one for a moment? Particularly when the dear lady and her child were in such need? And what place did such emotion have in her heart, when she had so newly discovered Duncan's loss?

One crewman took up the oars while the other shoved them off, jumping on top of the front as the boat cleared the last of the sand. He edged past her with a quiet, "Pardon, ma'am," and moved to sit beside his comrade on the widest bench between the oars. Together, they turned the skiff around and set off toward the anchored *Inverness*.

Verity gazed back at the heavily wooded slopes of North Carolina, thinking about the men and women in the tavern and on the streets. About the fury, the elation, the shouts for freedom. The fact that England had shot her own people. Colonists in rebellion, to be certain, but her very own. How the wife and child of a mayor had been forced to flee. About warnings and predictions of the future that had now evolved from potential to present reality.

Everything was about to change.

Between seeing to the ship and doing what he could to comfort Lady Channing, Ian found not the time to go in search of Verity until it was almost noon. It was in the stables that he found her, brushing down a gelding and whispering words of encouragement in his ear. Ian settled at the rail to watch her. The way she moved about, touching and soothing the horse, was almost a mesmerizing dance, and Ian reluctantly admitted to himself that he wished he could continue to watch her, unseen. Which was entirely improper, of course. He cleared his throat.

She startled and turned to stare at him, leaning on the top rail of the tiny stall. With the constant wash of the waves outside the ship and the creak of timbers, it was clear she had not heard his approach.

"Captain!" she said, putting her hands on her hips. "How long have you been standing there?" Tendrils of hair had come loose from their knot, framing her beautiful face.

"Long enough to decide you might aid me."

"Aid you?"

"With Lady Channing. Her daughter, at least, has given in to a morning nap. But the lady is as skittish as a deer among lions, which makes my men surly. Might you attempt your own charms?"

She gave him a rueful smile. "I shall do my best."

"Thank you."

With that, Ian turned to go. But just before she was out of sight, he turned to watch her reach for a bit and slide it in the gelding's reluctant mouth. She took hold of the reins on either side and forced the horse's head down, leaning her own forehead in to touch it to his, still crooning words Ian could not make out.

Go, man, he told himself. *Lest she catch you staring again.* But as he climbed the ramp and emerged on the deck, he wondered if it would have been worth the risk for but a few more seconds of watching her. Because there was something about Verity Banning that only made him want more.

Verity led the gelding out of the stall. She knew from experience that it settled her own nerves if she had another to consider first. Perhaps Lady Channing was a horsewoman. A bit of care for this fine mount might be just what she needed.

Verity passed Philip as she climbed the ramp. "Would you like me to join you?" he asked.

"That would be grand, Philip," she said. "That cream-colored filly is itching for some fresh air, I think. Do you believe you can handle her?"

He cast her a wry smile. "Well, I've not your ways, miss, but I shall attempt it."

As she reached the deck, the gelding pulled on the reins, his nostrils flaring. He tossed his head, whinnying with partial terror, partial excitement to see the miles of waves before him after the confines of the stables. "Easy, boy, easy," she crooned, stroking his neck while deftly stepping away to avoid his hoof crushing her foot. "There now, all is well. All is well." When finally the horse settled down, Verity looked around for Lady Channing. The woman was walking her way, head down, her hands worrying a handkerchief into a twist.

"Lady Channing!" she called, smiling when the woman looked up in surprise to see her and the horse on deck. "Lady Channing, might you give me some assistance?"

The woman frowned a bit and stepped closer. "How might I help?"

"I have a stable full of horses down below, all eager for a chance to stretch their legs. Are you an experienced horsewoman?"

"I am," she said, as if offended that Verity would even ask.

"Have you any experience with unbroken horses?" Verity pressed.

"I raised my own pony when I was a girl."

"Excellent." Verity handed her the reins. "Would you be so kind as to lead this fellow about the deck? I shall join you in a moment."

She stalked to the ramp and, when Philip emerged with the filly, took her reins from him. "Thank you, Philip. I can take her from here."

"Very well, miss."

She hurried to catch up with Lady Channing, who periodically stopped to wrestle the gelding into submission, then continued on. When she fell into step beside them, both horses eased. There was something about being fated to the same exercise that soothed them, Verity mused. Perhaps it was the same with people.

"Captain McKintrick said we should have you to South Carolina soon after our noon meal," she said. "He thinks your husband was right. There will likely be an England-bound ship or two there. Few will be eager to venture toward New England. They shall likely fill their holds with Carolina goods and be on their way across the Atlantic."

"He said the same to me," the woman said. "But, Miss Banning, do you truly think I ought to go? Should I not return and see if I might be of some aid to my husband?"

"I think your husband knew what he was doing when he sent you on your way," Verity said. "The best thing you can do for him is to remove yourself and your daughter from harm's way. Trust his friends to see to his care."

"There are precious few of them left," said Lady Channing. "Friends, that is. This last year . . . Ahh, if only we had left sooner. I begged him to go. Begged him. But he would hear none of it. Now . . ."

Verity said nothing as the woman fell silent. But she might as well have voiced her concerns. They were both thinking it. Would her husband be tarred and feathered? Ridden out of town on a rail? Or worse, hanged by the neck?

"Spirits were high among the rebels when we

left last night," Verity said. "But they likely will be more sensible this morning. Even the rebels will wish to behave honorably, by and large, and if your husband agrees to leave town, they will allow it. If they can obtain power without bloodshed, they shall opt for that."

Ian's poor cabin boy was assigned the unenviable task of following behind the horses, cleaning up manure and swabbing the decks after they were returned below. Verity glimpsed the gap-toothed Arnold, his face comically dismayed as he scooped up a steaming pile and threw it overboard. "The poor child," she said as she and Lady Channing passed Ian and his first mate, Michael, at the wheel. "May I give him some gift at the end of the voyage as thanks for his aid?"

Ian followed her gaze and then turned back smiling and shook his head. "Ach, no. 'Tis good for the wee lad. Best to learn that one can manage such things and live through it."

"I'd rather be assigned that duty than the latrine," Michael put in.

She nodded in full agreement. But then she considered the various items she'd purchased for her store. There was a puzzle game made out of horse nails; that would keep him busy on board ship as well as give him something with which to challenge the crew. She could just see him standing beside them, well knowing how to solve it, while they struggled. Or perhaps a backgammon board. "I should give him something to crow about and help temper his memories of the added work my voyage meant for him," she said to Lady Channing. "Or future voyages."

"So you shall sail with the handsome Captain McKintrick more than this once?" Lady Channing said.

"Perhaps," Verity said, shifting nervously under her penetrating gaze. What did she find so intriguing about that? "What with this new venture in Nevis . . . and if this potential war does not disrupt my plans . . . Well, yes. It would be a boon to have Captain McKintrick's assistance."

Lady Channing glanced at Ian's back. "He has a . . . *commanding* presence." Her catlike eyes slid to Verity, a small smile at her lips. "And the way he looks at you, my dear, is not merely as a potential merchant partner."

"Oh!" Verity said, blushing. Surely the woman was wrong. Only seeking a sorely needed diversion to her own life. It surprised her, how much she liked the thought of an ongoing partnership with Ian. But it was merely a sensible decision; she liked how the man ran his ship, not because of any romance.

He was a more strident captain than Duncan had been, she mused. Whereas Duncan had joked and cajoled—and when necessary, demanded—it was clear that to a man, none dared to question Ian's authority. They simply did as he asked, the moment he asked it. The majority had sailed with him before, and she knew that denoted respect. And while Duncan had been broad-focused, distracted at times by either story or sight, Ian seemed to miss nothing, from a knot that must be retied, to a sail that needed trimming, to a sailor's shirt that needed laundering. Verity found his keen attention to detail—knowing he seemed to catalogue everything about her as well—both unsettling and reassuring. He made her feel *seen,* so thoroughly that she felt conversely free and yet vulnerable too, exposed in a way. Half of her wished to escape him; half was glad that the confines of the ship forced constant contact.

"Will you join me in another game tonight, Philip?" Ian was asking when they came around again. Was he consciously avoiding looking at her? Or had Lady Channing's intimations put a foolish thought in her head?

"Glutton for punishment, are you, Captain?" Philip teased. He'd beaten him at chess every night they'd played.

"I may be a slow learner, but I'm dogged," he returned. "I'm convinced that if I play a bit more, I might learn all your tricks and finally have a chance to best ye."

Philip lifted a brow and cocked his head. " 'Tis your call, Captain. I only wish to salvage your reputation among your crew."

Ian barked a laugh. "If only that were true. Any

idea how my losses have become the talk of the ship when it is only you, Miss Verity, and young Arnold in my quarters each eve?"

Philip frowned, feigning confusion, then tapped his lips and lifted his brows. "Ship rats with loose tongues?"

"Ship rats indeed," Ian said. But he laughed under his breath as he said it.

Verity liked that about him. His humility and ease. And it surprised her, since in contrast she'd also witnessed his lack of tolerance for the ways his men failed him. In those moments when he discovered a sailor not giving him his very best, or worse, lying, he was fearsome, a man no one would dare challenge. He was utterly in command.

And yet after Lady Channing and her daughter were escorted to the deck of the first England-bound vessel they found, and they settled into curiously languid days on the sea, tacking back and forth against the wind and currents toward the West Indies, Ian seemed relaxed, lighter. The voyage was going perfectly, the winds a crisp four knots, the seas never so high as to be worrisome. Most days, Ian and the other crewmen helped Philip and her to exercise the horses. One afternoon, Philip paused with his horse to talk with a crewman, and Ian took his place beside her. He reached underneath the mare's chin and stroked it. "Ach, you're a bonny lassie, are you not?"

Verity smiled. "I've noticed your brogue is not as thick as your brother's," she said. "But it gets thicker around the horses. Or when you're weary."

"Or about a bonny lass, whether she be equine or human," Ian said with some exaggeration and a wink. He held her gaze a second too long for her to avoid blushing. How did he do that? Make her feel like a girl at her first ball with but a lingering look and playful word?

She shifted uneasily. What was this between them? Innocent flirtation? Or something more? And was it right for them to succumb to it, given that Duncan had only been so recently buried in their hearts?

"Duncan's became stronger because he sailed with our uncle, and I was still at school. Our uncle spoke a fair amount of Gaelic." He laughed softly in memory as he leaned over the rail, looking out. "That man's brogue was as thick as the English fog. Even I could not understand him a' times. And he was the one who taught us to ride horses, so I suppose that when I'm with horses, it rises."

"I see. And who did you learn to sail under, if not your uncle?"

"They were all Scotsmen. My uncle never had much to do with anyone he'd not known all his life. But when Duncan went to sea with my uncle as his cabin boy, I was too young to stay alone.

So they sent me to boarding school, where the English nuns dinnae take kindly to my 'backward tongue,' ye see. They fair whipped my hands every time I used the words *fash* or the like."

She smiled sadly at him, aware that he was again emphasizing his brogue for the sake of the story, but also sharing a tender memory. "I was sent to finishing school, but it was Protestant," she said. "From what I hear, most of the nuns who run schools are either saints or sinners."

"Nay, they are both," Ian said. "As am I. Both sinner and saint, every day of my life. They did the best they could. 'Twould be one thing to teach a group of fine young lasses at finishing school, but I would not envy the nuns the task of forming little hooligans into fine gentlemen. Would you?"

She smiled. "Never," she said, reaching up to pat her own charge's flank. "I will gladly take a horse to a little hooligan any day."

"Wise choice, lass," he said.

"Still," she said, daring to go on, "I find it . . . reassuring. The brogue. I think the horses like it too."

"Ye do?" he asked, his handsome ruddy-brown brows rising.

"Aye, lad," she said in good imitation of him, "that I do."

"Weel, weel, weel," Ian said in clear delight. "Do ye mean to tell me, lass, that there be a highlander's heart within that fine English form?"

She laughed and brought a hand to her mouth, feeling a blush bloom at her cheeks again at his casual, if playful, compliment. And as he turned to speak to his mate, she realized that for the first time in a long time she felt free and . . . happy. As she led her horse back to the corral, then turned to the rail for a few moments away from Ian—with whom she was becoming a bit too familiar—she considered all that led to this sudden sense of joy.

It surprised her, she acknowledged. It made her feel ashamed, in some ways, so soon after learning of Duncan's death. But as she stared across the whitecap waves, she knew he'd *want* her to feel such joy. To not begrudge herself a gift as some misguided act of penitence. She took a deep breath of the briny air and closed her eyes to feel the cool spray of the water, the wind drying it on her cheeks in seconds.

She felt the deep rock and sway of the ship, heard the pop of wind catching the sails. Listened as men relayed commands, teased and laughed together, high up in the rigging. She knew they watched her, wondered over her ways with the horses, and she overheard them commenting about the captain's keen attentions to the "pretty lass." At first it seemed an intrusion. But now she felt a growing pride as well as an acceptance of their presence—rather like the vervet monkeys of Nevis, hovering about in the trees, chattering, observing, scattering when she turned her attention their way. And for the first time, she glimpsed a bit of how the sea could capture a man's heart . . . or a woman's.

Thank you for this, Lord, she prayed silently, looking again to the waves. *This joy soothing my grief over Duncan. For this sense of purpose, these horses, this voyage, and* . . . She paused, frowned. But there was no shame in it, was there? To be glad of a new friend, a captain who could see her and her precious cargo through? *And for Ian,* she finished.

CHAPTER NINE

As much as she found their three-week voyage more pleasurable than she had imagined, Verity was thrilled when they'd left Jamaica and the islands began rolling by the stern—Anguilla, St. Martin, St. Barthélemy, Saba . . . At last she spied the rolling hills of St. Kitts and the conical shape of tiny Nevis in the distance. *Home,* she thought. And it surprised her, that word. As much as she'd told Keturah and Selah that she was coming to feel at home there, she'd always thought of Hartwick as her true home.

Hartwick, she thought with a pang. Now sold, their precious possessions in storage, the rest gone. The remaining funds—precious little, after all their bills had been paid—distributed between the three sisters. And all of Verity's now invested in horseflesh and cargo, heading back to Nevis. The place everyone she loved best now called home.

She was eager to let this next chapter of her life unfold. She'd oft thought it would include Duncan, dreaming that he might return to her and settle on Nevis's shore. But that had clearly not been meant to be.

Now, more than ever, she was glad that she had

set out to the mainland to begin her new business. It was good for her mind and heart to have so many tasks at hand, rather than to wallow in her grief. Over the last years, she'd seen so many die . . . from disease, from injury, even two men as a result of a senseless duel. Every other week, it seemed, they paid their respects by visiting either the cemetery at St. Philips or the slaves' plot at the Double T or at other plantations. "Take all that life offers you, Daughter," she remembered her father saying, "every day you have it. The morrow is a hope, not a promise."

Was that how he lived his life here on Nevis? Making the most of the life offered to him, even as he missed his wife and daughters at home? She hadn't spent nearly as much time with her father as her heart had longed for. But her father molded her still, even from afar. His dreams for the plantation and his plans to improve it were not unlike her own dreams for her mercantile, her trade in horses. And had not imagining Duncan's voyages to the mainland deepened those dreams?

Verity believed that God used everything and everyone in one's life to speak to them, if one allowed it. To teach, to mold, to influence, to guide, to encourage. If one was to make the most of this life, one had to remain open to it all, grabbing hold of the good, even in the midst of the grief.

Her eyes drifted over to Ian, then to the first

mate, and back to Ian. She startled, realizing what she was thinking. *The good amidst the grief.*

She studied him. She liked how the wind pulled some of his auburn hair loose from the tie at the nape of his neck. Ruffled and filled the open neck of his shirt. His covert smile as McKay said something in his ear that amused him. How his eyes darted from one sail to the next, encompassing the whole of the ship within seconds, narrowing in on particulars not up to his expectations and muttering corrections to Michael, which his first mate then turned and shouted to the crew. She would miss watching him at work, as she had Duncan. Both men were fully in command of their ships, but each clearly unique.

The good amidst the grief.

He looked over at her then, as if sensing her gaze. Gave her a tentative, curious smile.

She ducked her head and hurriedly left the deck for her cabin, suddenly glad for the need to gather her things.

There were two British vessels on patrol about St. Kitts and Nevis when they began to tack toward Charlestown from the far side of Saba. They sailed in formation, indicating trouble. "MacGuire!" Ian shouted to the crow's nest, not waiting for Michael's relay. "Any vessels of concern about?"

The skinny man took another look in all directions, lifted his spyglass to the west. " 'Tis most likely a Frenchie off of Statia that has their knickers in a wad, Cap'n!"

Ian gave a relieved nod. In times of relative peace, privateers were fairly rare in these waters. And while he had the guns, the sails, and the manpower to outrun many of them, he found himself anxious to get Miss Verity Banning and her horses safely home. It hadn't really occurred to him until that moment how it weighed upon him, her safety. But as he considered how he'd consulted the charts and the octant again and again—so much so that McKay had begun to tease him—he'd thought it was all due to this being the maiden voyage aboard his new sloop. Then he admitted to himself that it was more likely due to a certain maid aboard that drove him.

He wasn't a man to shy away from his own thoughts and feelings. His draw to the woman had been immediate. Still, it wasn't right. She had been Duncan's, and he had no right to her other than to be her guardian, her brother, her protector, her servant. *Keep it straight, man,* he sternly told himself. *There will be other bonny lasses in the ports to come. Ye need not this one.*

She strode across the deck at that point, face alight with Nevis in view, now so close. The isle was a beauty for sure, with her steep, green peak and many windmills, furiously churning. But it was Verity who captured him. With her long, curly brown hair, several loose strands dancing in the wind. Her fine profile. Long neck. Pleasing curves . . .

Keep it straight, man.

"Captain," Michael said, edging into his line of vision. He smiled in confusion and then curiosity, blatantly looking at Verity and then to Ian and back again.

"Somethin' you need, McKay?" Ian groused.

"Yes, Cap'n," he said, barely swallowing his grin. "Asking permission to come about. We're nearly past—"

"Yes, yes," Ian interrupted. "Come about!" he shouted, not waiting for his mate to repeat the order.

McKay crossed his arms and stood there, his grin spreading.

"Make yourself useful, posthaste," Ian growled. "Before I assign you latrine duty."

Disembarking the *Inverness* made Verity remember what it was like to leave Duncan's ship, the *Restoration*, and that first frightening day on Nevis. How different it was to arrive again now, two years later! And yet there was something similar too. An odd tug on her heart, a regret that her time aboard ship with a certain gentleman had drawn to a close.

'Tis for the best, she told herself sternly. *The last thing you need, Verity Banning, is for another sea captain to come courting you.*

But it was different, wasn't it? Ian wouldn't turn about and head for Europe and Africa. His goal was to establish trade between America and the Indies. Be anchored in these waters often.

Until he changes his mind. Or decides to go after Santiago, the privateer. Give him up. Allow these tender shoots of whatever is happening between you to wither.

She looked back to the *Inverness* and saw Ian, gesturing with wild hand motions between cargo and a crewman who apparently was not doing what he ought. The man scurried off to do what he was told, and Ian then turned to McKay to expend the remains of his frustration.

McKay put up his hands and nodded, and at last Ian heaved a sigh and began striding down the deck, all powerful motion and purpose, just as she reached the beach.

"Ahh, Miss Banning, back at last, I see," said Captain Howard, walking toward her, delight spreading his smile wide.

"Captain Howard," she said, electing to nod rather than attempt a curtsey on her shaky sea legs. She took Philip's hand and climbed from the skiff.

"I see that you were successful in your

endeavors," he said as she greeted Major Woodget and Lieutenant Angersoll beside him. "They appear a most fine herd. And mules too!"

She looked over her shoulder to where men were now leading the horses off the ship to a ferry, one by one, with Ian overseeing the process. "Indeed."

"I know our regiment will require at least four of them," the major said. "We had two expire last week of the colic and we were already two short for officers."

She gave him a demure smile. "Well, if you are at liberty to purchase at market price, you might soon be my first customer."

"Might?" He frowned playfully at her. "Come now, Miss Banning. You of all people would not dare to turn down the Crown's need."

"Of course not," she said carefully. "Although, as a new merchant, I must set off on the right foot or I shall not be able to afford to import more, eventually offering the Crown an even finer selection." She had to tread lightly—the king's men had been known to outright sequester mounts in times of need. But this man had been housed in her own home for some time; surely he would not dare to damage Keturah and Gray's goodwill by doing such a thing to her.

"Tell me, what news do you have of the Double T? Are my sisters well?" she asked anxiously.

"Quite," he said. "As is Gray and your people.

Though I suspect the mulatto child has missed you most."

She smiled. She had become quite close to Abraham in recent months. It had really begun when he found a baby monkey, alone in the jungle beside the remains of his mother, slowly starving to death. With the aid of mangoes, the boy had succeeded in coaxing the monkey into his jacket after a few hours and brought the vermin-laden animal home. It was Verity who had helped him nurse the baby monkey they dubbed "Biri" back to health and begun training him.

"Heavens, those two are magnificent," the major said, taking a few steps forward to admire the matched chestnut pair of geldings as they were led off the ferry to the beach.

"My new coach horses," she said smoothly, "a gift from a friend."

"A friend! Would that I had such a friend myself!" He turned toward her in wonder. "There is not a pair like them on the island. You shall be the talk of Nevis! Of St. Kitts too!"

"All the advertisement I shall need for my new mercantile. I intend to specialize in horses, carriages, and livery staples. Perhaps you may wish to come and call upon me in a week's time, when Banning's Bridlery is open for business. Open an account on behalf of the Crown?"

He gave Verity a surprised perusal and dabbed his sweating brow with a handkerchief. "Indeed."

The rest of the horses were off the ship now, Ian leading the last. He moved directly up toward Verity and the soldiers and handed the reins to her, then turned to greet the soldiers, with Verity making the introductions.

"Captain *McKintrick*," Captain Howard said thoughtfully. "Any relation to the Bannings' acquaintance?"

"My brother, God rest him," Ian said, crossing himself gravely and glancing toward her. "Duncan was on the king's own business when he was killed off the coast of Spain at the hands of a privateer."

"Frightful," Howard murmured. "A dreadful lot, those privateers. Please accept my condolences," he said to Ian, but Verity noted his concerned glances toward her. Living at the Double T, it had not taken him long to understand that Duncan McKintrick had been courting Verity. "And you as well, Miss Banning," he said.

It was her turn to bob her head in acceptance. "Thank you, Captain Howard. 'Tis most kind of you." This she said while thinking, *'Twas your king. Your king's foolish errand. Your king's demand . . .*

My king too, she corrected herself. *Are you not a loyal subject yourself? The great-granddaughter of an officer in the Royal Navy?*

Yes.

And . . . no.

Something had shifted within her as she received the news of Duncan's death. After being in the American colonies, seeing how they chafed under British rule and were now edging closer toward freedom. Perhaps it was collective, the officers' demand of lodging and meals, no matter how it taxed the resources of the plantation. Ian's own misguided attack on the soldiers in New York and subsequent imprisonment. And now the subtle insinuation that she had to sell the captain horses if he demanded it. Even though she was a woman of independent mind and character, she was first and foremost a subject of the king in the eyes of his men. Subservient, in the eyes of all men, really . . . except Duncan. And Gray and Philip. *And Ian . . .*

She glanced up at him and saw that he kept looking her way too. While he was cordially speaking with the soldiers, she knew he had brought the horse up to her as an excuse to intervene. To protect her, in some measure.

Captain Howard looked out toward Ian's sloop, then over to Ian and Verity, standing rather close together. His eyes narrowed. "Where are you off to next, Captain?"

"It depends on what I am able to sell here," Ian said, deftly avoiding mentioning St. Eustatius. British soldiers considered anyone who traded on the neighboring Dutch island as suspect, though they were powerless to stop it. "Perhaps

Verity shall assist me in selling it all and I shall take my ease on this pretty isle for a week before returning to the mainland."

"I see," Captain Howard said, again eyeing Verity when he noted Ian's usage of her given name. He frowned a bit. "I've heard tell that the trade is brisk over on St. Kitts too."

"Indeed. What news have you of these waters, Major?" he said, turning to the older man beside Howard. "Any enemy ships about? Privateers? We noted two vessels off of St. Kitts in formation, as if on alert to a wolf about the henhouse."

"No wolf that our navy cannot repel in swift order," he said, carefully offering nothing further. So there was some cause for alarm, but what?

"Glad to hear of it," Ian said.

"I beg your pardon," Verity said, "but I must see my horses to the mercantile corral and set about unpacking our goods."

"May we be of service, Miss Banning?" the major asked.

"Oh, no. I think Philip will have arranged all we need by now, and Ian's men have kindly offered their capable backs as well."

Captain Howard lifted his chin, lips pursed, and sniffed, clearly disliking her use of his given name too. She felt badly a moment, knowing she was using her familiarity with Ian to put the man off. But the last thing she wanted was for him to start calling upon her now that he knew Duncan was gone.

Is that it? Or is it because you would rather spend time with Ian?

No. Well, yes.

Send them all away, Verity. Remember yourself!

She reached for the reins in Ian's hand and gave him a curt nod. "Thank you, Captain. I'm certain you have much to see to aboard the *Inverness*."

He frowned in confusion. "Oh. Yes. But I'm happy to escort you to the mercantile."

"No need," she said with a light smile. "I well know the way."

"And as it happens, we are headed that way this instant," put in Captain Howard.

"Oh. Very well." Verity forced a small smile she hoped looked like some measure of gratitude. "I thank you, sir," she said to Ian with a deep curtsey, "for a fine voyage. And I shall look forward to our next."

"As shall I, lass," he said. He took her hand and bowed over it slowly, his last word so soft she barely heard it. It was his turn to glance toward Captain Howard with some concern, clearly wondering if she was dismissing him in favor of the soldier's company. "May I come to call this evening?"

"I fear I have so much to do I shall not be able to host," she said regretfully. Could they all not give her but a day to herself? But she knew she could not treat him quite so severely, despite the fact that they all were taxing her. "Perhaps tomorrow eve?"

He nodded slowly, his keen eyes moving to the soldiers and then back to her. "Tomorrow then. I shall look forward to it. Good day. Good day, gentlemen," he added.

The captain handed the horse's reins to one of the lieutenants behind him and offered Verity his arm. As they walked down the street toward her new mercantile and home—to which, she noted, he did not have to ask directions—he cleared his throat and glanced thoughtfully her way. "I am deeply grieved, Miss Banning, to hear of Captain McKintrick's loss. No doubt it pains you greatly."

"Indeed," she said. She felt torn. Half of her was moved by the man's compassion; the other half feared he saw an opening. "I think I shall mourn him for some time."

He frowned at that but nodded as if completely understanding. "A woman as fine as you does not lightly give her heart to another."

"No," she said with a sigh.

"So . . . your familiarity with this young Captain McKintrick . . . is that due to a sense of kinship between you?"

She lifted her brows in surprise. "Why, Captain Howard, I do not believe you and I are on such familiar terms."

"Oh, forgive me, forgive me. 'Tis only that, in these last months of residing in your family's presence, I find myself compelled by a measure of kinship and protection over you. And your sisters too," he added hastily.

She squeezed his arm and smiled, deciding to play upon this opening. "Thank you, Captain. We have always needed the care of brothers, being but three women on our own." She swallowed a smile as his frown deepened. Clearly, he already regretted the potential trap. "You are much like my dear brother Gray, always watching over us. I am so thankful for fine men like you in the world." She glanced up with some relief to see the mercantile come into view, with sailors and horses milling about. "Ahh, there 'tis! How I've looked forward to this fine moment!"

Philip came out of the shop, spied them, and came to greet the soldiers. "I'm glad to see you here, Miss Verity," he said, hands on hips and giving her a knowing glance. "The men are asking a hundred questions to which only you have the answers, I fear."

Dear Philip, always recognizing my need. He'd been a most suitable guardian and companion the whole voyage through. She slipped her hand from the soldier's arm and gave him a curtsey. "Thank you, Captain Howard. As you can see, I must be about my new business. Good day!" She hurried away from him then before he asked when he could come to inquire about his needed mounts, or worse, make a social call.

In seconds Verity was surrounded by five men, and she set to directing each. Then she called over to another, "Find the crates with my mannequins and displays. We'll need those unpacked first." She turned to a second. "Please be certain that the men put the four carriages in front of the shop in that small clearing, with enough room for customers to examine them from all sides. The horses can be settled into the stables."

The men set off to do as she bid. The shop was not large, but it was bustling with activity as the men discovered the crates she sought and began to pry them open, nails squealing. They were careful to preserve the wood, she saw, knowing that every crate would be reused by Verity to export goods herself or sold to another. Others were unpacking additional crates, and she set to directing each of them where to pile the goods inside. She would spend the day tomorrow setting up her shop, just as she wished. Today, if she could only begin the process, she would count it a success.

For a moment, however, she needed a bit of air and space. She climbed the steep stairs in the back to the small apartment she had set up before sailing for the mainland. There she noted that all was in order. A small room for a maid. A tiny kitchen. A parlor suitable for perhaps four people by the window, and down the hall, her own room and closet. She saw evidence then that her sisters had been here. There were curtains on the windows. A new vase on a shelf. Two new books on her bedside table, as well as a mosquito net hanging over her bed. That had been Gray, she decided. The mosquitoes tended to feast upon her brother-in-law, and he had insisted he install a net above every bed at the Double T. His care had extended to her here too.

She hadn't been lying about her gratitude toward Gray when speaking to the captain, she thought, as she fingered the fine netting. He had not only been good to Keturah, but was like a brother to her and Selah too. There was a part of her that wished she could rush home to them all. Yet they needed the room, what with the baby coming and the soldiers they had been forced to quarter.

And truth be told, Verity was ready to be on her own. To see to herself, for the most part, comforted by the fact that her family was within half an hour's ride if she needed them. It might be lonely, she thought, living here. But she'd have Trisa, the maid, Terence, her groom, Abe as stableboy, as well as a shop full of customers every day to keep her company. She moved to the window and opened the shutters wide to allow in the fresh air, thankful that from this part of town her shop took in breezes directly off the open water rather than the stinky harbor. She looked down at the bustling Charlestown streets full of sailors, merchants, travelers, and soldiers. No, it would be hard to be lonely here in town, with this many people nearby. Her shop and life would be so full she would not have time to miss her sisters or Gray or Philip.

Or Ian, she thought with a sick pang.

Duncan, she quickly corrected. And with that thought, the sick pang in her belly became a twist. What was happening in her heart? Her mind?

Who had she become? She had always considered herself extremely loyal. Now she was having feelings for Ian after but six weeks of knowing him?

But she had not spent much more time with Duncan. It had taken but six and a half weeks to cross the ocean from England to the West Indies. Yet that had been enough for them to begin a courtship.

Now here she was, ten months after seeing Duncan the last time. Six weeks after learning of his death. And six weeks into finding herself drawn to his brother.

Time to let them both go, she told herself. *You are home now, Verity. In Loyalist Nevis, far from the rebellion. Time to remember your loyal heart as well. Concentrate on the task at hand, not what might have been . . . or what could be. But what is, what is, what is.*

Chapter Ten

Ian counted the hours until he had permission to come to call upon Verity without seeming overeager. When they parted yesterday, she had seemed markedly different. Was it the British soldiers who swarmed about her like irritating gnats as soon as she was ashore? Or her concern for him, hoisting the Union Jack as he came to anchor off Charlestown, even though he'd flown the rebel stripes all the way to the islands?

It had left him unsettled, that. Flying the flag like a true Loyalist with nothing but rebellion burbling in his blood. But this was the course he had decided to take—and every crewman had agreed to follow. In order to make the most of these changing tides, and also aid the rebels, they would need to become shifting shadows. To a man, he had looked each in the eye and asked him to follow where he led them, regardless of consequence, and if he was unwilling, to disembark in South Carolina. To a man, every one of his thirty-two crewmen remained. He suspected a good number were due to Michael McKay and his lobbying for the growing rebellion. But some were due to their respect and admiration for Ian himself, and he took their vote of confidence as a measure of pride, like a soldier finding others were willing to follow him into battle.

For the first time, he felt worthy of such confidence.

Was it because Duncan, his elder brother, was gone? That he somehow felt the shift of familial responsibility onto his own shoulders, like a tartan-plaid blessing? Or because of . . .

Verity. Of how she looked at him. In wonder. Surprise. Pleasure.

But lastly, concern.

He thought again of his grandfather's pledge to support the cause of the king, the Crown, and all that it entailed. Of fealty. But then he thought of Duncan, of a few things he had said over the years . . . clearly, his brother had struggled too. Would he have thrown in his lot with the rebels? Or remained true to the mother country?

Not my mother country. Scotland is my mother country. Never England.

And with that, he was decided. It might cost him his ship, his freedom, even this fledgling desire to be worthy of Verity . . . whatever was to come, this was what God had brought him to. The quest for freedom.

If not for his kinsmen in Scotland, then freedom for his cousins in America.

Freedom.

That resolved, he managed to sell only ten

bushels of tobacco, and yet all of his hogsheads of flour, sugar, salt, corn, oats, and dried mackerel were gone within hours of arrival. Nevis and her sister islands were a hungry lot, and he could see how he could do a consistent trade without very much effort at all. The trick was to figure out the ratio of staples—such as corn or flour—to pleasures—such as tobacco—and supply each demand in appropriate measure. He was glad that Verity had insisted upon separate stores of all basics for her kinsmen on the Double T. From what he could see, they would need it.

Only his desire to see Verity kept him from hauling sail to St. Kitts and Statia to offer his remaining stores of tobacco in their markets. He found himself anxious to return to New York to find out how he might aid the rebel cause. Without Verity's cargo filling a good third of his hold, he wanted to ascertain what was most in demand, at what price, and where—be it Loyalist Nevis, French-held and thereby rebel Martinique, or the more worldly Statia.

It was but late April, and he figured he had until September to make as many runs as he could, pay off some debt, aid the rebel cause, as well as build up his coffers before he outfitted his sloop with additional guns and set off for Spain and Africa by way of England. After a visit with Marjorie, he'd head south. He would find that Santiago who had murdered his brother—and dispatch him to the fathoms of the sea—then load his hold with rare spices from Africa and return to the Indies and North American colonies to sell them.

Perhaps then, he thought, *this war will be more than a whisper, but rather a full-fledged shout of rebellion.*

Perhaps then, he added silently, as he approached Banning's Bridlery, *this lass's heart may have healed.* He opened the door and let his eyes adjust to the relative darkness after the bright tropical sun. Inside, two women were working on opposite sides of the shop—one a petite blonde, setting hats upon hooks on the wall, the second a statuesque brunette, her midriff round with child, moving a bulky crate atop another.

He hastened over to assist her. "Here, madame, allow me," he said, taking the crate from her.

She wiped her damp hair from her forehead and smiled gratefully. "Thank you, sir."

"Captain, madame," he corrected gently, turning to her, glancing around—hoping to spot Verity—and then back. "Captain Ian McKintrick."

"Ahh, yes," she said, her amber eyes widening and full lips parting in recognition. She brushed her chapped, work-roughened hands together and studied him more closely. "Duncan's brother, then. We have heard a great deal about you, Captain. A great deal. I am Mrs. Keturah

Covington. And this is my sister, Miss Selah Banning."

Ian smiled in delight and bowed over each woman's hand, saying the customary, "At your service." Why did it not surprise him that Verity's sisters would be hard at work in her shop and clearly accustomed to it? But the idea of Verity speaking about him to them? *A great deal . . .* the thought of it pleased him so that he had some difficulty finding his next words. He straightened and tucked his hat beneath one arm. "May I ask, is Verity about the shop?"

"She is," Keturah said, clearly not ready to dismiss him. Miss Selah edged closer too.

"I see," he said slowly, wondering what he would need to do to get past her sisters' scrutiny and to the lass herself. "It appears she left you two to set up shop, eh? 'Tis looking quite impressive." He turned to review the barrels of nails, the neat lines of reins and bits hanging from pegs, the sensible riding dresses, and piles of leather gloves.

"She has done fine work in her selections," Keturah said, following behind him. "Did you assist her?"

"Me? Nay. All I did was load her cargo in my hold and get her safely home. She is quite a unique woman, your sister. Very . . . competent."

"Indeed," Keturah said. "Fortunately she has a sound mind as well as a good dose of wisdom."

She paused, seeming to remember herself. "Captain, we were very sorry to hear of the loss of your brother."

Selah's blond curls bobbed as she nodded earnestly. "He was a fine man," the girl said. "A dear friend to us, really."

"As he was to many," Ian said, nodding soberly. "I thank ye for your condolences."

"Her affection for Duncan concerned me," Keturah said, turning to fiddle with a line of soap bars in a wide, flat box, even though they were perfectly straight already. "We well know the dangers the sea presents."

Ian understood then. She did not like it, the risk of loving a sailor. She wanted to protect her sister.

" 'Tis risky indeed," he allowed. "And yet have you not seen the dangers yourselves of living on-island? 'Tis my experience that there is far more disease in any given port than aboard a ship."

"Unless disease sneaks aboard a ship too," Keturah returned, lifting a formidable chin.

"True enough." Ian gave her a curious smile. "Still, you are a woman—women," he amended, glancing Selah's way, "who left the securities of life in England to travel here, unaccompanied by husbands, to see to your father's plantation. That does not seem the nature of someone averse to facing risk and danger."

Keturah sniffed and faced him, her wide, amber eyes unflinching. "There are some risks one must take, and others one might avoid. My sister risked her heart on a sea captain once . . ."

She should not do so again, he silently finished for her.

"I am here to consult with Miss Verity on what she wants me to retrieve for her on this next voyage," he said carefully. "I am to ship out tomorrow and will be gone for a month or more."

Keturah was now on the other side of the counter and rubbed the mahogany wood with a cloth. "Is that *all* you are here to see her about?" she asked, casting him a pointed look. "For, Captain, her heart is quite tender right now. As is yours, I suspect. And shared grief has a way of bringing souls together. At times that feels like a balm, and people often mistake it for something more."

Selah fidgeted beside her, wringing her hands and looking back and forth between them. "Keturah," she whispered with a frown knitting her delicate brows.

Ian laughed softly under his breath and turned his tricorn in his hands, considering Keturah. "Plainly, Verity learned to be forthright from you, Mrs. Covington," he said with a tip of his head, nothing but wry respect in his mind.

She allowed him a small smile. "As we all have unfortunately learned, Captain, life can be fleeting. I find it best to get to one's point rather than play about it."

" 'Tis refreshing to meet women such as you. I never was one to enjoy coy or disingenuous conversation."

"Good. Then we understand each other?"

He regarded her. "I understand that you have your sister's best interests at heart. As do I," he allowed evenly. "Speaking of Miss Verity . . . where might I find her?" he pressed.

Keturah held his gaze a moment and then reluctantly lifted a hand. "She is out back, working with the horses in the corral. She opens her shop tomorrow—Selah and I are only here to help with the finishing touches."

"And you have done a grand job of it," he said, nodding to each and sweeping his gaze around the room. "I imagine when I return, Verity will have sold every bit of it."

"I hope so," Keturah said, wrinkles of concern lining her forehead. This one, the eldest, clearly spent a fair amount of time fretting over her sisters.

"I think it shall all sell," Selah declared, "and she shall be anxiously awaiting new cargo from you, sir."

" 'Tis been a pleasure to meet you both," Ian said. "Perhaps we shall meet again when I reach Nevis next?"

"Perhaps," Keturah said. At the same time,

146

Selah said, "Oh yes! You must come to call upon us at the Double T!" The blonde ignored her sister's withering look and went to the door. "Verity will be glad you came to say farewell. Good day, Captain."

He grinned at her and settled his hat atop his head. The girl clearly wished to loosen the ties her sister had attempted to knot. "Good day, Miss Banning, Mrs. Covington," he said, then disappeared out the door.

He strode down a narrow alleyway between the stone buildings and breathed a sigh of relief as rock gave way to swaying cane, climbing up the hill. There were five windmills within view, denoting various plantations, and three grand homes within sight—the nearest rather expansive, the farthest in dire disrepair. The cane ended at the edge of a dirt road, and before him was nothing but an acre of burgeoning jungle brush and a path leading up and over a small hill.

He heard them before he saw them—the whinny of a horse, the steady clop of hoofbeats.

At the crest of the hill was a large corral, around which Verity rode one of the chestnut geldings, and she was dressed in . . . *breeches.* Ian stepped forward and leaned on the upper rail, putting one boot on the lower. He saw a small mulatto child perched on the top rail beside the stables, a vervet monkey scampering back and forth across his shoulders and arms as if the boy were some sort of tree. On the other side of the gate that led into the stables and leaning against the railing was an older Negro who met his eye and gave him a deferential nod. A guardian, he figured. Or groom perhaps?

Verity spied him and smiled. "Ian!" She eased the gelding into a walk and then slowed him until she could guide him closer. She praised the horse, reaching down to pat his cheek and stroke his neck with a soothing "Good boy," and, "That's my bonny boy."

"Boys cannae be bonny, lass," he said, reaching up his fist to allow the gelding to sniff him. "Only lasses can be *bonny*. Boys are *braw*."

"Is that so?" she said, sliding off the gelding's back with practiced ease and moving toward the rail. "Weel, if there ever was a bonny boy, is he not it?"

Ian laughed under his breath.

"And what of the infamous 'Bonny Prince Charlie,' laddie?"

"Well, lass, I hear tell that the man was a bit of a dandy," he allowed. "Perhaps that was it." It amused him, her attempts at the brogue. Made him think that she might have picked up a measure of his way of talking as they crossed the Caribbean. Or had it been Duncan? Even that thought could not dim his smile—he was too glad to see her.

"How does the day find you, Verity?" he asked,

scanning her dewy, sun-kissed cheeks and brow, their pink hue only seeming to make her green eyes more vibrant. He stroked the gelding's long nose.

"I am well," she returned. "And you? How go your efforts to sell your wares?"

"All but a bit of the tobacco is gone already. I thought I might head to St. Kitts or Statia tomorrow to sell the last of it, then set sail again to the mainland. But I could not depart before doing as you bade me to do—come and call on you."

"I bade you to do so, did I?" she said, her eyes and lips slanting up. "I seem to recall that it was you who asked it of me."

"Ach, is that how it was?" he said, rubbing his chin. "And here I thought some bonny lass was fearing I'd leave port without my giving her a mite of attention."

She smiled but then seemed to catch herself. She ran her hands down her shirt, attempting to smooth it, belatedly realizing she was in breeches. She lifted her hands. "What am I to do? One cannot train a horse to carry a rider if one does not ride said horse as a man does."

"Far more sensible, I would wager," Ian said, waving his hat as if to wave away her embarrassment.

"Yes, but the islanders do not favor it. My sisters and I wore my father's breeches when

149

we first came to work at Tabletop." She led the gelding over to the older man and handed him the reins. "Captain McKintrick, this is my new groom, Terence. Over there is Abraham, a fine stableboy and . . . friend."

Ian nodded to Terence and then to Abraham, who waved in greeting. The boy followed the older man and gelding into the stables. But inwardly Ian could not shed the image of all three sisters working the fields in breeches. It made him smile. No wonder the islanders were dismayed. And no wonder his brother had been enchanted.

"Thank you for coming to say farewell, Captain McKintrick," she said.

He frowned. Why the formality all of a sudden?

"I imagine you have much yet to do before you set sail, and I confess, I have a great deal to do as well." She looked away, clearly ill at ease.

Was Verity trying to get rid of him? Before anything became more . . . intimate?

"I shall be on my way shortly, Miss Banning," he said, trying out the name again to match her new, formal tone. Had it been Keturah? Had she cautioned Verity like she had tried to dissuade him? "But I wanted to discuss your needs from me on my next voyage. I can follow you so you can be about your chores as we talk. I assume you want me to return to the Carolinas for those two horses?"

She sighed and clamped her lips in a line as though not knowing how to proceed. "Very well. Meet me inside," she said, gesturing toward the stables.

Ian circumvented the corral and heard the bird screeching before he saw it. She was slipping a long leather glove on and waited for him to approach. " 'Tis best if you settle before I bring Brutus out of his cage."

"Brutus," he said, eyeing the fine falcon with feathers the color of his mistress's hair. "As in 'Et tu, Brutus'?"

"One and the same. After he clawed me for the fifth time, I named him so."

"And now? Does he still claw you?"

"Not me. Only those he thinks might bring me harm," she said, sending a playful smile his way. *Heavens above, they had only been apart but a day and he was already glad to see that smile again.* He resisted the urge to grin back at her like a sailor enchanted with a siren. "Keep still," she said, unlatching the cage and reaching in to allow the falcon to climb atop her wrist, still screeching.

They moved out of the stables, past the groom brushing down the gelding that Verity had just been working, and the curious noses of all the other horses. "Has your herd weathered the voyage all right?" he asked, matching her stride as she turned out of the yard and began picking her way up a path that led to a small garden plot—freshly overturned—and then up past the neighboring cane field that was already waist-high.

"They seem hale," she said, "to a one. May all our joint ventures be so prosperous."

Ian smiled. So there *were* to be further joint ventures. Perhaps her sister Keturah had not succeeded in persuading Verity to entirely avoid him. But then he was concentrating on catching his breath as the girl climbed the steep hill with more the constitution of a mountain goat than a lady of leisure. Not that there was anything about Verity Banning that hinted of leisure.

Finally, when she'd cleared the edge of the lowest field, she turned and looked out. He did as well, trying to conceal his rapid breathing and hoping his face was not flushed scarlet. He'd worn his tighter waistcoat, thinking he might cut a finer figure as they sat together and sipped tea. He should have known that that would not be a part of Verity's day. He liked that about her, that she was neither the genteel lady content to set about her needlework for hours in a dimly lit parlor, nor the less-than-genteel ladies who met his ship in every port. She was, of course, nearer to the women he'd known all his life in England—proper ladies—and yet there was a bit of the reckless in her too. Indeed, she was spirited.

Case in point, the breeches.

Philip had told Ian a little of the Banning sisters' story as they played chess each night. How they had set off to save their father's failing plantation, then succeeded at doing so. Here on Nevis he had pieced together Verity's story, how she had sold her inherited shares from the plantation to her elder sister and invested shares of their English estate in this new venture, all while hoping to discover what had become of Duncan. What would his brother have thought of this business? he wondered. Ian didn't think he would have entirely approved of it, having a wife so near the wharf, conducting business with menfolk day in and day out. 'Twas one thing for a lady to be selling dresses and fabric and such. 'Twas quite another to have her in breeches, selling saddles and stirrups.

But try as he might, Ian simply could not conjure up anything but admiration for the lass. Her hair—with its alternating hues of gold and brown—seemed enhanced in the sunlight, her forgotten hat bouncing on her back. And when she swung her arm out and set the bird to flight, watching in delight as the falcon climbed—allowing Ian to do nothing but stare at her profile—he decided he'd never met a girl so entrancing. *Ach, brother,* he thought. *I see what beset ye so. Why ye wrote to her. Why she was your intended. Do ye blame me for admiring her too?*

Ach, no. And there is more to this lass than what ye see, he could almost hear Duncan say.

She turned to him abruptly, clearly aware he was staring at her. He hurriedly looked to the sky and coughed. "He's a wonder, your Brutus."

"That he is. I missed him. And he, me. My sisters said he kept the whole plantation up for three nights running when first I was off. Made me promise to never leave him there again."

Ian laughed. "Will ye abide by that then? Sail with him in the hold from now on?"

"I suppose I shall have to. My sisters swear they shall never allow him on the Double T again if I am not in his company. Abraham gives him some comfort, but now he has that pet monkey, and Brutus would dearly like to eat Biri."

"So then you shall give my crew a new reason to speak of you in wonder. Not only as a horse whisperer, but as a master falconer."

She smiled shyly and squinted into the sun to watch Brutus turn a widening circle. His head was tucked, searching for prey among the cane fields. "This is Laurence Langley's field, the northwestern portion of the old Chandler Plantation."

"And he's given you permission to allow Brutus to hunt among the cane?"

"Every rat he kills buys me another friend among the planters. They hate the cane rats. They figure they lose precious pounds with every stalk they gnaw upon."

"Quite logical, that. And perhaps they shall come and spend those saved doubloons in your new store."

"One can hope," she said. Her smile faded. "I gather most are displeased that a lady of the island would take up such an 'unladylike' venture."

"So they say. But I saw a few lingering outside your window today as I approached. You have imported some of the finest leatherworks available within the Leewards, as well as some of the finest horseflesh. Dinnae fash yourself," he said, leaning toward her from the side, arms crossed. "They mean to simply make ye fret, so that when they come in at last—under the auspices of magnanimously 'helping a neighbor' with a sale—you shall be willing to do so at a deeper discount. Stick to your guns, lass. Make them come to ye, at your prices. Ye know what is fair. Wait them out as Brutus waits for just the right fat rat to emerge."

Her smile returned with his words, and she gave him a smart nod, her confidence renewed.

"I, for one, intend to return with more fine saddles and leatherworks, as well as those two fine horses you had the breeder reserve, so confident am I that my Nevisian contact will have sold through her wares by the time I return.

They may be playing a game with you, Miss Verity, but I have heard enough tales from Philip to know a Banning always finds her way to what she wants."

This teased her smile wider. "Tales from Philip, eh? Just what did he tell you?" Together they began to climb the path again, higher.

"Ach, the man was rather closemouthed actually, only giving me the bare bones. Loyal to a fault, that one. But it does not take a great deal of effort to discover your family's reputation among other Nevisians, if not from your guardian himself." He glanced back and saw Abraham climbing the hill behind them. He scanned the horizon for Brutus, saw that he was far off, then carefully allowed his pet monkey down among the cane. "I learned your sister hired a freed black overseer," he began more carefully, "much to the consternation of most of the isle's planters. And how she and Gray have hired other free men and women to work their fields alongside the slaves."

She sighed heavily and nodded. "As have I. Terence and Abraham are free. So is my maid, Trisa. It has not made our family popular among our neighbors, but it . . . well, it eases our hearts. Slavery . . . it does not sit well with any of us."

"And yet your neighbors cannot complain too loudly. Otherwise they only seem bitter because your plantation is producing so well."

"Indeed," she said thoughtfully, as if wondering

how he had acquired such detailed knowledge in his short amount of time on-island. "Be careful there, Abraham," she called. "Brutus is coming about. He still hasn't found his rat. I do not want him considering monkey meat instead."

The boy nodded, all big brown eyes that had a healthy tinge of . . . gold too. It gave him a rather startling appearance. It made Ian think about Keturah and how Verity herself had a bit of gold in her green eyes. And then how she had paused before calling the child "friend." Swiftly he glanced back and forth between the mulatto boy and her. Was he imagining things or was there a passing resemblance?

But when he looked back, Abraham had stopped abruptly in his tracks. His wide, gold brown eyes were not looking to his monkey or Brutus but between the cane stalks to their right, where two men were riding toward them.

Verity, in the midst of saying something over her shoulder, caught Abraham's frightened look and hurriedly followed his gaze. She pulled to a stop, with Ian beside her. Were they trespassing? He'd thought Verity said the neighboring planter welcomed her . . .

"Well, well," said a broad-faced man as big as Duncan. "If it is not the pretty Miss Banning. You're a mite far from home, aren't you?"

Ian eased forward a bit, liking neither this man's familiarity nor his vaguely threatening tone . . . nor the sudden pallor of Verity's cheeks.

"Mr. Shubert," she said, forcing false assuredness to her voice. "I have moved to Charlestown to begin a new business venture. What brings you this far north?"

The man looked Ian over, dismissed him, then looked back to Verity, his eyes sliding down her body. He huffed a laugh, as if delighting in her breeches. "Mr. Durant here is one of Mr. Langley's men. They're in the market for a new overseer, so he's giving me a tour. But I do have to say, this has to be the best part of the tour, eh, Durant?" He glanced back at his companion and then to her again. " 'Tis been a while since I've seen a Banning woman in breeches. A *very* long while."

Verity's breath noticeably paused.

Ian clenched his hands and willed himself not to go after the man and haul him off his horse. "I am Captain Ian McKintrick," he said and forced the men to look to him again, not Verity.

"McKintrick, you say?" said Shubert, eyes narrowing in confusion. "I've met another Captain McKintrick on a night that will live long in my memory." He lazily looked over at Verity again, his jaw tightening, and Ian took a step forward to block the man's view of her. What was it about this Mr. Shubert? Why did Verity fear him so?

"My brother," Ian said evenly, not bothering to

158

explain further. This was not a man who deserved explanations.

The two riders both widened their eyes, and Ian turned to follow their gaze. Brutus dived toward the field as if he meant to burrow ten feet under the soil. At the very last he lifted his wings to slow himself and then descended through the cane, screeching.

"Hoo," said Mr. Shubert with some appreciation, taking off his hat to beat it against his thigh and wipe his forehead of sweat with a sleeve. "I have missed seeing that bird hunt! Back over at Red Rock Plantation, the boys and I would lay bets on how fast it would take him to find a monkey or a rat. I wonder what he found just now."

"We best go discover it," Verity said. "I do not wish for him to get into anything sickly."

"I shall see to it, Miss Verity!" Abraham called, rushing down the path. "Keep Biri, will you?"

She paused, nonplussed, clearly robbed of her excuse to leave. But she bent to coax the baby monkey onto her arm.

"Heard tell you have some lovely new horse-flesh for sale," Shubert said, letting his eyes slide down Verity's legs again and back to her face.

"Now see here," Ian began, his pulse racing. What right had the man? Such audacity! *Never mind that the lass was in breeches.*

"I do," she interrupted, stepping past Ian and looking up at the men, hands on hips. "But you, Mr. Shubert, are not welcome in my shop. I shall not do business with either a leech nor a brute. And you, sir, are both."

"Just as defiant as your sister, I see," Shubert said. "Perhaps I shall take this post at Chandler just so I can accompany Mr. Langley into your shop after a long day in the fields. Surely you cannot afford to turn away a *neighbor* and a paying *customer*." Again he let his eyes move slowly down her body.

"Get off that horse," Ian gritted out. "I shall—"

Once more Verity stepped in. "Set foot in my shop even once," she said, "and I shall finish what I started at Nisbet."

The man's smirk turned to a glare. His companion tried to cover his laugh. "We shall see about that, miss," Shubert sneered. He glanced at Ian. "Mind yourself with this one, Cap'n. She's pretty as a picture but as menacing as a sea serpent, armed with that small dagger of hers."

With that, the men turned their horses and rode back in the direction they'd come.

Ian turned toward Verity and saw she was shaking. But what stunned him more was that she held a *sgian dubh* in her trembling hand.

CHAPTER ELEVEN

"Lass!" Ian said, aghast. He wrapped a hand around her waist, afraid she was about to faint, and hurried her down among the cane until Shubert and his companion were totally hidden from view. He eased the knife from her hand, then pulled her into his arms. "What is it, lass? Tell me. What did that man do to ye?"

She was trembling all over, giving into her fear now. He likened it to how he might face down a fearsome storm, and then at the end of it collapse on his bed, shaking as he recognized how narrowly he and his crew had escaped. "How is it that you have one of my brother's sgian dubh? Where are the other two?"

"My . . . my sisters," she said, panting against his chest, clinging to him. "Duncan . . . he came to us before he left that last time . . . said no highland lass was ever without one. Bade us each to carry one . . . at all times. I . . . He . . ." She staggered back from Ian, green eyes wild and confused. "What . . ." She shook her head and closed her eyes, turning partially away from him. "Forgive me," she muttered while shaking her head. Opening her eyes, she lifted a hand to her cheek. "I am not myself."

"Verity," he said, taking her hand and drawing it to his chest. "Tell me. Tell me all of it."

"Nay," she said. "'Tis not your concern. I must . . . I must find my way through this myself."

"Can I not be your friend? A listening ear at least?"

"Oh, Ian . . ." She raised her miserable eyes to meet his. "You and I both know that we dance about the edge of something more than friendship."

Her hopeful yet hopeless words—said with so little pretense—made him take a step back.

It was true, of course. But no one said such things. Not outright.

No one but a lass such as Verity . . .

"You are off soon for the mainland," she said, swallowing hard. "As I need you to be," she hurriedly added. "To bring me more goods, and more horses too." She set her hat to rights on her head and began walking down the path, gaining surety in her stride with every step. Abraham had appeared down at the bottom, monkey on his shoulder, and shrugged, apparently unable to find Brutus.

She paused again, clearly not wishing for the boy to overhear them.

"Shubert," Ian said grimly as he hurried to match her stride. "The man knew you carry the dagger. How?"

"I almost cut his throat with it at Nisbet," she said quietly.

"You did what?" Ian choked out. "He attacked you?"

"No. He attacked my sister. Both sisters. But it was Ket who talked me out of killing him." Wearily, she half turned away from Ian, looking out to sea but clearly envisioning that fateful night. "As a result of the attack, he lost his position as overseer at Red Rock. But he secured another position, on the southern end of the island."

And now he was potentially moving back here, to the north, Ian surmised.

A man who had attacked not one Banning, but two. His attack fierce enough that he was dismissed as overseer—a position difficult to fill for any planter—and banished from the parish.

They stood there, Ian wanting to know every detail while well aware that she had told him all she wished to. The rest he could ply from a local man deep in his cups at the Arrow & Anchor. No need to tax the lass further. 'Twas clearly a memory she wasn't eager to relive.

But the thought of her here . . . that man, anywhere close . . .

It made his heart pound with a steady rage.

She took a deep breath. Squared her shoulders. "I need you to be on your way, Ian. You have your own difficult seas to navigate ahead; these are mine."

He crossed his arms and considered her. "Aye, they are your own, lass," he allowed. "But I would not be honoring my brother's gift if I did not give ye something to help you navigate your own dark seas."

Her bright eyes narrowed, waiting.

"Duncan gave you the dagger. Now Shubert knows you have it, so there shall be no element of surprise. I take it he did not know you had it the first time?"

She paused, then shook her head a little.

"Now he does. Ye must learn to wield it as a proper highland lass might."

"I have a pistol too."

Ian pulled back in surprise.

She smiled at him, just a tad. "And I well know how to load and fire it. Gray saw to it."

"I like this Gray Covington more and more with each bit I learn of him."

She nodded. "You two would be fast friends."

" 'Twill help me to rest easier, knowing ye have a pistol with you behind the counter of the shop, or up in your bedroom, come nightfall. But the sgian dubh, there's a reason a highlander is never without one."

"Oh?"

Ian whirled and had his own in his hand in the same moment, crouched and ready, as if defending himself from her. "Aye," he said with a wink as he straightened, running his finger lightly across the sharp blade and looking with love at its hand-carved handle. The knives had been in his family for generations. He, Duncan, and Marjorie were each given a set of them. And Duncan had gifted his to the Bannings . . . to the Bannings. It made his heart falter a moment, then start to pound.

"They never need reloading," he said, touching the blade. "And 'tis far easier to stab an adversary in a scuffle than shoot him."

She nodded, still waiting.

"I shall have to leave ye, lass," Ian said, reaching up as if to tuck an errant curl of hair behind her ear, then thinking better of it and dropping his hand. " 'Tis true. I do not think either of us is ready to take this from a dance of the heart to something more. Not yet. But I cannot leave without training you a bit, as I did my sister, Marjorie. Would ye accept that at least? A few lessons? As a brother might teach his sister?"

She considered him. "I would. And thank you for it."

He cocked his head and sucked in his breath through his teeth. "Ye might well thank me. But ye also may curse me. Training with a sgian dubh inevitably leaves a body with a few bruises. I won't aim to harm ye, but ye must be able to understand what it is to defend yourself. Not play at it. But truly follow through."

She frowned and yet there was a welcome edge of a smile about her eyes too. "So you aim to draw blood?"

He laughed under his breath. "Nay. That would not do. But we shall wrap our daggers in cloth and pretend to do so."

Verity lifted a brow. "Then we best take to the shop and draw the curtains, lest we frighten away any potential customers, eager to avoid such violence."

Her sisters had left the shop when Verity and Ian returned to it. Her maid, Trisa, brought tea and a plate filled with cheese, meat, bread, and fruit. At Verity's bidding, the maid sat down on a stool behind the counter "to chaperone," as she put it, though a freed negress was hardly polite society's image of a proper guardian. Did Verity truly fear for her reputation? Or merely the idea of being alone with Ian? She thought little more of it, other than to surmise that, regardless of the reason, it was better to have Trisa here.

They began with the basics as they nibbled, with Ian teaching her how to flick her knife to her bare hand from a wrist strap, and then he bound it in a new fashion to her hand, pulled out a pair of fine kid gloves from her cabinet—big enough to conceal it stretched along her index finger—and cut a slit alongside.

"This way," he said and held her hand in both

of his, his brow furrowed in concentration, "you can swivel your palm and see what emerges?"

The blade glinted in the glow from the oil lamp, and she grinned.

"Feel the base of it against the curve of your palm?"

She nodded and swallowed hard, aware that she was allowing him intimacies she had not another. Not even Duncan. While he was teaching her, preparing her to defend herself, there was conversely an odd sense of her defenses melting to his touch.

Verity struggled to think of her potential adversary, not the way being this close to Ian made every bit of her skin sensitive to his own.

"You bring it up, like this," he said, carefully wrapping the tip in the rags and setting her elbow to her side, then bringing it forward like a battering ram to his belly. She fought to concentrate on his words, but had difficulty doing so, given her awareness of his broad, strong hands cupping her elbow and her wrist.

"Once, twice, thrice," he said firmly, totally absorbed by his task, not noticing her distraction. "If you must use a sgian dubh, be certain you do it well, lass. Again and again. Say it."

"Again and again." She took a swift breath and shook her head, reminding herself to concentrate.

"Imagine that leech Shubert before you. Now strike me. Again and again."

She managed to do so, stopping just shy of his belly.

"Good," he muttered. "Now again."

But as she rammed her arm forward, he grabbed her wrist and whipped her around, pulling her tightly against him. She struggled. *"Ian,"* she gasped. His chest spread wide behind her back, his grip on her wrist like iron, his other arm wrapped firmly across her waist.

Trisa rose, brow knit in consternation, but Ian waved her off. " 'Tis all right, Trisa. I mean your mistress no harm. Not truly. I only aim to prepare her to fight off Shubert."

That seemed to mollify the girl, after Verity nodded. She tentatively sat back down. But Verity's heart pounded, not because of fear but because of his proximity, his strength, the feel of his arm around her waist . . .

"He has you, Verity," he said in her ear. "Perhaps he's wounded, but you haven't hit anything vital. What do you do now?"

She squirmed weakly. Tried to remember he moved with her not as potential lover but feigned foe. *A brother. A brother,* she kept repeating to herself. She again attempted to break free of his iron grip, then tried kicking at his leg, which he deftly avoided. He still held her tight. She glanced toward Trisa, who stared at them, half alarmed, half delighted as if watching actors in a play.

"What do ye do now?" he demanded, gruffly pulling her even tighter against him.

"I-I do not know," she gasped in frustration.

"You ram your head back, into my nose. Feel it? Right here, near your crown? Tuck your head forward and then ram it back with everything ye have."

She made the motion, feeling him swing his head to the side to narrowly evade her blow.

He abruptly released her and stepped back, holding his nose and gaping at her, clearly thinking of nothing but their game of battle. "Ye've stunned me, lass. I'm bleeding like a rat in Brutus's talons. Now either kick me where it hurts a man most or run for help."

She lifted a brow. "You honestly wish for me to kick you where it hurts most?" She'd spent far too much time among stableboys and sailors, watching them wrestle, to be able to profess ignorance.

"Aye," he said, still pretending to hold his nose, actually stumbling toward her. "With your knee, fast and sure. Do it as if ye lift your foot to put it in a stirrup, the devil at your tail."

She brought her knee up, and he leapt aside, laughing in admiration now. "Good, good, lass. I want ye to practice all of that in your room for the next week, until each action comes naturally. Will ye do that for me, Verity?"

She was struck by the soft care in his eyes. "I shall," she murmured.

"Good girl," he said approvingly. "If the lout dare approach, ye shall be as ready as a highlander."

"A highland lass with a sgian dubh," she corrected, managing to arch a brow. Could he not see it? How she leaned toward him? Wished for . . . what?

He heaved a sigh and brought a hand to his chest. " 'Tis a sight that lights a fire in many a highlander's belly, that." But though his tone was playful, his gaze was intent. He paused. "Do ye truly think it wise, Verity? Residing here on your own? Or, knowing that man might be near, 'twould it be best to return to the Double T each night?"

"Nay," she said, "I shall have Terence and Abraham with me. Trisa too. If anyone dared threaten me, they would come to my aid."

Trisa nodded faintly.

"Good," he said, nodding, but clearly still uneasy. "Perhaps I shall fetch ye another dirk to be worn here." He gestured toward his armpit. "Or a fine boot blade."

"I think I shall do well enough with this," she said, fingering the knife with its intricately carved handle. "There are dangers everywhere. Even at my sister's home."

"Your sister's?" He frowned. "Do you speak of the soldiers? That Captain Howard and the rest? Surely they would not—"

"No, no. They pose no threat as Mr. Shubert does. At least as overtly. But there are other threats . . ."

Always other threats, particularly as women, she thought.

He nodded slowly, clearly wishing she would go on. But their farewell had already become far more than she had intended. She straightened.

"I need to do this. Show the town that I fear no man. Otherwise, how else shall they respect me when they come to buy my wares? Negotiate prices?"

He hesitated. "They would not."

"There you have it," she said.

Ian brought down his boot from the rounded cover of the trunk, straightened his vest, and reached to pull on his jacket again. "I confess this was not an evening like I'd expected to pass with ye, lass. Still, I'm glad of it."

She moved toward him, hands clasped before her. "As am I. Thank you for your care, Ian. For all you have done on my behalf. Blessings upon your voyage. I shall look forward to your return."

He gave her a small smile, reached for her hand and bowed over it. "*Ainnir as àille snuadh agus bana-churaidh as treise cridhe,*" he said, rising and reluctantly relinquishing her hand. He reached for his tricorn.

"And that means?" she asked, lifting her hands.

"Ach, I shall leave that for another time to tell you."

She crossed her arms. "You truly aim to leave me without explanation?"

"Truly," he said with a wink, and with that he set his tricorn on his head, grinned, and turned toward the door. "Good eve, lass," he said, pausing in the doorframe. He hesitated and reached out with both hands to hold himself steady. In that moment, she felt the pull and push of him from deep within. His own conflict.

As if half of him desired to stride forward and take her into his arms and half wanted to leave and never return.

"Take close care, Verity," he said, his tone sounding strangled.

"I shall. And you do the same, Captain. Until we meet again."

"Until then," he said. And with that, he seemed to recover his cavalier smile, cast her a two-fingered salute from his brow, and was gone into the night.

CHAPTER TWELVE

He'd walked five, perhaps six paces before he heard her door shut and the bolt slide into place. It felt like a slice to his heart—a sure separation—but he elected to consider it a solid wall between her and other interlopers while they were apart.

Even though he never turned back, he hoped she watched him leave from between the curtains. It had been enough, all that they had shared. Much had been said . . . far before 'twas time. But truth be told, as they weighed anchor and decided to forgo St. Kitts—setting sail for the more lucrative Statia—Ian had difficulty keeping his mind on what was ahead rather than what—and *whom*—he left behind.

Even given the distraction, they managed to sell their remaining stores of tobacco within an hour of arriving on the island. Then he and McKay walked the streets, becoming familiar with the merchants and studying what each sold, as well as what they might seek among his future imports. Many were Dutch and Jewish, but there were merchants from many nations along the streets—most noticeably, the French.

"Captain," Michael said, "my uncle asked me

to deliver a letter to a . . . *compatriot* here in Statia."

"A letter," Ian repeated, his eyes narrowing. "How did he know that we would be stopping on Statia?"

"I told him it was likely, given our cargo. But my task was to see if you changed your mind en route," he said quietly, pausing a moment as two ladies walked by, casting them flirtatious smiles. He turned to face Ian. "Are you still with us, Captain?" he said, lowering his voice. "Still ready to throw in with the Sons of Liberty?"

"I believe I am," Ian said, crossing his arms.

Michael smiled. "Then come with me." He ducked into Monsieur Bieulieu's—an establishment specializing in fine linens and soaps, as well as casks of wine. He waited for two customers in front of him to purchase their wares and leave before approaching the counter. "I am here for a small cask of your finest Bordeaux," Michael said. He took a coin from his small purse and offered it to the proprietor in the palm of his hand, exposing a fleur-de-lis tattoo on the inside of his wrist. "There are those in America who have yet to sample France's finest," he added. "Perhaps you have something special for us?"

The balding, round-bellied man studied his tattoo, gave him a hard look, then glanced to Ian and back. He took Michael's proffered coin. "Very good, monsieur," he said, slowly turning it between his fingers as if still considering whether he would sell him the wine or not.

Finally, he waved over a boy and leaned down to whisper something in his ear. The child looked at Ian and Michael, bit his lip, and disappeared out the back. The man waddled over to a side wall behind the counter and pulled out a small cask of wine, carried it to the counter. He set it before Michael. "See that you drink to my health, monsieur."

"Every time we pour a glass," Michael promised, hoisting it to his shoulder.

They turned to go. Once outside, Ian blinked slowly, as much over his confusion as to what had just transpired as a reaction to the bright sunlight. How had that helped the cause? Clearly something more had been conveyed between Michael and Monsieur Bieulieu, but what exactly? "Where now?" he grunted at Michael.

"This way, I believe," Michael said, gesturing down the street. They had gone but two blocks before Ian realized that two men were following them. Friends or foes? He and Michael shared a knowing look, and Ian let his dagger slide into the palm of his hand, all the while keeping up his pace as if nothing was amiss.

"Pardon, Captain," said a slight man from his left with a thick French accent. "May I have a word with you and your mate?"

Warily, Ian slowed and turned to face the man,

McKay at his shoulder. Michael slowly set down his cask. The two of them had fought their way out of more than one tavern, as well as taken down four sailors with fanciful thoughts of mutiny aboard their own ship a year past. There were few other men at his side he would've trusted more.

The smaller man smiled, and his thin brows lifted with his hands. "A word only, brothers," he said smoothly, eyeing Ian's clenched hand as if knowing what it held. The man glanced down the crowded street. "But not here." He leaned toward McKay. "We must speak in private."

Ian considered him, then his companion. They did not appear to be ruffians. Nor did he truly fear them—not with Michael at his side. They had a couple stones of weight and height on their side. He glanced at his mate, and Michael gave him a nod.

"Very well. Lead on," Ian said.

The two stepped ahead of them, and they turned several corners, walked down a long alleyway and then climbed a set of steps to what appeared to be a charming villa, with whitewashed walls and purple bougainvillea sending heavy boughs and climbing shoots across the entire expanse. The man knocked twice on the old wooden door and entered. " 'Tis only I, *Cheri*!" he called up the stairs. He set his tricorn on a peg and gestured to the empty seats of the small parlor.

The room was neat and tidy, obviously decorated with a woman's touch. His wife? Or mistress?

Ian sat down in the chair where he could eye the door and window, Michael at his side.

"You are Captain Ian McKintrick and his mate, Michael McKay. We have been awaiting your arrival."

Ian stiffened, and his eyes narrowed. But it was not him the men focused on . . . it was Michael.

"You can vouch for your captain?" said the Frenchman.

"With my life. You have something for us?" his mate asked.

"*Oui*. Just as you have something for us?"

Michael gave Ian an apologetic smile, tucked his hand beneath his vest and pulled out a letter, sealed with wax. He lifted it so that Ian could see the rebel's seal—the symbol with its coiled snake to signify subversives in America—before handing it to the Frenchman.

Ian leveled him with a stare, thinking of the elder McKay selling him the *Inverness*. Had they been that sure of him all along? And yet had he not expressed to Michael how he blamed the Crown for Duncan's death? Sold his ship to be free of any English investments? Flown the stripes of freedom on his mast all across the Atlantic?

The Frenchmen stood and handed Michael two

tiny letters from their own pockets—so small they had clearly been designed to be hidden. Ian and Michael rose too. "You shall head directly back to New York?" one asked, looking at them both.

"We shall," Ian said.

"Good. See to it that those notes get to Rupert Smith in the Dock Ward right away. It is of utmost importance."

"And if you get caught with either one," said the second, "be certain you swallow it."

"Sw-swallow it?" Ian sputtered.

"Swallow it," said the smaller man, clapping him on the shoulder with a cheerful smile. "Because if a British soldier finds it on you and reads it, you will likely find yourself on the wrong end of a noose."

"Now we must be off, and you as well," said the second. " 'Twouldn't be wise for us to be found together. We shall await your return."

He reached for McKay's hand and then turned tentatively toward Ian.

"What shall I call you?" Ian asked as they shook hands.

"Names are not important. Not in *our* business," said the man. "But if you seek me, begin at Monsieur Bieulieu's shop. Purchase a cask of wine, promise to drink to his health. I shall not be far."

Ian and Michael followed them out, where Ian

pulled him to a stop. When the other two men disappeared around the corner with a cheery wave, Ian turned savagely toward McKay and shoved him against the wall of the nearest house, his hands wound tight in his jacket lapels.

McKay's eyes filled with alarm. "Allow me to explain, Captain!"

"Quickly," Ian gritted out between clenched teeth.

McKay glanced down the alley, and with some reluctance Ian let him loose. No good would come from drawing undue attention.

"My uncle," Michael began, tugging the wrinkles out of his coat. "He thought you a sympathizer to the Sons of Liberty's goals. But we had to be sure. And everything I've seen of you, overheard you say, seems to have confirmed it. But Cap'n, my life, as well as many others"—he waved down the empty alleyway—"are now in your hands. Are you having second thoughts?"

Ian paused and took a deep breath, rubbing the back of his neck. "Regardless of my political decisions, you owed me the respect," he said, tapping on his mate's chest, "to tell me of this *before* it transpired."

"I'd meant to, Cap'n. Surely, I did. But every time I attempted it, you seemed preoccupied with the bonny Miss Banning."

That gave him pause. *The bonny Miss Banning.* "Still, brother. You might have found a moment.

Asked for it," Ian hissed, leaning toward him.

"Aye," said the man. "I might have. Forgive me, Cap'n. This is . . . uneasy territory."

Ian sighed and took a step back from his friend. He paced back and forth, rubbing his face, thinking. "What is it that you gave to them? Who wrote that letter?" he said under his breath.

"That is for my uncle to tell you," Michael said soberly. "I know not what it contained. I was merely the courier." He lifted his wrist with the tattoo.

"So 'tis done, then. We are revolutionaries. Spies for the Sons of Liberty?"

Michael stared him in the eye and nodded once. "Aye. Was that not what you intended? Flying the Union Jack into Charlestown, despite your leanings?"

Ian did not answer, wary of his mate for the first time. Was this a trap? A means to put his own neck to the guillotine?

His hesitation clearly made Michael wary too. "Was it not you who berated the king for sending your brother on a fool's errand? Blamed him for Duncan's death?" Michael asked, beads of sweat emerging on his forehead.

"Aye," Ian said, " 'twas me." He resumed his pacing, this time rubbing the back of his neck.

"Was it not you who said he wished he could make the king pay?"

"Aye."

"Was it not you who waxed on about the heavy-handed rule of the mother country? How she holds on to her territories not out of devotion but for the gains of taxation?"

"Aye," Ian said, waving at him in agitation. "Ye've made your point, man."

"So was it naught but idle speech?"

"Nay, 'twas far from idle!" Ian growled while casting him a furious glance.

"Then are you in, Cap'n?" Michael asked, crossing his arms, his concern easing.

Ian considered him. Thoughts of retribution soothed him whenever he thought of Duncan. Making the king pay. Making Santiago pay. Helping the Sons of Liberty and thereby striking a blow. But now . . .

But now there was Verity.

And it was one thing to consider the loss of his ship, even the loss of his life, in making things right on Duncan's behalf. But what would Verity have to say about it?

And yet, had not the girl seemed to be turning away from him yesterday on Nevis? Separating herself? Determined to make her own way?

He might do this. Nay, he *would* do this. But he would not involve her in it. 'Twas too dangerous. She had enough to handle, on her own in Charlestown, managing her new business, neighbors such as Shubert. But thoughts of the British soldiers who were so familiar with her and her family crowded in. Might she be privy to some intelligence at some point, vital to the cause? Might he find out a way to discover it, but without her direct involvement?

"I am in, Michael. Ye have my word on it. Now let us set sail for America," he said. "Tonight, in the safety of my cabin, ye shall tell me everything you know."

The night after Ian left, Verity was moving toward the door of her shop to lock it for the night when Captain Howard appeared on the other side of the glass window, his red uniform dancing in the wavy glass. Wearily, she turned the knob and opened the door partway. "Captain," she said. "I was about to close for the night."

Ignoring her obvious attempt to dissuade him from entering, he stepped forward. "Oh, I am so glad I caught you in time then. My men and I were hoping to peruse your horses before the sun sets. We meant to arrive earlier, but we caught a most disagreeable man in town doing something despicable. We were compelled to deal with him forthwith."

"Yes, well, might you return on the morrow? I was about to see to my supper."

He gave her a confused, wry smile while lifting his long, aristocratic nose to the air and inhaling deeply. "Why, it does not yet smell like supper is ready. Cannot your maid see to that whilst you see to us? Major Woodget shall be most cross with me this night if I have not made some headway on this front."

She paused, caught between her irritation and her need for a sale.

"Come now, Miss Verity," he pressed, leaning forward. "Your country has need of your service . . . and possibly a good number of your new horses. Do I not offer you the opportunity to serve as well as prosper?"

Verity willed herself to put on a smile. "Very well, Captain. Since you are so insistent, I shall lead you to them. Let me fetch my hat."

"Jolly good, Miss Verity. Jolly good." He turned to cast a smug smile at his companions, acting as if he'd won a wager. Perhaps he had, she thought with a sigh. For he was right in one thing. 'Twouldn't be wise to turn down a sale, no matter how high-handed and irritating she thought a customer might be. After all, not a single other person in Charlestown had dared to come to Banning's Bridlery that day, other than Keturah and Selah, who bustled about, filling the empty store with their light and cheerful banter. The two sisters were clearly bent on keeping Verity's attentions from the obvious fact that the island's populace intended to boycott her new store, deeming it unsuitable for a woman to run such a business. Perhaps if she sold the soldiers a few of her fine horses . . . well, she knew that jealousy and greed on the island oft broke the most stalwart of blockades.

That got her thinking about the matched pair of chestnut geldings. If she could train them to the yoke and leather, she could take afternoon rides each day around the island. Why, it would be a veritable rolling advertisement for her mercantile. The men might band against her as they had her sister, but in time their wives and daughters would compel them to break. Yes, one way or another, she would have this island's business in time.

Terence and Abraham left off their game of checkers at the small table they had set up in the shade when they saw her crest the hill with the soldiers in company. Captain Howard had brought along Lieutenants Angersoll and Cesley, the two soldiers who had presumably lost their mounts to colic. As they entered the stables, Brutus set to squawking in excitement.

"Shall I dispatch this menace forthwith, Miss Banning?" asked Lieutenant Angersoll, playfully handling the hilt of his sword as he observed her falcon in his cage.

"Not today, Lieutenant," she said idly. "You well know I'm quite fond of that bird."

Brutus quieted as they moved away and Abraham found a fresh sardine from the bucket to distract him. He'd left Biri to climb into the hayloft far from Brutus's quick eye. Verity knew that if the bird saw both his mistress and Biri in the stables at once, there would not be enough sardines on-island to keep him quiet.

The men followed her from one stable to another, where she discussed the merits of each mare and gelding. Lieutenant Angersoll soon returned to examine the mare with a white star on her forehead and white forelocks. Lieutenant Cesley hovered between a black gelding and a palomino mare. Verity encouraged Cesley to enter the stall and get to know the mare—which she thought more appropriate for him—while she talked to Lieutenant Angersoll about his needs in a mount.

"You are a fairly large man," she said, sizing him up and looking to the horses again. "With those long legs, you might be more comfortable on this gelding than that mare. Would you like to get more acquainted with him?"

"Yes, well," blushed the man, apparently a bit aghast at her forthright assessment.

"You must pardon Miss Verity's blunt description, Angersoll," soothed the captain. "Whilst it is uncommon for a woman to be dealing in horse-flesh, we are well used to the Banning women doing things their own way, right?" He turned to smile magnanimously at Verity, as if she should be grateful for his intercession. Yet if she was to make it on Nevis as a seller of horses, this sort of conversation would have to become rote.

She brushed past him and entered the stable with Lieutenant Cesley. "I've trained him to the bit but not the saddle. If you are sincerely interested in this one, I would have you come back each evening when you are off duty to become familiar with the horse, and he you. In time we can train him to the saddle too."

"Of what do you speak? Become familiar with a horse? I am a man with the king's coin to purchase any horse I wish," Cesley said, his eyes narrowing in confusion over her words. "And rest assured, Miss Banning, I have broken more than one pony in my day."

"And I am a seller of horses who only wishes to sell my fine mounts to those who are right for them," she said quietly, reaching up to rub the gelding's cheek. "My goal is for both of you to find satisfaction in the other. There shall be no breaking."

"Both?" He frowned. "Do you speak of the horse? I seem to not be—"

"I have become quite fond of each one, Lieutenant, on the voyage from the mainland. I am certain you understand," she said firmly.

The man blushed, stammered the beginning of one reply and then another. At last he simply nodded. "Very well, Miss Banning. I shall return on the morrow for my first lesson. For I aim to have this gelding. And if 'tis the only way—"

" 'Tis the only way, Lieutenant," she said with

a sweet smile, stroking the horse's neck. "For I am his guardian. And if you wish to assume guardianship . . . well, we shall see. We shall see."

CHAPTER THIRTEEN

Verity closed her store late Friday afternoon, having held off the British soldiers all week and selling nothing but a bucket of nails to a nervous slave, who apparently had not been able to find them anywhere else and in desperation ducked into her mercantile. Had even the slaves been warned about patronizing her store?

She told herself it did not matter; in time, many would turn to her. And each of the soldiers had his eye on a different mount—including Major Woodget—but none, to Verity's mind, had proven themselves worthy of taking them from her stables. Until they did, the horses would remain in her safekeeping. She knew she was behaving like a nervous hen over her chicks, but she could seem to do nothing else.

The next day, Verity rode Fiona sidesaddle to the Double T. She reveled in the glorious Saturday morning as she led the two chestnut geldings along behind her—both for exercise and to become more accustomed with the traffic of the road, other people, and the island in general. Terence followed behind on another horse while Abe and Trisa shared a second. Brutus winged his way, higher and higher above, and Biri perched on Abe's shoulder, chattering his excitement. She supposed that all of them were glad to be heading out of town, away from the bustle, the smells, the noises, and back to where there were few sounds but the wind washing through the cane, the splatter of brief, passing raindrops on jungle leaves, the banter of men and women heading out to the fields.

A family of vervet monkeys languidly crossed the road, the alpha male staring resentfully at them before disappearing into the brush. Verity darted a glance toward Abe in alarm. As usual, Biri watched his kind in mild, distracted fascination, as if he were more human than monkey. And she supposed that was what it meant to be adopted—to become more like those who loved you now, truly one with them, rather than those you'd once known.

They turned the bend of Round Road and passed Red Rock Plantation. Verity hoped her companions didn't see her stiffen, remembering Angus Shubert's loathsome intercession last week. She hoped Mr. Langley, owner of the Chandler Plantation, had found a better candidate for an overseer than Shubert. Indeed, since she had not seen the lout again, she dared to believe he had. As far as she was concerned, if she and her sisters could stay on the northern part of the island and Shubert the south, all would be far better off. But God help the women on the southern end . . .

Finally, she urged her mare down the Double T road, so glad to be home at last. She hadn't dared to return after she left Ian's ship. Not until she had spent some days in her new apartment and shop. It had been a discipline, an important one, but now her heart swelled at the thought of seeing her sisters, as well as the other dear faces of the Double T.

It was Mimba and Charlie who spied them first, climbing the hill toward the middle field, hoes perched on their shoulders. "Why, Miss Verity!" said Mimba. "Welcome home!" he cried.

"Thank you, Mimba," she said, smiling.

"And Abe! Your momma will be mighty glad to see you!" Mimba continued.

"As will I to see her," the boy said with a wide grin. He slid from the mare's flanks and took off running. Biri hopped from his shoulder and joyously scampered behind. There was no mistaking who was his master. As much as Verity had helped nurse him back to health, it had always been Abe who held the monkey's affection.

That was what she wished for her horses. To so meld with their new masters that they would not miss her or her stables for a moment. She figured that it was a might fanciful, such thoughts. But that was what captivated her—her horses, and those who would care for them. There was a part of her that seemed to sense what the animals felt, within, about her. And that both made her compassionate for their present as well as their future. With that in mind, she would do her best for each one, no matter how it rankled her potential customers.

She braced herself. Undoubtedly, she would happen upon Captain Howard, Major Woodget, and the younger lieutenants here. She was full of hope, however, because today she wished to lure her sisters away from the grand house for either a dip in the ocean or the waterfall pool or both. She'd dreamed of nothing else in the last few sweltering days in town, when the air had been uncommonly still and thick, the dust of the corral seeming to stick to every nook and cranny of her skin. Tossing and turning in bed, she'd dreamed of the falls, the black rock of the banks, the moss . . .

Ahead, she heard Mitilda's shriek of joy. As she entered the clearing before the main house, she saw the young woman pick up her boy and swing him around in a fierce embrace, the monkey prancing about them as if wanting to take part in the excitement. Mitilda leaned back, Abraham's cheeks between her palms, looking him over from top to bottom, then pulling him close to kiss each cheek. At last, she knelt and greeted the monkey. Biri scurried toward her outstretched hand, and she lifted him to her shoulder, where he chattered and nuzzled beneath her chin in his own method of greeting.

She laughed and looked up. "Miss Verity," she called. " 'Tis a fine day when you bring my son for a visit."

"Indeed," Verity said. "But you are always welcome to come and see him in town, Mitilda," she added, sliding off her mount with practiced ease, "or he to come to you on his own."

They stood there for a long moment.

"You know how it is, miss," Mitilda said, turning to watch her son as he chased the monkey around a bush. "So much to do."

So much to do, Verity repeated silently. Or was it that she was concerned, heading to town? Without an official errand from her mistress?

Tensions had been building over the last year, in tandem it seemed, with tensions in the colonies. It was as if the whites of the island feared that rebellion might be contagious, and the blacks—who outnumbered the whites nine to one—considered revolt. She'd witnessed how others harried Terence in town. His freed status seemed to agitate his tormentors; she'd heard them make up excuses to harass him. She'd glimpsed more of that same foolery with Matthew, Mitilda's brother, overseer of the Double T, and other freed slaves.

She decided to speak to Ket about giving

Mitilda reasons to come to town more frequently on Double T business. 'Twould be good for both mother and child to see each other more often. Abe was quite young still to be away from his mother for too long a time, although it had been Mitilda's suggestion that Verity hire the boy.

Her sisters came into view then, Selah hurrying down the stairs in joyous urgency, Keturah following in far slower fashion, given the advanced state of her pregnancy. How long did she have now? A month? Or less? Gray was there too, then Philip, each smiling down at them from the wide, new veranda.

The house had doubled in size from what her father had built. Even the kitchen was new—Ket, with great reluctance, had dismantled the ancient chimney, determined to have a smoke-free kitchen once again. But she'd saved many of the stones and sentimentally had the mason build them into the new chimney. Now there was an efficient kitchen, a long, more formal dining room with wide doors that opened onto the veranda for fine days or grand parties, a parlor that could seat a good twenty guests, a library, and six big rooms. Of which, Verity thought resentfully, three were taken by British soldiers.

As if on cue, Major Woodget, Captain Howard, and the two lieutenants emerged, faces alight at the prospect of guests. Verity's stomach twisted.

Was it not enough to see these men most every eve in town? Could she not come to visit her family and not bear their intrusion? But she forced a smile and accepted a kiss to each of her cheeks from the major and brief bows from the others.

That done, she turned to Ket and lifted the back of her hand to her sweaty forehead. " 'Tis dreadfully hot," she said. "I confess I'd hoped to squire you and Selah away for a dip in the pool."

"The pool?" Captain Howard repeated, eyebrows raised in sudden interest.

"Yes, 'tis a private pool," Verity said quickly. "Solely for family."

"Ah. I see," said the man, turning to view the ocean, choosing to ignore her slight.

"Verity," Selah chided quietly, taking her arm and leading her up the stairs. "Was such unkindness necessary?"

"No," she moaned. "Or maybe yes," she added in a whisper. "I have borne his company all week. Grant me a measure of grace, might you?"

"All week?" Selah asked as they entered the front parlor.

"All week," Verity repeated. "He has a mind to find a new horse. Two of his men have chosen theirs, and now he's succeeded in getting approval for another mount of his own. 'Tis given him license to come to call every evening. Right when I am most weary, hot, and cross."

"As you are today?" Keturah asked, coming in behind them.

"I was not cross. Not until I saw him here," she whispered. "Please. Might we steal away to the pool? Before they come in and demand our company all afternoon?"

Keturah lifted a hand to her dewy brow. Her cheeks had rounded with her pregnancy, as had her breasts and belly, making her the very picture of fertile femininity. It was as if every part of her burst forth. "Never have I seen you more beautiful, Ket," Verity breathed, taking her hand.

Keturah scoffed a laugh and turned fully toward her. "What? Me? In this state?"

"Yes, you." Verity smiled with her. "In precisely this state. Motherhood clearly agrees with you."

"I think so too," Selah said, sidling closer to Ket and wrapping her arm around her waist. "Is she not glorious?"

"Glorious," Gray affirmed, coming in behind Ket and wrapping his arms around her shoulders for a swift kiss to her cheek. "If you three are to escape to the pool, you must do so quickly. I shall distract the good Major Woodget and his men while you steal out of the kitchen."

"Oh, Gray," Verity said softly, "you are the very best brother-in-law in the history of brothers-in-law."

"Of course I am," he returned, giving her a wink. "Take your time, my lovely ladies. And return to the house restored. It shall make for a far better evening, shall it not?"

"It shall," Ket agreed, before kissing Gray full on the mouth.

Verity and Selah shared a delighted look and laugh, then all three scurried out to change clothes.

When finally they reached the pool clearing, Verity felt she'd reached the edge of heaven itself. "Oh," she moaned, hurriedly stripping off her clinging sweat-lined gown and turning her back to Selah to silently ask her assistance with her stays. "Do you know how often I dreamed of this moment while aboard Ian's ship? Or in town? It has been so cursedly hot."

Keturah let her dress fall—no stays beneath to hold her burgeoning belly—and moved to the side of the pool. She eased thigh-deep into the water, eyes closed in pleasure, then dived beneath, emerging ten feet distant, hair slicked back. She turned toward her sisters, reminding Verity of pictures of a self-satisfied otter, an animal she'd never seen outside of books. But it was as if she could fairly paste her sister's face on the broad-cheeked, completely content animal in the pictures.

Verity waded in right behind her. She dived, feeling the cold spring water cover every last inch of her. The chill both repelled and delighted her. She wanted it to seep into her skin. To feel the chill for hours. Because against the island's summer heat, it felt like a measure of protection, reprieve, relief.

She emerged farther than Ket had, closer to the falls, and laughed as Selah gingerly made her way in, shrieking at the cold. Gradually, Verity's skin numbed, and she floated on her back, watching the palm fronds dance above her, partially glistening in the sun, partially dark in shadow. Every time she came here, she felt her father's joy, his memory. For it had been here that he had come to wash, to rest. How was it that Mother had never wished to visit the island? Had it been fear? Pride? What had kept her from knowing this integral part of Father's life?

Verity could not fathom it now. Had Duncan still lived, there would have been a part of her that wished to travel with him to every port. To know, to experience what he did. But as soon as she'd thought of Duncan, Ian crowded him aside. Ian. What had he seen on St. Eustatius? Was he nearly back to the mainland now? It took but a week to reach the Carolinas. A week and a half to New York. Would the winds favor his return in a month? Mayhap less?

Was she wishing for his return?

She let herself sink in the depths of the dark pool, waving her hands and allowing the air to escape her lungs. In the silence she descended.

Deeper, deeper. *Oh, Duncan,* she thought. *I cared for you so. I'm so sorry I shall never see you again.*

She thought back. Struggled to remember the breadth of him. His ways.

But it was Ian who filled her mind. With his darker auburn hair and green eyes. Those eyes . . . so keen. Aware of every little thing about him. Of her. And others.

Verity pressed upward, back to the surface, gasping for breath.

"Ver?" Keturah called from the bank. "Are you quite well?"

Verity considered that. "I am well," she panted. "Quite? No."

Selah edged toward her, the girl's blond curls in sleek subservience for once. "Not quite, Sissy? What ails you?"

Verity sighed and moved toward the bank beside Ket. She turned onto her back, reaching for handholds among the vine and rock that would keep her in place. It had been here that they had convinced Ket of her true feelings for Gray. And how had that turned out? Was it not the right place for all things, frank and simple, between sisters?

"What ails me?" Verity repeated. "What ails me?" she railed, rubbing her face with one hand. "I came to care for one brother. A fine man, lost to me. And now . . . and now . . ." She rested her hand on her forehead as if checking for a fever.

"And now you've come to love another," Ket said simply.

Verity turned to stare at her sister. "What did you say?"

Ket leveled her amber eyes back toward her. "I said," she intoned softly, "that you've come to love another." Ket reached out her hand, and reluctantly Verity entwined her fingers with her sister's. " 'Tis all right, Ver," she said, eyes full of tears. "Knowing Duncan as I did, I think he would consider it a blessing. You, finding Ian. And he, you."

"You think so? Truly?" Verity whispered. "It is not a . . . betrayal of sorts?"

"No, not in this way," Ket returned, pulling Verity's knuckles to her lips for a kiss and squeezing her hand. "It is quick, for certain. But love comes when it wishes."

Verity smiled in confusion. "Was it not you who attempted to dissuade him when he was in Charlestown?"

Keturah attempted an innocent look, but Selah's expression verified Trisa's story.

"There is no hiding it. Trisa told me how you veritably told the man that I risked my heart once on a sea captain; I should not do so again. And truly, a part of me agrees . . ." She looked away from her sisters, up into the swaying palms above them. "It leaves me conflicted. These feelings for Ian when I felt much the same for Duncan."

"Is it not a blessing?" Selah asked softly. "To be so loved not once, but twice?"

Verity sighed, letting her sisters' words seep into her soul. Keturah had been blessed with Gray's love, but she had not been so fortunate with her first husband. Was it true? Had Verity been so blessed, to be loved not once, but twice? Did Ian truly love her? There was an undeniable attraction between them, though no such words had been expressed. Indeed, not even Duncan had confessed his love in the ten letters he'd sent to her. Attachment, fondness, yes. But love? It had been there, Verity thought. They simply had not had enough time. And now, with Ian . . .

Oh, Duncan, would you truly have blessed this?

A trade wind in the palm fronds above them, the breeze rippling the water of the pool and giving her wet shoulders and neck a delightful chill. But in that moment, it was as if Verity could feel Duncan's blessing.

He had been a good man. A generous, big-hearted man.

And Ian . . . she'd been rather curt with him that last night. After his encounter with Keturah, did he leave Nevis thinking there was not a chance of anything but friendship between them? And did she want to begin a relationship with him, given his growing hatred toward the British, his determination to hunt down Santiago, and his fiery, passionate ways? Was he the right match for her?

Try as she might, she could not come up with someone better. She remembered that last night with him. How it felt for him to be holding her, even in pretending to fight. Had she not thought of it every night since as she practiced with the sgian dubh?

"So . . . how long does it take to sail to the mainland and back?" Selah chirped, breaking into her reverie.

Verity laughed and then sank beneath the blessedly cold surface again. But as she remained submerged, her ears, her senses dulled, stopped up . . . She thought clearly, *five weeks. A week en route, a week in port, three weeks back.*

Five weeks.

Come back to me, Ian, she urged through the spring pool . . . waters that flowed into the Caribbean . . . that met the Atlantic . . . the very water that lapped at the *Inverness*'s own planks even now.

Come back to me, she thought. *And let us see where this shall lead.*

CHAPTER FOURTEEN

Ian watched as the waves washed against the *Inverness*'s planks like a silent link between himself and Verity. 'Twas foolish, such a fanciful thought. But still it remained, that thought of a watery map between New York and Nevis.

The image of it trailed behind him with each step he took down the old wooden wharf as the scents of brine and tar assailed his nostrils. The mood was different, six weeks hence from his last visit. People eyed him warily, as if protecting themselves as well as the port. The Battles of Lexington and Concord had intensified the resentment between Loyalists and Patriots. The promise of retribution, coming to set the American colonists back in order, hung in the air like a misty threat. But this time something deeper permeated every citizen, every seaman, every merchant, every slave and servant who hovered about.

There is no longer the threat of war, his mind railed at him. *'Tis here like a swelling wave.* The battles had set the world on edge. But with the English acknowledging the threat of the rebels here, and because he did not hoist a British flag from his mast, he was now under more austere observation than ever before. Heretofore he'd dropped anchor, registered with the wharfmaster, paid his fees, and been granted access to the wharf. Now he hovered on the very edge of the harbor with other vessels from other foreign lands, as if he might be an unwelcome suitor, only granted access because his hold was filled with rum and sugar.

And they were wise to be wary.

If only they knew.

He came bearing precious cargo and commerce for the colonies. But the letters he and Michael McKay carried? They were clearly for the good of this fledgling country . . . and the downfall of her overlords.

He and McKay strode down the gray planks of the pier, sea gulls circling madly about. But their eyes were not on the birds but the twelve British soldiers, fully armed and stationed outside the harbormaster's office.

"Steady," he muttered to McKay, as much for his own sake as for his first mate's. They had sewn the small letters into the bottom hem of their jackets. "The key is to appear as if nothing is amiss." But he heard the Frenchman's advice echo in his mind. *If caught, swallow it.* That'd be difficult, given their current location. He'd heard of a man caught swallowing enemy correspondence, and the man had had his throat cut down to the gullet, where the Brits fished the paper from his esophagus. McKay and he had agreed—if they were caught, they'd prefer the noose to being filleted.

The harbormaster approached, a middle-aged man with spectacles perched on the end of his nose. "Papers," he said, reaching for Ian's ledger.

"Last port of entry, Captain?" asked a fresh-faced lieutenant to his right.

"Statia, briefly," he answered casually. There was no sense in hiding it; they'd clearly see it in his logbook. "I had a few hogsheads of tobacco to sell after a long stop in Nevis where I sold the majority of my cargo."

The soldiers had tensed at the mention of Statia, but eased a bit with the naming of the British-held isle.

"Did you have cause to speak to anyone on St. Eustatius?" asked the lieutenant. A man by the name of Ainsley.

"Only those interested in purchasing my tobacco. As I said, it was but a brief stay. My cargo was full of Nevisian sugar and rum, and I was eager to return to the mainland."

The harbormaster signed the logbook and handed it back to him. "Four soldiers shall accompany you back to the ship and review your cargo."

"Review it? For what cause?"

"To be certain there are no arms or ammunition buried within those hogsheads of sugar," said the lieutenant.

"You suspect the Nevisians?" Ian asked, lifting a brow.

"I suspect the French who frequent St. Eustatius, among other islands," the lieutenant replied.

"Do what you must," Ian said easily. "You'll come away with nothing but sticky fingers for your trouble."

The lieutenant's face softened a bit. "I'm certain you understand, Captain. Given the rise of the rebels here in the colonies, we cannot be too careful. I have strict orders, especially with ships not flying the Union Jack." He paused. "May I ask why you have not registered this ship as a British vessel?"

Ian considered him, tried to put a hold on the words building in his mind, but was unable to suppress the rising tide. "My brother captained a British vessel and was pressed into service, whereupon he met his death," he bit out, struggling to keep his rising rage from further tightening his tone. "I intend to make a fortune in trade between the Indies, Americas, and England, not fight for either side in the present squabble."

"That's a rather mercenary view, Captain," the lieutenant chided. "What of your duty to your country?"

Ian shrugged. "I believe my brother's life was duty enough."

McKay shot him a sidelong look, but Ian's eyes remained on the lieutenant. He'd heard the edge in his own words, and now he'd likely drawn undue attention.

The lieutenant turned to face him fully. They were about the same age, the same height. Ian itched to bring his sgian dubh to his hand, but such an action would be foolish just now.

"Search them," the lieutenant ordered, his eyes not leaving Ian's. "Then search every inch of his vessel."

"Lieutenant?" asked a private, as if wondering if he'd heard correctly.

"Summon twelve others and search it!" he barked.

Ian clenched his lips as he was gruffly turned toward the wall of the harbormaster's office, hands sprawled above him, and roughly searched. He did not dare look at McKay, silently cursing his own tongue. *Couldn't keep quiet for but a wee moment longer, could ye now, laddie? Always have to have the last word, do ye not?*

More soldiers went trotting down the pier and streamed onto the deck of the *Inverness*.

"You shall not find anything amiss," he said to the lieutenant at his side. "I am but a merchant."

"We shall see, Captain," said the man through

narrowed eyes. This close up, he could see they were an eerie gray-blue.

Fine spy you turned out to be, man, he chastised himself. The young soldier behind him ran his hands down every inch of his breeches. For a heart-stopping moment, his cheek was right beside the hem of his jacket where the tiny letter had been sewn.

"Such ill treatment!" McKay said, moving suddenly to distract the man.

He was swiftly pressed back by two soldiers.

"Can ye not see why the Americans chafe under such a heavy hand?" Michael went on.

"McKay!" Ian said. "Stand down."

The lieutenant shot a glance between Ian and McKay and back again. "Take your ease, sailor," the lieutenant said. "We are here for the good of this land, not her detriment."

Ian turned back to the wall. His mate had succeeded in intervening at just the right moment. The man behind Ian had risen and idly completed the last of his search.

Two hours later, after being led back to the *Inverness*, the soldiers rose from the hold with nothing to show for it other than the sticky fingers Ian had promised. Meanwhile, the lieutenant and another man had gone through every paper and ledger in Ian's cabin.

Ian and McKay waited outside on the deck

where they had been commanded to remain, under armed guard. Ian paced, adopting the role of a wrongly accused innocent, hands on hips. When Lieutenant Ainsley emerged from his cabin and methodically set his hat on his head, he gave Ian one last long glance. "We found nothing, but I suspect that is our lack of sleuthing prowess," he said, stepping forward, nose to nose with Ian. "My intuition is fairly keen, Captain. And my intuition tells me there is something off about you and yours."

"And yet ye have found naught. Leave off, Lieutenant, and I shall be about my business and away from this harbor as soon as possible."

"Do not return anytime soon," he said. "You have a bad smell about you, Captain. I have issued orders not to allow you to return once you depart. And you shall not be allowed to export any goods."

Ian started. Had he heard the man correctly? "What? What right have you?" Two men grabbed his arms, holding him back.

"Yes, Captain. Those in rebellion here think they are quite clever. But we have the means of choking them into submission." Ainsley smiled when he saw the frustration in Ian's eyes. "You think you are above the reach of England? That by simply striking the Union Jack, we can no longer make demands of you?" He shrugged and folded his arms. "We cannot. But these are yet British waters, and New York a British city. We can make certain that only our loyal friends benefit from commerce here. And you, Captain, are clearly no friend to England."

Chapter Fifteen

At the end of two weeks of visits, Verity agreed to sell the British soldiers their desired horses. She did so out of the need to end the persistent Captain Howard's excuse to call upon her daily, as much as the desire to make her first significant sales. People had begun to enter her store, looking over their shoulders surreptitiously as if fearing they might be caught. But few purchased more than minor items. She had to open the dam to selling the rest of her stock of horses; she was well aware that come month's end, Ian might arrive with more, and she would need both the funds to pay him and the room to place them. It made her anxious, thinking of him choosing all that might arrive in his hold, as well as how her new horses might fare en route. But Ian had watched her carefully with the breeder, seen how she wanted them treated aboard ship. She was reasonably sure that he would do well in representing her.

As expected, Major Woodget, Captain Howard, and their men drew many an admiring eye atop their new mounts. Eager to please her, the captain rode far and wide in those first days after securing his new mare. "I have told every person of import from here to Gingerland that 'tis Miss Verity Banning of Banning's Bridlery I thank for this fine new mount," he said, leaning slightly over her store counter as she polished it with a rag and oil.

"You are most kind, Captain," she said, giving him a gentle smile.

He seemed to take that as encouragement. "As I was about this afternoon, Lady Browning of Marlowe Point extended a kind invitation."

"Oh?"

"Indeed," he said, flashing her a grin. "There is to be a soiree at her plantation tomorrow eve. I would be most glad, Miss Verity, if you would accompany me."

She frowned a little and parted her lips, searching for the words to dissuade him.

"Before you say no," he said, lifting a finger, "let me go on. I am well aware that your heart is still bruised over the terrible news of Captain McKintrick. I do not wish to press you. But I thought we might attend together as . . . friends," he said, then ducked his head with a smile. "Would it not be good for your business to arrive in your own fine new coach, drawn by your beautiful pair of geldings?"

Verity set anew to the work of polishing her counter, thinking it over. The man didn't know that there was more than one Captain McKintrick in her heart. Even so, he had made a good point. She'd been thinking that the geldings were ready for a significant outing. And if they appeared in that grand mahogany carriage, she was reasonably certain she could sell the four others she had within days. Island society was like that, even more competitive than at home in England, given their constant interaction on a landmass that only measured thirty-some square miles and had only two main roads.

It would be the perfect excuse.

"Come now, Verity," the Captain said, moving down the counter to be closer to her. "I shall be nothing but the perfect gentleman."

She swallowed hard. Woodrow Howard considered himself the consummate English gentleman. But his eyes, his demeanor . . . there was something about him that always put her off. Something assuming about him, as if their relationship were inevitable in a way. As if he'd decided he was in no great hurry and needn't press her, because who would be better for Verity than him?

And perhaps his assumptions were understandable. Many thought a man in British uniform a fine, steady catch, compared to the many drunkards and womanizers among the plantations. Was it fair of Verity to determine there could be nothing between them when she had never truly given him a chance? When last she left Nevis, she'd still considered herself devoted to Duncan McKintrick. When she returned, she fancied she had feelings for Ian. Perhaps a night at a soiree, on the arm of a friend, might help her discern what she was feeling further, and if she found no reason to doubt it, give her a moment to end Captain Howard's constant attempts at flirtation.

Only one thing gave her pause. Marlowe Point was down south, in Gingerland. Angus Shubert was there too. Did she really want to be anywhere near him? Still, the chance to be among society and show off her horses and carriage . . . and with the days slipping by . . .

"I would be most pleased to accept your invitation, Captain," she said, speaking quickly before she changed her mind.

His brows lifted in delighted surprise. "You shall?" he said, his voice cracking. He coughed, cleared his throat, gathered himself and straightened his shoulders. "Quite so. Very good, I mean. So then—shall I come around at six? I assume you wish for us to take your fine new carriage rather than hiring one?"

"Yes, yes," she said eagerly. " 'Tis a grand idea, showing off my new team and carriage. Thank you for that, my friend."

His smile faltered a bit at her use of *friend,* but he nodded. "Very well, Miss Verity. I shall be here promptly at six. I shall look forward to it."

He bowed, and she gave him a brief curtsey.

She showed him to the door and shut it behind him, relieved as she turned the lock and flipped her sign to *Closed.*

Trisa edged out from the back room. "You truly aim to go to the party with that one, Miss Verity?"

"Not alone," Verity said with an edge of a smile. "With luck, the Brownings invited my sisters and brother-in-law as well. Whereas the rest of the island finds fault with Gray and Ket's decision to hire freed slaves, the Brownings have always been kind to us. Fetch Abe, will you?" she asked, turning to pull a fresh sheet of paper out from under the counter. She reached for her ink and quill. Quickly she penned a note to Keturah, describing her dilemma . . . and her request.

As much as Ian felt the urgency to sail to North Carolina as fast as he could—and secure Verity's horses and saddles before word from Lieutenant Ainsley preceded him and the Brits blocked his exit—he had to see through the delivery of their missives and find out how he might best aid the Sons of Liberty in the months to come. All week long, Michael had sought an audience with the rebels, but with his grandfather out of town, he had not found a way into their web. At last, Michael had heard from him.

This commerce-choking threat was but Britain's latest move, determined to press the rebels back into subservience. Yet walking the streets of New York, Ian observed many locals in open rebellion—a woman spitting at the redcoats as they marched past, a shopkeeper flipping the Closed sign on his door just as soldiers approached. Even a prostitute turning her back on a redcoat holding a heavy bag of coin.

He'd found a sodden, illegally printed pamphlet in the street with threatening, angry words from John Adams. Another from John Locke, resurrecting old language about "limited government." Still another from Benjamin Franklin. On corners he saw soldiers piling these pamphlets on the ground and setting fire to them. But he knew in homes and apartments and offices and stores, many more could be found.

The rebellion was in fact gaining strength, and this latest attempt to kowtow them would surely fail. 'Twould be grim in the meantime for certain. Trade was the lifeblood of any settlement or city. But there was something different among these people, something only hinted at in the islands. In the islands, Brits still thought of England as their home, no matter how long they'd lived in Nevis, St. Kitts, Jamaica, or Montserrat. Here, while an American might speak with a British accent, 'twas American soil he or she claimed as home.

He and McKay entered a tavern as if they had nothing on their minds but a mug of ale and some hearty food for dinner. After they'd supped, Michael looked at him and asked under his breath, "Shall we slip out the back now? I know the way from here. Our contacts shall be waiting."

"Nay," Ian said, motioning for another round of ale to the barkeep. "We've had a man shadowing us since we left the wharf. We need a way to distract him before we go."

McKay wisely turned back to his pewter mug and lifted it to tap against Ian's. "To your keen eyes," he said. "I had not seen him."

"He's but a wee man, easy to miss."

"I knew you'd be well suited for this, Captain. There 'tisn't much that escapes you."

"Much? That intimates that I do miss some things."

"Precious little, and seldom anything important," McKay said, taking a swig. "Now, what do you propose as a distraction?"

Ian drank from his mug, thinking. Then a pretty barmaid entered from the back, just starting her shift from the looks of it. The voluptuous girl with a stack of blond curls atop her head tied on a clean apron, knotting it at her waist before bending to pick up several dirty dishes and placing a hand on a man's shoulder, laughing and bantering with the four at the table.

"Aye, that lass'll do," he said to McKay.

His mate looked over his shoulder to the maid

and then back to his mug. "Pretty as a peach, that one. Not a man in here who doesn't have his eye on her already."

Ian pulled open the drawstring of his money pouch and fished out a doubloon. McKay let out a low whistle. "It might not take as much as that, Cap'n."

"But I am not paying for 'might not,'" Ian said. "I am paying for 'as good as done.'"

They waited patiently for the girl to draw near. At last, she brought over a pitcher and leaned over—as much to show off her ample cleavage, Ian thought, as to see their mugs refilled. She cast him a mischievous, flirty glance. "May I get you two gents anything else?"

"Perhaps," Ian said. He opened his hand, giving her a glimpse of the gold coin in his palm. "But not food nor drink."

"Ach, I am not that sort of woman, sir," she said, leaning back in dismay. "If you have need of company—"

"Nay, nay," Ian said, feeling the burn of a blush at his cheeks. "'Tis not that that I wish to pay you for, lass. 'Tis the fact that we find ourselves in need of slipping out the back door unseen. Alas, a man bedevils us, trailing our every step. He is sitting in the corner, to the right of the front window."

The girl kept her blue eyes on Ian's, as cool under pressure as an old sailor facing a tempest.

For the first time, he saw she was not the naïve young girl he'd first surmised. She was wise beyond her years, probably reared in this establishment. "I believe we understand each other, sir," she said, sliding her hand beneath his and grabbing hold of the coin. "Give me but a moment. You'll know when 'tis time."

She topped off his and McKay's mugs, making it look as if they intended to do nothing but sit right there until the proprietor kicked them out. Ian clapped McKay on the shoulder and began to tell him a story about Duncan, solely for the excuse of keeping an eye on the maid, who weaved her way between tables. She stopped to talk to one group of men after another, nodding and smiling, picking up more and more dishes as she went, her stack becoming progressively precarious.

"Get ready," Ian whispered with a grin to McKay. There was a shout, a shriek, and a tremendous clatter as the huge pile of pewter plates and mugs in the girl's hands and arms went flying. The man in the corner ended up covered in the leftover stew from several bowls and rose, swearing at her; men at every table stood to come to her aid while Ian and McKay eased past the far side of the group, slid down the hall, and exited through the back door.

They hastened down the alley, crossed the street, turned a corner and went down another alley. McKay paused to hurriedly purchase a loaf of bread—ostensibly so they looked like two mates out to fetch themselves a bite to eat—and then led Ian half a mile distant. When a patrol of British soldiers approached from the opposite direction, McKay tore off a hunk of bread and handed it to him. He and Ian stepped into the street, allowing the soldiers to pass, each biting into the bread and nodding to the redcoats. Thankfully, the soldiers barely spared them a glance.

"Here," McKay said, tugging at Ian's elbow. They entered a narrow alley, the buildings three stories high on either side. At the end, McKay knocked on a door—four knocks in swift succession, followed by three more, this time with a rest between each rap of his knuckles.

Nervously, Ian glanced down the alley as they waited. After what seemed like an interminable period of time, they heard the slide of a lock and the door creaked open an inch. An old woman stared at them. "Who are you?"

"Friends," Ian said.

"Michael McKay," said his mate. "And this is my captain. I can vouch for him. My grandfather, Joseph McKay, sent us."

The old crone opened the door wider and gestured for them to step inside. "Make haste, boys, a'fore someone sees you."

They paused in her tiny kitchen. "Well, up the

stairs with you," she groused, pointing to a steep staircase.

"Thank you, ma'am," McKay said.

They climbed the rickety stairs, which felt as though they might give way at any moment, and emerged into a larger parlor filled with men. As one, the men turned toward the newcomers and grew silent. One of them, a middle-aged, gray-haired man with a tremendous gut, rose and asked, "Is that the McKay lad?"

"Indeed," Michael said, moving forward to extend a hand. "But it has been some years since I have been called such, Mr. Smith. And this is Captain Ian McKintrick. We arrived a week past from Statia and have a letter for the cause."

"Well, out with it, man," he said. "Let's see it."

Ian was already pulling off his jacket, as was McKay. Both set to ripping out their hems, eager to be free of the tiny letters that had threatened their undoing. *I hope it was worth all that,* Ian thought.

He handed his letter to Rupert Smith, apparently the leader, who leaned toward an oil lamp and broke the red wax seal. "This is news of aid for our lads via the French," he muttered, still reading. "There is a shipment of rifles and munitions set to arrive down the coast in three days' time. We are to arrange a diversion, so the vessel can smuggle the weapons to the beach."

McKay snorted. "That'll take more than a comely barmaid," he said.

"Or ten," Ian said.

"You've done well, my lads," said the portly man. He patted McKay on the shoulder and nodded to Ian. "Very well. Can you find reason to travel to Statia again? If so, we have a missive you might take to our friends, and they might have another for you. The cause is in need of as much detailed reporting as we can obtain—troop movements, naval reports, and the like."

"I can get your letter back to Statia," Ian said, "but the British shall not welcome my return to New York. I was not flying the Union Jack, and there's an officer there who has decided I shall not be allowed to export goods any longer."

"That'll not last long," said the man. "The Loyalists will be as strangled as the Patriots if they start interfering with commerce. They shall create a large ruckus over that." He paced back and forth, chin in hand. "Still, it might be useful to find a compatriot in an established Loyalist, one who has a bit of the rebel spirit in him. Can you do that, lads?" He looked from Ian to Michael and back again. "If you can do that, the British officer shall be forced to grant you entrance as well as exit. You'd be able to observe the movements of British troops and vessels, and report to us. The alternative is to make your way in through one of our secret smuggling inlets. But 'twould not be nearly as beneficial or timely as if you could gain entry past Sandy Hook."

Ian bit his lip. He knew a Loyalist who might be willing to sail with him . . . as well as betray her country for the cause.

Verity Banning.

With her cousins in New York—a well-known, fine family with deep Loyalist roots who had many friends on Long Island—she could likely gain them entry, even if he came upon Lieutenant Ainsley again.

But the question made him pause. Was he really ready to risk Verity's safety on behalf of the cause?

Moreover, would Duncan have ever done so?

CHAPTER SIXTEEN

Gray entered her store at half past noon.

"Why, Gray, what brings you here?" Verity asked.

"I am bent on a surprise for my wife and a boon for my sister," he said.

With that, he waved in Gideon and Cuffee, who each carried a hogshead of sugar on their shoulders, part of last year's bountiful harvest that Gray had set aside for bartering. Coin was notoriously short on the islands, and Verity had prepared herself to accept trade as needed.

"My goodness," she said. "For what is this?"

"I am taking my wife and sisters to a party this eve," he replied, giving her a sly smile. "I hear tell that one sister needs protection from a certain redcoat with dubious intentions."

"Oh, I am fairly certain of his intentions," Verity said. "They simply do not match my own. But what do you aim to purchase, Gray? Horses or—"

"That fine black carriage out front," he said. "Ket tells me you aim to keep the mahogany one for yourself."

"I do."

"Will this be sufficient?" he asked, gesturing

toward the sugar. "Perhaps if McKintrick can take it north on his next voyage?"

"Ah, 'tis more than enough, Gray. Thank you." She clutched her hands at her chest and grinned. "With two of the finest carriages arriving at Marlowe Point this eve, the Banning-Covingtons shall be the talk of the whole island. Men shall be at the store come morn, begging me to allow them to purchase one of the other carriages. They shall not be able to resist them."

"Indeed, they shall not," Gray said with a wink. He turned to Gideon and Cuffee. "Hitch my team to the black carriage out front, would you? We need to return to the Double T and get cleaned up before the party tonight."

"Right away, Master Gray," said Cuffee. Gideon followed him out after casting Verity a shy smile.

"Do not fret over tonight, Ver," Gray said. "We shall accompany the captain here to collect you. There shall not be a moment where you must endure his company without your sisters'—or my—aid."

"Oh, Gray," she said, reaching across the counter to squeeze his hand. "How I adore you."

He laughed, his tanned forehead wrinkling in surprise. "Then I have done my job well. Thank you for the fine new carriage, Miss Banning," he said and feigned a formal bow. "At last I can escort my bride in style to a soiree."

"And it shall be a much smoother ride for her," she said, following him outside.

"A boon to be certain."

Verity watched with pride as Gray climbed into the open back of the sleek and curvy carriage and sat down on the tufted, cushioned seats. In his work clothes he did not cut quite the right picture, but she knew that come eve, he would. Especially with Ket and Selah alongside him.

"Until this eve, dear one," Gray said, giving her a jaunty wave.

"Until this eve," she said. Then, folding her arms, she watched as Cuffee climbed up beside Gideon, flicked the reins, and the old mares began hauling the carriage down the road toward the heart of Charlestown. She grinned, knowing Gray and the new carriage would draw many an eye, just as he clearly had planned. *Watching out for me even now,* she mused.

"Miss Verity!" Trisa called up the stairs. "They're here!"

With one last look in the mirror, Verity gathered up her emerald skirts and descended the stairs, carefully planting each slippered foot before giving it her full weight. The shoes were brand-new and rather slick on wood, not having their first scuffs yet. But they were a beautiful brocade, dyed by the tailor to match her new gown. Trisa had curled and pinned her hair in an elaborate pile atop her head, and she'd donned a pair of tear-drop pearl earrings that had belonged to her mother.

But it was not for Captain Howard that she had dressed to look her very best. It was to so thoroughly impress everyone who saw her in her carriage that they would wish to do as she hoped—vie to purchase the others.

"Verity?" called Ket before she was halfway down the stairs.

"Verity, we must be off!" called Selah.

"She comes, Lady Ket, Miss Selah," Trisa said. "See there?"

Verity heard the squeak of the door and the heavy-booted steps of what she had come to know as the captain's. Her dear sisters had made certain they were inside before he had a chance to enter, doing as she'd asked . . . running a blockade. She hurried over to her sisters, greeting each of them with such glee, she pretended not to even see the captain.

But at last she was forced to turn toward him.

"Miss Verity," he said, giving her an elegant bow. "You are a vision."

"You are too kind, my friend." She gave him a slight curtsey. " 'Tis nothing but the wondrous work of Tailor Paxton."

He made as if to reach for her hand, but Ket smoothly interceded, oohing and aahing over the fine sateen and embroidery of the bodice.

"Paxton really has outdone himself. And I with nothing to wear but this tent of a gown," she moaned.

Verity smiled at her sister. 'Twas truly a tent, of sorts, her bulbous belly and the doctor firmly refusing any further attempts at stays. But it was a pretty golden silk, and again, Verity decided her sister fairly glowed. "Ahh, Ket, you are beautiful in anything you wear these days. You could be wearing sackcloth and you would still have every man stealing glances in your direction."

Ket laughed. "Only that fine carriage you sold my husband could lure me out for another social gathering before I have this child," she said, taking her arm, Selah the other, and leaving the poor captain in their wake.

"And your geldings and your own carriage!" Selah breathed. " 'Tis the prettiest in all the Leewards, I wager. May I ride with you? Captain, you do not mind, do you? 'Twould be such a pleasure!" She blinked innocently at him, her big brown eyes beseeching him.

"Of course you may," the man said slowly, clearly torn. Escorting both of the eligible Misses Banning would make many others mad with jealousy. And yet he had clearly envisioned time alone with Verity on that fine leather seat, she surmised. She hid her smile and accepted Gray's gloved hand, helping her up and into her carriage. Terence was in livery, looking every bit the genteel driver. Little Abe was in livery too and clung excitedly to the back of the carriage. Selah was next, and then the major shook hands with Gray, and her brother-in-law moved back to join Ket in their own fine carriage, driven by Gideon and Cuffee.

"Carry on, Terence," Verity said. "On to Marlowe Point, if you would."

"Right away, Miss Verity." Terence had only to flick the reins and the geldings set off excitedly.

The horses were young and still a bit green to the carriage yoke, but she smiled as they settled into the matched gait just as she had trained them. Abe had braided their manes and tails for the occasion. She thought of Duncan, who had intended these horses for her, she recalled. Had he imagined taking her to a party like the one tonight? Perhaps as a wedding gift to her?

They had never spoken of marriage. Indeed, their courtship had not encompassed anything other than fervent glances of longing and kisses to the hand or cheek. A few walks together, a sister always trailing behind as a chaperone. But there would have been no other rationale than a wedding to give her something as extravagant as this pair of fine horses.

It sent a pang of sorrow through her, remembering him. His generous heart, his earnest attention every time they were together.

But 'twas not meant to be.

And what was odd now for her was that as much as the thought grieved her, she'd come to know Ian in a way that perhaps surpassed anything she had with his brother. Ian had chosen to see Duncan's gift through. He could have sold the horses in New York and pocketed the money as part of his own inheritance. Instead, he had paid off the remaining sum due and brought them to her, honoring his brother's unspoken wishes. An act of honor as well as generosity.

Ian. Where was he? How did he fare? How she missed him.

"Goodness, Miss Verity," intoned the captain, "why so glum?"

"Oh!" She startled and forced a soft smile. "Not glum. Only a bit melancholy. I was wishing one Captain McKintrick was here to see this beautiful pair of horses he gifted me, and the other Captain McKintrick here to see them pull the new carriage he helped me import. If all goes as planned this eve, I will owe them both a great deal."

"Ahh, yes," the captain said, his jaw shifting as if in agitation. "I am certain it would have pleased them as much to be here with you—and Miss Selah—as it does me."

"You are such a kind friend to escort us this eve, Captain," Selah said, leaning forward with a brilliant smile. She was in a light blue gown that hugged her curves and seemed to accentuate her chocolate brown eyes.

The captain shifted in his seat, clearly disliking but another of the Bannings referring to him as *friend,* but what could he say? Surely there were worse ways they might refer to him, and friendship denoted something closer to what he desired, did it not? She turned to watch passersby on the boardwalk gape at them as they rolled by, many of them pointing. Smiling, she lifted a gloved hand to wave.

Already the evening was unfolding just as she had foreseen. And with Gray and Ket behind her in the second carriage, they practically formed a parade. Dear, dear Gray! Daring to spend some of their precious sugar stores in order to aid her, in more ways than one. And Ket, coming out when she clearly wanted nothing more than to remain in a hammock at the Double T, doing her best to rest and cool off, come evening, after another wearisome day. Yes, this was what it meant to be family, to support one another.

They paused here and there to pull to the side and let the other carriages and wagons heading into Charlestown pass by. But most of the plantation owners and their wives were heading to Marlowe as they were. By the time they reached the sprawling plantation owned by the Brownings, the sun was beginning to set behind them, making Montserrat glow in the distance, and beyond it, Martinique. "Oh, is it not beautiful?" Verity said. " 'Tis not often we get to see the view from this side of the island."

"If one might call *that* foul island in the distance beautiful," the captain sniffed.

Verity smiled. "Oh, come now, Captain Howard. Were Martinique English soil, would you admit to its beauty?"

He softened as he looked at her, letting his eyes follow the lines of her neck and cleavage and then hurriedly return to her face. "Mayhap if they saw the error of their ways."

She hid a smile and looked to the fine railed fence that lined the entry to Marlowe. Red bougainvillea had been planted at regular intervals, giving it a grand, uniform appearance she'd not seen on any other plantation. Most opted to adopt the abundant yet discordant mix of yellow bells and crab claw and white jasmine along their lanes, as well as fruit trees. Here at Marlowe, there were no trees. All in all, this side of the island was far more arid, the rocks more apparent than the encroaching jungle. It felt wider on this side of the isle too, a flat sprawl of land on a slow rise that led to the lush green hills and volcanic peaks.

Terence pulled the team to a stop, a line of carriages now waiting to be received at the grand house at the end of the lane. From here they could hear the roar and wash of the waves and see porous-rock storehouses lining the beach.

"I wonder if it nettles the French, such bounty,

within view," the captain said, gesturing outward. "In many ways, Nevis still reigns as the Queen of the Caribbees."

"Most have found their own strengths, from what I have gathered," Selah said, waving gaily at the Welands, who had turned to gape at their new carriage and team of horses. "They no longer envy the other, but rather strive to make the most of their own."

"Until they aim to make their neighboring isle their own," the captain added. "Mark my words, ladies. 'Tis a good thing the Nevisian Assembly called for aid. With the rebels daring to fire upon our men up north, you shall soon see the Royal Navy at her finest. But you need not fear," he continued. " 'Tis precisely why we are here. To protect you. And if your slaves get any foolish notions of insurrection with enemies afoot, we shall put a swift end to that as well."

Verity swallowed hard. She found such idle talk irritating, and Selah, even more so. Had the man not gathered even that much in all these months on the Double T? And with Terence and Abe right here in the carriage, clearly taking in every word? Even as a freed man and boy, they loved many others who were yet slaves. Thankfully, they were at last nearing the house, and the sudden silence amongst them was not as apparent. They could hear the strains of music over the waves, louder than ever, and Verity gave into a smile of exultation. How long had it been since she had been to a proper party? Months, she realized, what with setting up her shop and traveling to America and back.

Thoughts of the voyage brought Ian's tanned face, his sun-kissed auburn hair, his dark green eyes to mind, unbidden. What might he look like in a proper necktie, long coat, and breeches tucked into polished boots? Duncan had always appeared a bit too broad in such attire, a bit trapped, like Ket might appear in stays, given her pregnancy. But Ian, with his more lithe form, why, he'd be more similar to Gray in stature, cutting a fine figure . . .

"Miss Verity?" asked her escort, clearing his throat.

She startled and belatedly remembered herself and where she was. Mr. and Mrs. Browning stood behind the captain, clearly too taken with the beauty of her carriage and team to note the distraction of her one remaining occupant. Cheeks ablaze, she reached forward to take Captain Howard's hand and lifted her skirts, demurely descending.

"Goodness, Miss Banning, wherever did you obtain such a lovely carriage and team?" said Mrs. Browning, kissing both of her cheeks.

"Oh, perhaps you have not heard," she said brightly. "I have opened a shop in town, offering only the finest horses and carriages in the

Leewards. My brother-in-law has another that was imported but two weeks' past," she said, gesturing behind them. "We have three others on display at Banning's Bridlery. You must come by at your earliest convenience."

"Oh! Really!" she said, clearly torn between excitement and hurriedly concealed dismay over the idea of a mercantile run by a woman.

" 'Tis a fine carriage and team indeed," allowed the reserved Mr. Browning, bending over Verity's hand. "You shall be the talk of the party."

"My hope precisely," she said, daring to give him an impish smile. " 'Twould be good for my business, yes?"

"Indeed," he said, returning her smile.

"Well done," Captain Howard said under his breath as he led Verity and Selah to a corner, awaiting Ket and Gray. "If you keep enchanting each of the planters here, your remaining goods shall be sold before you return to town."

"From your mouth to God's ears," Verity whispered back.

The man wasn't entirely intolerable. At times he could be very civil, endearing even. But other times . . . Again, she thought of Ian. How she wished it were he escorting her. The chance to dance with him. Maneuver among the people in attendance, discover an avenue in each to connect them with Verity and aid in building her business. Captain Howard was doing his best. But Ian was so fiercely keen in understanding each man or woman's strengths.

Where was he now? In New York? Or on to North Carolina? Or even tacking back toward Nevis? Her heart began to pound at the thought. No, it was too soon for that. Surely he had not yet left the mainland.

She and Selah greeted the young Mr. Fredrickson, the Takaitus family, and a few others who refused to ignore them, as many others were doing, silently punishing them for the decisions they had made at the Double T in regard to hiring freed slaves. Servants circulated with flutes of champagne, trays of canapés, and grilled shrimp.

Verity had just taken a bite of a shrimp when she nearly choked.

Before her stood Angus Shubert, dressed not as an overseer but like one of the most fashionable men in attendance. She blinked and stared, certain she was imagining things. But indeed it was him, grinning at her as he held the lapels of his jacket in meaty hands.

"Well, if it isn't Miss Verity Banning," he began. "Not in field breeches tonight, are you? And Miss Selah to boot! Your other sister cannot be far, can she?" He leaned left and right, looking for Ket, before returning to Selah, eyes running down the length of her blue gown.

Selah sucked in her breath and moved a bit behind Verity, who said the first thing that came to mind. "I-I did not expect to see you here," she said, despising the slight tremble in her voice. She was quick to clear her throat.

"No, I imagine not," said Shubert. "You half expected me at Chandler, right?" He turned to a servant and exchanged his empty champagne flute for a full one, drained it, and set it on a nearby table. "I turned that offer down, as enticing as it might have been to be your neighbor again. You see, in an odd change of fortune, I am one of the gentry now."

"Oh?" she managed, silently wishing that Gray, Ket, and Captain Howard would see who had engaged them, but resisting the urge to turn and search for them. A predator sensed fear, and she refused to give this one any hint of that. She knew it would only bring him pleasure.

Selah seemed to gain strength from Verity, managing to step forward beside her again.

He looked from one to the other of them and swung his heavy head back and forth. "You two have always been as pretty as a picture."

"Thank you, Mr. Shubert," Verity said wanly. "Now, if you will excuse us . . ." She moved around him, but he stepped in front of her.

"No, not yet." He'd gripped her wrist, then hurriedly dropped it, seeming to remember himself. "Are you not curious as to how I am at last in the center of one of these parties rather than hovering somewhere near the stables? Or why

I did not accept the position of overseer at the Langleys' plantation?"

"No," she said, looking coldly up into his eyes. "I am not curious about any part of your life, Mr. Shubert. As far as I am concerned, the less I know about you, the better I shall sleep."

He grinned. "Because thoughts of me keep you awake at night?" he asked suggestively, leaning closer. "You wouldn't be the first girl who dreamt of me."

"Oh? Others have suffered night terrors at the thought of you too?" she bit out under her breath.

"Now, that is unkind, Miss Banning," he said, tucking his chin and feigning hurt. "And given that I might be shopping in your new mercantile tomorrow, you'd best watch yourself."

" 'Tis you who should watch himself," she hissed. "And do not bother stopping by my shop. I shall never sell a thing to you."

Gray arrived then, along with Captain Howard. "Shubert," he growled, stepping between Verity and the man. "You know better than to approach any of my family. Not after what you did."

"Oh? That?" Shubert's lips twisted in derision, and he made a cutting motion with his hand as he glanced at Selah. "That is water under the bridge."

"Not for us," Gray said. "Be certain you stay on this side of the island, and we shall keep to ours."

Shubert laughed. "That shall prove impossible now," he said, sliding his hands in his jacket pockets as if utterly at ease. "For I married the Widow Everly yesterday." His eyes scanned the room. "And I reckon that makes me the most powerful landowner here, with holdings across *all* of Nevis." He leveled a smile at Gray.

Gray paused, visibly shocked. "Widow Everly?"

"Why, Mr. Everly passed only two weeks ago," Selah breathed, gloved fingers over her round lips.

"This is a hard place to be a woman living alone," Shubert said. "I was willing to come to her aid in that regard."

"And she without an overseer, I had heard," Ket added grimly, now at Verity's other elbow.

"Why hire an overseer when you can have one in a husband?" Shubert said, lifting his hands and grinning. " 'Tis like killing two birds with one stone, I say."

Verity frowned. Who likened marriage to killing?

"I do not care whom you charmed into marrying you," Gray said, leaning so close to the man that his nose was mere inches from Shubert's. "You stay away from my family. Do you understand me?"

"Or what?" Shubert scoffed. "You shall not succeed in banishing me again. I am *one* of you now, Covington. Actually, I have far more power than you, given your poor choices and reputation with how you handle your slaves. I will go where I wish. See whom I wish." He leered in Verity and Selah's direction.

"Now see here," Captain Howard said. "You forget yourself, man!"

"Oh, I do not forget myself, Captain," Shubert said, eyeing each of the Bannings and Covingtons slowly. "I do not forget anything. No wrong done to me. Nor how I swore I would get even one day."

A servant came by again, and Shubert took another flute of champagne from the tray, drained it with several loud gulps, and raised his empty glass to them all in salute. "A pleasure catching up with my old neighbors. Now, I must see to my new wife, as well as my fellow councilmen."

CHAPTER SEVENTEEN

"Fellow *councilmen?*" Keturah muttered, gripping Verity's hand—discovering with some surprise that she had a sgian dubh clutched between her fingers—and wrapping an arm around Selah's shoulders. "Have they gone mad, accepting Angus Shubert?"

"Vincent Everly left a seat open," Verity said. "Perhaps it is but temporary."

"Whatever would have possessed Mrs. Everly to marry him?"

"I know not," Verity said, feeling as shaky as Selah appeared. "I have heard she had a weak constitution, even before Vincent died."

"Weak constitution or addled mind?" Ket asked under her breath, leading both sisters to a settee. "Tea, please," she asked of Gray, "for all of us?"

He nodded and set off, but not before he whispered in the captain's ear. The man's shoulders straightened, and he looked about. A soldier set to guard duty, Verity surmised.

"I heard she has taken to frequent doses of laudanum," Selah said, keeping her voice low.

"What do you wager Angus Shubert helped her to obtain it?" Ket asked.

"What do you wager Shubert threatened to accept the Langleys' offer at Chandler unless she agreed to marry him?" Verity nodded. Surely that was it, for there wasn't a lady of society on-island who would have ever considered Shubert's hand in marriage, addled in the mind or not. Let alone the richest. But the Bannings and Covingtons well knew how difficult it was for a woman to hire a good overseer.

"All the while, he was angling to be the new owner of the biggest plantation on Nevis," Ket gritted out.

Together, the sisters watched as Shubert met his new bride—fifteen years his senior—and bent to whisper something in her ear. The woman, even in her finery, looked frail, as if she had not eaten in days. She had been pretty once, likely the talk of the island in their father's days. Now her cheeks were sunken, her eyes hollow, the stark bones of her clavicle making her appear more a ghostly skeleton than living flesh and bone.

"Perhaps he learned something more of her other than a penchant for laudanum," Keturah said. "That man would do anything to get ahead."

"And he has succeeded handsomely in this," Verity said, blinking several times in shock. "From overseer to councilman? Master of the Downing Plantation? That plantation manages, what, two or three hundred acres?"

"Four," Keturah corrected. "And 'tis not only here in Gingerland. Even before Vincent died, it was he who was always best poised to buy other plantations going under. He has land in every parish of this island—Figtree, Windward, Saint Thomas, Cotton Ground, even our own Saint Paul."

"And now it all belongs to Angus Shubert," Selah said with an audible swallow. "All the slaves on those plantations . . ." she breathed, mentally calculating, brow furrowed in concern. "What do you suppose they number? Six, seven hundred?"

"Far more," Keturah said grimly. All three sisters were remembering the cruelty the slaves at Red Rock suffered when Shubert was overseer there. How it chafed at him, the manner in which the Bannings and Covingtons treated their own . . . and now hired only freed slaves. "I bet a thousand, all told."

Selah sucked in a breath. "A thousand souls at his mercy," she repeated in a whisper. She'd gone white, looking at the man, his huge form easily seen through the crowd. Likely remembering that terrible night when he had almost raped her. Would have raped her had not Gray, Duncan, and her sisters arrived in time. Keturah covered Selah's hand. She, too, had been manhandled by the brute.

If Shubert could do such things to her sisters,

ladies of stature, what could he do to every negress under his control?

Verity looked back to Shubert, now weaving between other guests, pausing to make conversation. The rest of the gentry did not quite know how to handle his arrival in their midst either . . . and yet if their success at the Double T had taught them one thing, it was this: Profiting on a plantation made inroads with every family on the island, regardless of how others might resent them. There was simply no way around it. If one succeeded, the others hungered to learn how they did so. To ignore those who prospered was to risk one's own profits. And year by year, despite his harsh methods, Shubert had helped make every plantation he served profitable.

If Keturah and Gray could be at least marginally accepted, despite their unconventional ways of operating the Double T, it wouldn't be long until Shubert's transgressions were buried and talk centered on what he was doing right.

Verity heaved a sigh. "At least he's still primarily down here. Far from us, rather than at Red Rock or at Chandler."

"Yes, but he no longer feels the confines of his banishment," Selah said, taking with trembling hands a cup from a tray offered by a maid beside Gray. "Can you not see it in him? Clearly, he feels he can go anywhere he wishes on Nevis."

"And he has the rationale to visit any parish, any day he wishes now," Ket said.

"But he is a married man," Verity tried. "A councilman. He shall have to comport himself accordingly."

"Will he?" Ket asked bleakly. "I do not think we can count on that."

Verity shivered, thinking of the man's promise to come to her store tomorrow.

He might be coming. She could not stop him from doing so. But she and Ian's training with her sgian dubh could make short work of any threat he brought to her doorstep.

She hoped.

Captain Howard returned with her to the store where he'd left his mare in her stables. The Covingtons paused in Charlestown too, giving her as much coverage as they could, but Verity urged Selah into their carriage and on to the Double T. "Go on now," she said. "Ket needs to get home. I shall be fine." Both Keturah and Selah looked utterly spent after the evening's festivities, but they hesitated, glancing toward the captain, waiting expectantly by Verity's shop door.

Hearing them pull up, Trisa, God bless her, lifted a lamp in the window and disappeared, presumably to greet them downstairs. "Go on," Verity repeated. "Trisa will see to my needs."

And give me an adequate chaperone, she added silently.

Ket reached over and squeezed her hand. "I hope you sell every horse and carriage tomorrow. I heard it from more than one woman that there are many considering an improvement in either carriage or horse."

"And once they visit your fine shop," Selah said, "they shall not be able to help themselves from perusing the rest."

"Let us hope," Verity said. But her sisters' confidence bolstered her own.

As their carriage pulled away and Trisa opened the door, greeting her and the captain with lamp in hand, Verity turned to the man. "Thank you for a fine evening, Captain." She glanced over her shoulder. "Abe will be here in but a moment with your horse."

He paused. "Are you so eager to be rid of my company, Miss Verity?" he asked softly.

Trisa bowed her head and slipped inside, leaving them in partial privacy and darkness. Yet the door remained open.

The captain lifted his hand and, with a feather-light touch, traced her cheek. "Is there nothing in you . . . nothing that makes you find favor with me?"

Verity swallowed and bowed her head a moment before looking back to him, saying nothing. He was a decent man, merely lonely.

Stationed here on the island for the foreseeable future. Why was it that her heart longed for one sea captain after another?

"Is it McKintrick, then?"

She nodded. "Yes."

"The first? Or the last?"

"Both, really," she said gently. "I find myself grieving Duncan, and yet anticipating Ian's return more than I thought I would."

He stiffened, put his hands on his hips, and looked down the empty street of the town. "You have an understanding with the captain? Upon his return?"

"No." She shook her head. There had been nothing formal said. Only a binding of her heart to his from within.

"I . . . I see."

"Oh, Captain Howard," she said, impulsively reaching out to touch his arm. "I do appreciate your friendship. Surely you can see that." When he continued staring at her gloved hand upon his arm as if transfixed, she hurriedly dropped it.

"I do," he said gravely, then placed his tricorn atop his head as Abe brought his mare around the corner of the shop. Every bit of his movements spoke of sorrow, defeat. And while that saddened Verity, to bring him such pain, she found relief in the clarity of it too.

Perhaps now he would leave her be. Find

another woman in town who might return his affections.

"Good eve, Miss Banning," he said, bowing curtly in her direction, one hand atop his hat, one atop his heart. "You did me an honor this evening, accepting my company."

" 'Twas you who honored me, Captain. Blessed me. Assisted me. Thank you."

"Anything for a friend, eh?" he said, a new edge of bitterness to his tone. He climbed onto the mare, took the reins from Abe, and turned the horse so he could face Verity again. "Tell me, Miss Banning. What happens if this McKintrick fails to return to you, as did the last?"

Verity's mouth dropped open. "Why, Captain," she breathed, eviscerated by his words, "I understand pain, but I never figured you to be cruel in the face of it."

"Is it cruelty, Miss Banning?" he pressed, his voice thin. "Or reality?" He looked up at the front of her store and around, as if taking in the silhouette of the peak and the broad swath of stars. "Here on Nevis we've learned that time is oft in short supply, Miss Banning. And those who are wise make the most of what they have, when they have it, before 'tis gone."

He referred to himself, of course.

"I am well aware of how time can be short," Verity said, "and I find that choices are a gamble, Captain. Every one. But with each one I make,

I strive to do as my heart and my God directs. I can do no other."

He held her gaze a moment longer, and then he turned and was swallowed by the darkness. In time, the steady sound of his mount's hooves on cobblestone faded, usurped by the island's nightly hum of crickets and tree frogs. She took several steps away from the shop, looking up to the silhouette of the peak, the stars that blanketed the sky. "Oh, God," she whispered, "this choice was of you, was it not?"

And at the thought of the captain's suggestion, that Ian might never return, as Duncan hadn't . . . she hugged herself and closed her eyes. Was Woodrow right? Was she being foolish, fanciful, longing for another man who might not return, when a decent man was right here, right now, clearly ready to court her?

"Miss Verity?" Abe asked, tugging at her hand with his small one. "You all right, Miss Verity?"

"No, Abe, I fear I am not," she said.

The child—her half brother—took her hand in both of his. "Mama always says that things seem darkest when it is dark outside. Sleep on it, and come mornin', your heart will be brighter with the new day."

His earnest tenderness made her smile. "Your mother is a wise woman, Abe."

"Yes'm. I've heard her tell it to more than one sad person. Why are you sad?"

251

"Sad? No. Concerned is more like it. Concerned I made a mistake this night."

"Well, Mama always says that a mistake can be made right, if one has the gumption to make it so. And sometimes you have to risk making a mistake in order to get anywhere. Look at me. I risked a mistake in accepting this job as your stableboy."

"Yes, you did, Abe." Verity smiled. "And what say you now? Was it a mistake, moving with me to Charlestown?"

He shrugged. "Not that I can see, yet."

Trisa came out then too, offering Verity her shawl. She wrapped it around her shoulders, and then Verity allowed the two of them to lead her inside. And as she locked the door and carried her lamp up the stairs, she thought she agreed with Abe. *I did not make a mistake with the captain. At least as far as I can see yet.*

Chapter Eighteen

When Ian arrived off North Carolina's shore, there were no British vessels within sight. He and Michael hurried to call upon the horse breeder, and in addition to the two Verity had picked out earlier, hastily chose sixteen more mares, geldings, and two stallions, figuring even if any of them failed to meet Verity's expectations, they could sell them on Statia—and given their empty hold, they needed every one they could claim. But by the time they had led the horses down to the harbor, there was a British clipper at anchor, forty men in red uniform now milling about the harbormaster's office and the wharf, interrogating every captain scheduled to set sail.

Mr. Darby swore under his breath and pulled up short with the lead horse, Ian right behind him. Ian had informed him of the lieutenant's threat in New York—and Darby, clearly a rebel sympathizer, well knew what it might mean for his business. After all, Ian was reasonably certain that the man was getting half again as much for his horses for export than he would by selling them to others in the Carolinas. "Come this way," he said, turning a corner and moving down an alley and around the block. Once clear of the houses, he turned to speak with Ian and Michael. "We will not get these horses loaded today. But we could in the wee hours at Shelter Cove, about ten miles south of here. Might you register your departure with the harbormaster and meet us under cover of darkness? That clipper appears set for the night. She's likely the only one on patrol in these waters."

"Likely," Ian repeated, his tone droll. *But if she isn't . . .*

"How would we recognize the cove?" McKay asked.

" 'Tis just south of Yount Cove, the one with the long point and lighthouse. Shelter Cove has a lone tree on her own point."

Ian took a deep breath, considering. He knew that if he was caught smuggling, the British would have cause to see him swinging from the nearest tree. They'd barely made it out of New York with food and water for the men on board. And yet if there really was a war about to begin, he needed this cargo—and its profits—to continue to aid the cause and fund future voyages. He eyed Michael, and his mate gave him a single nod, arms crossed.

"Can you get a ferryman to this cove," McKay asked the breeder, "so that we can load the horses?"

"There is one nearby. He'd come to our aid for a fat purse."

"We shall leave that to you, then," Ian said. "The *Inverness* will be in that cove awaiting you and these horses come nightfall. Do we have a deal?"

"We do," said Mr. Darby, offering his hand.

Ian shook it. But as they parted ways, he wondered if he had just purchased himself a world of trouble, as well as a small herd of horses.

"If we are caught . . ." he muttered to McKay.

"We simply must not," said his mate.

The morning after the party, Gray and Philip were outside her door when Verity opened the store. She blinked twice, surprised. "Gentlemen," she said. "Good morning."

"Good morning," Gray said with a grin, following her inside.

"Are you here on a social call or to purchase something from my fine establishment?"

"Perhaps both," Philip said, picking up a wide-brimmed hat and trying it on.

"All right," Verity said slowly.

Gray leaned a hip against her counter and crossed his arms. "You gained a fair amount of attention last night, as you hoped."

"And?"

"And we thought you might like some aid in manning the store when the entire island's gentry arrive," Gray said.

"That is optimistic," Verity said, crossing her own arms. "What you truly mean is that my sisters would not have given you a moment's rest, fretting over me and the potential of Angus Shubert coming by. Right?"

"Well," Gray said, swallowing a grin, "that too."

"So you intend to spend hours here? The day?"

"As long as it takes," he allowed. "Ket would be here herself, but the evening taxed her. And Selah didn't wish to leave her alone."

"Of course not. Gray, listen. I shall be perfectly all right here on my own. I have Terence and Trisa . . ."

He shook his head. "Sorry, Ver. You know how it is. I can either suffer your irritation or my bride's."

"And you choose mine," she said with a short laugh.

"There you have it," he said cheerfully. "Marital harmony is at times a delicate balance."

"Especially when said bride is heavy with child?"

His grin widened and he nodded. "What can we do for you?" he asked, rolling up his sleeves. "Put us to work. We are at your disposal."

"Well, I do need a new barrel of nails from the back. And would you and Philip be willing to hang a shelf for me? Even on the ladder, 'tis a bit too high for me to reach."

The two men set off to do as she directed. "Such foolishness," she was muttering, thinking them overprotective, when Mrs. Willis arrived, with Mrs. Browning on her elbow. They entered tentatively, as if there were something inside the shop that might bite them or smelled distasteful. But as they looked about—a sidesaddle catching Mrs. Willis's eye, a brocade carriage cushion Mrs. Browning's—their mood softened.

The bell at the door rang again, and a couple Verity recognized but had not yet met entered the shop, inquiring about two mules. Gray came in from the back, carrying the barrel of nails, Philip with hammer in hand. Both men's faces lit up when they saw she had customers.

"Gray, would you mind escorting this couple to the stables? They'd like to see our mules. Terence can take it from there."

"Certainly," he replied, setting down the heavy barrel beside the half-empty one with a thud.

She turned from them as he introduced himself and went over to Mrs. Browning. " 'Tis a lovely cushion, is it not?" she said with a smile. "Filled with horsehair, so it should be quite durable. I also have this one, over here." She led Mrs. Browning to a second, leather-covered version.

"Ahh, yes," said the older woman. "Our own is quite threadbare. But then I was also admiring your carriages outside, miss. Mr. Browning should be here any moment . . ."

The bell rang again, and Mr. Browning did indeed enter the store, followed closely by Angus Shubert.

A chill ran down Verity's spine, but she concentrated on the Brownings, pretending she had not seen the hulking man on Mr. Browning's elbow. Shubert was taking off his hat, looking about the store and whistling under his breath. Philip edged into her line of vision, hammer still in hand, and she dared take a calming breath.

"We are interested in one of your carriages outside, Miss Banning," Mr. Browning said. "Might I inquire about the price?"

"Certainly," she said, gesturing toward the door. "Let us go and look at it together. There are many fine features that no one outside of London or New York has yet seen." She led the way, hoping and praying that Shubert would stay inside, but he followed them out.

"I, too, am interested in a carriage. This one over here," Shubert said. "My new wife is accustomed to the finest in everything."

"Allow me to assist the Brownings, and then we can speak further, Mr. Shubert," Verity said.

The Brownings, sensing the tension between the two, tensed as well. Mrs. Browning wound an anxious hand through the crook of her husband's elbow. Philip stepped even closer to Verity.

"Go on, then," Shubert allowed, crossing his arms.

Nervously, Verity began walking with the Brownings around the perimeter of the new model, pointing out the suspension system that allowed for smoother rides, the wide double wheels that helped "ensure that one might not be left stranded on Round Road. If one wheel breaks, the other is likely to carry the day," she told them. As Verity moved on, she became more comfortable, pointing out the iron-reinforced tongue, the tufted seats, the solid floorboards and door. When finished, she named her price—an exorbitant sum, ten times what she'd paid—and then carefully schooled her face to await their decision.

Mr. Browning looked soberly at his wife's expectant expression and, just as Verity hoped, turned back to her and smiled. "We shall take it."

"Excellent. If you wouldn't mind stepping inside with me, I shall write up your bill of sale."

"Write one for me too," said Shubert, again stepping forward. "You sold me as well."

"That one is twenty percent more, Mr. Shubert," she hedged.

"Fine. I shall pay it."

The Brownings glanced back and forth between them.

Verity paused. She'd intended never to sell a thing to Shubert. But perhaps it would be most expedient to agree to the sale and send him on his way. After two weeks of selling little but nails and three horses to soldiers, could she really afford to turn him away? After all, he was not asking for horses, only the carriage. And with both him and the Brownings seen about the island in their new carriages, surely she would sell the remaining one within days. "Very well, Mr. Shubert. I shall prepare your bill of sale next."

She quickly turned away before his smile of victory could fully form, leading the Brownings inside, just as Mr. and Mrs. Thompson approached. She saw to the Brownings' bill, answered the Thompsons' questions about a child's saddle for their nine-year-old son, and once they had left, looked up to see Philip waiting, a heavy purse in hand. He set it carefully on the table. "This is Shubert's payment for the carriage. Or shall I say Lady Everly's payment?"

Verity heaved a sigh and lifted the pouch, pulling open the drawstring to inspect the pile of coins within. The Thompsons had arranged to pay her in sugar, as had Mrs. Willis, and she had to admit it was good to have someone pay in coin for once. On Nevis, coinage was notoriously in short supply. Those who had it had an advantage and could often obtain a better price in the midst of negotiations. And yet she hated the sense of being grateful to Shubert for any reason at all.

"Is he waiting outside?" she asked.

"No," Philip said grimly. "He announced that he would return 'sometime in the next week' with his horses to take the carriage home to Downing."

"Sometime in the next week?"

Philip nodded, obviously as nonplussed at this notion as she was. The thought of Shubert arriving anytime of the day . . . *Why, Gray and Philip could not remain as her guardians for all that time. They were needed back at the Double T.* She already chafed at their being away from the plantation today. The Double T was run as lean as could be; there was always far too much work to do and far too few available to accomplish it.

Gray arrived back with the couple interested in the mules. "They like what they saw. They're also interested in the pretty mare with the white socks." He made quick introductions, and Verity took an instant liking to them.

"If you will return to the stables with me," she said, "we can talk about the mare. I am a bit protective of my animals," she added over her shoulder. "I hope you can understand."

"I understand," Mrs. Pickering said. "I raised a mare from a filly as a child. She was more a sister to me than my flesh-and-blood sister was ever kin."

Mr. Pickering gave her a quizzical look, while she and Verity shared a conspiratorial smile. It was then that Verity had a hunch she would sell them the horse. Still, she followed the routine she'd practiced with the soldiers—having

Terence bring the mare to the small corral and then watching the couple with her for fifteen minutes to be certain. After observing their tender and gentle actions, Verity knew the Pickerings would be fine master and mistress—for both the mare and the mules. Smiling, she led them back to the store.

And when she got there, she found it filled with at least twenty others.

Chapter Nineteen

On land, Ian followed the young lieutenant and his men who had been sent out by rowboat to examine their empty hold. He leaned against a pillar and waited for them to complete their search of his ship from stem to stern, arms folded, jaw clenched. *What right had they? To impede the flow of trade?*

"Do your superiors believe this will win you allies among the colonists? Cutting off their lifeblood?"

" 'Tis not my superiors, but theirs who have created this trouble," sniffed the lieutenant, bending to scratch out a signature on his ledger and handing it back to Ian.

"The fools shall only infuriate them further. Strengthen their resolve," Ian bit out.

"Careful, Captain. You must not speak poorly of England or I shall throw you in the town jail for the night to think better of your rebellious ways."

Ian clamped his mouth shut.

"Where shall you go next?"

"Perhaps to France," he replied through clenched teeth.

The lieutenant stilled and studied him, in an instant looking older and more resolved. "If you return to these shores with French stamps, prepare to forfeit your cargo and your ship."

"Oh, I shall not be returning to the Carolinas," Ian growled, turning away from the young man and climbing the steps before he had been properly excused. "I will find some other place to ply my trade. Where there are fewer lobsterbacks about."

"Captain! You forget yourself!" cried the lieutenant, scurrying up the steep stairs behind him.

Ian drew himself up and faced the man squarely. "I spoke not of England, only for the desire to see fewer of her men on these shores. But forgive me. I am speaking out of turn. Be on your way, Lieutenant, and I shall be on mine."

The lieutenant's brow furrowed. Clearly, he knew Ian intended to try and obtain goods to export, despite the law, but then what could he do about it? He inspected Ian's empty holds himself. "See that you set sail and do as you've said, Captain. Do not return to this harbor whilst I remain posted here."

Ian gave him a small nod and watched as the men climbed out of his ship and into their long rowboat. But even when the *Inverness* was under full sail, he paced the decks like a caged tiger. If they were unable to make the rendezvous, if they couldn't obtain the horses, his hold would be utterly empty. The New Yorkers had purchased every barrel of rum and sugar he'd brought in, but he owed a great portion of those profits to the four plantation owners who had hired him, including Gray and Keturah Covington. To return to the islands empty-handed, to not have the funds either to aid the rebels or chase down the man who had killed his brother . . .

He sighed and leaned heavily against the starboard railing, watching as the green, hilly banks and wide sandy beaches went by. Had he erred terribly? Was it truly his place to aid the rebels, or should he have swallowed his pride and hoisted the Union Jack? What would Verity think if he arrived back in Nevis with an empty hold? And yet thinking again of the imperious ways of the redcoats in both New York and Charlotte, their shortsighted belief that strangling her subjects would force them into subservience . . . *Nay, that was not the sort of monarch to whom he wished to bow.*

Independence. Freedom. Justice. The triple-threaded cord that bound every rebel to the next had seemed to wind its way around his heart too with this voyage.

McKay came to stand beside him, leaning on the rail as well. "Captain?"

Ian sighed. "If they manage to curtail the rebels' ability to export as they have mine," he said under his breath, "how shall they fund this war, brother? And if I arrive in the Indies without even a single horse in our hold, how shall I continue to fund our voyages and carry missives for our friends?"

"Judging from the missive we delivered, the rebels already have aid. Via the French, I'd wager. And we shall not have a single horse," said McKay, clapping him on the shoulder. "We shall have eighteen."

Ian smiled and took another breath. Michael's belief in their plan bolstered him. "Best not to spend time trying to figure out how to face the morrow's storm, eh?" he asked.

"Not when there are tricky seas at your bow this very night," McKay returned.

By nightfall, Verity had sold all the carriages and half of everything in her store. Trisa brought tea to her small sitting area, where Gray, Philip, and she had slumped into chairs after closing the store below.

"I shall gladly take a day of planting cane to a day in your store," Gray groaned, putting a hand to his head. "The constant negotiation! The demands, left and right! The henpecking among women! This is truly what you wanted, Ver?"

Verity giggled. She was as weary as they, but she was also exhilarated. All her carriages, sold? Half her store, packed up and away? Serious interest in every horse and mule she had left?

She'd been largely paid in sugar and rum, but when Ian returned . . . When he returned, he'd find a way to export those payments and make a handsome profit. She grinned, thinking of sharing with Ian, telling him about her success. "Yes. This is *exactly* what I wanted."

He lifted a brow and shook his head as if she were mad. Philip appeared to agree. "Clearly, God formed you with a different head than my own, or it would ache as mine does now."

Verity sniffed the air. "It smells as if Trisa has supper on. Do you two care to eat before you return to the Double T?"

"No, thank you," Gray said, rising. " 'Tis best to return to my wife and the plantation. You will remain inside? Locked up and safe, even if Shubert comes to your door?"

"I shall ignore every wolf who ventures to my door," she promised.

"Tomorrow, Philip and Selah will return to aid you. I am needed at the Double T."

"Of course," she said. She battled the thought of saying it was unnecessary, but seeing Shubert today, the threat of his return . . . She turned to Philip. "Thank you for today. For helping me as you did in the store, but most of all for standing beside me in dealing with Angus Shubert."

"But of course, miss," he said with a kindly smile and slight bow. "I shall return at sunup."

"I dislike this—the need for your aid. Clearly you are as needed as Gray at the Double T."

He held her gaze. " 'Tis never a sacrifice to come to your aid, Miss Verity, but rather an honor."

"You are a good man, Philip. You both are," she said, walking with them to the door.

"Lock this door behind us," Gray directed sternly.

"Just as soon as your big booted foot is out of the way, it shall be done," she said with a jaunty grin.

"Terence is in the storeroom?"

"Indeed, he is. And I shall give him a loaded weapon," she said quietly. "But do not tell Angus Shubert I am doing so."

The men smiled at her and stepped outside, but she noted that they waited close by until she had done what she promised and bolted the door. She laughed—half amused, half irritated—and waved them off.

When they'd turned toward their horses, she dropped the curtain and moved to the back storeroom, where Trisa was handing plates of food to Terence and Abe. Both man and boy had cots there, as well as a washbasin and pitcher and trunks to hold their belongings. " 'Twas a good day, friends. Thank you for all you did to make the day a success."

All three gazed back at her and then toward the

corner, where her payments of sugar, rum, and eggs had been stacked and stored.

"Guess the dam broke, eh, Miss Verity?" Terence said.

"Yes it did," she said. "The only shadow on our day was Angus Shubert, who promised to return soon for the carriage he purchased."

Terence and Trisa shared a look. News on this island traveled fast, though never as fast as among the slaves or freed folk. They didn't want to be anywhere near Shubert.

"I want you to have your pistol ready, Terence. Loaded, please. And I know it's cooler in the stable hammocks, but I would like you and Abe to sleep on the cots here in back tonight."

His middle-aged, wrinkled eyes narrowed over her concern, but he nodded. "Yes, Miss Ver."

She'd asked him to sleep inside once or twice before, but never with a loaded pistol.

"Trisa and Abe, keep your daggers under your pillows. I shall do the same."

"Yes'm," said Trisa.

Abe nodded.

"Thank you. Do your best to get fast to sleep. Perhaps tomorrow shall be as busy as today, and I shall have need of your aid from sunup to sundown again."

"We shall be ready, Miss Verity," Abe promised, and the earnestness in his high, childlike voice made her smile.

"Good night."

"Good night," Abe and Terence said. Trisa followed her out and up the stairs to see to her and Verity's supper. Most nights the girl ate with her too.

Many plantation owners on the island objected strongly to giving their slaves or servants weapons. But there were plenty other owners who routinely trusted their slaves by giving them weapons to help protect them from either outside invaders or those among their ranks with dark thoughts of rebellion. Verity trusted these three with her life. And with the thought of Angus Shubert coming to her door, demanding entrance, she wanted her people to be armed.

She had just sunk into the small parlor's lone wing-back chair, the one she favored by the window, when she turned to glance outside, hoping to see a last hint of sunset reflected in the clouds high above. She closed her eyes, relishing the sweet breeze that flowed in, easing the stifling upstairs room with the promise of the night's cooler temperatures, and then she slid to the floor before the window, arms folded on the sill, eyes still closed.

She heard Trisa enter the room and set her tray on the nearby table. "Miss Verity?"

"Yes, Trisa," she muttered. "I shall be there in a moment."

"Miss Verity," the girl demanded in a hush.

Frustrated, Verity opened her eyes and glanced up at her. "What *is* it?"

But the girl's wide eyes were trained on something outside. She took a step backward, clearly frightened.

Verity whirled back to the window, scanning every line of the buildings across the street, the trees beyond. And it was only then that the outline of Angus Shubert moved away from the building against which he'd been leaning, idly watching her.

Aghast, she slammed the window shut, whipped the curtains closed, and scurried away from it. When she came to rest at the far wall, Trisa sank to her knees beside her, arms wrapped around her shoulders, trembling.

They sat there for several minutes, hearts racing, waiting for him to begin pounding on the shop's front door. But no such pounding occurred.

"Shall I go get Terence, Miss Ver?" Trisa whispered.

Verity shook her head. "No. Shubert is not coming to our door tonight. He *wants* a reason to return," she said, figuring it out as the words formed in her mind. "He wants me to know he has a reason to return. He *likes* to spread fear."

Verity scrambled to her feet and paced back and forth, chastising herself for her cowardice, for so clearly showing him exactly what he wanted, slamming the window and curtains closed like that. But she was so weary from the day, so dreadfully weary.

She went back to the chair and sat down, resisting the urge to peek out the window again, knowing that if he was still out there, he'd like nothing better. Turning to the table, she forced her spoon into the bowl of fish stew, shoving one bite into her mouth after another, knowing she would need sustenance if she were to fight well. And with each bite she swallowed, she resolved to outsmart Angus Shubert, to find a way to bring him down. Had she not done so once? Could she not do the same again?

But the first time he had been but an overseer.

Now he was a councilman.

A councilman by marriage, an inheritance, she reminded herself. It was a temporary position, only until next February when it would be decided if he could remain a member of the council. February, she mused. Nine months away. How much havoc could the foul man wreak in nine months' time?

Far too much, she thought bleakly. *Far too much.*

CHAPTER TWENTY

They had twelve of the eighteen horses loaded onto the *Inverness* when they spotted torches onshore and heard the shouts of men over the waves. They were in uniform lines. *Soldiers.*

"Make all haste, men!" Ian cried downward. Below him, the ferryman and three others had managed to bring the ferry loaded with horses to his ship. Alarmed by his tone, they followed his gaze, surmised what was happening, and began whipping the reluctant horses, rushing two more of them up the narrow gangplank.

Ian watched in horror as a stallion still on the ferry whinnied in terror and rose up on hind legs, his hooves slashing a mare's back in front of him. Another stumbled and fell into the water, disappearing for a heart-stopping moment before rising with a great splutter, sloshing about. Ian cried out in exasperation. *One down,* he thought.

But as he looked to shore again, his eyes widened. There were two longboats with many torches aloft, cresting the waves closest to shore. British soldiers.

"All hands! Haul sail!" he bellowed. They had

to go now. With however many horses they had loaded.

"All hands! Haul sail!" Michael echoed from his side, seeing what Ian had seen. If those soldiers reached them and arrested them for smuggling, they'd all be hanging from the old oaks like Spanish moss come sunup, necks akimbo. "All hands! Haul sail!"

It was night, the wind sparse. But if they were to catch the breeze, with all sails, they'd quickly outrun the longboats. The question was, how many more horses could they coax aboard in the seconds that remained? He ran to the railing again, watching with bated breath.

More whips cracked, one after the other. He recognized the breeder's voice. Two others. And as the sails unfurled, the ferries drifting away from them in the diminishing light of the ship's starboard lanterns, he counted three horses remaining, shifting on the abandoned ferry platforms, as if they couldn't decide if they were relieved to be left behind or frustrated. The one that had fallen into the sea was already making her way toward shore, her strong, wide head momentarily visible in the light of the moon.

Fourteen aboard. We missed four, he thought forlornly.

But then, *Fourteen! We have fourteen! Two more than when I brought horses last to the Indies with Verity!*

Belatedly, he thought of the breeder and the ferrymen and peered over the side to see them climbing up the ship's nets, leaving their ferries behind. He laughed and shook one man's hand after another.

"Hope you do not mind a few stowaways, Captain. Couldn't stay behind," said the breeder, climbing over, chest heaving from the effort.

"Nor could we," said a ferryman.

The other heaved himself over the rail and then glanced back with rounded eyes, watching his life as he had known it literally disappear beyond them.

"I do not mind stowaways," he said, grinning, "so long as you are ready to join the crew. And if you dinnae mind a trip to the tropics."

"I always wanted to see the islands," said the first ferryman.

"Will those soldiers inquire at your home about where you might be?"

"Perhaps," said the breeder. "But I instructed the wife to tell them I was away in search of more stock if I didn't return home this night."

"And I instructed mine to say I was down in South Carolina," said the first ferryman. The second was the only one who appeared alarmed at that thought, clearly new at the smuggling business.

"Want me to find a spot to drop you farther

275

south, man? You can make your way home by land."

He eagerly agreed.

Ian glanced up at their billowing sails, then back at the longboats growing small in the distance. The soldiers had not been near enough to identify the *Inverness*. They had fourteen horses. They were escaping with their lives. Not all was lost. And there was no naval ship in the vicinity, preparing to give chase.

Nay, much had been gained, much granted.

And moreover, he thought, steering southward, *at long last I am heading back to Verity.*

By the end of the tenth day after the Brownings' soiree, Verity's shop had been virtually stripped, leaving only the stores of goods in which she'd been paid, three buckets of nails—which she was certain she would sell in the coming weeks— and a set of teacups and pot to which no one had yet taken a shine, for some reason. The rest of the shop—every bridle, rein, saddle, hat, riding costume, and more—had been sold. Every mare, stallion, and gelding had been claimed as well. Only one mule remained in Verity's stables, the new owners yet building a corral.

She picked up one of the lonely, ignored porcelain cups and looked it over. "Someone had to be the odd man out. Sorry, little tea set," she mused. She turned to a slate and picked up a piece of chalk, considering what to write. Then she carefully printed:

SOLD OUT. AWAITING NEXT SHIPMENT. CLOSED UNTIL ARRIVAL OF THE *INVERNESS*.

Verity stood back and read it over. Satisfied, she carried the slate to the front window and carefully propped it there. The glass was wavy, but she was certain most would be able to make out the words.

She took up a second slate and wrote the words:

THIS CARRIAGE BELONGS TO ANGUS SHUBERT. HE IS FREE TO RETRIEVE IT WHEN HE WISHES. —MISS V. BANNING

She smiled as she looked the message over. How irritated he would be to find her gone. In the days since he'd purchased the fine carriage, he'd done naught but come to spy on her each eve, and she surmised he used his ownership as rationale to be near her any moment he wished, taunting her, keeping her on edge. She was relatively certain he'd not seen her in the window after the first night. In the subsequent nights, she'd taken to looking out at him from the hallway window or the corner of the shop's wide front window under cover of darkness. Tonight, she boldly opened the door, half hoping he was watching as she strode toward the lone carriage in front of her shop, perched the sign on its bench, and then languidly returned to her shop as if she had not a care in the world.

Each night, watching Shubert watch her, she'd begun to feel stronger, less afraid. The man coveted power and was used to using fear to gain it. She was determined to find any way possible to show him she did not fear him. He was a brute, a selfish and sick man. It made her feel horrible, thinking of poor Eleanor Everly, his invalid wife. What was her life like now? Was she in a continuous fog of laudanum? Or did she awake periodically to the nightmare who was her husband? Did he manhandle her as he had Keturah and Selah?

A shiver ran down Verity's back, and she said a quick prayer of protection for his new wife. "Trisa?" she called. "Ready?"

"Yes, Miss Verity," said the girl, hastening down the stairs, bags in hand. The girl was clearly excited—as was Abe, skipping in from the storeroom—to be returning to the Double T for a time.

Word had come. Keturah was even now laboring to bring her child into the world, and every passing minute made Verity mad with worry.

"Where is Terence?" Verity groused in irritation, pacing. He'd been gone for half an hour. He'd been sent to bring the horses and carriage around, nothing more. What was holding him?

Abe frowned. "I do not know, Miss Verity. I shall go and see."

The boy was in motion when Verity reached out and grabbed his wrist, her thoughts catching up with her. She glanced to the window. It was dark outside now, the last vestiges of dusk leaving the horizon a dark purple.

"Miss?" Abe asked, frowning and looking to where she held him fast. Biri, on his shoulder, chattered at her, as if objecting to her delay too.

"A moment, Abe," she said quietly and moved to the window. Slowly, she edged the curtain aside. She saw Angus Shubert in none of the deepening shadows. Still, the hairs on the back of her neck stood on end. Something was terribly wrong. She could feel it. Terence never tarried; he should have had the team hitched and brought around a quarter hour past. What could be keeping him?

Brutus is probably acting up, she told herself. *I have not given that bird nearly enough hunting time lately.*

She turned to Trisa and Abe. "Lock the door behind me. If I do not return in five minutes, run to town and fetch the sheriff."

Abe nodded, and Trisa frowned. "Miss? Let us come with you," she said.

"No," Verity said. "You are to keep the boy safe. Promise?"

"I promise," said the girl, her arm around Abe's shoulder.

"Arm yourselves, both of you," she said, even as she brought her dirk to hand. Terence had carried the pistol to the stables. No shot had been fired . . . Was all this simply her imagination run wild?

Please, Lord, she prayed as she unlocked the back door. *Let this be my imagination. Only my imagination.*

She continued to chant those prayers as she climbed the steep, well-worn path to the stables. In front of it was her carriage with the matched pair of geldings in their yoke and yet hobbled, ready to go. The lone mule brayed a welcome, and Fiona pranced around the perimeter of the corral. It was the fact that both remained in the corral—rather than standing, tied behind the carriage as they ought—that made Verity pause.

She neared the stable door. "Terence?"

Brutus, hearing her, squawked in excitement. But Terence said nothing.

"Terence! Where are you?" Verity called, alarm building in her chest. She pulled the door open wide.

Someone grabbed her from behind, covering her mouth with a meaty hand before she could scream. She knew his smell—the dank, weeks-old odor of his sweat. Could feel the wide breadth of a chest that could only be Angus Shubert's.

But she could not see him. He bodily lifted and carried her deeper into the stables.

And while every bit of her mind was going through Ian's lessons, sorting through to see what she should do first, every single one fled as her eyes settled on a horrifying silhouette.

Terence, hanging from a rafter in the stables, his neck at an unnatural angle. His feet and hands hung limply. Slowly, strung on the rope, his body circulated, a gruesome sight.

And with that slow circle, her knees seemed to fail her.

Shubert laughed lowly, catching her in her swoon. "Easy, easy," he said, pulling her limp body closer.

She was horrified, but seemed unable to do anything but stare at Terence. Her friend, her dear loyal servant. *Dead?* She fought for breath. Fought sudden nausea. Fought to think clearly.

"You see that?" Shubert whispered in her ear, his breath hot and humid. He gestured toward the body.

Terence's body . . .

"That there is evidence of what is to come, little miss. You think you have power here? You and your sisters think you can thumb your nose at how things ought to be done? Well, you're wrong, little Miss. So wrong. Tell me you're wrong. That you see the error of your ways. Agree to do as I direct, and I may let you live."

Verity's eyes narrowed. For the first time, her heart seemed to beat again in her chest.

She blinked. Once. Twice.

Remembered the dagger in her hand.

"Error?" she mumbled, trying to buy time. To think about all that Ian had taught her.

"Yes, that, speak to me of that," he whispered, inhaling deeply at her neck. As if in an attempt at seduction. She swallowed rising bile. "Tell me you see at last how things ought to be. That men rule this island, and women and slaves are to be subservient. Tell me that, and I shall let you go. If you wish . . ."

He bent and kissed her neck with wet lips. It took all she had in her to remain still, getting a firmer grasp of the dirk in her sweating hand, staring at Terence's limp form, willing herself to be strong.

"You are a man of power," she said, shifting her feet to gain better balance.

"Yes!" he said in delight. He pushed his nose into her hair, inhaling deeply again. "Say that again."

"You are a man of power," she gritted out. "But you *ought not to be.*"

It was only as he stilled that she leaned forward and with a cry rammed her head back into his nose.

She heard—and felt—the sickening crack. He cried out and stumbled backward, away from her, and she away from him. But all she saw was his hand striking the lamp and sending it flying, oil spilling, and in its wake, flame.

Flames catching straw, railing, wall paneling.

Then, in a panic, she remembered Terence.

Now free of her captor's grasp, she rushed toward her faithful groom, madly trying to lift him up by circling her arms around his thighs. "Terence!" she screamed. "Terence!"

She looked up into his lifeless eyes, but some part of her thought if she could only lift him long enough, ease the tension on his neck, he might come back. Sputter, cough, gasp for breath.

"Terence!" she cried, tears running down her cheeks as she strained under his weight. "Terence!"

Dimly, she heard Shubert curse her, then the door of the stable slam shut, the sliding sound of something heavy. But her eyes were on her friend. Belatedly, she remembered the blade in her palm. If she could not lift him, could she cut him down? Coax breath back into his body once he was lying prostrate?

CHAPTER TWENTY-ONE

They'd dropped anchor just before sundown, yet it took a good hour for Nevis's harbormaster to reach them for his inspection and allow them entrance.

Ian was so anxious he insisted on taking an oar in the longboat, often out-stroking the sailor at his right.

"Easy, Cap'n," McKay said. He grinned in the deep shadows of the lamp held aloft at the front. "Miss Banning shall be there, be it dusk or dawn," he added under his breath.

"So you say," Ian grunted, bending, pulling, feeling every muscle tense in his stomach and back.

"How far could she roam?" McKay teased. " 'Tis an island."

"She's a Banning. Those women came from England to Nevis without benefit of brother or father or husband. Only the three of them. What in that makes you say that one would not possibly leave this island, if so moved?"

McKay remained silent a moment. "Because her sisters remained behind?"

Ian smiled at that. "Aye. That might be the *only* reason."

"The only one?"

"The only one. Truly, these women are uncommon."

"And one more uncommon than the others?"

"To my mind, yes."

"Thus the heavy sail all the way from the Carolinas to Nevis's shore? The failure to stop at Hispaniola to see if we might sell some of the horses?"

"Verity shall purchase every horse we brought," Ian groused, irritated that his mate questioned his wisdom. "And if not, we shall sell the remainder on St. Kitts or Statia."

That satisfied his mate. More than anything else, he knew now that Michael wanted nothing more than to aid the rebel cause. And to do so, they needed two things: Verity's help, and a visit to Statia.

Not that Michael's needs were foremost in his mind. Nay, God help him, he felt as if he could barely stay within his skin, so urgent was his need to see Verity. Was she still awake at this hour? Might she think him rude, coming to call, unannounced, after dark? Perhaps he ought to wait until morning . . .

But it seemed a stark impossibility. He knew he would likely not sleep a moment, awaiting the sun. Best to err on the side of impropriety than go mad before dawn, he mused. Something told him that Verity would forgive him. And something else told him he had to get there as quickly as he could . . . his heart? Or was it the Almighty?

So as soon as the longboat ground into Nevis's gravelly sand, he leapt out, McKay fast on his heels. Half of him wanted his mate with him—always a wise course in a new port—half wished to be alone. Thus the man's trailing gait both gratified and irritated him.

The town was not large. In minutes he reached the southern edge and Verity's shop, holding the lamp high. He smiled, noting the lone remaining carriage—she'd clearly succeeded in selling the others—but then frowned when he read the slate on the seat, which said the carriage had been claimed by Angus Shubert.

"Cap'n?" Michael said.

He turned from the carriage to his mate.

The tall man gestured with his chin to beyond the store. "Smell that?"

Ian inhaled.

Fire.

He took off around the store, even as the back door opened, Abe and Trisa spilling out, gaping at him and McKay as they dashed past. "Where is Verity?" he cried, knowing even as he heard Brutus shriek.

"Up there! Terence too!" Abe cried, running behind.

They reached the stables, saw the hitched geldings madly attempting to break their hobbles, clearly smelling the fire too. Flames were already breaking through the left side of the stable roof.

"Verity!" Ian screamed. "Verity!" He and Michael turned toward the stable door. It was blocked by a heavy stone. They shared a quick look—each wondering why someone would have done such a thing—before Michael shoved it aside.

Fishing a kerchief from his pocket, Ian covered his mouth and entered the smoky stables, fire primarily on the left but spreading fast. Flames licked across a rafter above him, but the dense smoke made it impossible to see further.

"Verity!" he called. *"Verity!"*

There was no answer other than the falcon's shrieking, piercing cry doubling in time. His cage hung to the right. "Go!" he said to Abe, pointing the boy toward the bird. "Get Brutus out!"

"Verity!" His eyes teared up as smoke engulfed him.

McKay was right behind him, hand on his shoulder.

"Verity!" he cried again, but just then his toe hit something soft but solid. A breeze washed through the open door and cleared some of the smoke, although it also fanned the flames. Horrified, Ian bent over Verity's limp form, dirk in hand, her head resting on the chest of Terence's dead body.

Quickly, he searched for a pulse at her neck,

silently chanting, *Please, Lord, please, Lord, please, Lord . . .*

He felt a faint lift and drop in her veins and released a sigh of relief. Then he moved to Terence, but with one touch he knew the man had been dead for some time. He ran his hand along the man's oddly angled neck, discovering the broken vertebrae. *Hanged?*

Fury raged through him as he gathered Verity in his arms, piecing together a possible cause for the horrific scene before him. Someone had hung the poor man and locked Verity inside the burning stables. She had tried to save him, cut him down, then succumbed to the smoke.

He carried her out while Michael brought Terence's body. Outside, he set her down, gasped and coughed, taking in deep drafts of air. But his sole focus was on Verity, who was ghastly pale in the flickering light of the burning stables.

"Breathe, lass," he begged, leaning to touch his forehead to hers. "Breathe, please breathe."

For interminable moments she seemed to remain utterly still, as if hovering between this life and the next, ascertaining which might be best. Abe approached, the monkey on his shoulder, chattering, the bird in his cage, still shrieking his outrage. Fiona and the mule, relatively safe in the corral outside the burning stables, brayed and whinnied as they circled, madly trying to find an escape. The geldings, five feet away, stomped and tugged at their hobbles.

"Hear that, love?" Ian said urgently, holding one of her hands in both of his. "We are all here. Abe, Trisa, me. Your animals. Come back to us. Breathe, love. Breathe . . ."

As if finally hearing him, she coughed. Coughed so mightily she might have been sick. Gently, he eased her to her side, hating the sound of her struggle and yet celebrating it too. She was alive! Alive! Tears, unbidden, crested. *Thank you, Lord,* he prayed silently. *Thank you, thank you, thank you . . .*

Trisa rocked back and forth, Abe in her arms, kneeling beside Terence's body, the two of them silently weeping. He reached out and rested a consoling hand on her arm a moment, then atop Abe's head. "I am sorry for your loss. We shall find out who has done this and see them punished."

He shifted his attention back to Verity. She was slowly moving, grimacing, coughing as she struggled to open her eyes, tears creating streams through the soot that coated her face.

What might have happened had not he and Michael arrived in the harbor tonight? Decided not to come, given the late hour? A shiver ran down his spine. And after it a cold, hard shudder of resolve. That stone had not rolled in front of the door by itself. Who had hung Terence? Set the stables afire? Left her there to die?

Neighbors began arriving in housecoats, calling out in alarm for buckets of water, for everyone to come to their aid in fighting the fire. But Ian stayed close to Verity. She was waking, eyes fluttering open, green-gold eyes—glorious eyes—finding his. Wondering. Confused. Then glad, so impossibly glad to see him that he gathered her in his arms, regardless of who was there to see it. "Oh, Verity. *Verity,* what a fright you have given me."

"Ian," she said woozily, lifting a hand to his cheek. "You've returned?" Then her eyes widened. "Terence!" she cried, her voice raspy. "Terence!"

"Shh, shh. Oh, Verity. I am sorry. You did what you could for him."

Tears ran down her cheeks, streaking through the soot coating her skin. "Dead," she whispered. Then she closed her eyes and shook her head in such exquisite sorrow that it threatened to break him.

"Would you be so kind, Ian," she began, every word an effort.

"So kind?" he repeated when her words trailed off.

"So kind," she mumbled drowsily, "as to see us safely to the Double T?"

"Of course," he promised as the first bucket of water was belatedly thrown on the burning stables, now fully engulfed in flames.

He gathered Verity in his arms again and lifted her into the carriage, where Trisa awaited, glancing back to the stables. "Tie up the mare and mule," he said to Abe, "and set the bird in back of the carriage. Let us get Miss Verity to the Double T at once."

"Yes, sir," said the boy, wiping tears from his face. McKay climbed onto the driver's seat and grabbed the reins.

Ian turned to the neighbors. "The stable will burn to the ground but isn't likely to spread. Even so, keep watch on those rising embers. I need to get Miss Banning to her sisters. Somebody go after the sheriff. This was no accident. Miss Banning's man was murdered, and the one responsible meant for her to die in there too."

The twenty or more who had gathered parted to let them pass, silently aghast. And as they passed, Ian stared at the sign on the lone carriage before Banning's Bridlery. Someone had clearly murdered Terence and left Verity to die in the stables.

And yet there was this carriage with Shubert's name on it.

Was it a testimony of his innocence, or a convenient exhibit for his defense?

CHAPTER TWENTY-TWO

Ian kept his arm around Verity's shoulders all the way to the Double T. She responded to his first few questions, but when he decided to let her rest, she drifted off, cradled against his chest. Michael drove, keeping his eyes to the dark road and the billowing jungle on either side, as if expecting further attack. Sitting beside him, Trisa kept her arm around Abe, the boy's shoulders shaking as he wept for Terence. Brutus's cage was strapped to the carriage behind them, covered with a cloth, and the bird had finally fallen silent, as if aware he kept grim company with Terence's motionless body. Biri, the boy's monkey, perched on the back of the front bench.

But even with all this around him, Ian had a hard time concentrating on anything but Verity's long, thin, soot-smudged fingers splayed across the white of his shirt just above his left hip. Her head, resting on his chest, just beneath his chin. He knew it was not entirely proper, allowing her to settle in so, in the midst of her unconsciousness. But God help him, it felt good, so good to hold her. To feel her womanly presence, the rise and fall of her steady breathing, the reassuring thump of her pulse. Two coils of her long brown hair had fallen from the knot at the nape of her neck and waved across his chest. He could have settled her in the corner of the carriage, but he could not find the strength to let her go.

He had come so close to losing her. So very close.

Still, when they turned down the drive of the Double T, he was relieved. Here, she would be safe, looked after. He would get her settled with her sisters, summon the major and his men, and ride back to Charlestown to speak to the sheriff. They would find Angus Shubert this very night and hear testimony of his whereabouts, or find others who might have seen something. Because he knew he could not leave Verity alone on this island again—not if there was someone who was determined to kill her.

Michael pulled the carriage to a stop, and a groom came running with a stairstep in hand, hurriedly tucking his shirt into his breeches as Ian carried Verity down from the carriage.

Mitilda emerged on the porch, and when she saw who had arrived, she sent a small girl running inside. She hurried down the grand front steps to gather up Abe in her arms. "What is it?" she asked, moving toward Verity and Ian. "What has happened?"

"Oh, Mama," Abe cried. "They killed Terence!"

"Verity!" Selah cried, racing down the stairs. "Captain McKintrick! What has happened?"

He strode past her and up the steps. "She is all right, Miss Banning," he said. Verity moved and groaned in his arms as if struggling to awaken. "Or will be. She has suffered a terrible fright and inhaled a great deal of smoke."

Selah turned with him and raced up the rest of the steps, holding her skirts in one hand. "Follow me. We shall take her to my room."

Major Woodget met them at the door of the parlor, his face a thunderous mix of rage and fear when he saw Verity's limp form. Philip and the two other soldiers rose from the parlor settee. But when a woman let out a long, tortured cry, every one of them stilled.

What was going on here? Why did every man in the room wince at the sound but not leap into action?

Ian glimpsed Gray at the top of the stairs, shirt untucked, hand on the back of his neck, pacing outside the far room's door.

Then it came to him. *Keturah,* he surmised. Laboring.

He glanced at Selah. "Forgive me. I had no other thought than to bring her here this night. To you."

"Of course. This is where she belongs," Selah reassured him. "Come. The midwife is with Ket. I shall see to our Verity." She led him up the stairs, where Gray had seen them and waited with renewed consternation lining his face.

"What is this? Verity?"

"She suffered an attack," Ian muttered to him as they both followed Selah. The last thing Keturah needed now was to overhear things that might tax her. "Her man, Terence, was killed. The stables set afire. The smoke overcame her."

Selah moved aside a mosquito net above the wide bed, allowing Ian to settle Verity atop it. "I fear she shall get your bedding rather dirty," he said sorrowfully.

"Never mind that," Selah said, bringing Verity's legs up onto the bed.

Mitilda arrived with a fresh pitcher of water, a basin, and a pile of clean rags. Trisa followed close behind. Selah turned to the men and herded them out. "We shall see to my sister, gentlemen."

Wanting to stay by Verity's side and yet knowing she needed the ministrations of these women most, Ian reluctantly followed Gray out. Selah closed the door firmly behind him.

Down the hall, Keturah let out another long, keening cry, and Gray closed his eyes and winced, as if feeling her pain. Ian clamped a hand on his shoulder. "Ach, it shall soon be over, man. And you shall have a braw son or bonny daughter."

Gray gave him a wan smile, but then his brow

wrinkled. "Will you be heading back to town to look after this foul business?"

"Straightaway." He glanced over the rail to the group of soldiers, pulling on their red coats, as well as Philip and McKay. "They shall all be glad for the task."

Gray laughed under his breath and nodded. "If there is one place a man feels most useless, 'tis in the home of a laboring woman."

"We shall chase down Verity's attacker. You have my word on it," Ian said over his shoulder, rushing down the stairs now.

"And I shall aid you," Captain Howard said, lifting his chin. He'd been speaking with Abe, getting the boy's story. "After all, this is our island."

His island, not mine, Ian surmised. Establishing territory. Clearly, the vision of Ian arriving with Verity in his arms bothered the man for more reasons than one. And with a hold full of smuggled horses, the last thing Ian needed was the captain—or his superiors—asking to see his papers.

"I so appreciate it, Captain," Ian said with a deferential bow. "Lead the way."

Two grooms had brought fresh horses to the house, and when the soldiers mounted, Ian noticed that all four were on horses he had helped Verity import. Who had purchased all the others? And where would they put the fourteen he'd brought on the *Inverness*, what with Verity's stables burned to the ground? Construction on a replacement would have to begin immediately, and the horses kept in corrals until it was done. He could see to that.

"Let us ride directly to the sheriff," Major Woodget said.

"I believe Miss Banning's neighbors shall have summoned him," Ian said. "It was asked of them as we parted."

"Good." The captain's mare danced nervously beneath him. "Then let us go directly back to the scene of the crime, where you shall tell us everything you know."

"As you say," Ian said.

The soldiers led the way, and with a brief shared look with Michael, they followed, Philip behind them. In half an hour, they were back in town and discovered many people hovering about, most behind Verity's store. The stables were nothing but smoldering ruins now, people still arriving with buckets of water to douse the embers.

How close had they come to discovering two bodies among the ashes? Hot tears laced his lashes, surprising him, shaming him. *Verity.*

Ian loved her. Honestly loved her with everything in him. How could she have so thoroughly captured his heart in the short amount of time they had shared together?

Michael set a hand on his shoulder. "You all right, Cap'n?"

"Fine, fine," Ian said with a cough.

"The boy said that he had not seen anyone in the stables," Captain Howard was saying to the sheriff, the other men gathered round. "But that Angus Shubert had been about every day. Watching the store, the servants said, but never entering."

"Why?" Ian asked.

"The man is a brute," Philip put in. "And Miss Verity has shamed him more than once. He revels in taunting her."

"I saw it for myself, on my last sojourn to Nevis," Ian said. "He approached Miss Banning. Threatened her."

"Threatened her? How?" asked the sheriff.

"Well," Ian allowed. "Not overtly. But his intent was clear."

"Angus Shubert has managed to secure a level of power since you have been away," Major Woodget said. "Married the Widow Everly, become master of Downing Plantation, as well as found himself a councilman by means of taking Mr. Everly's seat until the next election."

Ian sucked in his breath. He remembered how Shubert had frightened Verity that afternoon in the fields. How she feared he would be the overseer of the neighboring plantation. Which was worse? Being a neighboring overseer or wielding the power that Downing afforded him?

This was worse, he decided.

A brute with feigned power was worrisome.

A brute with true power was a very real threat.

"He purchased one of Miss Verity's carriages," Philip said, "but said he would pick it up in the next week. He did not return for the carriage."

"Instead, he left it here, presumably because it provided him an excuse to be in proximity any day—or evening—he wished," Captain Howard said. "The boy said Miss Banning had spotted Mr. Shubert outside her window nearly every night. She tried to hide it, not wanting to frighten the boy and the maid, but they knew regardless. He was not watching the store. He was watching her."

"So you say," said the sheriff, arms folded, chin in one hand. "There might be any number of reasons for the councilman to be about Charlestown's streets."

"Come now, Sheriff," Philip said. "You know the story as well as I. The man attacked Miss Verity's sister at Nisbet Plantation. And it was Miss Verity who put a stop to it. That has always been a burr under his belt."

"I have spoken with him about that night," the sheriff said, tilting his head to one side. "He said he was not himself. Deep in his cups. Have we not all been there, once or twice?" He laughed and looked around. Half the men laughed with him. Philip, Michael, Captain Howard, and Ian did not.

"Shubert was more himself that night than any other," Philip pledged gravely. "He and his men savagely beat the overseer of the Double T and—"

"Now, now," the sheriff cut in. "The way I heard it, that was a story your slaves spun. There was not one white witness, was there?"

Philip clamped his lips shut, clearly fuming. "So you suppose it was one of the slaves that so beat that overseer?" he asked, incredulous. "A freed man whom—"

"A freed man who invites trouble," the sheriff said, waving his hand in a downward motion. "If you people over at the Double T do not want such mischief, then perhaps you should consider hiring a proper white overseer."

"Matthew Rollins is one of the best overseers on this island, and you know it," Philip said, pointing a finger at the sheriff's chest. " 'Tis due to him and his knowledge that the Double T outproduces so many others. And that has always made the others jealous, including Angus Shubert."

"All right, all right, Philip, settle down," drawled the sheriff. "All this evidence is circumstantial. Councilman Shubert has clearly done some things wrong in his time, but think on it, gentlemen. He has all a Nevisian could want. Land. Stature. Why attack Miss Banning? Why murder her servant? Leave her to die?"

"Because she has thumbed her nose at all he holds dear," Ian said. "He wants people to fall in line, to do as he says—admire him for what he has or what he wields. Bow to his power. The Bannings—and all those at the Double T—never have."

"Did Miss Banning say it was Councilman Shubert who attacked her?" the sheriff asked.

Ian shifted and frowned. "She was barely conscious for the most of the ride to the Double T."

"We are wasting time," Captain Howard said. "We must find Shubert this instant. Ask him where he was this night, and if he has witnesses to verify his story. As much as it might put you in an awkward position, Sheriff, he should be your lead suspect. Or he will provide an alibi that will support your 'honorable councilman' stance, and we will immediately move on to others. Perhaps other men who purchased from Miss Banning's store or had a run-in with Terence?"

Philip shook his head. "No one ever had a run-in with Terence. The man was as affable as any I ever met."

"He was a freed man," Major Woodget said. "Councilman Shubert is not the only one on the island who chafes at that prospect. Many fear that it inspires . . . *unrest* among the others."

Silence settled over the group. It was true that Shubert was not the only one.

"Let us do as you suggested," the sheriff said. "Find our newest councilman and hear his story. My men and I shall ride for Downing, where I expect to find him taking his leisure rather than up to any foul play. You others can search the town for him."

Ian studied him, so much of island politics becoming clearer to him with each statement the sheriff made. He was a lawman, but in truth the planters owned him. And if he was forced to arrest and jail the most powerful planter on the island . . .

The sheriff lifted a finger of warning to each of them. "On the off chance you *do* locate Mr. Shubert, mind me—you may waylay him until our return, but you *must* not harm him. Understand?"

Reluctantly, Ian agreed with the others. But as he and Michael strode away, he muttered, "If we do find the man, keep me from killing him, would you? If 'twas him, if he dared to try to murder my Verity, I shall—"

"Your Verity?" Michael whispered, casting him a wry grin.

His question made Ian pause. Then he nodded. "Aye. Mine. At least I hope the lass will agree to it, in time."

Mine. Saying the word solidified both his love for her and his desire to do right by her.

Including hunting down the man who had left her for dead.

CHAPTER TWENTY-THREE

Major Woodget and his men made their way down one side of the street in Charlestown while Ian, Philip, and Michael did so on the other. There were a total of eighteen taverns in the tiny town—Angus Shubert might be supping in any of them.

They were just leaving the fifth one when Michael whistled and gestured over his shoulder. Ian pulled to a stop, Philip at his side, and saw that there was a side room, a maid now entering it with tankards of ale in either hand. The men made their way around the crowded tables to the swinging doors of the side chamber. With a nod, Michael peeked inside. Of the three of them, he'd be the least recognizable to Shubert.

Casually, he turned back to them as if he had not seen a thing. But under his breath he said, "He is in there. With three other men."

Ian pushed aside the urge to charge in and grab hold of the lout. Verity needed him not to give in to his most base desires for retribution. Instead, she needed him to find a way to remove this man from power forever. That began with the Brits apprehending Shubert, not him. "Fetch

Major Woodget, would you, Philip?" he asked. "Michael and I shall make certain Shubert does not leave this room until you return."

"Straightaway," the man said, immediately on the move.

Ian and Michael stood to either side of the doors, keeping watch on the room. Just then the doors slammed open and Angus Shubert stepped through, the slight lurch to his steps betraying the number of tankards he'd emptied. Ian grabbed hold of his jacket lapel and swung him around hard against the wall. "You are staying right here, Shubert."

"Let me go at once," Shubert snarled. Ian noted crusted blood lining one of his nostrils. "No one dares to manhandle a councilman!"

Ian released him and lifted his hands. "Forgive me, Shubert. But I must insist you remain here. My friends and I have some questions to ask of you."

" 'Tis you," he said, recognizing Ian. *"McKintrick."* His eyes narrowed, and a slow smile spread across his face. He lifted a blood-stained kerchief to dab at his nose, which had resumed bleeding. "You have questions to ask me? About your girl, perhaps?" He leaned toward him. " 'Tis a wonder who will lift her skirts for a *councilman* when her man is away at sea."

Ian gritted his teeth, trying to hold back, but he could not help himself. Again he grabbed hold of the man's lapels and slammed him against the wall. He was pulling back a fist to pound him when Michael grabbed his wrist.

He looked back, enraged. Michael gave him a shrug. "You made me promise, Cap'n. No killing the man, right?"

Ian let out a growl of frustration, turning back to Shubert. "How 'bout I not kill him. Only leave him with something to remember this night? Somebody already started on his nose, it appears."

"Go on," Shubert taunted, utterly at ease. "Give me your best. Then I shall watch you hang come morning." He leaned forward, spittle from his wide lips splattering Ian's face. "Because no one harms a councilman and lives to talk of it."

"Come along, *Councilman* Shubert," Woodget intervened, grabbing hold of Ian's wrist, forcing him to stand down. The major gestured toward the side chamber as Captain Howard neared the table. "Perhaps we might have a word with you in private?"

Ian dropped his other hand and turned away, hands on his hips, shaking his head and fighting the visceral urge to teach the foul man a lesson he wouldn't soon forget. He'd gotten close enough to smell woodsmoke on the man. There was little doubt he had been in Verity's stables. Given the summer heat, no other fires were ablaze on Nevis.

McKay waited with him a moment, as if not trusting him, and then they followed the others inside. Remembering what Verity needed most, Ian positioned himself on the far side of the room.

Woodget gestured to a chair, but Shubert moved to the corner, unbuttoned his pants and relieved himself in a chamber pot. "Now, what is this all about, Major?" he asked over his shoulder.

"There has been an attack on Miss Verity Banning and her man. Her servant was killed— hanged from the stable rafters—and Miss Banning only barely escaped a subsequent fire with her life."

"Ah. Heard something of it," he said, finishing his business and turning to plop down on the chair catty-corner to the major. "The tavern was abuzz."

"Were you anywhere near Miss Banning's mercantile this evening, Councilman Shubert?"

"Near? No. Passed by, sure. Only one way to get between my plantation and taverns like this, and 'tis past the girl's shop."

Captain Howard lifted his chin. "It appears you purchased one of her carriages. Why have you not laid claim to it?"

Shubert lifted his hands and gave the man a small smile. "I am a busy man, Captain. Much occupies the planter who manages more land than any other on Nevis, and now with my new duties as councilman—"

"I can only imagine," Woodget said dryly. "So you are here in this tavern conducting business?" he asked pointedly.

"Of a sort," Shubert said, his smile widening.

"When do you anticipate laying claim to your carriage?"

"When I find the time." Shubert's smile faded then. "I thought it would be a boon for Miss Banning. A sort of advertisement, the whole island aware that she had sold it to me."

"Boon or curse?" Ian muttered to Michael.

"What did you say?" Shubert growled.

"I said it was good for her purse," Ian said evenly.

Shubert's eyes narrowed.

"Miss Banning's servants said you had taken to watching the shop and their apartments each night," Major Woodget said.

Shubert huffed a laugh. "I become a councilman and suddenly I am the object of every woman's secret wishes." He lifted his hands, palms up, and leaned back in his chair.

When Ian began to step forward, Michael reached out an arm to block him.

"As I said, there is only one way between my plantation and this tavern, which happens to be my favorite."

"Why have you not been seen on horseback,

then?" Ian asked. "Surely you do not walk from your plantation to town each eve."

Shubert gave a small shrug. "I like to have a few ales, a bit of supper, and then go for a walk before I have a few more. Then I ride to Downing. Ask anyone here. 'Tis my routine."

"And you chose a tavern but eight establishments away from Miss Banning's store?" Ian asked.

Major Woodget raised a hand, irritated by his interruptions, but Ian's eyes remained on Shubert.

"Why not?" Shubert asked, smugly crossing his arms. "I purchased it several days ago. 'Tis mine now."

Woodget drummed his fingers on the worn table. "Were you here all evening, Councilman Shubert? Or did you take that walk after a few ales tonight?"

"Tonight?" Shubert said, pursing his lips as if he could not quite remember. "Nay, tonight I stayed in. Got waylaid by a comely wench, as well as two young men who needed to discuss something with me."

"Will those men agree to that account?" Woodget asked.

"Yes. Yes, I believe they will."

"Do they work for you?" Ian asked.

Shubert nodded. "They sharecrop my land." He leaned forward across the table. "But then this is my establishment. Practically everyone here works for me, one way or another."

Convenient, that, Ian thought.

"Summon them, would you, Councilman?" Woodget asked.

Shubert stared hard at the major and then lumbered to his feet, went to the double doors, and looked about. "Andrew! Arthur!" he bellowed. Then spotting them, he waved them inside.

Moments later, a young man of about seventeen and another of about twenty came in, hats in hand. They looked nervously about at the soldiers.

"Gentlemen," Shubert said to them. "Tell these good men that you were with me all evening—"

"Mr. Shubert!" Woodget cried, rising to his feet.

Shubert feigned innocence. "What is it?"

"You may as well have told them exactly what to say!"

"Oh." He pretended regret. "You're quite right. Gentlemen, please tell these good men about our conversation here in the tavern this evening. How we've spent hours together discussing—"

"Outside!" Ian roared, aghast at Major Woodget's bumbling progress. Had the man truly never interrogated another? Like so many other nobles fancying themselves warriors, had he merely purchased his military commission? Or

worse, was he intentionally trying to aid Shubert?

Major Woodget rose from the table. "Yes. Let us speak of it outside. You, Councilman, I ask to remain right here."

"Of course," said Shubert.

Ian followed the major and one of his underlings into the cool island evening, leaving Philip and Michael to keep an eye on Shubert. He couldn't trust himself in the same room with the man a moment longer.

Around the corner, Woodget drew the two young men to a stop, the other soldiers on either side of him. Ian walked around the tavern toward the back, and just around the corner he leaned against the building, arms folded, straining to hear the men's conversation over the cacophony of the island's jungle.

"Now out with it, gents. Was Shubert truly with you in the tavern for the entirety of the evening?"

"For much of it," said the older one.

"Much of it?" Woodget pressed. "So you cannot swear that Shubert was inside this tavern all evening?"

"Please, sir," began the younger one, "you heard him. Please do not make us go against Mr. Shubert."

The older one chimed in, "Our mother is sick, terribly sick. And Mr. Shubert, he promised we could have another month on our land. We need to bring in our cane, sir. If we do not, we cannot afford to pay the doctor."

Woodget paused, then said, "I am deeply sorry for your plight. But I must have the truth. Was Shubert with you, or within your line of vision, all evening?"

"Yes," said the older one hurriedly.

Woodget sighed. "You would swear to that?"

"Yes," said the man again.

"And you, lad? Would you place your hand on the Bible and swear the truth of this tale?"

Ian peeked around the corner. The younger one paused, glanced at his brother, then back to the major. "Yes," he said weakly.

Ian let out a scoffing laugh under his breath and shook his head. He'd interrogated more than a few men over the course of his years aboard ship, and he'd seen many protect another. Woodget would get nothing from these men. They would testify to protect Shubert and in turn protect their mother.

Woodget asked where their plantation was, their names, and then dismissed them. Ian hurriedly returned to the tavern from the opposite direction, following the soldiers inside. Woodget wearily sat down again beside Shubert. "I have one more question, Councilman."

Shubert motioned for him to go on.

"Why is it you reek of woodsmoke?"

The question gave Shubert pause. "I . . . I was

examining the tavern's chimney. It appears we need a sweep."

"And if I were to go to the kitchen and ask the cook about it, without you there, would she tell the same tale?"

A slow smile crept over Shubert's lips. "She was out fetching water at the time. I was alone in the kitchen."

Woodget gave him a hard look. "I see."

Shubert's smile grew, because he did indeed see.

"What of your nose?" Ian asked, leaning on the table. "Who tried to break your nose this night, if all about you are friends, not foes?"

Shubert stared back at him. "You remember my speaking of a 'comely wench' earlier?"

Ian's pulse doubled. Verity. He was speaking of Verity. But he decided to wait Shubert out, even before he felt Michael's hand of warning on his shoulder.

"I was distracted by her form," Shubert went on, drawing a suggestive curve on the table with one meaty finger, "and in a most embarrassing moment I ran directly into that swinging door there." He looked up at Ian and grinned. "But I wager I am not the only man that girl has made look a fool."

Ian closed his eyes and turned away. "Come," he muttered to Michael. "I cannot stomach a moment longer here with this one."

Shubert had the audacity to laugh as they exited the tavern.

His mate followed him out, Philip right behind them. In the alley, Ian began pacing, hands on hips again. There was nothing more to be done this night. Shubert had an alibi, and he'd given them nothing solid they could pass off to the sheriff as evidence.

"What now?" McKay asked.

"Let us ride back to the Double T," Ian said. "I need to know if Verity is all right. That is the only good that can redeem my sour mood. For if I remain here with him . . ."

"Aye, Cap'n," McKay said. "Come along, then."

Verity awakened as swiftly moving clouds turned peach with the rising sun. Groggily, she considered the view, slowly coming to understand that she was at the Double T, not Banning's Bridlery. One memory after another flooded through her mind until she sat up with a start. "Terence!" she screamed, her throat tortuously dry. "Terence!"

She began to weep, remembering. The fire. Cutting down his dead body. Hoping against hope that he still lived . . .

Selah opened the door and rushed in, her hair about her shoulders, her dressing robe open in her haste to get to Verity. She flung herself atop the bed, enfolding her older sister in her arms, cradling her head as she wept. "Oh, Ver! I am so sorry. So dreadfully sorry," she crooned.

"How . . . When . . . ?"

And then he was there, in the doorway, hurriedly glancing down at the floor, avoiding looking at them in their varied states of undress. "Forgive me," he said. "I heard you cry out." He turned away.

"No! Ian! A moment, please," she cried, tears streaming down her face. She looked helplessly to Selah, who rushed to a wardrobe, pulled another dressing robe from it, and wrapped it around Verity's shoulders. Then she pulled the blankets up to her chest, tied her own dressing robe more firmly about her waist, and went to Ian, who hovered just outside the room.

"Come in, Ian," she said softly. "She wishes to see you."

"Forgive me," he said to Verity, entering tentatively. "When I heard ye cry out, lass, I forgot myself. All I could think of was getting to ye."

" 'Tis all right," she said, reaching out a hand to him.

He went to her bedside and sank to his knees, still clutching her hand. "Oh, Verity. How I loathe it, seeing ye in such distress." He kissed her hand, and she could feel the dampness of his own tears upon it.

"But 'tis to you I am indebted, yes?" she asked,

sniffing. " 'Twas you who brought me out of the stables? I remember little, but I do remember that."

"Aye, lass," he said, looking into her eyes. "You gave me a terrible fright."

"And Terence . . ." she said mournfully. Her eyes widened. "What of Trisa? Abe?"

"They are well," Selah said. "Here with us."

Verity leaned back against her pillows, clearly relieved.

"Terence was gone before you discovered him, I expect," Ian said.

She shook her head, covered her mouth, and looked to the window. "Nay. When I got to him, he was still warm . . . Still warm, Ian! If only I had arrived sooner!"

Selah sniffed from her chair beside the bed and dabbed at her eyes.

"If you had arrived sooner, perhaps you would have been killed as well," he said carefully. "Whoever murdered him would not have wanted you as a witness."

Her heart started pounding as another memory came back to her. "It was Shubert," she said.

"You remember him, Verity?" he asked eagerly. "You saw him?"

"Yes!" Then she frowned. "Well, no. I did not actually see him, but 'twas him! I am certain of it. His voice, his hands . . ." She looked to Ian, urgently needing him to believe her, but it was his turn to look away, jaw muscle pulsing.

After a moment, he looked back to her. "You said 'his hands.' He grabbed you, then? Man-handled you?"

"Yes," she said, tears beginning to flow again as she nodded. "Grabbed me from behind. I had my dirk in hand, just as you taught me, Ian. But seeing Terence, hanging there . . ." Her voice cracked, and she gave into a moment of tears. Selah returned to her side and handed her a fresh handkerchief.

"Tell me," Ian gritted out. "Tell me all of it. Everything you can remember."

His fury made her shrink back. "Do you . . . Ian, do you blame me?"

His brows lifted in surprise, and his face softened. "Nay, lass, nay. Any anger ye sense from me is purely for the blackguard who attacked ye." He took a deep breath, realizing that in his fury his brogue grew thick. "You say 'twas Shubert. Help me by telling me everything you remember. Perhaps there's some detail that will give the sheriff rationale to hold him until the judge reaches Nevis again."

Verity licked her lips and with a trembling hand reached for a glass of water. After drinking thirstily, Ian helped her set it back on the table.

"It's all right, Ver. Tell us, what you remember," Selah said, taking her hand. "Every bit you can remember."

"I-I ran up behind the shop," she began. "I noticed that Terence had the geldings hitched and ready but had not brought out Fiona and the mule, which I thought odd. I called out for him, and when he didn't respond, I began to worry that something was very wrong. When I entered the stables . . ." She swallowed hard, and Selah took her hand, encouraging her to go on. "Shubert grabbed me from behind. He covered my mouth and lifted me, carrying me deeper into the stables."

Ian rose and paced, dragging his hands down his face.

Verity's heart raced at the memory. Selah drew closer, but Verity looked to Ian. "I was remembering what you taught me, Ian."

Her words seemed to center him again. He returned to her bedside, kneeling and taking her other hand.

"I was preparing to fight my way out. But then . . . Ter-Terence had left a lamp hanging, about a third of the way down, on a peg to the left. He was . . . he was just outside of the circle of that light, deep in the shadows. When Shubert carried me closer, I saw him. When I saw him, I . . ." She shook her head and then rubbed it, feeling the ache building there. "Seeing Terence, it was as if any thought of fighting back melted from my mind. All I could think of was him."

She shuddered at the thought and hated that it brought forth more tears.

"And then?" Ian pressed.

"He kissed my neck, tried to get me to bend to his will . . ."

Ian's face was again a mask of fury, but this time she knew it echoed her own outrage toward Shubert, not frustration with her.

"And then?" Ian said again.

The next memory made her smile through her tears. "Then I finally seemed to remember myself. I leaned forward, and with everything in me, I rammed my head back directly into his nose," she finished proudly.

Selah laughed in surprise, and Ian grinned along with her. "Aye, lass, that was very good. Very good," he repeated, remembering the blood crusting in Shubert's nostrils.

"I was set to turn and stab him, but as he fell he must have caught hold of the lamp. It went flying, and with the spilling oil went the flame. And in that moment, all I could think about was Terence again. Lifting him from that awful noose. Perhaps helping him breathe again. Then, when I couldn't, cutting him down."

Ian nodded and squeezed her hand, even as Selah clung to her and wept for Terence anew. "You did it, lass. You got him down in the end."

"And then . . . I must have fainted?"

"Aye. The smoke likely overcame ye."

"And Shubert? He left me there to die?"

"Did his best. Likely wanted to get away before he was seen. God be praised, McKay and I arrived in time."

"You saved me," she breathed.

"Ach," he said dismissively. "If I had not, your maid or neighbors would have."

"Perhaps," she said. She took a deep breath and let it out slowly. "But now we can go after Shubert. Get the sheriff to arrest him."

Ian frowned. "I fear 'tis not as simple as that."

"Why?" Selah cried. "You just heard all of it. He attacked her!"

"We saw Shubert this night. He has an alibi. Two young men who swear he was with them all night."

Verity's breath caught. *The lying snake . . .*

"Shubert has them over a barrel. They have a sick mother, and they owe Shubert money. He has given them another month to bring their cane to the mill and pay him. He says he broke his nose by running into a tavern door when he was . . . *distracted*." His jaw muscles tensed again. What was he leaving out? "And you— Verity, you never actually *saw* him, did ye, lass?"

Verity paused, shocked anew, then shook her head slowly and looked to the window. Accepting the truth of it. That the man, a man who had attacked Ket, Selah, and now her might get away with it again. "He shall be twice as bad now," she said quietly. "He likes to watch me. Taunt me. Let me know he is near."

"But I shall be near too," Ian pledged.

"For how long?" she asked. "Until the *Inverness* must sail again? No sea captain can make a living by remaining at anchor."

"For as long as it takes," Ian said, "to bring Shubert to justice or see him dead."

CHAPTER TWENTY-FOUR

The three of them were silent for a long while, each lost in their own thoughts.

"Something else transpired last night, Ver," Selah said carefully, "something that may lift your spirits."

"Oh?"

Selah rose, nodding earnestly. "Mmmhmmm!" she said with delight, fairly bursting.

"Well, what is it? Out with it!" Verity cried.

"Last night," Selah said, taking her hand in hers, "you and I became aunties."

"Aunties!" Verity threw off the bedcovers. "Ket!"

She was up and out the door in seconds, with only one thought on her mind. She ran down the hallway, pausing just outside Gray and Ket's bedroom, hand on the doorknob. But then Mitilda opened it. Seeing them there, she opened it wider with a grin. Gray was on the bed, fully dressed, beside Ket, who looked weary but happy. She smiled when she saw her sisters, reaching out one hand to them. Both hastened to her bedside.

"Oh!" Verity cried, hand to her mouth. For

the babe in Keturah's hands was so beautiful, so new . . . "He? She?"

"She," Keturah said, smiling down at her daughter in her arms.

"Oh, she is perfect, Ket," Verity cooed, leaning closer, tearing up.

"Is she not?" Selah said, crowding in too. "Simply perfect."

"May I hold her?" Verity asked.

Ket nodded and lifted the bundled babe to her. Verity settled the child in her arms and turned so she could better see her in the morning light streaming through their window. "She barely weighs a thing," she said, running a fingertip across the babe's smooth brow. Her breaths came swiftly as she slumbered, her eyes moving beneath almost-translucent lids. "You precious, precious little thing," Verity said, lifting her up to kiss her sweet face. She turned back to Ket. "And you? Are you well?"

"I am," she said, but her brow was beginning to knit as she took in her sister's appearance. "Why is it you are here, Verity? And smelling of smoke?"

"Oh," she said, turning away so her face did not betray too much. 'Twas best not to upset a new mother, she knew. There would be time enough for Ket to learn all of what had happened. "I suffered a slight mishap at the mercantile. Selah took me in and saw to me as you labored. All will be well, in time. After all, I have a niece."

"We have a niece," Selah said, pressing in, demanding a turn to hold the babe.

Reluctantly, Verity relinquished the child to her sister.

"What will you name her?" Verity asked.

Keturah looked to Gray, took his hand. "Madeleine Hope?" she asked.

Gray laughed under his breath. "Keturah has decided, and I have no objections to such a lovely name for such a lovely creature." It was his turn to demand a chance to hold her. With a sigh, Selah handed the child to her father.

Verity stared at the four of them—her closest, dearest family—and joy seemed to push back against last night's tide of terror and anger. It did not drive it entirely away—only helped her put it in a proper place in her heart and mind. She would not let Shubert steal into her thoughts now. She would not. As much as he would delight in that . . . she would not.

She strode over to the window, looking down past the waving cane to the sea beyond. But Terence, dear Terence . . . *Oh, Lord, not Terence.* Guilt rushed through her. He had died because of her. And because of how the Double T aimed to employ emancipated slaves. She was almost certain of it.

Would others die too as they fought to live life

the way God wanted them to? Yet what other choice did they have?

I am so sorry, Terence, she thought, closing her eyes. *I am so very sorry.*

They would need to lay his body to rest that afternoon. Watch as his friends sang the songs of old and covered his burial mound in seashells. Pray that he was at rest, true rest now, in heaven.

She glanced back at the Covingtons, such a sweet trio. No, for this moment at least, she chose to revel in the glory of answered prayers, here in the flesh. After all, Keturah had thought herself barren, her long years of marriage to the horrible Lord Tomlinson begetting her nothing but misery and abuse, no children. But now with Gray—who loved her sister with his whole heart—they knew the full meaning of blessing.

"Would that you will bless the rest of us too, Lord," she said under her breath.

That night, Ian found Gray in the parlor, contentedly pacing with the baby, smiling down at her face. For once, Major Woodget and the men seemed to have made themselves scarce, seemingly unnerved by a new babe in the house. Or had it been Keturah's piercing cries the night before? As much as it had rattled him too, he had heard the birth pangs of women before. His sister, Marjorie. An aunt. Women in every port. To him, birth was as much a part of life as death, and both seemed to come in equal measure.

"Gray, may I have a word?" Ian asked.

"Come," the besotted man said, gesturing distractedly toward a settee.

Ian swallowed a grin. Given the man's elation as a new father, perhaps this would be the perfect moment to ask Gray what he must.

"May I offer you a drink?"

"No, thank you," Ian said. "I must remain entirely sober, given what I have to say."

Gray's eyes narrowed, and he turned toward a crystal carafe. "Perhaps 'tis I, then, who shall need a drink."

"Perhaps."

Instead, Gray came around the settee and, resettling his sleeping daughter in his arms, finally dragged his eyes from her face to meet Ian's. "Does this have to do with Verity? And Shubert?"

"Well, yes. And no," Ian said, wishing he had his hat in hand. He needed something to occupy his nervous fingers and sweating palms. He could not remember the last time he had been so on edge. "I have come to beg your permission to court Verity. As her brother-in-law, I figure you are as near a guardian to her as any."

Gray smiled and nodded slowly. "There is no need to beg, Ian. You are a fine man, and I know Verity already has a tender place in her heart for you."

"Truly?"

"Truly."

Ian did not know why he had pressed him. He had discovered that much himself. But it felt good, reassuring, to hear it from Verity's guardian.

"Besides," said Gray, "as you know, the Banning women seem to do whatever they wish, regardless of what the men in their lives direct. 'Twas Keturah who demanded we marry, even before I could afford to build her this proper home."

Ian blinked in surprise. He'd thought the house had been Gray's all along.

Gray laughed. "Ah, yes. There you have it. Best to know the truth of such things before you begin courting a Banning. But I will tell you this, man. There is none finer than Keturah, Verity, and Selah. None finer."

"They are indeed different from any women I have met yet, in any of my travels. Refined and yet . . ."

"Not? Not conventionally, anyway," Gray said easily, taking no offense. "But it takes a different kind of strength in a man to stand alongside them. They seek not a man to direct them or lord over them, but rather one who will celebrate their strengths, even as he does his best to protect and love her. And I shall not abide a man who will do anything less for my sisters-in-law. Do you believe you fit such a description?"

Ian nodded. That made sense to him. A different kind of strength . . . for a different kind of woman. "I am that sort of man. At least I shall strive to be should I win Verity's affections."

Gray considered him. " 'Tis an adjustment, for most of us. But I see it in you, Ian. What Verity would need in a beau."

Ian smiled and took a deep breath. What would come next was much harder. "There is something else. Something that might change your mind about me."

"Oh?"

The child whimpered, stretched, and then settled again, completely distracting her father. Seeming to remember himself, Gray again turned to Ian.

"When last in America, I was refused permission to export from her shores."

Gray frowned. "For what reason?"

Ian tried to swallow but found his throat dry. "I struck the Union Jack and have refused to raise it."

"Because of your brother?"

"Aye. I blame England for sending him on a fool's errand. But there is more. I am taking up the Colonial cause."

Gray rose slowly. "You mean the rebel cause."

"Aye," Ian said, rising too. "If you could see what is transpiring there, Gray. How they are choking the colonies." He turned and began pacing the room. "Now after Lexington and Concord, it shall be twice as bad. There are rumors of England sending many more troops to put down the rebellion."

"So then it shall soon be over. You're on the wrong side, man. If—"

"No. I dinnae think so, Gray. It shall not soon be over. And if they turn away anyone who refuses to fly the Union Jack at their mast from import or export, what shall happen to all the merchant ships that supply the West Indies? Think on it." He gestured to the window. "Half the ships that bring cargo here and other islands are not English vessels."

Gray sank to his seat again. "The fools," he growled, rubbing his forehead. "They shall starve us. We cannot keep ourselves, let alone the fieldhands, fed for very long. Our store-houses here at the Double T will last only a few months."

Ian nodded. He knew this would come as bitter news.

"So Britain makes another callous decision, forgetting her own in the process." Gray sighed. "But what of you, Ian? What of this makes you think I might change my mind about approving your courting of Verity?"

"I could not leave American shores without a thing in my hold. I have a crew to pay and a desire to sail east to track down the blackguard who killed my brother and bring him to justice. So I managed to obtain fourteen head of horses under cover of darkness."

"You . . . you *smuggled* them out?" Gray asked.

"Indeed," Ian whispered. "Moreover, I intend to do it again if necessary. I intend to do all I can to aid the rebels. Pass along information, help the rebels obtain weapons. Britain has overplayed her hand, and—"

Gray abruptly took to his feet again. "It brings me great displeasure to say this, Ian. But you must leave now, and you may not pursue Verity's hand."

Ian's heart plummeted even as he stood there, frozen. "Please, hear me out."

"I have heard quite enough. Do you not see it?" Gray ran an agitated hand through his hair. "Already we are pariahs on this island. There are many who distrust us, many who would see us dead or gone rather than prosper. They deeply resent our success to date."

"And yet your success might give you a voice, make others think," Ian tried.

Gray laughed derisively. "Are you blind, man? This island is rife with Loyalists. They count on Britain for protection." He let out a second mirthless laugh. "Why else would we put up with the likes of Major Woodget and his men? Because we must," he hissed, leaning toward Ian. "Because our neighbors demand it.

And after all the ways we have challenged their beliefs, their way of life, we shall not challenge them on this front. Condoning Verity's courtship by a smuggler. One who aims to openly aid the rebels . . . No, it cannot be. Those on Nevis would understand your desire for retribution against the man who murdered your brother; they would not understand your new allegiance to the rebel cause."

Gray shook his head in dismay, seemed to gather himself, sighed and stared down at his daughter. "I must make the wisest decisions I can, Ian, now more than ever," he said wearily, lifting the tiny Madeleine. "For her. For my wife. For my sisters-in-law too. As you said, I am the closest to a guardian they have. And I shall do my best to protect them on every front."

Ian nodded, swallowing hard against the sudden lump in his throat. Gray had reacted in the worst possible way he had imagined. Sending Ian away when he was so close to accepting him, denying his request to court Verity. Yet he could understand the man's position. Respected him, really, for making such a hard choice. "I understand," Ian managed, turning to leave. "Might ye give me a moment to tell Verity myself?"

"Nay. 'Tis best for me to do so. I am sorry, Ian," Gray said, following him to the door. "I think highly of you. Of your brother too. Thought it quite satisfying, the idea of a McKintrick at Verity's side. Perhaps after the conflict is over . . ."

"Aye, perhaps," he said, feeling queasy as he walked out of the parlor and retrieved his hat and coat from beside the door. *After the conflict is over.* The man did not know. He couldn't know. He simply thought that this would be resolved in the colonies over the course of the next few months. They had not experienced the long-simmering rage over lack of representation and high taxation, the powerful desire to drive out the British oppressors. Nay, this would not be a conflict over and done with in a few months' time. This would be a protracted war lasting years. Gray thought he understood the American colonies, as a partially empathetic uncle might upon hearing news of an errant nephew trying to make his own way in the world but upsetting his parents in the process. Still, he was only doing what he deemed best on behalf of the family, trying to protect them all, and Ian could not argue with that.

"There is the matter of Verity's horses I obtained for her. She specifically chose two of them, the last we were in the Carolinas."

"She shall have to do without them," Gray said firmly. "She cannot accept a shipment of smuggled horses. 'Tis too risky."

Ian stared at him. Both of them knew she would be furious. It was, of course, her last possible import for some time, brought to her at great cost. For the first time, Ian felt shame in it . . . in how his actions might expose her to danger. What had he been thinking? Purely because she seemed open to the idea, but was that enough? Or had he failed as her protector from the very start?

"Be well, Gray," he said, turning away.

"And you as well, Ian," Gray said, closing the door behind him.

As Ian hovered on the edge of the stairs, he felt the warmth of the house at his back dissipate as the cool of evening enveloped him from the front. He heard someone laughing from among the slave cabins, a great belly laugh. A playful shriek. A toddler wailing. It was enticing, this island, the people here, and yet it clearly was not his home. Had not God made that perfectly apparent?

Settling his tricorn on his head, Ian nodded to himself, resolute about the path ahead. If there was but one benefit of not winning Verity's hand, it was this. He could fully serve the rebel cause now and track down the privateer who had stolen Duncan from the both of them. And before leaving, he could make sure that Angus Shubert never hurt Verity, Keturah, or Selah ever again.

He took a deep breath. For the first time in a long while, he did not fear death in the pursuit of his causes. That had been weighing on him, he realized, as he began the long walk back to

Charlestown. He had worried that he would bring Verity further grief if he never returned to her, just as Duncan's death had brought her grief.

As of today, he was free of that burden. She might grieve his parting now, the potential of their love, but nothing like a wife mourned a new husband, lost.

But will you not then free my heart, Lord? he prayed, striding up the road and wiping away embarrassing, furious tears. *If this is of you, then free my heart too.*

CHAPTER TWENTY-FIVE

Verity had not seen Ian all day. After Terence's funeral, she had returned home to hold little Madeleine for hours, the both of them dozing, having each survived a trauma of her own, she supposed. Then Selah had demanded she bathe and don a fresh gown of Ket's for supper. And before they went downstairs, Selah set to curling her hair and pinning it up, "So you shall look as pretty as a picture for you-know-who," she whispered in her ear.

Verity had batted her sister away but giggled as she did so. The idea of looking pretty for Ian, for seeing his eyes light up when she came into the room . . . Yes, for that, she was willing to sit still for another hour as Selah finished her ministrations. Ket's gown was a bit big on her, a bit long, but it was clean and beautiful, and she knew the copper brown would bring out the gold in her eyes. Would Ian notice this too?

She had to remind herself not to race down the new staircase, taking each step as the lady her mother had taught her to be. Down below, spying her, Major Woodget, Captain Howard, and the two lieutenants both rose to greet her, as did Gray.

But Ian was nowhere in sight.

She did her best to disguise her disappointment as Captain Howard came to her, bowed, and kissed her hand. "You are resplendent, Miss Banning," he said. "You have made a most remarkable recovery!"

"Owing to my sister's kind care," she said, turning to Selah. She felt badly for a moment, forcing the men's attention to her pretty little sister, yet she could barely tolerate him at the moment, so desperate was she to find where Ian had gone.

She took Gray's elbow. "Did you invite Ian to return for supper?" she asked quietly, leaning close.

"What? Uh, no," he said, fairly pulling away from her, which was odd. He always seemed to like her sisterly affections. "He had to be . . . off."

Verity frowned. But then Keturah arrived, up out of her childbed far too soon. She and Selah turned to their sister in chagrin, but Ket smiled at them benignly, as utterly at ease and at peace as the Madonna depicted with her Holy Child in every painting from around the world.

Mitilda came in then, inviting them all to the table, for supper was ready. Together, they enjoyed delicious turtle stew, roast mutton, roasted potatoes, and mango cobbler for dessert.

Sated, Verity leaned back in her chair and looked again to Gray, who had been oddly quiet throughout the meal.

He summoned Nellie to the table, the new nursemaid, and gently offered little Madeleine to her. The woman eased out of the dining room as Gray returned his attention to those around the table. "I have some unsettling news for you all," he said gravely but quietly, clearly not wishing to be overheard by the household servants. "This day I learned that in response to the recent battles with rebels, Britain may begin to reject merchants in American ports who refuse to fly the Union Jack."

"And so they should," grumbled the major.

Verity heard Keturah suck in her breath and saw Selah cover her mouth. They understood. Why, was not half of their exported goods brought to them by ships sailing under flags other than the Union Jack? Was this why Ian was not present? Had he finally taken a stand against the English yoke that had been chafing him of late? It had to have been him who told Gray this news, what with his recent return from America. Had it so unsettled Gray that he sent Ian away?

"What this means is that we may be in for some challenging days ahead," Gray continued. "We have stores that shall supply the Double T for a few months, but no longer than that."

"Then we shall pray that this conflict does

not go on for very long," Captain Howard said.

"And yet we must prepare for it in case it does," Gray replied.

"I have contacts in Liverpool," Major Woodget said. "I would be most happy to intervene on your behalf. Arrange for food, lumber, whatever you wish."

"That is good of you, Major," Gray said. "Let us send word at once."

All of them knew it would take six weeks, perhaps longer, to get word to England. Six more weeks to return to the island, and only if a ship was ready to sail at once.

"If America truly cannot export, Nevis shall need many supply ships en route to us from England," Philip added. "To say nothing of the other British Isles."

"Or the rebels shall see how they cut off their own nose to spite their face," Major Woodget said smugly, "and all shall return to normalcy."

"Or is it the British who have cut off their nose to spite their face?" Verity asked quietly.

"Verity!" Keturah said, aghast.

"Forgive me," Verity said quickly, not wishing to upset her sister, so soon out of childbed. "I spoke out of turn." *But I did not speak untruth,* she thought.

"You must curb your tongue," Major Woodget said. "These are not times for young women to say whatever is on their minds. Nor men for that matter. Our king is at last taking these rebels in hand, and his subjects will readily support him. If not," he said, pointedly looking to Verity over the edge of his crystal wine goblet, "they risk being labeled rebels themselves."

The table grew silent.

"We are the great-granddaughters of Alfred Banning, a commander in the Royal Navy," Keturah said, rising. "You shall find nothing but Loyalists in this house."

The men had risen with her.

"I beg your pardon, Mrs. Covington," the major said. "I spoke merely out of a desire to protect your house, not threaten anyone in it."

Keturah gave him a demure nod. "Yes, well. Now I must return to my chambers. I fear the evening has taxed me far more than I thought it might. Sisters? Might you attend me?"

Selah and Verity immediately moved to do as she bid, each following her out and then taking an elbow as she climbed the stairs.

"What were you thinking?" Ket hissed at Verity.

"I thought of speaking the truth," she hissed back.

"Speak the truth to us, not them."

"When? When are we not saddled with their presence? When might I speak to you or Selah freely? Solely in the confines of our rooms, it seems."

"So be it," Ket said. "Speak to us in our rooms, then."

Verity sighed heavily and bit her tongue before she said something—in the hallway, in the privacy of their rooms—she would later regret. Ket needed rest, peace. Not politics.

It was Ian's sudden absence that had left her in such a cantankerous mood. She had so anticipated seeing him, of perhaps strolling along the front lawn to look at the stars. She adored being outside at night, and in town it was not nearly the same as being here on the Double T.

She and Verity helped Keturah undress and climb into bed. They heard Madeleine's mewling cry before Nellie tapped on her door. "You may enter," Ket called.

The maid brought the babe in. "Begging your pardon, Lady Ket, but the babe is hungry. Do you wan' me to find a wet nurse? All the fine white ladies do."

"Well, not this fine white lady," Keturah said, gesturing the woman forward. "I shall feed my own child as long as I am able. There is something gratifying in it."

She parted the neckline of her gown and brought the squalling child to her breast. Verity cast a surprised look in Selah's direction. Blushing, Selah looked away.

"What of it, sisters?" Keturah complained. "Is it not as God intended?"

"Yes, well," Verity said, shifting, as anxious as the maid appeared to be. Not a one in their set had ever suckled her own babe, even in England. *But leave it to Ket to do it her own way.* "Go on now, Nellie. You've done your best by Lady Ket. I shall bring the babe to you when she is done."

"Yes'm," said the woman, scurrying out of the room at once.

"I *must* feed her," Keturah said, answering their silent argument. "You have seen my husband. He is utterly besotted. If I am to hold my baby at any point in the day, this shall be my only defense."

Verity laughed and settled in beside her, daring to look upon their special intimacy. It did appear . . . warm. Tender.

Then Gray eased into the room. Selah hurriedly cast a dressing gown over Keturah's shoulder. He glanced at her, bemused. " 'Tis not my beautiful wife and babe I have come to see."

"No?" Ket asked distractedly, peeking under the gown at her daughter.

"No." He fell into a sitting chair as if utterly exhausted. " 'Tis actually for your sister that I have come." His eyes moved to meet Verity's, and her breath caught. What was this? "Perhaps we could have a word alone?"

"Gray Covington," Keturah chided, "you know as well as I that anything you have to say to one of us sisters ought just as well be said to all."

"A man might try, might he not?"

"Out with it," Ket said, waving off his complaint.

But then his hesitation, and the long silence that followed, drove every bit of jovial mood from the room.

"Gray?" Verity said. "Say what you must. You are frightening me."

He rose and came over to her, offered his hand. Tentatively, she took it. "You know I have your very best interests at heart, do you not?"

She looked up into his earnest eyes. Never had he done wrong by her. Always love, always protection, always support. She nodded, but trepidation filled her.

He covered her hand with his other, sorrow filling his eyes. "Ian came to me today," he said, again hesitating.

Ian? "Go on," Verity said, finding his pauses infuriating now.

"He asked to formally court you."

She frowned even as her heart leapt. Formal courtship? But why Gray's sorrow? "And what did you tell him?"

"I told him I would be glad of it," Gray said.

The tension poured from her, and she smiled, wanted to laugh . . . until she focused again on her brother-in-law's grim expression. "Gray? What is wrong?"

He sighed, glancing back at the closed bedroom door, then to Verity and her sisters. "There was

344

more he had to tell me. He has thrown in with the rebels, Verity. Admitted to his being involved with spying and smuggling."

Keturah gasped.

Selah clamped a hand to her mouth and slumped onto the bed.

But Verity remained still. "And?"

Gray frowned. "You *knew* of this?"

"I surmised it," she replied. "And I have come to think . . . I approve." She pulled her hand from his and gestured toward the door. "How can you stomach it, Gray?" she whispered. "The heavy hand of His Majesty bears a terrible weight upon your own household! They eat your food, drink your wine, and to what end? Do they aid you in the fields? In the stables? No. They merely sit about like proud peacocks, prepared for a fight that may very well never come to our shores."

She rose and paced back and forth, looking from one surprised face to the next. "I have been to New York, my dear ones. Seen and *felt* the chafing of the yoke England places on America's shoulders. I have been to places where the presence of the king's soldiers is seldom seen. And those places?" She lifted her chin, remembering the outskirts of Charlotte. The light step in the people's gait, the camaraderie. " 'Tis something special. Different from anything we have yet to experience here or in England."

She looked to Ket. "Consider Madeleine. How

she might be as a child or as a young woman. Would you wish her to love you freely? Or force her to love you?"

She waited, looking from Ket to Gray, then to Ket again.

"Well, freely, of course," Ket answered.

"Do you not see? England believes she can force her children to love her. And when they do not, she punishes them. What good can come of that? Love, devotion, loyalty . . . they must be freely given. Has God himself not taught us that in the Holy Writ? Otherwise it is naught but a form of slavery."

"Verity!" Keturah said. Yet by the look in her eyes, she was beginning to understand.

Selah stared at her but nodded slightly, her big brown eyes shifting. She was thinking, hard.

Verity turned to Gray. "What did you say to Ian to send him away? Where is he now?"

He shook his head. "No. I shall not let you do this."

"You must, Gray. Tell me all of it," she insisted.

"No," he said loudly, then looked over his shoulder in fear.

"See that?" she hissed, grabbing his arm. "You fear the very men who are here to 'protect' you."

"Because I do not wish for my sister-in-law to be labeled a *rebel*," he said quietly, shaking off her hand.

Verity could see that he had acted in the only

346

way he could see fit—to protect her. She looked back to Ket. "I must know, Sissy. All of it. This is my life. Not his. Not yours. Mine. I am a woman grown. Let me make my own decisions."

"Even if it means you might face the gallows?" Ket said, her voice as wan as her face.

"Even then," she said. "The longer we tarry, the more likely that will be," she warned. "Give us a chance."

"Us?" Ket asked.

"Me. Ian. Together. I love him, Ket. God help me, I love him with everything in me." She looked at Gray. "He ran into that burning stable to save me. Do you *truly* think he does not have my best interests at heart?"

"I think he did not stop to think about how pursuing his own interests might put you in harm's way," Gray said. "And once faced with that, he did the honorable thing."

"He withdrew his request to court me."

"He accepted my refusal with grace."

Verity shook her head, disappointment and fury washing through her in equal measure.

" 'Twasn't your place, Gray."

"If not me, then who?" he said, his brow wrinkling.

"When you fell in love with Keturah, who stood between you? You who did not have the funds to build my sister a house," Verity pressed. "Did I? Did Selah?" She well knew the answer, as did he.

"Verity, he admitted to being a *smuggler.* To bringing horses to these shores for you . . . horses illegally obtained."

She took in a long, deep breath and held it. "And you stopped him."

"Of course I did!" Gray said, throwing up his hands. "He himself saw the shame in it."

"The shame in it? Those horses may very well be the last bit of business my mercantile has for a long while. I have put all I have into Banning's Bridlery, Gray. As you yourself put everything into Teller's Landing."

He lifted his chin and crossed his arms. "You need not fear your future, Verity. You shall always have a place here with us."

Verity let out a cry of frustration, entirely unladylike. Her sisters stared at her in shock. She looked back at them, feeling the separation yawn as clearly as dry earth breaking under the summer sun.

"Ket . . . Selah," she said beseechingly. "I must go after him. I love you both, as I love you too, Gray," she added, glancing at her brother-in-law, regardless of how angry she was with him. "But 'tis as clear to me now as it was when Ket felt the need to come to the islands. It felt like a mad plan to us then too, yes?"

Selah rose, wringing her hands. "And yet we chose to do it together. With God's blessing."

Verity nodded, considering her words. "Yes.

Together. But now I feel God's blessing in *this*. I shall go to Ian. Aid him in his cause—and the rebels too—in order to win the Americans their freedom. And in time I hope that you all shall be in it with us. If not, I shall understand. After the conflict is over, we shall find our way back to one another."

Her voice cracked on the last word. Was she truly going to do this? Leave her beloved sisters behind in order to pursue the man she loved? And join him in furthering his cause? One that was swiftly becoming her own?

Yes. Because it felt right. Moreover, *righteous.*

England was dear to her, a country to whom she would always be grateful. Yet what right had England to lay claim to lands across an entire ocean—here or elsewhere? Of course, she doted on the West Indies, and the Indies on her! The wealth flowed back and forth. But what of the Americas? Or East India? For them, the Crown was nothing but a heavy yoke.

England has no right, she decided. And one way or another, by Ian's side she would assist in the cause to end her oppression.

Chapter Twenty-Six

Ian found Michael sitting on the *Inverness*'s beached longboat, and wordlessly he summoned Michael along. Together they strode directly down the street and into the tavern owned by Angus Shubert. They found the man where they had left him earlier—in the side chamber, deep in his cups, a tavern wench on his lap.

Shubert rose when he saw them enter, paying no heed to how the girl tumbled to the floor. Ian bent and helped the lass to her feet. "Go," he said under his breath. "I aim to make him pay for more than this."

She scurried out of the room. Watching their exchange, two men stumbled after her. Two others remained, one on either side of Shubert.

"What do you want, McKintrick?" he slurred. "You came after me yesterday and failed. Why not board your ship and be off with you?" A joyless smile crept across Shubert's face, his eyes mere slits. "Is it that you fear your girl shall turn to me once you're gone? After all, once a wench has a taste of me—"

Ian vaulted across the long table, casting himself in a slide directly into Shubert's chest with one foot, his wounded nose with the other, not caring a whit how it would end.

Shubert fell backward, Ian half atop him.

A piercing pain shot up his shoulder and neck, down his arm. But as soon as he was down, he was turning, shifting, finding his feet again. With his elbow, he struck the lower back of one of Shubert's companions, making the man arch and stumble forward, then turned toward Shubert, narrowly ducking the man's fist.

He rammed his own into the man's bleeding nose, again and again. If Verity had failed in breaking it, he would not.

Shubert shuddered, staggering as he backed up with each blow.

Ian grabbed hold of his filthy jacket and slammed him into the far wall, his head bouncing off it in pleasing fashion. Dazed, the man stood still a moment.

"Your days of delighting in the torment of women are over," Ian hissed, drawing back his fist.

"Captain McKintrick!" cried a woman behind him. "Release him at once!"

Ian glanced back. He blinked twice, not quite certain he wasn't imagining it. "Verity? What are you doing here?"

He felt Shubert pulling away a second before he turned back to his adversary. And as he did, he felt all four meaty knuckles of the man's fist meet his cheekbone, sending him sliding back over the table and onto the floor.

Verity hurried over to Ian as Michael grabbed Angus Shubert's shirt and flung him out of the small side chamber and into the main part of the tavern. She could hear wood cracking, men shouting, pewter mugs clanking against the hard floor. But she remained focused on Ian.

His eyes narrowed, as if he fought slipping into unconsciousness, and then widened. "Verity? Lass, is that truly you?" he asked, reaching up to cup her cheek.

Michael returned to the side chamber, hovering over them. "You all right, Cap'n?"

Ian blinked slowly and stared at Verity as if she were but a vision.

"Mr. McKay," Verity said, "it seems you and your captain made some poor decisions this night."

"I would not call it that."

"No?"

"No," Ian said for him, seeming to regain a bit of his equilibrium. "Not if our decision was to—" he paused and laboriously struggled to sit up, wincing as he covered his shoulder with one hand—"to suppress your tormentor's ability to torment you and yours further."

Verity hid her smile. Was it anything more than what she herself wished?

"Still, Captain McKintrick, 'twould be best for us to be off to board the *Inverness* posthaste. If the sheriff arrives and finds Councilman Shubert injured and lying on the tavern floor, he shall most certainly escort you to the jail."

Ian stared at her quizzically. " 'Best for us' did you say?" Again, he looked a tad woozy and set to squinting at her.

"Yes, us," she said with a firm nod of her head. "Now, help me get him up, Mr. McKay. We must be off and away from this tavern immediately."

"Right you are, miss," he said, reaching for Ian. Together they got him to his feet, and when Ian wobbled, McKay bent and heaved him over one shoulder.

"Follow me," she said, not waiting for his assent. She moved into the main tavern, where everyone present looked from Angus Shubert's unconscious form to them and back again. There would be no exiting the establishment without everyone seeing them as she hoped. Even so, she elected to lead Mr. McKay out the back door, assuming that one of Shubert's comrades had ridden for either the sheriff or the assistance of British soldiers. They'd likely arrive via Round Road in front.

She pushed through the double doors into the kitchen and out past two cooks, one kneading bread on a table, the other stirring a pot on the cookstove, then out the back. She held the door for McKay. Ian winced and groaned as they stood in the back alley.

"This way," she said. "Hurry." They weaved their way through a warren of tight alleys, stone houses and shops, until they finally reached the road that ran along the beach all the way to the harbor. She was thankful the night was at last full dark. If necessary, they could ease back into the alleys if anyone came their way, for she knew that British soldiers or the sheriff and his men would be carrying a lamp or torch. So far, no one else seemed to be anywhere but in town.

They were approaching the harbor's empty slave-trader platforms and stores when Ian demanded they stop. "Set me down, Michael," he said. It didn't take more than one request for McKay to do as he was told, laboring for air as he was.

Ian struggled to remain steady on his feet, covering his sore cheek with his hand. She could not see much, what with only the moonlight to guide them, but she could see that Ian was in pain.

"You are badly hurt," she said, stepping toward him, lifting her hand.

But he blocked her with his arm. "Nay, do not, lass. Do ye not yet see?" His tone was tortured. "We cannot do this. You with me. Me with you. Gray forbid it."

"I know." She swallowed hard. "And yet here I am. Choosing otherwise."

Ian peered deeply into her eyes. Then he frowned. "It brings me no pleasure, you spiting your brother-in-law."

"They shall come to see my way of thinking. In time," she said, sidling closer to him. "My sisters are already halfway there. For I told them all that I was with you, Ian McKintrick. With you."

"With me?" he asked lowly. "Me? Not my *brathair*?"

"You," she said, reaching up a tentative hand to trace his temple, his ear, then wind her fingers through his hair. "No matter where you lead me. Because you, Ian McKintrick, have my heart."

Michael coughed and eased away, walking backward. "I shall ready the longboat, Cap'n," he said. And while neither of them glanced his way, Verity was certain there was a smile behind every word.

Ian leaned his forehead toward hers. "Me, lass?"

"Yes, you, Ian," she said, and with that she lifted her lips.

For a brief heart-stopping moment, he hovered, his own lips barely grazing hers, contemplating. Then, decided, he drew her to him, kissing her. Kissing her more thoroughly than she had ever been kissed before, wrapping his arms around her, clinging to her as if he couldn't hold her tightly enough.

When he released her, she took a half step back, panting for air, considering him, weighing his reaction. "Was that your decision, then?" she asked.

"Decision?"

"Shall you take me with you?"

He laughed, sounding confused. As if he was one-third aghast at her audacity, one-third wildly hopeful, and one-third against it.

Seeing her firm resolve, he moved in, testing her. Wrapping an arm around her waist again, he pulled her to him. "I shall not see your good name besmirched. If ye wish to come with me, Verity Banning, 'tis only as my bride. That being against your brother's wishes, 'tis surely to be a trial of its own."

"You wish to marry me?" she asked.

"With everything in me," he replied, his face a mere inch from her own. "Would you have me, lass?" He swallowed hard, pulling slightly away. "I am not Duncan, and I am on a rebel's path . . ."

"You are not Duncan," she agreed. "But you are Ian, my Ian. 'Tis true," she said. "I was falling in love with your brother when he left me last. He was a fine, fine man. But you are as fine a man. You are the one I love now. And I think . . ." She paused and looked away toward the moon, the sparkling sea. "I think Duncan would bless this. This love between you and me."

"I believe he would too." Ian hesitated, then

let her go. With some effort, he knelt down, still holding her hand in both of his. "Would you then have me as your husband, lass? Stand beside this rebel against the Crown? Because you must know now that that is my aim—to aid the Sons of Liberty, regardless of the cost. And with that in mind, I cannae promise to keep you safe. But I promise you this: I would give my life tryin'."

They remained where they were for a long moment, staring into each other's eyes.

"And if I agree," Verity said at last, "when would the nuptials take place?"

"This very night," he said hopefully. "McKay can perform the ceremony, if'n I name him acting captain. And lass, if you are my bride this night, I do not intend to spend time on deck."

"So be it," she said with a slow smile.

He pulled back a tad, as if startled. "Truly?"

"Truly."

He abruptly stiffened, rose as if it pained him and paced away, then back. "Verity. Are ye in your right mind, lass?"

"Are ye in yours?" she returned, mimicking his brogue. "Ye have a hold full of horses you cannae unload here, it seems. A woman who can help you sell them on Statia. A woman who can even help you gain entrance and trade again in New York, or Long Island, I wager, given her Loyalist cousins. Moreover," she said, edging closer to him and trailing her hands up his chest, "a woman who loves you. Did you truly think ye would succeed in leaving such a woman behind?"

He laughed then, hands on hips, bending backward with great merriment, then staring at her again. He lifted a hand to her cheek. "I give you this last chance, lass. Ye propose to leave behind your beloved sisters, your brother, your baby niece, your shop . . ."

"Hopefully, but for a time," Verity said. She covered his hand with her own and lifted his palm to kiss it. "For you," she added. "I am forever with you. Do you not see, Ian? 'Tis you I want. More than anything else. I shall pray that the good Lord returns me to my family in the future. But my present? Well, as far as I can see, that belongs beside you."

Ian was certain that 'twas no girl's dream of a wedding. Naught but Michael to conduct the ceremony with two men as witnesses at the prow of the ship. No flowers. No fine dress. No beloved fellowship surrounding them.

But to him, it was as if he were living a dream.

A lass as fine as Verity Banning willing to take one such as him, a ship captain with nothing but illegal cargo in his hold. A man sent packing by her brother-in-law. The younger brother of the man she once loved. A man she had lately retrieved from a squalid tavern floor.

And yet somehow she looked up at him with nothing but love.

"This is God's own grace," he said, lifting her hand to his lips and tenderly kissing each knuckle. "That one such as you should love one such as me."

"This is love," she returned. "Testimony of what I wish for the rest of our lives, Ian. One of mutual sacrifice, dying to self in order to build what is better, together."

Michael and the crewmen shared a long look, as if wondering what madness had befallen the couple. But Ian and Verity? They continued to gaze at each other with nothing but love, hope.

And with that, he leaned down, cupped her precious face in both his hands and kissed her. Kissed her until he felt her body ease, melting into him. Then he scooped her up in his arms and carried her down the length of the ship as the other sailors cheered, all the way down to his cabin door. He set her back on her feet. "This is it, Mrs. McKintrick. Your trunks are in my cabin, your bird and trade items from the store are in the hold. Are you ready, lass? If so, then call for McKay to weigh anchor."

"Mr. McKay!" she called over her shoulder, eyes still on Ian.

"Yes, ma'am?"

"Weigh anchor, Mr. McKay. Let us be away from Nevis before they come after us."

"You heard the cap'n's wife, men! Weigh anchor! Haul sail! You there! Stop looking for the next order from the cap'n! He has a wife to bed!"

Verity gasped, but Ian only laughed. Once more he picked her up in his arms, then pushed open the door of the cabin and carried her inward.

Once again the men cheered behind them.

"Ian!" she cried, her face hot with what she knew was the deepest blush of her life.

He merely grinned at her as he kicked the door closed behind them.

And as he lowered her gently upon the bed, Verity decided that if she was to be the captain's wife—standing alongside a smuggler, a rebel, an enemy of the Crown—well, she best get used to such no-nonsense, brash ways.

For to survive, such ways would become her own.

CHAPTER TWENTY-SEVEN

Early the next morning, Verity walked about the captain's quarters, taking stock of the place for the first time. Taking into account what was Ian's, what had to remain, what might change, in time . . .

"Over here, Miss Banning?" McKay asked, her trunk on his shoulder, gesturing with a jaunty smile to the corner on the far side of the bed.

She felt the heat of her blush. "That will do well, Mr. McKay," she said. "But ought you not refer to me as Mrs. McKintrick now? Or Verity?"

After lowering the heavy trunk in the corner, he straightened and turned to her. "May I call you Verity, miss? Missus," he amended hurriedly. "But Mrs. McKintrick it shall be around the crew."

"Yes. I would very much like it if you called me Verity. May I call you Michael?"

"Please." He lifted his chin. "Verity. You are a fine woman. And your husband? He is a fine man."

"Yes, he is," she agreed with a grin.

"My prayer is that you shall forever serve the other. For last night, despite his love for you, he was willing to sail away without you, because he thought you would be better served if he did so."

Her heart stuttered, then pounded, remembering how close she had been to losing him forever. "Because Gray sent him away?"

Michael glanced toward the door, hearing noises outside. "He is an honorable man, your husband. Even though he has chosen to fight for the rebels. And that will chafe at him once we return to British-held shores."

"I am aware," she said. Had it not been his way, to refuse to fly the Union Jack, even if it might have gained him easy entrance in New York, North Carolina, Nevis? And yet he had flown no flag, despite the consequences. Not that he had raised the new, yellow Gadsden flag with her coiled snake.

'Twas not his way. The way she had decided to follow, to join in taking his hand . . . Together, they would need to raise the Union Jack to the wind again, jointly accepting the responsibility of appearing to support England while doing their best to eventually send her home.

"He wants nothing more than your safety, Verity," Michael said, offering his hand. "And as his first mate, I want the same. I shall protect you with my life," he pledged.

Verity teared up, taking the man's hand. Such a promise! It bespoke of a deep bond between him and Ian that he should pledge what Ian had.

In a charming gesture, Michael pulled her knuckles to his lips and kissed them, then dipped his forehead to touch them as well—as if in fealty—just as Ian entered the cabin.

He drew up short, watching them with shrewd, sharp eyes. Then he shifted and dropped his jacket onto a hook as if a highland lord, Verity mused, expecting nothing more of his men. In turn, Michael moved past him and out the door, with nothing more than a nod as he did so. Ian shut the door and slid the bolt through the latch.

She blinked as Ian strode over to her, drawing her close. "Listen," he began. A call rang out, then others. "We near Statia," he whispered in her ear, bending to kiss it. The top. The crest. The curve at the bottom . . . sending delicious shivers down her neck.

"Yes," Verity whispered back.

"Say it now, if ye wish to remain, lass. I shall honor it, fully understanding. And agree to an annulment. From here we can hire a boat to return you to Nevis's shore. Because by nightfall I shall be on my way back to America, bent on either assisting the cause with smuggling or finding a way in as a spy."

"And if I do not wish to annul our marriage?" she asked, hands sliding up his wide, strong chest, his neck, through his hair. "If I am still as certain today as I was last night that I am to be your helpmate, in every sense of the word?"

"Then kiss me, lass, telling me this is not a dream, but my future."

She looked up at him, staring into his eyes. Cradled his face between her hands, then on tiptoe softly, slowly kissed him. "I love you, Ian McKintrick. May God himself light our way forward. Because I do not wish for another day apart."

He ran his fingers along her hairline. "Not a day, lass. Nor a night," he added with a suggestive grin. "I pledge it. Together. Forever. So long as I have breath in my chest, I am yours, Verity Banning McKintrick."

While Ian wished otherwise, he knew they had to move as soon as the sun peeked over the eastern horizon. There would be time enough on the voyage, he thought, to spend long, languid hours with his wife in the privacy of their cabin. But right now he had to help her sell the horses and meet with their contact as quickly as possible.

After all, he didn't want to remain in Statia's harbor for long. Angus Shubert had power now, and wealth. If the Brits were not compelled to come after the McKintricks on Shubert's behalf, he might take it to mind to hire a mercenary to do so. No, 'twas best to see to their business and set sail for the open sea before nightfall.

He leaned in to kiss her on the temple. "As

fetching as I find you, I aim to see to our business and be away from here before Shubert can send anyone after us."

She reluctantly agreed. "Do you know where we might sell the horses?"

"I have an idea, yes. Dress and I shall get us a bit of bread and tea."

She nodded, and he slipped out the door.

Outside, his crew cast him furtive, knowing looks. One grinned and gently slapped the back of his hand against his cohort's belly before folding his arms and staring at Ian, his grin growing wider.

"Must I find something useful for you to do, Brighton?" Ian barked, half amused, half irked at the man's insolence.

"No, Cap'n," said the man, sun-lightened eyebrows lifting. He scurried off down the deck, but he was still smiling as he went.

Ian turned to his friend. "Decker, go to the galley and ask the cook for a pot of tea, two cups, and a loaf of bread. Bring it to my cabin."

"Yes, Cap'n."

Ian moved to Michael, who stood at the wheel. They were cruising just off Statia's coast. "Spot any British patrols?"

"Nay," Michael said. He, too, had a bit of a knowing grin behind his eyes, but he had the good sense not to let it reach his lips. "Shall I head to the harbor now, Captain?"

"Yes, take us in. If there's a spot in the wharf, 'twould be best to tie up. Easier to off-load the horses."

"Aye, Captain. I shall do my best."

"Good man, McKay." He paused. "Think we would do better selling the horses to Monsieur Bieulieu or Mr. Schwartz?"

"Schwartz," Michael said. "If your goal is a fair price and speed. Are we of the same mind? We need to conduct our business and then head back out without delay?"

"Aye, we are of the same mind. Schwartz it is, then. Today is his lucky day."

Ian returned to his cabin. Entering, he saw that Verity had donned an emerald gown. She sat on a stool, plaiting her hair. After closing the door, he crossed his arms and stared at her.

She smiled up at him. "What is it?"

"Nothing. Or everything," he said with a laugh. "I think 'twill take me some time, lass, to become accustomed to a wife in my cabin. All this . . . beautiful femininity at my fingertips."

She waggled a finger at him. "Not at your fingertips at the moment, Mr. McKintrick. For we have work to do, yes?"

"Yes," he said with a regretful sigh. Perhaps his expression betrayed more longing for her than he had intended.

She completed her braid and pinned it neatly at the nape of her neck. While he liked how it left her beautiful profile free, there was a part of him that ached to undo it and see her hair again in a mass of curls about her shoulders. She looked quizzically at him and shook her head. "The horses, husband. Think on the horses with me. Do you know of someone who might buy them all outright?"

"I do. He shall give us a fair price, though not as much as we might have received were we not in such haste."

"It shall kill me to see those two beautiful mares sold at less than the best price. After all you went through to bring them to me."

"It cannot be helped, my love. Next time we shall do better, I promise you."

"And what of my sugar? My rum?"

He frowned. "What?"

"My sugar and rum from the store. I had the goods loaded in your hold yesterday before I went to find you in town. Shall we sell them here or in the colonies?"

He gaped at her and then laughed. Then he pulled her to her feet and into his arms. "Ye are a marvel, Mrs. McKintrick. 'Tis due to your foresight that we shall be able to sail to America and go about the business at hand."

"Only because you managed to bring the horses with you."

He kissed the top of her head. " 'Tis the beginning of a grand partnership, I believe."

"In more ways than one," she said, smiling up at him.

"*Qu'est que c-est? Vous avez apporté une fille?*" the shorter man barked in French when he opened the door. *What is this? You brought a wench?*

Ian grabbed hold of the man's jacket with both hands and brought him close to his face. "Are you speaking of my wife?"

Verity stepped closer, pure calm. "The wife who has Loyalist cousins who might grant us access to New York?"

The man's eyes shifted to Verity, and he slackened. "You would do that, Madame McKintrick?"

"For the cause? Yes."

The tension in the room eased a bit. Ian released him.

A woman called from upstairs, "Do you want wine, François?"

"No names, I told you!" he yelled. "Leave us be!"

The five of them sat down—François, his unnamed compatriot, Michael, Ian, and Verity. But she noticed that all of them sat on the edges of their chairs, ready to spring to their feet, regardless of how they appeared.

François leaned forward. "You were able to deliver the last letter to the intended recipients?"

"We did," Ian replied evenly, tapping his thumb on the table.

"You think you can get in another?" François asked. He fidgeted and glanced around the room. "The British tighten their lines as we speak."

"I do." Ian looked toward Verity. "She speaks the truth. She can gain us access that no others can."

François leaned back in his chair and let out a sigh of relief. "The last we sent after you . . ." He made a circular motion in the air with his index finger. "From what I hear, they did not fare as well." He looked hard at Verity. She struggled not to wriggle under his gaze. "You put her in danger, this wife of yours. Making her your lead."

Ian tensed again. His jaw muscle pulsed.

"It is decided," Verity said. "I am decided. My husband would gladly keep me someplace safe, but the cause demands sacrifice. For every one of us to do all we can to help. And this is a way that I might help."

François stared at Ian the whole time she spoke. "If she is discovered, she will be hanged."

Verity stood. She squared her shoulders. "If I hang, I hang. This cause . . . standing beside my husband . . . I am his loyal wife, even as I am America's newest loyal advocate." She shook her head and then paced back and forth, hand to her temple. After a moment, she paused. "How might I do anything less than this? And what is it I offer anyway? All I shall do is grant access. 'Tis Ian and Michael who shall do what is truly dangerous."

"Are you certain of that, Madame McKintrick?" François pulled out a pipe and began stuffing it with tobacco. "You are young. You are quite pretty. You shall not go unnoticed."

Verity straightened her shoulders. "Thank you, monsieur. I intend to use that to our advantage."

François stared at her, pipe suspended in the air, and then laughed. So deep, so long that the others around the table eventually joined in.

All but Verity.

She remained still. Staring back at him. "I am not a frivolous, empty-headed sort of woman. *Je parle Francais, Latin, et Anglais. Je peux le faire!*"

I speak French, Latin, and English. I can do this!

François gave her a long, appraising look, then set down his pipe and glanced at Ian. "You approve of this, Captain?"

A slow smile spread across Ian's face. "I am a new husband, François. But I know this. My wife is a Banning, and from what I can gather, there are few in the West Indies like them. 'Twas her sister who took over Tabletop Plantation on Nevis."

François's eyebrows lifted. Clearly, he'd heard of her sister's success. "But that was due to her marrying her neighbor."

"Partly," Verity said, sitting and leaning forward across the table, fingers nestled beneath her chin. "But only partly. We Banning women have minds of our own."

Ian guffawed at that. It was forced a bit, clearly meant to disarm these men, and yet it worked. Verity leaned back in her chair and remained silent.

François sobered and finished tamping down the tobacco in his pipe. He rose, moved to the fireplace, bent and brought a splinter of wood to the bowl of his pipe. Inhaling quickly, smoke soon billowed forth. He turned to face the group, the smoke so thick that he was only partially visible, as if an apparition. "Madame, you venture where few women have gone before," he said. He puffed a few times and let out a luxurious cloud of smoke. His small, dark eyes returned to her. "You are truly willing to sacrifice your life, your future, for the cause? Why not remain on Nevis, in the safekeeping of your sister's household?"

Verity strived to keep a steady expression, but her eyebrows lifted. "Because, monsieur, my husband—a man whom I love most sincerely—is a spy," she said in French. "A smuggler. A warrior for the cause . . . a cause I support as well."

François tried to hide his smile as he inhaled on the stem of his pipe, but largely failed. "Tell me how you intend to gain access to a country with increasingly guarded borders."

Chapter Twenty-Eight

Ket spotted Angus Shubert through the kitchen doorway as he rode his horse down the drive, accompanied by the sheriff and two soldiers, as well as two other men, all astride their own horses.

"Ket," Selah said in a frightened whisper, seeing him too. She had been kneading bread at the table, only pausing when she noticed that Ket was pulling her sgian dubh from her waistband, hiding the small knife in her palm.

" 'Twill be all right," Ket said to her.

"But the men are all in the fields."

" 'Twill be all right," Ket said again. "The sheriff and soldiers will keep Shubert in line." She turned to Nellie. "Just in case, take Madeleine upstairs to our room and bolt the door."

"Yes'm."

"Sansa, lock the door behind us."

"Yes, Lady Ket," said the servant, reverting to her old title as she stared out the window in terror. There was not a black man or woman on the island who did not know of, and fear, Angus Shubert.

Selah palmed her own knife and was right

behind Ket as they strode out to meet the men.

As one, the visitors pulled up on their reins.

"Gentlemen," she said, shielding her eyes from the sun and concentrating on the sheriff. "What brings you to the Double T?" She let her eyes drift over to Shubert, her pulse tripling when she saw how battered his face was. Had that been Ian's doing? She pretended not to notice.

"Mrs. Covington," the sheriff said, neatly dismounting. "We have come to call upon your sister. Miss Banning was seen in town last night and may have been witness to the criminal beating of Councilman Shubert here."

"I see," Keturah said. "Unfortunately, Verity does not reside here any longer. Did you go to Banning's Bridlery? She lives above the shop now."

The sheriff, a man of about forty with keen eyes and gentlemanly mannerisms, squinted at her. "Yes, ma'am. We checked there. The shop appears closed. And Miss Verity's boy, well, he seems to be here."

Keturah stifled a groan and glanced over her shoulder to Abraham, who stood outside his mother's cottage, watching them.

"Abraham missed his mother," Ket explained, "so Verity gave him permission to spend some time at the Double T with family. After Terence's murder"—she looked pointedly at Shubert—"and the fire, Verity thought it best not to endanger any

376

more of her help until the perpetrator was found."

"Well, now," said the sheriff, "cases like that are quite challenging to resolve. There were no witnesses, you understand. No one who saw anyone but Miss Verity, her maid, and the boy there that night."

Ket glanced again at Angus Shubert. Even though one eye was swollen shut, his face a mass of bruises, his nose still swollen, she detected a hint of triumph in his expression and posture. She clenched her knife tighter. It was he who had killed Terence. She was as certain of it now as Verity had been.

"Enough," Shubert barked. "Call your sister out here."

"I cannot," Ket replied. "As I said, she is not here."

Shubert's good eye widened. "I told you, Sheriff. The girl ran off with McKintrick. Up and sailed away in the middle of the night."

Ket frowned. "Of what do you speak, Mr. Shubert?"

"Councilman Shubert," he corrected, enunciating each syllable and leaning forward.

"Councilman," she allowed, giving the word no tinge of respect. "It does you no honor, beginning a rumor about my sister." She turned to the sheriff. "I can tell you that Captain McKintrick asked my husband for permission to court Verity. My husband told him no."

"What's this?" Shubert asked. "You and the McKintricks have always been thick as thieves. Why send this one away?"

"Because Captain McKintrick admitted to being a rebel sympathizer," Ket said, using the words she and Gray had agreed upon. "Being a Loyalist, Gray could not abide by it. So he sent the man on his way."

Shubert frowned, bringing a hand to his chin, but the soldiers all murmured among themselves. To them, what Ket said was worthy rationale.

"You can inquire of Major Woodget yourselves when he returns from St. Kitts. He and his men quarter with us. Ask them of our political stance, and if he thinks Gray would accept a rebel's pursuit of his sister-in-law's hand."

One of the soldiers whispered something in the sheriff's ear, and the sheriff nodded. "Very well, Mrs. Covington. We shall inquire of the major upon his return to the island. What of Captain McKintrick? Do you know where he intended to sail?"

"I do not."

He paused, then added, "Miss Verity has not been seen in town. She is not here. Is there not a slight chance she has eloped with the captain?"

"My sister?" Ket shook her head. "While Verity has a mind of her own, I can assure you that she is a lady, through and through."

The sheriff tucked his chin. "I see."

"Being a lady did not keep you from marrying beneath you," said Shubert. "Way I heard it, you did so with naught but a few negroes as witnesses. Nothing proper about it. Why might your sister not do the same?"

Keturah turned cold eyes on him. "I do not think you wish to speak of improper marriages, Mr. Shubert. Not when I have heard tell that you took Mrs. Shubert's hand in marriage when she was barely conscious."

His good eye narrowed, and he clamped his lips shut. He stepped toward her and rammed his finger in her direction. "This will be your undoing, *Lady* Ket. I aim to take every one of you Bannings and Covingtons down," he said, glancing at Selah. "Beginning with Verity and her lover."

"Her lover!" Keturah said. "You shall not—"

"And after I do," he interrupted, continuing to advance, "I shall buy the Double T and run it as our people have done for centuries. Not in the disgraceful manner you've adopted."

With each phrase he'd edged closer and closer to her, but she refused to back away.

"Yes, when this land is mine—and mark me, it shall be mine—I will take your slaves in proper hand and make certain all the freed sort are loaded on a ship and sent elsewhere. Stories of how things are done here on the Double T make our own slaves restless."

Keturah glared up at Shubert and slowly shook her head. "You shall *not* have this land. You shall never lord over our people. Because I shall die before I see that happen."

A smile teased the corners of his lips. "We shall see, then, Lady Ket. Any of you care to place a wager with me?" He glanced back at the men. The soldiers and sheriff shifted uneasily. The two others grinned. But Shubert was eyeing Ket and Selah again. "You will face hard times at some point. Comes with running a plantation. You've seen it yourselves. Mudslides. Hurricanes. Disease. And when you have nowhere else to go, you shall be forced to come to me."

"Never," Ket pledged.

"Never say never, Mrs. Covington." His grin widened, and he looked over his shoulder again. "My wager is this. These two shall be on their knees before me, begging me to buy this plantation, within three years' time."

"Never," Selah said, stepping forward. "We shall be paupers before we ask anything of you."

Shubert turned toward Selah. "Well, I'll be. The little miss is coming into her own. A spitfire, just like her sisters. I like a woman with fire in her veins," he said, hitching up his breeches. "Too bad I'm a married man now."

"Come along, Councilman," said the sheriff. "I think we are done here."

Shubert looked them both over again and then

reluctantly turned to his horse and mounted. "Tell them, Sheriff."

Clearly irked, the sheriff said, "If you hear from either Miss Verity or Captain McKintrick, I expect you to report it to me immediately."

"Of course," Ket said, her mouth dry. Selah nodded.

The men swung around and rode up the drive, disappearing among the swaying palms and thick foliage of brush and trees.

Breathe, just breathe, Ket told herself. And it was only then that she felt the warm drip of blood between her fingers. Opening her hand, she saw that she had been clenching the dagger so hard, she'd lanced her palm in two places. But even as Selah gasped and led her back to the kitchen to dress it, Ket could feel only relief in seeing Shubert exit the Double T.

And pray that Verity and Ian were far—very far—from his reach.

Four weeks later, the *Inverness* closed in on New York, and Verity wondered if her Harrington cousins would back up their Union Jack as promised. A month into her marriage, she felt stronger, more settled as Mrs. McKintrick. But was she truly ready to utilize her family ties to get into a city rigorously guarded by the Royal Navy? François had told them that three generals were en route to America along with thousands of troops, determined to put down the rebellion before it became a full-fledged war. They had likely arrived by now.

'Twas one thing to consider spying.

'Twas quite another to see it through.

And for the first time, as she stared at the coast just off the starboard side while Ian called for the crew to stow the aft sails, slowing them down, preparing to anchor, her heart seemed as heavy as that curved chunk of iron. For ever since they left Statia, she had known she would need to call upon Albert and Roberta Harrington to gain them access. Perhaps trade to boot. But staring at the coast, for the very first time, she thought of Albert and Roberta and their small babe—her cousin and his wife and child—not as an entry pass but as her family. Family she planned to deceive.

She shuddered, and Ian turned toward her, a question in his eyes. "Ian, you know as well as I that I meant to use my relations as a point of access."

He studied her and then slipped an arm around her waist, pulling her close. "Aye, lass. And now that we are upon their doorstep, you wonder . . ."

She nodded, tears lining her lashes. It both shamed and confounded her. What was this? So late? Why now?

"My grandda spoke of Culloden. He always said 'twas one thing to speak of battle. Another to look your enemy in the eye across the field." Ian bent and kissed her temple. "Ye now are almost looking the enemy in the eye, but fret not over your kin. They shall know nothing of what we are about."

"Even if we are caught?"

He paused to consider that. "They shall know the truth of it then. But we shall make certain that they can claim ignorance."

"I loathe the thought of causing them hardship. The British . . . there may be repercussions for them even harboring the enemy if we are caught."

"Then we must not get caught, lass. We shall slip into that port and, in a few days' time, slip back out. Look at it. The city is engulfed with people, despite the conflict. These new British troops make it all the more a tempest in a teapot. Do you think they shall truly pay attention to us?"

Together they scanned the busy wharf filled with ships, boats, and skiffs of all sizes. And as they did, Verity understood he was right. Walking along the gray planks of the wharf were redcoats, Loyalists, likely some Patriots too. People only trying to get through to the next day, the next week, the next year, hoping all would work out for the best. But what would be best was for the British to return to their own shores. For the Americans to be free to pursue life, liberty, and happiness.

She'd spent the bulk of her time on the voyage reading every pamphlet that Ian had collected. The writings of Locke. The treatises by Adams and Franklin. Political pamphlets illegally printed and covertly distributed. If there were brave souls willing to put themselves out there to do that—to write down their inspired ideas, to print them, to distribute them—how could she shirk her responsibility? All she had to do was introduce her new husband to the Harringtons. Spend a night or two in their home. Secure a hold full of exports for Ian.

And smuggle the missives in from Statia—as well as more back out if it was requested of them.

They had already collected valuable information on various ships of the Royal Navy by cruising along the coast of America to New York. It appeared the majority of them were concentrated in New York, but there had been patrols along the coast of the Carolinas too, obviously bent on attempting to frighten the rebels—who had no formal naval fleet of their own—and prevent smugglers. The thought of it made her blood boil again. What right had they to choke off the Americans' lifeblood in trade?

"I am afraid, Ian," Verity admitted, lifting a hand toward the Union Jack that flew from the main mast. "But I am decided. This is the path I am to follow."

"The path we are to follow," Ian affirmed. "We

shall lie at anchor in the harbor, go ashore, pay the wharfmaster our fees, then be on our way to the Harringtons' house. There you shall stay while I see about delivery of our missives."

"No, Ian. Take me with you. You shall seem far more innocent with a wife on your arm."

He frowned. She was certainly right. Yet he preferred keeping her out of any potential danger.

"It may be safer for me to remain behind, Ian, but not for you, without me. And I do not care to lose my new husband to the gallows. My heart . . ." She hesitated and brought a hand to her swelling throat. "My heart could not take that. You wish to protect me? Protect my heart."

He groaned and pulled her closer. "Ah, lass. What am I to do with you?"

"Make a proper spy out of me," she said, grinning. "Are you to take the letters to the same place as last time?"

"Nay. 'Tis never in the same location. Too dangerous. I am to go to the Dock Ward near Hanover Square, a section of the city held by the Sons of Liberty."

"We are to go to the Dock Ward."

He grimaced. "There we are to find a beggar with a red scarf, who shall send us to the new location."

"And if that beggar is not present?"

"Then we shall wait until tomorrow."

"And if he is not there on the morrow?"

Ian pulled her closer. "Then, dear wife, we shall think on it and pray that the good Lord shows us what to do next. From what I can tell so far, spies often dinnae ken what their next step will be until they lift their foot and search for the right landing spot."

They came around the point where the harbor opened up before them, and Verity gaped. There were nearly a hundred ships! The sailor in the crow's nest called down the names of the ships and their nationalities. Most were from England. But there were also men-of-war from Germany, and a schooner from Spain.

Ian tensed, his forearm becoming like iron beneath her hand. She stared up at him quizzically, but he was looking to the mast.

"Talisker!" he shouted. "What was the name of that last ship?"

The sailor brought his spyglass back to his eye. "The *Juliana* of Spain, Cap'n!"

Ian tore away from her and began pacing the deck, rubbing his face, the back of his neck.

"Ian . . ."

But he was shaking his head, muttering to himself. And he'd grown deathly pale.

"Ian."

He turned wild eyes upon her and finally stopped pacing. "Do ye not know the name of that ship? Have I not told ye? Of her captain?"

A Spanish vessel. Her heart began sinking even before he finished what he had to say.

"Captain Alejandro Diego Santiago," he bit out, his hands circulating as if in a grand introduction. "A privateer. A mercenary, now, I wager, working on behalf of the cursed English," he hissed in her ear, resuming his pacing.

Verity turned back to the rail, sliding her hands outward to keep herself from fainting.

Alejandro Diego Santiago.

A privateer. A pirate. A murderer.

The one who had killed Duncan.

CHAPTER TWENTY-NINE

Ian strode over to Michael, who watched him with questioning eyes over the *Inverness*'s wheel, and leaned in close to the first mate's ear to whisper something in confidence. Michael's head shot up, and he studied the horizon, at last spying the offending ship. While a blush of fury climbed his neck and cheeks, he managed to remain much calmer than Ian—shouting orders to the crew, keeping them on task to bring the *Inverness* to rest in the harbor.

Verity bit her lip. She remembered Ian's promise well, when they had first met. To hunt down the privateer who had murdered his brother and see that the man faced justice. She had seen what he had done to Angus Shubert. Witnessed him, when challenged, putting crewmen in their place with swift, decisive action.

In this case, there was no doubt in her mind that her husband could resort to murder, if it came to it. She simply had never considered that it would happen here. This enemy had been cruising the Barbary Coast as well as Spain's, taking advantage of merchants for years. How had he come to be in the English fold? Why? Were the

British paying more for assistance in corralling the Americans than he could make as a privateer? Or had the British caught him, and this was part of his penance for seizing Duncan's ship? His life? Service in patrolling American shores? Or did he use an alias, disguising his past?

She thought through all the different scenarios that might explain his presence. And ways to keep her husband from him.

"Ian," she said as he paced nearer to her again, chin in hand. She reached out to stop him.

Reluctantly, he slowed, practically shaking he was so tense.

"We must keep our minds on the task at hand. We must," she urged. "Have you not told me that a distracted spy is the first to be caught?"

He clamped his mouth shut, the veins along his temple pulsing with rage. And yet he remained focused on her, as if her words had to seep through many layers of sand before finally filtering through.

"Do you wish to get even with this Santiago?" she said. "Then bite the hand that apparently feeds him."

Ian moved to resume his pacing but then stopped and glanced about. His agitation was drawing the attention of every crewman.

"Come," she coaxed. "Let us go to your cabin, away from prying eyes."

He allowed her to pull him inside their cabin,

where she embraced him once the door closed. He was stiff, his heart pounding in his chest, his skin hot to the touch. But he remained still.

"It could be that we might not even cross paths with him in the city," she said, looking up into his eyes.

"But I wish to cross paths with him, Verity," he gritted out.

"To do what, Ian? To kill him? And then be thrown in jail, or worse? What is it you want more? To serve the rebel cause or to take justice into your own hands?"

"Both."

"You cannot."

"I must!" He ripped away from her and ran a hand through his hair. "Did I not promise ye I would?"

She folded her arms. "You promised a grieving girl, yes. But 'twas not a promise I solicited."

"Do ye not want retribution for Duncan?" he thundered.

She remained still. He was like an avenging angel, righteous in his anger. Yet he was not angry at her, only with the one who had stolen Duncan from them both.

They stood there for a moment. Then she slowly lifted a hand to his cheek, staring into his eyes with love, willing him to feel that more than the present fury overtaking him. "Ian," she whispered.

And with that he seemed to melt, tears lacing

his long lashes. He half groaned, half cried, pulling her into his arms. In turns, writhing away and then nestling close. Partly wanting the comfort, partly rejecting it.

Through it all, she clung to him. "Ian, Ian, Ian," she whispered, hoping his swirling thoughts would center on her calming voice. At last, it seemed to work and he grew still.

She pulled back to look him in the eye again but held firmly to his arms. "I want this captain to face justice, Ian. I do. We were robbed when Duncan was taken from us. But God has seen us to this place. Seen us find our way to each other. Might we trust Him to see justice through when it comes to Captain Santiago?"

Ian grimaced and closed his eyes, then lifted his face to the ceiling, considering, then looked back to her. " 'Tis not the way of a Scotsman, lass. When someone wrongs our kin, it must be set right."

Again, she lifted a hand to his face. "But cannot God himself set it right?"

"Of course He can. Or has He set me in this place, in this hour, to see the task through? Who else might I spare heartache, grief, if I send that monster to the depths?" he asked, pointing toward the side wall of the cabin in the direction they'd last seen Santiago's ship. "I promised ye, lass. I promised the Lord Almighty himself!"

She shook her head slowly. "Oh, Ian. Do you

not see?" She took his hand and put it over her heart. "You might have once gone after Santiago. Done what you feel you ought. But now . . . now, Ian. You have pledged your heart to me; before God you promised it. To love, honor, and cherish, as I did for you. To my mind, that is the reigning promise between us. Not the one you uttered as you set Duncan's affairs in order. And if you go after Santiago, if you are caught and hanged because you murdered a Spanish captain serving the Royal Navy . . . how will that show me I was loved, honored, and cherished? No." She shook her head in solemnity. "Ian Douglass McKintrick, if you do this, it shall be on your account only. Not mine. Because my heart wants nothing more than to spend years at your side. Not to be left a widow after a mere month of marriage. And are the stakes not already high enough?"

He stared down at her, his face rife with confusion. Again, he acquiesced, nodding and pulling her close with a sigh. "Aye, lass. I hear ye. 'Tis your heart I shall guard. Your future. I pledge it," he said, his voice a bit strangled.

And for the first time, she wondered if she believed him.

Because, deep down, she was not convinced that his heart had caught up with his promises.

Ian stifled a groan when he spotted the gray-eyed Lieutenant Ainsley standing beside the bespectacled harbormaster, who was seated at his desk inside the office at the end of the pier. Michael's step faltered, and Verity looked up at each of them—clearly noticing their hesitation—but Ian pressed on.

He smiled and offered a hand to the lieutenant, as if greeting an old friend rather than a man who had practically torn his ship apart, looking for contraband or evidence against him.

Lieutenant Ainsley tepidly returned his handshake. "Captain McKintrick. You have returned." He picked up a ledger and perused it. "I had not received any reports of ships arriving under anything but Spanish or German flags."

"Indeed, sir. The tides have turned for me yet again. On this last trip to the West Indies, I was blessed to take a Nevisian bride," he said, smiling down at Verity and patting her hand on his arm. "May I present my wife, Mrs. Verity McKintrick. Verity, this is Lieutenant Ainsley, and the harbormaster, Mr. Gladstone. And you gentlemen remember my first mate, Mr. McKay, of course."

Verity curtseyed prettily as the lieutenant bowed.

His gray eyes followed her, curiosity making them sparkle. A bit of a smile teased at the corners of his lips as he returned his gaze to Ian. "So you have come back to the English fold? With a Union Jack at your mast and a pretty Nevisian bride on your arm?"

"I have," Ian said. He tucked his chin in what he hoped was a conciliatory expression. "On my last trip, grief had my mind a tad addled. I am happy to report that love has healed what ailed me."

"That'll do it," cheered on the harbormaster with a grin. "A proper wife will always set a man's mind straight."

"Among other things," Verity put in proudly, and all of them laughed.

Such a fine girl, Ian thought.

The lieutenant appeared charmed by her and a bit mollified, but still not entirely ready to give Ian full clearance. "So what brings you back to New York, Captain?"

"Well, trade, of course. My hold is full of rum and sugar that I hope to sell here. My wife is reluctant to leave her sisters, still in Nevis, farther behind than the colonies. So I suppose I shall establish a consistent American-West Indies trade."

The harbormaster and soldier again stared at her.

She smiled shyly, playing the role as they had rehearsed. She brought a hand to her throat, playing with the delicate pearl choker nestled there. "We have spent two years on the island, going on three, rebuilding my father's plantation. 'Tis become home in a way . . . as much as any place other than England can be home. So as much as it pleases me to accompany my husband to the colonies here, I shall be glad of it when Nevis is once again within view."

"Entirely understandable," the lieutenant said. "Is it your family's plantation that has filled Captain McKintrick's hold with sugar?"

"A few hogsheads are from the Double T, but many are from other plantations, traded for horses and leatherworks I imported several months ago."

The harbormaster's grizzled brows rose. "*You* imported?"

"Aye," Ian said, gazing down at her proudly. "Not only is she beautiful and from a fine English family, she has a head for business as well."

"Banning's Bridlery, I called it," she said, smiling up at Ian. "Although I shall have to rename it now, since I am a properly married woman. Ian helped me bring in every bit of the supplies I had in my store. And gentlemen, you cannot imagine how grateful the English gentry of the island were for our service. Why, they hadn't seen such goods in decades!"

"I can only imagine," said the harbormaster in surprise. Clearly, he'd never met a female operating such an enterprise before.

The lieutenant's gray eyes went to her hand, still on Ian's arm, tracing the lines of her pearl wedding ring, Ian thought. "How long have you two been married?"

"A little over a month," Verity said, giving him a shy smile.

"I see . . ." He picked up the ship's logbook from the desk and opened it, paging backward. He looked up at Ian. "You had your first mate conduct the ceremony?" he asked with a frown. His attention flicked over to Verity. "Did you not wish for the sisters you mentioned to be present?"

"It was all very sudden. Hardly ideal. But my Ian was shipping out, and in the moment I simply knew it was right. My heart had become his." Again, she looked up at Ian with such adoration that he had a hard time not escorting her outside for a proper kiss. "And when a woman's heart is in a man's hands, that woman makes certain he does not leave her without it."

Her disarming humor made the rest of them laugh.

Lieutenant Ainsley smiled and shook his head. "You appear to have married quite the woman, Captain McKintrick."

"You have no idea, Lieutenant," Ian said.

But as he returned to scanning the logbook, the lieutenant's smile faded. "You made another stop at St. Eustatius," he said coldly, looking to Ian. "For what reason?"

"To sell horses," Ian said, struggling not to appear nervous. He'd known this would be the hardest part.

"I see nothing here in your logbook of obtaining

397

any horses. And as I recall, you left New York with an empty hold."

"I did. Until I stopped in Mexico for fourteen head. I could not return to Nevis with an empty hold. Not if I meant to claim this bride."

The lieutenant was not dissuaded by Ian's subtle attempt to shift his attention back to Verity. He was again perusing the logbook. "There are no notations about a stop in Mexico."

"There are many *puertos* in Mexico that do not have a fine harbormaster, let alone require paperwork. I was moving quickly, Lieutenant, my mind solely on returning to Nevis."

"And why did you not sell those horses in Nevis?" asked the man.

"Because I had recently imported twelve others," Verity interceded, "and had a contact on Statia who had inquired."

"I can assure you, Lieutenant, that I shall be nothing but aboveboard in my trading as we move forward," Ian said. "After all, I have a wife . . . and a country to support now."

"So you sold those horses on Statia?"

"I did."

"But 'twas *your* idea, Mrs. McKintrick?"

She gave the lieutenant a gentle smile. "I know 'tis difficult to imagine, Lieutenant, but among the islands, 'tis common to trade as you must. Whilst we do our best to trade only with the English and her allies, we are but tiny islands in the midst of a vast sea. Provisions and friends are at times months away. To avoid starvation and to remain solvent, necessity demands occasional, well—*bending* of the rules." She lifted a finger when he began to stutter an angry reply.

"That said, as I understand it, as the great-granddaughter of the Royal Navy Commander Alfred Banning, and the cousin of a staunchly Loyalist family residing right here in the city—the Harringtons—perhaps you know of them?"

Lieutenant Ainsley's mouth clamped shut. Clearly, he had heard of the Harringtons.

"Yes, I see that you do," Verity hurried on. "With such credentials, I would venture to say that my husband shall have full clearance to export and import as he wishes, which will allow us to curtail our trade with those on islands the English consider . . . unsavory."

"Do I have your word on that, Mrs. McKintrick?"

"You do."

"And yours, Captain McKintrick? No more visits to St. Eustatius?"

"You do," Ian said with a nod of deference.

The officer's eyes roved over McKay and back to them. Then he abruptly shut the logbook and handed it to the harbormaster. "Proceed. I shall summon a carriage and escort you to the Harringtons' home myself."

"There is no need for—" Ian began.

"No, no," said the lieutenant slyly, holding up a hand. "I insist."

"But, Lieutenant," Verity said, "I have not had a moment to send them word that we would like to come and call. We have only just arrived."

"I am aware, Mrs. McKintrick. I merely enjoy reunions among family. 'Twill be my joy to see you to their door."

So they had not completely fooled the man. He clearly wanted to test their story by witnessing their reunion. Ian could only hope that the Harringtons would welcome them with open arms . . . and none of the suspicion *this* one carried in spades.

Chapter Thirty

When they exited the city, Ian leaned forward. "Pardon, Lieutenant, but this is not the way to the Harringtons' home."

"They have moved since you were last in New York," said the man seated across from them. " 'Tis lovely country, is it not?"

"Indeed," Ian said. They stared at the huge estates they passed by, interspersed between miles of verdant farmland.

When they turned off the road and onto a long, tree-lined lane that approached a grand country home, Verity gaped and looked to Lieutenant Ainsley in confusion. "Are you quite certain this is my cousin's new address?"

"Rest assured, Mrs. McKintrick," he said, "we are in the right place. Your cousin's fortune has most assuredly seen an upturn. He is our newest city alderman. With the office came the ability to purchase this estate."

"I see," Verity said. "What a pleasant surprise."

"Is it not?" Lieutenant Ainsley said, exiting the coach and extending his hand toward her.

Belatedly she accepted it, took her skirts in her other hand, and floated down the groom's provided steps as her mother had taught her. *Mother,* she thought. Mother smiling, clapping over Verity's clumsily performed harpsichord piece as if she were Handel himself. *Mother.* She would have loved to be here. She hoped the Harringtons would welcome her as they had before, despite the awkward, unannounced surprise of their arrival.

She had gathered this was Lieutenant Ainsley's intention, such awkwardness. He only wished to witness the extent of it. She thanked God that she had been with the Harringtons just this spring. Surely they would be a bit shocked seeing them at their door, and yet they would show nothing but a warm welcome toward their kin.

After getting the nod from the lieutenant, a second man knocked on the door. It was only then Verity realized that Ian's hand was holding overly tight to her elbow and that they were surrounded by British soldiers. She swallowed hard.

An elderly butler in livery opened the door, and his round, droopy-lidded eyes did their best to widen in the face of so many crimson uniforms surrounding them. "May I be of service?"

"Yes," Verity said. "I am Mrs. Verity Banning McKintrick, and this is my husband, Captain Ian McKintrick. We have come to call upon my cousins. Are they at home?"

The man perused the soldiers again before returning to Verity. "Master Harrington is away.

Mrs. Harrington is at home but was not expecting visitors." He shot her a harrowing look down his nose. "Might I escort you to the parlor to see if she is willing to receive you?"

"Indeed. We have but only arrived. I would have sent word, but the kind Lieutenant Ainsley here insisted that he escort us directly to the bosom of my cousins."

"I see," he said, seeming to have overcome his agitation. "This way, please."

He brought them into the grand home, and Verity paused. There was something in the scale of the entry, the sheer size of the house that sent her hurtling back in time to Hartwick Manor. Nothing in Nevis had compared to it. Most buildings on the island were fairly new, the older structures having rotted or been leveled by hurricanes within the last twenty years. This was a home—a mansion—that had stood for far longer.

They were escorted into the large parlor, its ceiling twenty feet high and lined with brocade panels. Verity took a seat on a beautiful settee. Ian stood beside her, his tricorn under his arm. Lieutenant Ainsley did the same with his hat in the room's opposite corner, where he could observe both their hostess and the McKintricks upon their meeting.

Despite the fact that she had seen Roberta not three months before, Verity felt a cold trickle of sweat roll down her spine. *Do not rehearse disaster,* she told herself silently. A phrase she had learned from Keturah. But what was one supposed to do if disaster was clouding one's mind? *Imagine anticipation. Resolution.*

Roberta arrived finally, bustling in with surprise and delight on her face. "Oh, dear cousin!" she cried. A maid followed behind, and Verity grinned when she saw that Roberta had delivered a chubby, curly-haired angel now nestled in the maid's arms.

"Oh, congratulations, Roberta!" she said, embracing her cousin before turning to the nursemaid. "What did you name him?"

"Francis. Is he not a giant among babies?"

Verity laughed. "Indeed. Mrs. Roberta Harrington, may I introduce my husband, Captain Ian McKintrick. We were married a month past and have only just arrived in the harbor by ship. We meant to send you word before coming to call, but Lieutenant Ainsley insisted on escorting us directly to your doorstep. I beg your pardon for the intrusion."

"Intrusion?" Roberta drew back in dismay. "Look about us, cousin. We have nothing but rooms upon rooms in this home. You simply must stay with us during your visit to New York. Please say you will."

"We would be most delighted, thank you," Ian said.

"And with my duty done, I shall be off," Lieutenant Ainsley said, shifting his tricorn in his hands. He glanced at Ian, then Verity, clearly not mollified, but robbed of any excuse to remain. "Good day, Captain and Mrs. McKintrick."

"Good day, Lieutenant," Ian said. "Would you be so kind as to send your men in with our trunks?"

Ainsley hesitated and then tucked his chin. "But of course. Good eve, Mrs. Harrington."

"Good evening, Lieutenant. We are to host an officers' ball in a few days. Consider yourself invited. Bring a pretty girl on your arm."

He pulled on his chin. "A tall order in this town, where there are far more men than eligible women."

Verity tilted her chin and tapped it. "You cut a fetching figure. I wager you have a chance."

His brows lifted and he laughed, this time more outright. He glanced at Ian.

They shared a tentative smile, and Verity's heart lurched. It was happening. They had made their way into the city with their missives for the rebels intact. One was in the hem of her broad skirts, the other in her petticoats. They'd guessed that no soldier would dare to search her as thoroughly as they might her husband or his first mate.

Lieutenant Ainsley bowed to each of the ladies, placed his hat on his head, and strode out the door, not looking back. Verity did not doubt that he would return for the ball—with a pretty girl on his arm or not—solely for the rationale to observe them further.

She turned to Roberta as the butler closed the tall doors of the parlor behind him, leaving them alone. "So," she said lightly, "Albert is now an alderman? Much has transpired since I saw you last. You left behind your doubts about the Crown's right to rule here? Taxation?"

Roberta paused, but then a catlike smile pulled wide her lips. "For all intents and purposes," she whispered, sinking down beside Verity in a whirlpool of silk skirts. She took her hand, and her blue eyes twinkled as she looked at Ian. "I know who you are, Captain. It is thanks to you that the rebels were able to secure ammunitions. It is thanks to you that they knew General Cornwallis was en route."

Ian rose, alarm in his eyes.

"No, no, sit," she said, smiling, looking at Verity and back to Ian. "You need not fear, dear ones." She lifted her hands. "You are in the company of family who wants to see America free as much as any other Patriot. But Albert was persuaded to profess his loyalty to the Crown in order to help his fellow Americans in the best way possible, to hear firsthand what our enemies are planning." Her smile widened. "And you cannot imagine all he has learned already."

· · ·

Verity leaned back in surprise. She looked to the closed door through which Lieutenant Ainsley had disappeared just minutes before. But Roberta was already on the move toward a corner desk. She uncorked a bottle of ink, lifted a quill, and hovered over the paper a moment before beginning to write in mad haste.

"How long will you be in port?" she asked.

"Two, perhaps three days," Ian said.

Her quill scratched across the paper and then she paused to dip it in ink again. "Might you stay longer? A week perhaps?" she said as she wrote. "There is much to pass along to our friends, yet we have not found a satisfactory route to get messages to them without arousing suspicion." She glanced over her shoulder, eyes round with earnestness. "You two are a godsend. We have so much to share! So much that will aid the cause. But Albert believes he is frequently being followed, and once or twice I have wondered the same."

Verity and Ian could do little else but nod. She was with them? *They* were with them—both Roberta and Albert? Verity did not know what to say. She did not want to impede upon the progress of Roberta's letter, which was perhaps even more important and timely than what she carried in her skirts and petticoats.

She lifted a cup of tea to her lips, not quite

tasting it, simply trying to imagine her prim-and-proper cousin's wife, a young mother, the mistress of this grand home, willing to put it all at risk in order to help the cause. Her resolve and courage strengthened Verity's own.

Reaching the end of her page, Roberta sat back from the missive, letting it dry. She turned to them, any trace of humor gone from her expression. "You two fully understand the gravity of this mission? Both what might be accomplished and yet also the risk involved?" She gestured over her shoulder. "Only yesterday, Albert learned of General Burgoyne's primary mission goals, troop numbers, and armament. He has been going mad trying to figure out a way to send this on and tasked me with the effort. Now here you are, like messenger angels."

"Indeed," Ian said. "We understand the risks, madame. And if we can aid the rebels in bringing an early end to Burgoyne's mission—" he stopped to look at Verity, waited for her to nod her agreement before finishing—"then we accept the risk as worthy."

"Excellent," Roberta said, turning to sand the letter to absorb any remaining wet ink. "Where are you to meet your contact?"

"The Dock Ward, near Hanover Square. A beggar in a red scarf?"

She nodded as she folded the letter and dripped wax on the fold, then stamped it with a family herald featuring a lion. "You shall need a reason to be near there should someone follow you as well. I would suggest that tomorrow you escort your wife, Captain, to the haberdashery named Charlotte's a block to the west of the Dock Ward. While your wife tries on one hat after another, for she is quite particular and will be sending both clerks after countless hats trying to find just the right one"—she winked at Verity—"you might slip out the back door for some 'fresh air.' Ask the proprietor, Mr. Mosely, where to go for a pleasant stroll. He shall likely suggest you exit through the back and walk to a little park a block distant. He did so for Albert when we last visited."

To Ian, Roberta said, "Before you do, go to the front window and study everyone outside. See if anyone loiters, keeping an eye on the store; they may well be watching you. From the back of the haberdashery, head east down the alley, then north three blocks and then east again to the river. Be certain you are not followed. If you are, simply return to the haberdashery, and we shall find another way. But if you are in the clear, give our contacts both this"—she reached back to grab hold of her letter—"as well as what you have brought from the French."

Verity gaped at her. "Cousin, such intrigue rolls off your tongue with great ease!"

Roberta smiled. "Never had I imagined this

would be my lot in life. But I confess, I enjoy it ever so much more than the dull necessities of running this massive home and fulfilling the role as the newest alderman's wife. Still, as I said, Albert's new position is bringing us the most spectacular information. Indeed, together, I believe we can help turn the tide of this impending war before it even begins."

"I hope you are right," Ian said.

"But what if you are discovered?" Verity asked.

"God shall see us through," Roberta said. "For it must be He who has placed each of us in these positions. And if not us, then who?"

CHAPTER THIRTY-ONE

"Smile, my love," Ian said, taking her arm. "We are simply two newlyweds out and about on a beautiful autumn day in New York." They reached the bottom of the mansion's front steps and the Harringtons' own carriage, pulled by a beautiful, massive Friesian gelding.

Verity could not stop herself. She stepped forward to the magnificent animal with his glossy black, braided mane, and cooed, "Well, good day to you, handsome boy," she said, stroking the horse's cheek. She looked up at the driver. "He is a fine, fine horse. Is he difficult to manage?"

"At times," said the driver. "He does not care for yapping dogs. But he seems to favor pulling the carriage."

"He would be happiest if you gave him full rein and the chance to gallop, I wager," she said, running a gloved hand along his sleek neck and admiring the thickness of his chest.

"Quite so, ma'am," said the driver with some surprise.

She looked back to her husband, who wryly shook his head. "I can take the horsewoman away from her stables, though not far from the nearest horse."

"Indeed." Verity took his hand in her own, her skirts in the other hand, and climbed into the carriage with its tidy concealed steps that folded away beneath. "Anyone who knows me would expect such a thing, would they not?" she said as Ian settled in beside her.

"Very true," Ian replied, smiling down at her as the driver set off for the haberdashery in Hanover Square. "Your color is quite high, Mrs. McKintrick."

"Is it?" Alarmed, she put a hand to her cheek.

" 'Tis." Ian squeezed her hand. "But do not fear it. I find such a look quite fetching. A perfect day to purchase a beautiful new hat for my bride."

She smiled conspiratorially at him. If he thought her fetching, she did not have anything on him. They had gone that morning to shop for him, purchasing a new shirt, coat, and breeches—which were tucked into shiny black leather boots—as well as a finer coat and shirt for the ball tomorrow night that the tailor was now altering. If anyone had bothered to follow them about, they must be dreadfully bored. And it would make their visit to the haberdashery all the more believable, as it was simply more of the same.

Yet Verity shivered at the thought of anyone following them. Again and again she resisted the urge to look about, to see if anyone bothered to trail them. They had not detected anybody, but that was not to say potential spies could not still be close by. Judging from Lieutenant Ainsley's suspicious reaction to them yesterday, Verity would not doubt if the man had set someone after them himself, despite their warm welcome from the good alderman's wife.

They moved down the busy streets, every bit as refined and varied as London's own. Patrols of British soldiers were visible every few blocks, most congregating to talk and laugh among themselves, utterly at ease in this city that Verity was coming to view as occupied by the enemy. For that was what it was—an overbearing, tyrannical army forcing others to bend to their will. What reason had they to be here, so far from their own land? Dictating with whom these people might trade? Forcing them to pay taxes for governance they had not requested? They were little better than the ancient Romans, greedily claiming all that fell into their view as their own, and making the conquered pay for it.

At Charlotte's Haberdashery, the driver pulled to the side, drew up on the reins and secured them. He climbed down and opened the narrow door, allowing Ian to descend first. Ian paused and looked about him, always vigilant yet appearing from the outset naught but the doting husband. While he offered his hand to her, Verity could see his eyes shifting first over her left shoulder, then her right. But then his attention was solely on her, smiling at her with pure satisfaction. She knew it was part of the afternoon's charade, but she could feel the heat in her cheeks. Her husband was simply so handsome, no one could deny it. It still brought her up short, on occasion, that he was truly hers, and she his.

He gave her a puzzled look as the driver hurried back to his seat, clearly embarrassed at witnessing such intimacy. "What is it, wife?"

She heaved a sigh. "I am startled to find that I seem to fall more deeply in love with you, husband, with each passing day." She took his arm and they began walking together toward the store. "See that you are not caught," she whispered, "for that would be a most tragic end to our tale of love."

He turned to her at the door and took her hand. He brought it to his lips and kissed it, all the while staring into her eyes. "I shall return to see your selection of just the right hat as quickly as I can."

She grinned, knowing the clerks inside were likely watching. "This is a new side of you, Captain McKintrick. I never knew you so favored the finer things."

"No?" he said, opening the door for her. "Witness the fine lass I chose as my wife," he whispered in her ear as she passed him, using a gravelly tone that sent a shiver of delight down her back.

She was surrounded by hats of every sort. Verity could see numerous bonnets, wide hats meant to be tied at the back of the neck, as well as tiny, ornamental confections to be worn at the top of a highly stacked coiffure. She narrowed in on that option. If she were to keep the haberdasher's hairdresser busy coming up with the right curl and stacks, that would give Ian hours in which to complete his task.

Ian followed behind her, with Roberta's sea green ball gown that she had lent to Verity wrapped in linens to keep it clean. In a bag on his other arm were the stays and panniers—all of which she would insist on donning in order to choose the right hat—and all of which would take time.

The proprietor—a lanky, hawk-nosed gentleman named Mosely—met them at the door. He was dressed in a rust-colored coat, embroidered along the lapel in the same color, just enough embellishment to make him stand out. He wore his own hair, but it was rolled at both temples. "Good day," he said, learning their names and smiling in appreciation when he discovered who had sent them.

He took Verity's arm and led her to a room with more than two hundred hats on display. "Tell me what you seek, madame, and I shall see that you are satisfied." Over his shoulder he snapped his fingers, and a girl set off to the back room, presumably to fetch something.

"That is most assuring," Verity crooned. "We have only just arrived from the Indies, and my cousin graciously invited us to attend the officers' ball. I have borrowed this gown from my cousin, but I wish for the right hair and hat to make it my own."

"Completely understandable," said Mr. Mosely. "We have a woman who does the most exquisite turns with a lady's hair. Would you care for me to summon her?"

"Oh, that would be grand," Verity said. "And if 'tis not too much trouble, I would like to don this gown so that together we can create the perfect look, head to toe. After all, my new husband shall be meeting a great number of important people at this function, and I cannot afford to present myself as anything short of a jewel in his crown."

Ian gave her a wan smile that faded quickly— part of the act they had rehearsed. "Is it truly necessary, darling, to go to such lengths? We shall be here for hours. Why not simply show the good Mr. Mosely your gown and—"

"And leave here with a hat that is good but not the perfect accent to my hair?" Verity asked huffily.

"No, dear, but—"

"Or have all the New York ladies talking of my poor choice behind their fans?"

"Of course not," Ian sighed, looking a bit beleaguered. "That would be most shortsighted. Take all the time you need, my love." He nodded at the proprietor. "Please, Mr. Mosely, proceed."

Clearly accustomed to accommodating fussy women, Mosely gave him a knowing glance over his spectacles and gestured to a seat in the corner. "My girl shall be along shortly with tea," he said. "And for you, good sir, I shall bring you something a mite stronger."

"I would appreciate that," Ian said, stiffly taking a seat and propping his new silver-tipped cane against the wall beside him.

A girl in a white bonnet and crisp white apron arrived to show Verity to a dressing room. Half an hour later, after assistance with the wider panniers and tight stays that brought her waist in and made her hips appear twice as wide, she was in the gown and laced up. She emerged into the main room of the shop, and Ian stood, smiling at her. "Pretty as can be," he announced.

"Ah, not quite yet," said Mosely, lifting a finger. "You have yet to see what we can do to enhance a woman's beauty, Captain McKintrick." He moved to a tray and poured an inch of liquor into a crystal glass. "A bit of liquid patience," he said, offering the glass to Ian.

"Good man," Ian said, toasting him. "Clearly

you have dealt with more than one husband in this shop."

Mosely gave him a smile more from his eyes than his lips. "More than one for certain." He turned to Verity and gestured to an older woman behind him. "This is my hairdresser, Mrs. Oren. She does the hair of every fine lady in town and has agreed to fit you into her schedule to make you ready for the upcoming ball."

"That is most kind of you, Mrs. Oren," Verity said with a nod.

"Your gown is a stunning color and shape on you, Mrs. McKintrick. What good fortune that Mrs. Harrington had it for you to borrow. Tell me . . . to which of these hats are you drawn?"

Verity swept around the room, admiring first a wide, lace-trimmed bonnet.

"Ahh, but I fear 'tis not quite right with the gown," Mr. Mosely said. "That is meant for a more demure day dress."

"Oh, of course," Verity said. "What of this large one over here?" She pointed to a grotesquely decorated hat, loaded with faux green grapes and vines. "It has some green in it."

Mr. Mosely pinched his nose and looked at her as if she were sincerely trying his patience. He glanced at Ian as he sipped, then sucked in a long breath and turned back to her. "Mrs. McKintrick, if you would be so kind as to take a seat here," he said, gesturing to a stool. "Allow Mrs. Oren to attend your hair, and I believe you will gain insight as to how fashion has changed whilst you've languished in the Indies."

"Oh! Of course!" she said, dutifully taking her seat.

Mrs. Oren moved a table in beside the stool and set out a myriad selection of hairdressing tools. In short order she had unpinned Verity's long sable hair and combed it out. Ian rose as she did so, meticulously studying each hat and bringing the occasional selection to Verity to judge. With each one, Verity found a reason for fault. He reached the center window and continued to pretend to search for the right hat, but Verity knew he was now searching the street for anyone who might be watching them. To distract Mr. Mosely, she asked him how long he had been in business, what had drawn him to become a haberdasher, why it was named Charlotte's . . . anything she could think of to keep the man's attention on her, not Ian.

"What about this one, darling?" Ian asked, lifting a perfectly horrible crimson hat with a red silk cardinal perched on a branch. "Perhaps it would contrast with the gown?"

"Perhaps it would be best if I suggest the right ensemble?" Mr. Mosely said, taking the hat from him—a hat that Verity claimed she despised— with an indignant air.

"Ach, well," Ian said, blinking in surprise, clearly trying to keep a straight face. "I suppose

I dinnae ken a good hat from a poor one. May I make use of your privy and then get some fresh air out back? By the time I'm through, perhaps you shall have transformed my wife as Mrs. Harrington promised."

"That we shall, Captain," Mr. Mosely said eagerly. "The privy is down the hall and to the right. The back door leads to an alley. A block to the west is a fine little park if you would like a place to stroll."

"Excellent," Ian said. "I shall return shortly, wife, and see what magic these two have conjured."

Verity watched him walk out, her head held firmly in place by the formidable Mrs. Oren. And as he disappeared from view, she began to pray.

CHAPTER THIRTY-TWO

Ian spotted the elderly man in the red scarf, with an upturned hat held out toward passersby. He took a final look around, confident that no one had followed him—after all, he'd taken three loops around the small park and seen only two pairs of women, followed by their chaperones.

He hurried across the street, dodging between oncoming carriages, wagons pulled by mules, and men on horseback. Even this far from the center of town, the city clearly thrived, none the worse off for the war as yet. He settled into a pace he hoped bespoke of a further goal, then paused and fished in his pocket for a coin when he reached the beggar.

"Down on your luck, man?" he said, just as François had coached him.

"Cannot be farther down than this," he returned, arching his back with a hand to it as if it ached.

"Perhaps you ought to consult a doctor about that," Ian said.

The man's red-rimmed eyes met his as he recited the code words, "Doctors take a heavier coin purse than I have."

"This might help," Ian said, dropping a silver farthing into the man's hat.

"Right kind of you, sir." The man glanced around at the people about him. "There's a doctor two blocks south of here who might see to my aches and pains."

"I hope he shall," Ian said, already on the move, silently repeating the directions. *Two blocks to the south.* Would he know where to go from there? His eyes scanned the three- and four-story brick buildings about him, some of which seemed to be precariously leaning. Laundry was hung from lines strung between the buildings. The streets smelled of refuse, and worse. Rats scurried through piles of garbage. Clearly, he had left the finer part of town and entered the less desirable.

Which was good, he told himself. Soldiers and Tories would not favor such a place.

He sensed the two men behind him as he walked. He took a turn before he'd reached the two-block mark, not wishing to lead the enemy to his contact's door, and gripped his cane tighter. He carried no sword or pistol—given he had no cause—only his hidden dagger. But the cane might prove a decent weapon if it came down to fighting his way out and running to retrieve Verity.

The men followed his every turn and closed the distance between them until Ian was forced to whirl around and face the two. "What is this?" Ian ground out. "Why do you follow me?"

One was shorter, stockier. "We are but curious, sir. What is a fine gentleman like yourself doing in this part of town?"

Ian studied one and then the other. Were they friends? Or foes?

"I was curious as well," he replied. "I wished to know if there is a doctor close by who might help the old beggar with the red scarf. The man seems to be in great pain."

The shorter one folded his arms and nodded. "There is a doctor about. Let us show you to his door." The two took the lead, gesturing for him to follow.

Withdrawing the sgian dubh from his waistband in one hand and gripping the cane in the other, Ian grimly followed. Was this a trap? Or were they but scouts, an outer protective layer for the rebels somewhere within the tenements of this block?

It was with some relief that they returned to the building where he saw a faded sign beside the front door. *Marcus Chellis, Doctor of Medicine.*

The shorter man rapidly knocked on the door three times, paused, then followed with two slower knocks. In a moment, the door cracked open.

"Gentleman here to see the doc," said the shorter man, his companion apparently mute muscle.

The door opened, and Ian saw it was a comely maid, a girl of about sixteen in a neat apron and bonnet that made her blue eyes fairly shimmer. She reminded him of Verity's younger sister, Selah. "Follow me," she said, allowing her eyes to drift down his fine new coat and back up to brazenly study his face.

He turned to close the door behind them and saw the two men had already disappeared. Scouts for certain.

The girl led him into the kitchen, where three men sat eating a meal of stew and ale. Together they looked up at him, and Ian recognized Michael's grandfather, as well as the leader of the last meeting he'd attended, Rupert Smith. The third was a stranger.

"Why, if 'tisn't Captain McKintrick!" enthused the elderly McKay, rising with a grin. "Come, come. Have ye brought my Michael wit' ye, lad?" he asked, clapping him on the shoulder and looking to the hallway expectantly as Ian shook the hands of the other men.

"Not this time, no. I have but slipped away from my wife at the haberdashery in order to bring you these." He used the small dagger to slice through the inside hem of his new coat, fished out the two missives—one from the French, the other from Roberta—and handed them over. As soon as he was done, the blonde gestured for him to give her his coat, making a needle-and-thread motion to tell him she would mend it.

The men pulled over a candle from the mantel and set about frantically reading, passing the letters around the circle.

"General Washington needs word of that one," said McKay, pointing to Roberta's note. "And General Arnold that other. This," he said, lifting the third to Ian, "we could have used a month past." He rose and threw it in the fire.

What did that mean? Ian wondered. "We came as fast as the *Inverness* could carry us."

"Aye, laddie, I wager ye did," McKay said. " 'Tis the curse of time, this business. We are perpetually behind."

"Perhaps I can provide a temporary reprieve," Ian said. "For my wife is cousins with Albert Harrington, and he and his wife are dedicated to the cause."

The men shared a gleeful look. "Aye, laddie," McKay said. "We are aware of the Harringtons."

"We have reason to tarry a week here in the city," Ian went on. "Perhaps while we idle, we can bring you more information in a far timelier manner. Mrs. Harrington said they come by information almost daily but have not had a way to reach you because of those who keep an eye on them."

"I can imagine," said Smith. "For their sake alone you cannot come here again. There are those who shall remember you, especially in your finery." He put chin in hand, thinking. "Does Mrs. Harrington assist at the workhouse in Fly Market on occasion? Provide blankets or food or medicine? I've seen many a gentlewoman do so."

Ian shook his head. "I do not know."

"Could you convince her to take on the task?"

"Possibly."

Smith rose and went to a cabinet, pulling out two bottles. "This," he said, holding up one, "is invisible ink. And this," he added, holding up the other, "makes it visible."

Ian drew back in surprise. "Truly?"

"Truly," he said, grinning. "Now the Harringtons can write a letter in invisible ink, and should they be caught, there'd be nothing to see on the page. But it still might arouse suspicion if they had a blank piece of paper on their person. So I prefer they use *this*." He retrieved another bottle labeled *Alum* from the cabinet. "Mixed with a bit of vinegar, they can write messages on hard-boiled eggs, with your women carrying them to the workhouse as an act of charity."

"No one would think twice about it," Ian said.

The man nodded.

Ian studied the bottle of alum, wondering how it worked.

"On the outside," continued the man, "the eggs appear untouched. But once we peel them, the messages shall be visible on the flesh of the egg."

"Do ye believe your wife or Mrs. Harrington would be willing?" McKay asked.

Ian sat back in his chair. "The question is, am I willing to put my wife in that position?"

McKay leaned forward on the table. "*Ach*. The lass is already up to her ears in eels, lad. What harm would there be in this? They're eggs fo' the poor!"

Ian bit his lip and turned the bottle in his hand, considering. " 'Tis entirely invisible? No one would know anything had been drawn on the eggs?"

"Unless a man holds it in just the right light," McKay said. "Which is another reason to use the eggs. You could judge it for yourself before the lasses are on their way. So far, not a woman working for the cause has been caught. Granted, there have been but two, but I dinnae think the Brits yet suspect we would resort to such tactics."

Ian nodded thoughtfully. "So, eggs on the morrow, should Mrs. Harrington be willing. In three days' time, a ball is to take place at the Harringtons'. Perhaps you can arrange for someone to be there to meet my wife, Verity, should we have more information to pass on?"

"Aye," McKay said. "The lass who now mends your coat? We shall send her as additional kitchen help—for both the workhouse tomorrow and the ball in three days. The workhouse always takes anyone they can find, and I know the woman who manages staff for such a grand party. When the clock strikes eleven, tell your Verity to ask for a cuppa fresh tea at the door of the kitchen, claiming a dry throat. I'll be sure my girl is there to attend to her."

"Understood."

"The girl will tell her where to meet the following day should ye have more information. Ye yourself can maneuver about, attempting to overhear anything relevant. The deeper the men get in their cups, the looser their lips shall become."

"Agreed."

"Mind ye, lad. Have the *Inverness* manned and ready to set sail at a moment's notice," McKay said gravely. "These are dangerous waters, here in the city. And out there, the Royal Navy patrols. If ye or your Verity are caught . . . ach, weel, you'd best haul sail and do your best to outrun every redcoat you see."

"I cannot flee back to Nevis. I ran into some . . . trouble there. And if I go to Statia, I shall not be able to return to New York again. There is a lieutenant attending the harbormaster who already suspects me."

"Then your days of bringing us information from the French might be at an end, laddie. We shall find other ways for ye to aid the cause. Ye must sail to Philadelphia. Introduce yourself to the Continental Congress there. Offer your ship in service. Randolph, Franklin, Hancock, and the rest will be glad to receive ye."

"They are forming their own navy?"

"As we speak," said McKay. "General Washington is outfitting six ships at his own expense. In the meantime, perhaps ye can be a privateer, doing your best to hassle the Brits for once."

Ian lifted a brow. "Perhaps. I would need to get Verity to safety first."

"Take the lass to Statia. Or Martinique."

"I should not leave her in Philadelphia?"

"Nay." He glanced back at the other two. " 'Tis only a matter of time before every city along the coast shall face battle. We've encountered skirmishes to date. But the Continental Army is rising, and with the aid of information like this," he said, waving the letter from Statia, "they have a better chance of showing the British that we mean to see them gone for good."

The other man stepped closer. "General Arnold is soon to make his way to Quebec. He aims to win that territory so that the Brits cannot retreat there. We have French support, as well as the Indians. But this other letter," he said, pointing to the one from Roberta, "would indicate that the British know what he is about, despite his attempts to covertly gather supplies and troops. See what you can discover about that at the party, eh?"

The blonde arrived and wordlessly handed Ian

back his coat and then disappeared through the same door.

"Consider it done." Ian slipped the bottle of ink in his pocket and then paused at the door. "Might I ask a favor?"

"Indeed, laddie," said McKay.

"There is a Spanish schooner in port. Do any of you know of her captain, a man named Santiago?"

McKay looked back at his compatriots, but all three shook their heads. "What is it ye wish to learn?" the old man asked Ian.

"The reason he is here, and why the British have embraced him," he said.

McKay nodded and studied Ian. "Ye have run across this man before?"

"He is the privateer who murdered my brother, Duncan, before taking his ship. My brother who served on behalf of the Crown! Now here he is, likely dining at a British general's table," he spat, shaking his head.

McKay's grizzled brows drew together. "Ach, that's a terrible thing, laddie, a terrible thing. But I ask ye—can ye set it aside for now? On behalf of the cause? There shall come a time for retribution. But for now, more than anything we need what ye and your wife can provide. Can ye avoid this Santiago in the coming week?"

Ian inhaled deeply, thinking over his words. The man was right, of course. Echoing what

430

Verity herself had urged him to do. *Lord, help me,* he prayed silently as he left the men behind. Because it would have to be the Lord himself who stopped Ian if he came face-to-face with Captain Santiago.

Mrs. Oren had added a round ball of woolen bunting and wrapped Verity's hair around it, essentially adding a foot of height to her hair. " 'Tis not perfect yet," said the small woman, standing back to admire it, "but perhaps you can imagine now what it shall look like?"

"Yes," Verity breathed.

Clearly pleased, Mr. Mosely stepped forward with a tiny sea green hat encrusted with white, pink, and purple shells and three long and wide white feathers. A group of soldiers marched past the front window, and Verity eyed them anxiously, wondering how much longer Ian would be.

"Mrs. McKintrick?" Mr. Mosely said, waiting for her response.

She hurriedly lifted her mirror again, wondering how such a ridiculous look had become the height of fashion. "Is it not perfect?" she said, forcing a smile. "Perfect for a sea captain's bride, yes?"

"Exactly what I decided," Mr. Mosely said, clapping his hands in delight.

The bell over the door jingled as new customers entered the shop, giving Verity a welcome

431

reprieve. She'd forgotten what it meant to keep up with the latest fashions. Her stays bit into her rib cage, her panniers seemed unwieldly—fairly trapping her in the chair with their width—and her hair . . . why, how was she to dance without fear that the whole thing might topple to one side?

In Nevis, the ladies did their best to keep up with English fashion. But there, the heat kept such nonsense to a minimum. There, she might don Roberta's fine gown and perhaps the panniers—indeed, they might provide welcome ventilation beneath the skirts—but if the heat and humidity did not make short work of Mrs. Oren's hairdressing, the wind surely would. Suddenly, she had such a terrible longing for the islands— for her sisters, for the Double T, for the green of the cane and palms, for the salty scent of the ocean on the breeze—that it made her feel ill.

She lifted a hand to her cheek.

"Ma'am?" asked Mrs. Oren. "You appear ghastly pale." She hurried over to the pot and poured a cup of tea, then hastened back with it.

But then something made Verity's heart lurch.

A young woman speaking to Mr. Mosely had just introduced her friend and their escort.

A Captain Alejandro Santiago.

CHAPTER THIRTY-THREE

Verity froze and then choked on a sip of her tea, swallowing it wrong.

Mrs. Oren patted her on the back. "There, there, Mrs. McKintrick," she said. "Are you quite all right?"

"Yes," Verity sputtered, then shook her head. "Please," she said, "I think my stays are too tight. Might you assist me?"

"Yes, of course," said the woman, escorting her to the dressing room. Behind them, Santiago laughed—a deep, genuine laugh. Why had she thought he would sound more . . . shrill? Maniacal?

From the door of the dressing room, she dared to look back. He was flirting with both of the young women, pretending to try on a ridiculously dandified hat, which set the girls into a fit of giggles. He smiled at them and then looked over the head of the one to his right, directly at Verity.

For a moment their eyes locked, and Verity forgot to breathe.

He was handsome, and for some reason that made her furious. She had imagined him ugly, grotesque even. The personification of his evil deeds. He gave her a tiny smile and nod, curiosity rife in his dark-lashed eyes as he returned her stare. His expression was pure flirtation. Nothing onerous. Only light. As if he had not a care in the world. As if he had not murdered the man who had once been her intended.

Swallowing hard against the rising bile in her throat, she hurried into the room, past the waiting Mrs. Oren, who looked to Captain Santiago and back to her again, wondering what might be transpiring.

"Was the hat to your satisfaction, then?" Mrs. Oren asked, following her into the dressing room.

"Indeed," Verity replied, relieved when the door closed behind the older woman. But she was terrified her husband would enter the shop again and find Santiago there. She forced herself to find appropriate things to say. "Please have Mr. Mosely wrap it up for me. And might you come to the Harrington home on Fifth Avenue the morning of the ball to attend my hair?"

"Not in the morning, but I could attend you at one."

"One. Excellent." Verity sat down and buried her trembling hands in her skirts as Mrs. Oren carefully unpinned the hat.

"Would you like me to leave your hair up, Mrs. McKintrick?"

"No, thank you. Let this remain a special surprise for the ball, yes?"

"Of course. I'll go fetch my brush and comb to set it back into your net."

After the woman left the dressing room, Verity rushed over to the door to peek into the shop even as she madly tried to untie the laces behind her back. If she could get undressed and into her own gown, she might be able to intercept Ian before he entered the place.

Because despite his promises, she did not trust that if he faced Santiago now, here, he would not let his fury rule his heart. She herself faltered, one moment thinking of Roberta's excitement over finally having a means to pass along critical information to the rebels—and they should do naught to ruin that opportunity—the next thinking that the man had no right to be going about his life, flirting, shopping, as if he had not done such terrible things to others. Wanting Ian to come immediately. Then thinking that would be the worst possible thing. If Ian were to attack Santiago, he would be thrown into jail . . . perhaps the same one where she'd first met him.

Verity turned to lean against the wall, remembering how he'd been then. Lost in grief and anger . . . and how far he'd come. He had a direction now. A cause to fight for other than a personal vendetta. Duncan was already lost to them. Together, they could protect many, many American men who still lived.

The cause, she told herself as Mrs. Oren entered

the room again. *The cause. Concentrate on the cause.*

Mrs. Oren quickly and efficiently took down her hair and put it in a knot, securing it under a net that she pinned in place. Then she helped her out of Roberta's ball gown and back into her own day dress, which she could lace up herself, given that the laces were low on the back. Verity hurriedly pulled on her short boots and buckled them, then stood, wondering how she might address Captain Santiago or if she ought to at all.

But as she left the dressing room, she saw him holding the door for his two female charges. They were leaving, still chattering away. He closed the door gently behind him, and once again their eyes met and held for a moment. This time he did not smile. In fact, there was a trace of sorrow in them, she thought—or had that been just a trick of the wavy imperfections of the glass?

"He is quite a man, that Spaniard," Mr. Mosely said. "He has brought more than one young lady by to purchase a hat. I wager it has made him the sweetheart of New York."

"Oh?" Verity said.

"I have not met a young lady yet who is not impressed by such a useful gift."

"I can only imagine," she said, bringing her purse to the counter.

"He tried to purchase your fine seashell hat."

"Wh-what?"

"Yes," Mr. Mosely said with satisfaction in his tone, fingering the little hat and raising it to the light. "He has quite an affection for my art. He asked who would be wearing this particular piece." He gingerly set it back in its box, surrounded by crumpled fabric to keep it centered, and then fastened the lid.

"Did you tell him my name?" Verity asked, her voice noticeably anxious.

He glanced up at her. "Why, yes. I did. Did I err in that?"

"No, no," she said. But inside, she was screaming yes.

Her mind spun . . . And yet perhaps it was just as well. If Santiago knew there were other McKintricks about, perhaps he would be cautioned. Avoid her and Ian, if possible. Because if he surprised Ian . . . She shuddered to think of what might happen.

As if summoned by her thoughts, Ian opened the shop door a moment later. With one look at her pale face, he hurried over to her. "Are you well, Verity?"

"I am," she said. "Only a tad queasy. Mr. Mosely has found me a fine hat. Might we return to the Harringtons' so that I might rest?"

"Of course," he said.

They exited the store, and Ian got her settled in the carriage. Once the sounds of horses and creaking leather covered their conversation, he leaned closer to her ear. "Verity, what is amiss?"

"I . . ." She paused. What good would it do for him to know that she and Santiago had stood in the same shop? That Santiago knew of her identity? 'Twould only make her husband fear for her safety, when the Spaniard seemed to wish her no ill will. "Oh, 'tis nothing. Just a case of angst disturbing my digestion. I am so glad you are safely returned, Ian. You were gone a terribly long time."

"Forgive me, love," he said, lifting her gloved hand to his lips. "But it seems you managed it all right? They did not ask about me?"

"No. I think they were relieved to have you gone. And then . . . other customers arrived, and that proved a beneficial distraction."

"Indeed. Providence reigns."

"Indeed," she agreed. She looked to the side window, as if captivated by the people and traffic of the city, while she considered Providence, and why, given the many haberdasheries in the city, Captain Alejandro Santiago entered this one, on this day.

Keturah sat on her chair by the windowsill that her father had meticulously lined with shells of all sorts, and she had managed to save as they remodeled the house. She thought of him collecting each shell and thinking about his

438

wife and three daughters far away, even as she wondered after Verity now.

Outside, she could hear the gentle roar and *whoosh* of the ocean's waves, washing across the sand, as well as the breeze through palms and cane, and the jungle's familiar cacophony of sounds—crickets and tree frogs, for the most part, with the occasional angry chatter of monkeys. Inside, she could hear Selah, playing haphazardly on the harpsichord in the parlor. She was even less gifted on the keys than Verity, despite her avid attempts. Directly below, Mitilda chastised a poor kitchen maid for being lazy. Down the hall, she heard Madeleine cry as Gray set her down for the night—as he had promised—shooing Ket away. She smiled. The man doted on their baby girl, and she found herself jealous in turns with being grateful for his attentive care of their babe.

Gray eased into their dark room and closed the door behind him. He moved across the new, wide floorboards—which still emitted the faint, sweet odor of freshly hewn lumber—and over to her. He leaned a hip into the opposite corner of the windowsill, ignoring the poking of the shells, to look over at her. "I so love seeing you here, Ket, with the moonlight streaming in, the shells before you. You are beautiful."

She grinned and tucked her head, embarrassed. "Me? 'Tis been quite a day. Hours in the kitchen, sweating along with Mitilda and Sansa. I could have used a bath at the pool or a dip in the sea."

"It is not too late. Shall we go for that dip?"

"To the ocean, or the waterfall?"

"Whichever you like," he said easily.

Ket considered him. "Madeleine . . ."

"We can ask Selah or Mitilda to listen for her."

She pulled back in surprise. "What would they think of us, going out at this hour?"

"That we wish a reprieve from this infernal heat. Come," he said, rising and extending his hand to her. "I think a dip in the sea is what we *both* need."

"But then we shall return covered in salt."

"And we shall take a bucket of water from the sluice at the bottom of the yard and wash it from our bodies." He pulled her closer, his broad hand at the flat of her back. "Come, love. Your mind has been toiling day and night since Verity left us. See if this might bring you ease."

"Very well," she sighed as she allowed her husband to lead her by the hand down the hall, pulling her along like a half-willing captive.

They paused downstairs where Mitilda was seeing to preparations for the morning's break-fast, with Sansa now scurrying to do everything she asked. Abe had wisely retired to either his mother's cottage or the stables.

"Mitilda," Gray said.

Her pretty oval face whirled in surprise. "Master Gray?"

"Ket and I wish to take an evening stroll. Might you keep an ear out for Madeleine?"

"Of course, sir."

"Thank you. We shall return in an hour."

Then he continued to pull Keturah along and out the front door, her face burning hot. "Honestly, Gray, what shall Mitilda and Sansa think?"

"They shall think," he said, drawing her closer and wrapping an arm around her shoulders, "that we are stealing away for a much-needed moment alone. The right of any married couple."

Nearer the stables, they could hear Major Woodget and his men had arrived. Gray led her to the far side, cradling her in his arms and putting a finger to his lips as if they were spying children. She smothered a giggle into his sweat-stained shirt, glad for it. The last thing she wanted was to have to make polite conversation with British soldiers this night.

Major Woodget exited first, muttering over his shoulder to the men behind him and then pausing to face them. "Now that they are in New York, the generals shall put this rebellion down in short order. Britain shall prevail, and the colonies shall once again acknowledge their master."

"Then we shall be excused from this godforsaken island and return home," Captain Howard added.

Keturah recognized the slur in both their

voices. They'd been drinking. And outside the house, where they believed they could speak freely, their words were not hidden behind social niceties. She did not think Howard always hated it here, but Verity's spurning and suspected elopement with Captain McKintrick had seemed to leave him fairly despondent. Men on the island far outnumbered the women. With Verity now a McKintrick, his dreams of marrying into a plantation family had likely died. But to call this beautiful island *godforsaken?*

"Hard times are ahead for certain," Lieutenant Angersoll chimed in. "I've heard tell that supplies will be twice as expensive for these planters in a week's time, thrice in a month. Without the American colonies supplying them 'twill be difficult."

"Difficult?" asked the captain, wavering a bit in the moonlight. He looked up toward the house. "Soon they shall have to decide between feeding themselves and feeding their slaves."

They stumbled toward the house while Ket and Gray remained where they were, stunned by the man's harsh words.

They had talked about it as a possibility; the soldiers now seemed to think it quite probable.

"Gray," Ket whispered.

"No," he said, pulling her close, rubbing her back. "It shall not come to that."

"But if it does . . ."

"If it does, then we shall find a way through. Seek other means to find supplies. In the meantime, I think we must dedicate several more acres to our gardens of corn and squash."

She nodded. "A wise plan. But what do you mean, about other means to find supplies?"

"I am saying this island forces me to rethink my convictions every time I seem to have settled. I am saying that we already do not do things on the Double T as others on Nevis do."

"I know that," she said, a bit irritated, only wanting him to go on. To say more. Because surely—

"I am saying that I *like* how we are operating the Double T. I like that in ten years, every man, woman, and child on our land should have emancipation papers in hand."

"As do I."

He began leading her down toward the beach. "And perhaps I acted in fear and haste when I sent Ian McKintrick away."

"Oh, Gray, you did so to protect Verity. To protect us."

"Aye. But now . . . now we may have need of a smuggler in the family."

She stopped and turned to him, trying to see his face in the spare moonlight, and laughed. "You would resort to that? Smuggling in supplies?"

"If it kept us and our people from starvation, yes. Of course I would."

She blinked up at him, her heart faltering. "I love it here, Gray. I love these people. I love this island. I love this life. *Our* life. Despite the difficulties. The ugliness. Do you think we can truly make it through?"

He took her hand and intertwined his fingers with hers, then brought it to his chest. "Keturah, God has brought us through so much already. Why would He fail us now?"

She pulled back a few inches, thinking. "He would not," she said at last, shaking her head.

"Three years ago I was broke. A bachelor with a bad reputation and not a penny to my name . . . only the deed to the land here. Now I am a planter, with visitors seeking advice on how to make it in the Indies, with a beautiful wife, an enchantress of a daughter, and a fine estate. What have the last three years brought you?"

She tried to tuck her head, but his firm hands would not allow her to look away. She closed her eyes, considering. "Three years ago I . . . I felt beaten and discarded. A girl seeking refuge, of sorts, back home at Hartwick. And now," she said, admiring his broad shoulders, "I am by the side of my one true love, on land I love, among people I love."

When they reached the beach, Gray turned to her, taking her in his arms and tracing the lines of her temple, cheek, neck. "Do you not think, beloved, that a God who can take a penniless second son and a discarded beaten wife, and bring them to this, *this* . . . do you not think that He can see us through whatever might come in the future?"

His words resonated in her heart as truth, but they also struck fear. Had they not sacrificed enough already? Had their toil—both internal and external—not been enough? "But what if we are discovered?" Keturah whispered. "We quarter British *soldiers,* Gray. Will they not question where we have obtained our supplies?"

Gray lifted both her hands in his and slowly, reverently kissed each one. "Ket, I ask you to trust me and the God who has seen us through to this day, and shall see us through future days. I know you wish to plan it all out. But sometimes, love, 'tisn't possible. Sometimes we simply must live day to day and see how He leads. Here is my promise," he said, pulling her closer. "No matter what comes—trial or treasure, failure or triumph—we shall face it together. Together, Ket."

She closed her eyes and once again leaned her forehead against his. "Together," she whispered, gaining strength in the utterance of each syllable.

CHAPTER THIRTY-FOUR

When Ian had suggested the plan that evening to Verity, she did not even let him finish. "Of course," she said, reaching out to study the bottle, then holding the ink to the waning light.

"That's it, lass? No hesitation?"

"No," she said, shaking her head. "Better me than you. I could not survive another few hours like I spent in the haberdashery, hoping and praying you would not be caught."

He frowned. Now 'twould be his turn to do the same.

"And McKay is right," she went on. "Women are seen as far less suspicious to the Brits." She set down the bottle and moved to the window, remembering all the people they had seen in the streets. Men hurrying home from work or late suppers, a few couples out for a stroll . . . and many redcoats. So many. The city was flooded with them.

Ian went over and wrapped his arms around her from the back, kissing her temple. "What are ye thinkin', lass?"

"I am thinking of all the people," she said.

"Which people?"

447

"Of all those soldiers, in particular. I have been steeped in the cause of late, thinking of little but what the Americans desire and need. But did you see the soldiers today, Ian? I mean, truly see them?" She remembered six redcoats passed by, laughing and teasing one another. Some pudgy, some lean. Some barely with facial hair, others with full beards. "They are men. Someone's brother, someone's son, someone's friend, each one of them."

"Aye," he said soberly, nestling his head against hers. He could feel the tearing within her, the conflict.

"The weapons we helped the Continentals to obtain might be used against those very men," she said under her breath. "One might die by a bullet we helped supply."

"Aye," he repeated. " 'Tis a nasty business, war. Both sides will lose brothers, sons, friends. But when there is no other recourse, there is no other recourse."

She nodded slowly, as if it pained her.

"Come. Albert has asked us down for a nightcap in the library." He pulled her gently away from the window. "Perhaps he has some wisdom to share with you, as a Loyalist turned rebel."

They left their room and walked together down the grand staircase. The house was quiet this eve, the servants largely in their quarters after the day's work. Only the butler with the hound-dog eyes, William, remained on duty in the hallway outside the library.

Inside, Roberta and Albert were sitting in twin wing-back chairs by a low-burning fire. For late June, New York was experiencing a colder wave of weather and so the fire was welcome. Before them was a tea tray with a silver pot— steam dancing out its spout—cups, and several delicacies. Spying them, Albert stood and Roberta after him.

"Welcome, cousins," Albert said. "I am glad you can join us."

Once Ian and Verity sat down on the settee that flanked the wing chairs, William asked, "Is there anything else you require this evening, Mr. and Mrs. Harrington?"

"No, William," Albert said. "Thank you. We shall see you in the morning."

"Very good, sir," he said, closing the double doors of the library behind him.

"So tell us of your visit to the haberdashery!" Roberta said, watching as Albert rose and tiptoed toward the doors. "Were you quite successful?" she asked, eyes wide, encouraging them to share the details.

Albert was listening at the door, making sure William was not hovering nearby.

"Quite," Verity replied, looking between her and Albert. "I found the most adorable little seashell hat to go with your gown. But I am not at all certain if I like how Mrs. Oren intends to do my hair."

"Oh, you simply must trust Mrs. Oren. She will give you the latest style."

"And if I do not care for the latest style?"

Now Albert was slowly turning the knob and opening one door, peeking out, then closing it again.

"Then ask for another!" Roberta said.

Albert hurried over to them and pulled his chair closer to the group. "All right, we are safe. All are in their quarters for the night, and this room tends to muffle sound quite well. Still, let us keep our voices down."

Ian and Verity nodded.

"You wish to know what transpired today," Ian said.

Their hosts eagerly assented.

So he told them of his meeting and pulled the bottle of ink from his pocket. "They wish for you to write pertinent information on hard-boiled eggs, then send them with Roberta and Verity to the workhouse tomorrow."

"Well, well, what do you know?" Albert said, lifting the bottle and turning it over as if searching for a label. "Does it truly work?"

"Apparently. They very much want any information you have and believe this is the best way to convey it."

Albert's thin eyebrows went up. "Most ingenious, really."

"Do you have additional information? Something valuable enough to put our wives in harm's way?" Ian asked.

"Come now, Ian," Roberta said. "We shall not be at any risk. We shall only be doing our charitable duty." She grinned and reached out an excited hand to Verity. But Verity's demeanor did not match hers.

Albert saw it too. "Do you not wish to take part in this, Cousin?"

"No, I do," she said sadly. " 'Tis only that I've been struggling a bit of late. Now that we're here. Now that I feel how very real it is. 'Tis no longer simply an idea . . ." She swallowed hard and bent to pour her own tea, waving off Roberta's attempt to intervene.

Albert nodded. " 'Tis a trial of its own, to understand that the battles at Lexington and Concord were but the beginning." He rose and stepped over to the fireplace, resting a hand on the high mantel. "I fear I shall be of only temporary aid in this role. There are already those who grow suspicious about the Patriots' ability to discover Loyalist secrets. I can only pass along two, perhaps three more pieces of key information, given that I am in such a small sphere of civilians who know what I do. 'Twon't be long until they look to every council member as a potential spy."

"Should you need an escape route in the next few days, you may utilize the *Inverness*," Ian said. "Even now, I have McKay outfitting her for a voyage anywhere we need to go. But after that . . ."

"After you depart, we would need to find our own means of escape," Albert said soberly. He cast a heavy glance in Roberta's direction.

"How did you and Roberta come to support the cause, Cousin?" Verity asked. "How did you choose the Sons of Liberty over England? Even to the point of risking your very lives?"

"We did not do so lightly," he said softly, his voice barely audible over the crackle and pop of the fire. "Especially when we knew Roberta was with child." He returned to his seat then, sighed heavily and leaned forward, his fingers steepled together as he continued. "It is no small thing to go against England in this. To go against other cousins," he said, looking directly at Verity. "But in the end, we decided we had no choice."

"Because?"

"Because if one studies history at all, one can see what is plainly transpiring here. Eventually, all empires come to an end. They overreach. Their people demand too much. The empire tries to comply with all the demands—both their own insatiable hunger for more territory and their people's—and at last their capability comes to an end." He raised his hands. "They simply cannot afford to fund it all." Letting out a long sigh, he paused and then added, "We are witnesses to the end of the British Empire. They have reached their apex, reached too far, spent too much, and now they shall begin to recede. Much like the Greeks and Romans did before them."

"And we wish to be on the side that remains," Roberta interjected. "Both sides shall be wounded in this war. Neither Tory nor Loyalist shall escape unharmed, leaving many to mourn. We believe in the end, however, it shall be the Continentals who will emerge the victors, and we with them. We were torn for a time, but Francis's birth helped solidify our thoughts. We fight for his future more than ours, for this new country that one day shall be wholly his own."

Verity nodded.

" 'Tis also our hope, Verity," Albert said, "that the more we can aid the rebels, the faster this conflict may come to an end. If the British see that they battle a dedicated force with resources of its own, perhaps they shall be dissuaded from continuing to try to hold on to this land."

"That is a sizable *if*," Ian said. "The Scottish fought them for generations."

Albert sighed heavily again and sat back in his chair. "Indeed."

"The Patriots shall require the strength to survive defeat in battle and yet continue to fight to win the war," Ian said. "Do you think they have that within them?"

He himself did, but Ian still wanted to hear Albert's spoken affirmation. Especially since he was about to permit Verity to take such a great risk.

"They do," Albert said. "We do," he corrected himself, reaching across to take Roberta's hand. Together they looked to Ian and Verity.

This is Verity's choice, Ian thought. She was the one wavering, possibly having second thoughts. Gray's words came back to him. *"They seek not a man to direct them or lord over them, but rather one who will stand beside them, celebrating their strengths."* So he took her hand in his and waited.

Verity looked down at her lap for several long seconds, then to Ian, and at last to her cousins. "Then let us do what we can to aid you," she said.

Verity took two baskets from William, each with a dozen eggs and a loaf of bread beside them, and waited as he handed Roberta two more. Albert had left for the office at the same time he left every day, and Ian was sitting in the library, pretending to read the paper, putting on a lackadaisical act for the servants.

Verity knew that, deep down, he was mad with worry; he'd been up before the sun, pacing before the window. He'd tried to talk her out of going. *"I must do this."* Tried to talk her into letting him accompany Roberta instead. *"How would that appear?"* Tried to suggest he take the eggs directly to the men in the Dock Ward. *"They told you that you were not to visit them there again. You are too recognizable."*

Finally, he'd taken her hands in his and leaned down until his forehead touched hers. "Are you certain that this is what God would have you do?"

"I am," she said.

He considered her for a long moment. *"Ainnir as àille snuadh agus bana-churaidh as treise cridhe."*

"You've said that to me before," she whispered. "Will you now tell me what it means?"

"It means you are a most beautiful lass, with the strong heart of a warrior," he said.

The heart of a warrior, she reminded herself now, even as her own began a staccato beat.

Swallowing hard, she called to him from the hall, trying to sound casual for the servants' sake. "We shall be back in a few hours, Ian."

"Very well," he called back, as if disinterested, turning the page of the *New-York Gazette* and continuing to pretend to read.

They exited the house, and a young, slim coachman in livery assisted them into the Harringtons' luxurious coach. Half an hour later, they'd left the country and neared Fly Market. Roberta leaned forward to ask the coachman to stop and let them out. He swiftly obliged and assisted them down the stairs. "Wait for us here, if you please," Roberta said. "We shall be but an hour or two."

"Aye, ma'am," said the coachman.

They strode down the sidewalk, soldiers and men tipping their hats in deference to them. At first, Verity could not look them in the eye, memories of last night's doubts still vivid in her mind. But then she thought if God was truly leading her in this, she had to be brave and count the cost. And counting the cost meant fully recognizing each person she passed, whether they be a British soldier, a boy hawking newspapers, a woman with a tray of dried fish, or a couple of gentlemen on their way to work.

Be with us, Lord, she prayed silently. *Bring this all to a swift end. Save us all . . . on both sides of the conflict.*

Once they reached a stretch of empty sidewalk, she asked quietly, "How did you manage to secure all those eggs?"

"I boiled them as soon as you went to bed last night," Roberta said, still facing forward.

"And Albert wrote on each one?"

"Only those in the baskets with the red linen beneath. 'Tis those we must get to our contact."

Verity nodded, feeling her heartbeat pick up. They each had one basket with red linen, one with blue. Sharing the burden. "Perhaps I should carry both of them. In case we are caught. Think of little Francis, Roberta."

"No," she said with a gentle smile. "We are in this together."

They turned the corner, and Roberta slowed. Ahead was a checkpoint, it appeared, with twelve soldiers standing about, blocking the street and allowing pedestrians through one gate, wagons through another, after questioning each one.

"Chin up, smile," Roberta said cheerfully. "We are only about doing good work for the Lord, looking after the less fortunate," she reminded Verity.

"Indeed. Have you been to this workhouse before?" she said under her breath.

"No. I have been meaning to for months, but with the baby . . ."

"Use that," Verity said. "Men do not like to discuss childbirth."

Roberta laughed under her breath. There were three people between them and the soldiers, waiting to get through.

Two.

Then one.

She could feel the sweat beading on her upper lip, even though it was rather chilly out again this morning. Another bead ran down her spine, beneath her stays. She glanced at Roberta and then emulated her smile, the tilt of her shoulders. She was feeling more confident by the moment.

But then she saw Lieutenant Ainsley walking by with several other men, crossing the street on the other side of the blockade.

He started when he glimpsed her, and she fought the impulse to groan.

Roberta stepped forward, Verity a half step behind as she watched Ainsley approach out of the corner of her eye.

"Good day, ladies," greeted the young captain, smiling at them both and then glancing at what they carried.

"Why, Lieutenant Ainsley," Roberta said with a bright smile, "good morning."

"Good morning," Verity murmured.

"What brings you to Fly Market, of all places, ladies?"

"We are headed to the workhouse, to aid them in serving the poor their breakfast," Verity said, raising her basket. Now she saw the benefit of carrying a completely innocent-looking basket of eggs. She pulled back the blue linen, and Ainsley peeked at them.

"Perhaps you ought to leave this work to others, ladies. There are quite a few rebel sympathizers in this neighborhood," he sniffed, looking over his shoulder with distaste.

The checkpoint officer eyed Roberta and Verity with renewed consternation.

"We know not of each soul's political stance, Lieutenant," Verity said sweetly. "Only that they are hungry and that our Lord calls us to feed the hungry." Again she lifted her basket a bit for emphasis.

"May I?" Lieutenant Ainsley said, gesturing toward her blue-linen basket.

"But of course." She hoped she looked more confused by his interest than concerned.

Lieutenant Ainsley lifted the cloth and peered more closely inside it. He grabbed an egg, turned it over, and then threw it to the ground.

Roberta and Verity gasped.

The soldier cried, "Lieutenant!"

The women held their breath as Ainsley bent and retrieved the egg, perused its cracked shell, blew the dirt off it, then casually peeled it and took a bite.

If he did the same from each of the baskets . . .

If he glimpsed the markings inside . . .

"Only making certain there was nothing hidden inside, soldier," he said with a conspiratorial grin. "The rebels are getting progressively more clever. Last week at this very checkpoint, we found a basketful of eggs that had been blown out, with tiny messages inside them. Make certain that each of these ladies' eggs have the heft of a hard-boiled egg before you grant them passage."

"Yes, sir," the man said, awkwardly gesturing to the women for their baskets. They handed them over.

Ainsley folded his arms and looked to another

underling. "Break open each of those loaves of bread too, in at least four parts. Some have been known to bake messages into a loaf."

"Lieutenant, is this truly necessary?" Roberta asked with a frown. "Given my station?"

" 'Tis not *your* presence here that gives me pause, Mrs. Harrington, but the company you keep," he said while staring at Verity. "Would not your husband celebrate such vigilance in keeping our soldiers safe?"

"Of course," she replied with a sigh. "Just get on with it, would you? We must get these to the workhouse in time for the morning meal."

"I imagine the poor would be glad for it, day or night. It shall not go to waste, Mrs. Harrington." Verity tried to hold Ainsley's gaze and not to look at the soldier behind him, patiently handling one egg after another, now going through Roberta's basket. Another soldier swiftly broke the bread in fourths and, finding nothing, did his best to set the pieces back together in the basket.

"Nothing here," said the bread man, handing back the baskets.

"Nor here," said the other, doing the same.

Still, Ainsley stood in their way. "Have you done such charitable work before, Mrs. Harrington?"

"I have not," she said, shifting the baskets on her arms as if they were a burden. "As you well know, our fortunes have improved of late. But having been heavy with child, I could not do as God asked of me. Now I can."

Ainsley sniffed again, lifted his chin, staring at one and then the other. "Very well, ladies," he said, waving them onward. "Go and do your good work. Good day to you both."

They nodded and strode through the makeshift gate. Verity felt the man's gaze upon her back as she walked side by side with Roberta.

"Mrs. Harrington!" he called. "Mrs. McKintrick!"

They froze, then forced themselves to turn slowly back toward him. Verity's heart was pounding out of her chest. Did she look as frightened as she felt?

"I shall see you on the morrow!" Ainsley said cheerfully.

Roberta blinked slowly, not understanding.

"The officers' ball? I am very much looking forward to it."

"Oh, yes," she breathed. "We shall look forward to your company," she added with a demure curtsey.

Twenty paces later, heads together, Roberta said, "Can you breathe yet?"

"A bit," Verity said and forced herself to take deeper breaths now.

"Good girl. Now smile and tell me of Nevis and your sisters as we walk. Albert says they are each as delightful as you."

Verity did so, talking about her sisters and the Double T and her mercantile, all the way until they reached the workhouse.

"You know what our contact looks like?" Roberta asked, opening the tall, heavy door.

"I think I shall when I see her."

"You think?"

It was her turn to encourage Roberta. "Trust me," she said with an impish grin. But as they faced the masses of people in line, her smile faltered. Why, there had to be over two hundred people in the hall! But Ian had said to search for a girl working in the kitchen who looked like Selah but with blue eyes.

She caught a glimpse of a tall girl with blond hair carrying a tray to the serving table, but she looked not at all like Selah. Then a pleasing-looking blonde who was shorter, but when Verity approached her, she saw she had hazel eyes, not blue. They edged to the back of the dining area and over to the kitchen, and then she spied her. Ian had been right. She looked so much like Selah, it almost stole her breath. So beautiful!

The girl was setting a giant pot on the table, where a brunette dipped a ladle in and began to serve. The girl was turning back to the kitchen when she saw them approaching and walked directly to them.

Blue eyes. It was her.

"We brought some food to contribute," Verity

said. "Shall we each set out a basket of eggs and bread straightaway? You could keep the others in back until you have need of them."

"An excellent idea," said the girl, meeting her steady gaze as she took the red-linen-covered baskets from each of them.

"May we stay and help serve?" Roberta asked.

"Do as you please, ma'am," she said with a bob of her head, then disappeared into the kitchen.

"Come with me, Verity," Roberta said, edging between two matronly women and taking up a fork to serve slices of ham. Beside her, Verity grabbed a spoon and started ladling beans onto plates.

"Thank you, ma'am," said a boy, his face streaked with dirt, looking with wide eyes at the generous plate in his hands.

"You are most welcome," Verity said. And as she looked to the next group of people who approached—an older man, two young girls anxiously holding hands—she was particularly glad for this mission. It felt good to be helping others, on dual levels. And if Ainsley spoke the truth, if she was surrounded by rebel sympathizers, that was all the better.

CHAPTER THIRTY-FIVE

Selah eased out of the kitchen, her arms heavy with two baskets laden with freshly baked bread. The slaves and freed men and women who worked the Double T had been in the fields for a terribly long day, what with Matthew bent on getting through the weeding before an impending storm closed in. Already the palm fronds strained to and fro in the gusts of wind. She could feel the moisture in the air, though no rain had yet fallen. Matthew had been right. The day had the feel of a tropical storm about to settle directly over the island and pour heavy rain all night. Come morning, the fields would be too soggy to work, the roads impassable for days.

But as she approached the cabins, she began to hear strains of song just over the edge of the wind rushing through the cane. Gray and Ket had built a larger gathering house in which some field hands slept on either end, but in the center was simply a roof and flooring with no walls, allowing protection from sun and rain and yet granting maximum ventilation. It was here the eighty slaves and freed people of the Double T tended to gather, spilling out on either side for particularly important moments. And tonight appeared to be important.

She moved through the outer edge of the group, greeting each one by name, distributing bread as she went. "A bit more to see you through the night," she said, over and over. "I know you worked so hard this day."

But it was a man continuing to sing that drew her further inward. It was with some surprise, after she made it through the final circles of people, that she discovered a young white man at the center. He held a closed Bible in his hand and was teaching them all a hymn, his voice a pleasing baritone. He was moving from one person to the other, smiling into their face and tapping each one on the shoulder, the arm, the hand.

" 'Rock of Ages, cleft for me, let me hide myself in Thee. Nothing in my hands I bring, simply to Thy cross I cling. Naked, come to Thee for dress; helpless, look to Thee for grace. Foul, I to the fountain fly, wash me, Savior, or I die!' "

Gradually, every person in the building looked to Selah, not him, and only in that moment—such was his fervor—did he see her. His words faltered, and he drew himself up, clearly surprised. "My friends," he said, a slow, lopsided grin spreading across his thin but handsome face, "you did not tell me the Double T was the home of an angel. And look! She bears gifts! A bit of bread!"

Selah smiled and handed one basket to Sansa, the other to Gideon, so that they could distribute the rest, and walked over to him. "I am Miss Selah Banning. Who are you, sir?"

"Jedidiah Reed, lately of Hispaniola, a new arrival to Nevis," he said with a bow.

"And what brings you to the Double T, Mr. Reed?" she asked. He seemed kindhearted—his joy was fairly contagious—but these were her people. She did not want anyone taking advantage of them.

"My God has called me to witness to all I can reach, and my welcome had worn out on Hispaniola," he answered regretfully. "My funds were enough to purchase passage here, so I considered that to be the Lord's direction for my next step."

"I see," she said, not at all understanding. This man had set sail and spent his last farthing to reach Nevis? How would he care for himself now?

"Do you have friends on Nevis?"

He lifted his big hands. "I make friends wherever I go, miss. The Lord directs me to them."

"I see." She believed in the Lord's direction. Surely she did. But the way this Mr. Reed spoke of it . . . "And why did you come to the Double T?"

"I asked about in Charlestown. More than one

said that the Double T was filled with the kindest souls on the island."

"Well, that is quite gracious of them to say. But what is it you want, Mr. Reed?" she asked, stepping closer to him. "Are you here to charm these good people out of the little money they have?"

He blinked down at her. He was quite tall and lanky. A bit . . . awkward, despite his handsome face. And young. Not much older than she.

"I have not asked these brothers and sisters for a penny. Nor will I."

"Then why are you here?" Selah pressed.

He grinned, the suddenness of it disarming her. "How can such a pretty little girl be so fierce? You remind me of my mother's terrier."

Men and women broke out in laughter all about them as word spread about what a *terrier* was.

"That's our Miss Selah," called one.

"She's tough, our Miss Selah," said another.

She pulled back, surprised. Half amused, half offended. "Well, you . . . you, Mr. Reed, remind me of a wolfhound!"

He laughed and crossed his arms. "Listen to me, Miss Selah—"

"Miss Banning, if you please. My friends call me Selah, and we, sir, are not yet friends."

His brows raised in alarm. "I seem to have offended you. I am most sorry for that, Miss Banning. I am here not to take advantage of these friends. Only to spread the Good News."

She faltered, took a step back. She had heard of such men. "Why, you . . . you are a *Methodist!*"

That made his crooked smile spread wide, and then he began laughing again, this time so hard that he bent backward. "You say that, Miss Banning," he said, tears in his eyes, "as if I were a convict rather than a Christian."

Her cheeks burned. She had not meant to sound as such.

"Who said you could be here?"

"I did, ma'am," Matthew said, climbing the steps behind her. "And Mr. Covington too. Is it not well with you, Miss Selah? The man was keeping our minds off the storm."

"Oh. You did, Matthew?" she added awkwardly. "Yes. Oh, of course. Of course. If you deem it best."

"I do," said the overseer with a gentle smile. "No harm in hearin' a little of the gospel preached, is there? There are many souls here on the Double T who have never heard the Good News."

"No. No, there is no harm in that," she agreed.

"Please stay, Miss Banning," invited Jedidiah Reed. "Join us."

"Oh, I cannot. I best get back to the house before this storm lets loose. A good evening to you all, friends." She started moving through the crowd.

"There she goes, your resident angel," said the young preacher. "With her arriving with so much bread in hand, it reminds me of a favorite story. One day long ago, many had gathered to hear Jesus preach. Many came. The old. The young. Both men and women. So many that there were thousands! But toward the end of day, someone realized there would never be enough for them all to eat. A boy brought forward a basket with but a few fish and a loaf of bread in it . . ."

Selah strained to hear more over the rushing wind but could not. Resolutely, she kept striding toward the big house, no matter how much her heart encouraged her to return. Half of her was intrigued by Mr. Reed, half agitated. It had been her practice to spend part of each day and eve with the plantation's field workers, tending to wounds, lending a listening ear, soothing babies, teaching the little ones their alphabet. Now she felt . . . displaced.

Matthew seemed glad of the man's company. They all did. When it was Selah they normally welcomed so gladly.

Are you so selfish, Selah? she chided herself. *Can you not be glad for your friends, that they might have some welcome company on this stormy night? And perhaps hear of the one true God for the first time?*

She entered the kitchen and went to the parlor,

where she found Gray and Ket. As usual, little Madeleine was nestled in her father's arms. "Do you know who I found out in the meetinghouse?" she asked, hands on her hips.

"The young Methodist minister," Gray said calmly, lifting a finger to his lips, apparently fearing her upset would awaken the slumbering babe.

"Yes!" She turned to Ket. "A *Methodist,* Ket. Are you not alarmed?"

"Alarmed by someone sharing Scripture and song with our people?" Ket asked benignly. "I am not. Are you? And for once, this is something the other planters favor. Only last week at Saint Philip's, I heard Mrs. Jackson bemoan the need to share the faith with the slaves. That it was our 'Christian duty.' Perhaps this Mr. Reed shall garner us some portion of favor on-island."

"No doubt Angus Shubert shall find fault with it," Selah said.

"Or perhaps he shall have to remain quiet for once," Ket said, keeping her voice low. "I doubt he has warmed a church pew in some time. And you know how many of the other planters are on Nevis. They may be up until the wee hours of the morning drinking rum—"

"But come Sunday morning they drag themselves to church," Selah finished for her. It was true. And met with her sister's calm assurance, all her irritation and concern seemed to leak out of her. She collapsed onto the settee. Then she quickly rose, pacing before the window, peering out toward the windswept palms.

"Matthew said he seemed a good sort," Gray said. "Told me he would keep an eye on Mr. Reed and send him packing if he did anything other than what he said he would do. You need not fear a wolf among the sheep. The shepherd is close by."

She nodded but continued her pacing. Perhaps that was it. *She* was accustomed to being the shepherdess. There was something in the man, or perhaps the way the others gathered about him, that had made her feel . . . displaced. There was that word again.

I am jealous, she admitted to herself. Once more she sank onto the settee.

"What is this I hear?" asked Major Woodget, coming into the room. "Something about a wolf among the sheep?" He gestured toward the window as he shrugged off his red coat.

"We have a young minister with us this night," Gray replied. "Speaking to the slaves."

"Ahh, I see. With this storm about to erupt, I wager he shall be here for some time."

"That could be," Gray said.

"With supplies running low, is it wise to accept additional guests, Gray?" he asked.

"This Mr. Reed has yet to sit at our table," Ket said, picking a stray thread off her skirts and letting it fall to the floor. *Unlike the major and his men,* Selah silently finished for her.

"Tell me," Gray intervened smoothly, "were you able to inquire about additional supplies through the regiment stores in town, Major?"

Major Woodget gave Ket a hard look, but she did nothing but cast him an innocent smile in return. Only Selah had heard her rant against the soldiers as they formed the last of their flour into the loaves of bread she'd distributed among the field hands. Gray had promised to go to town in a few days—after the storm—to see if any new shipments had arrived. But she held out little hope. Nothing had arrived in the last two weeks. With word of the impending shortage, every plantation owner on every island of the West Indies was hoarding each and every hogshead full of staples he could find.

"Will Mr. Reed require a bed this night?" Selah asked. "Perhaps we can offer him the couch in Gray's office."

"No need," Gray said. "Matthew tells me that Mr. Reed intends to sleep in the meetinghouse. Insisted on it actually."

She got up and stepped back to the window, noting how the wind was now bending the trees in arcs, and part of her wondered if this storm blowing in had brought Mr. Reed with it.

CHAPTER THIRTY-SIX

"You must wear this choker, Verity. It looks stunning with that gown," Roberta said, fishing it out of a drawer in her wide *coiffeuse* and handing her a velvet-covered box. They sat together in Roberta's dressing closet, each attended by a *coiffeur*. Roberta's hairdresser appeared content as she wrapped her mistress's shoulders in a cape and prepared to powder her hair with small, silver-inlaid bellows. In contrast, Mrs. Oren appeared sullen after resignedly agreeing to make Verity's hair only half as tall as it had been in the shop *and* leave it unpowdered.

"Oh, you are too kind," Verity said, opening the box. She gasped in surprise. The choker featured a large diamond with three strands of pearls. "Roberta? Are you certain?"

"I am. 'Twas a wedding gift from Albert, so be sure not to lose it on the dance floor. And return it to the box at night's end, would you? That box is almost as valuable as the necklace," she said with a laugh but gave Verity a pointed look.

The box . . . there was a message hidden in the box, Verity surmised.

"Of course. Thank you so much for your generosity."

Her hairdresser went on to apply paint to Roberta's skin—a layer of blanc with an artful application of rouge to cheek and lip. But being a married woman, she hesitated over the offered *mouches* or beauty mark. "Ah, well, some say if you place one on the right cheek, it means you are with the Tories. So carry on!"

Mrs. Oren began fastening the new hat atop Verity's hair. Roberta turned to her and cooed, "Oh, that is what I have been missing! Perhaps I shall make a stop at the haberdashery for something similar, for the next time I don that gown." Her attendant had moved on to use a bit of kohl to darken her brows.

"You shall do no such thing," Verity said. "You may have this one after the evening's festivities are through. 'Tis the least I can do as thanks for allowing me to wear your gown and choker this night."

"Pshaw," Roberta said with a wave of her hand and a glint to her eye. "It gave me the ideal reason to wear my new gown, even though that one is perfectly fine."

At long last, Mrs. Oren was done. She stood back to admire Verity in the mirror. "I must say, your hair looks very lovely after all, Mrs. McKintrick."

"And it is all due to you," she said, casting the hairdresser a smile.

"Now then. What is it you require in paint?"

Verity contemplated her image in the mirror with a sigh. "A bit of rouge perhaps for my cheeks and lips. Some kohl for my brows. But after weeks on the sea and on Nevis, I fear it would take every bit of Roberta's blanc to cover this tan."

Partially mollified, the hairdresser opened the jar of paint, which smelled of sandalwood, Verity thought. Perhaps its source.

"I think your tanned skin looks quite exotic," Roberta said. " 'Tis no wonder Captain McKintrick fell in love with you at first sight. How could he do anything but? Half the room shall do the same tonight at the ball when you appear."

"At first sight?" she scoffed. "Whoever told you that?"

"He did," Roberta said smugly. "He told me all about the first day he met you, and how ashamed he was, given his poor countenance and circumstances."

Verity nodded. " 'Twasn't the finest of meetings. But we . . . we were both different then. God has taught each of us a great deal in the past months. Healed us, directed us in ways we could not have imagined."

"All the way to New York from Nevis. I am so glad of it." Roberta squeezed Verity's hand. "I shall be most despondent when you must ship off again."

"Perhaps it shall not be for long," she replied for the benefit of their hairdressers.

"Oh, I do hope you are right."

Yet they both knew that, once she and Ian weighed anchor, a reunion in New York was unlikely until the war was over, and only if the Sons of Liberty won.

Once alone, Verity removed the liner of the jewelry box and found the hidden letter. This she tucked into the top of her stays, knowing she could easily fish it out later—and few men would dare search for it. Then she need only ask for a cup of tea at the kitchen when the clock struck eleven, and the blonde from the workhouse would appear. She planned to pass off the note as she took hold of the cup.

Would that work? Would anyone see the exchange?

Lord, protect us all, she silently prayed, exiting Roberta's dressing closet and returning to her own rooms. There she found Ian, who had donned his new rust-colored silk ball coat and breeches, with embroidery on the waistcoat beneath, as well as a powdered wig. He crossed the room and took her hand, bowing over it as he looked up at her. "You, my love, are utterly enchanting."

"And you look like a painting out of Versailles."

"Do you think?" he asked, turning slightly left and right as if seeking further admiration. His eyes narrowed at her. "How did you escape the powder?"

"By agreeing to the bunting in my hair. That was the least Mrs. Oren would accept. Anything less would have compromised her reputation."

He smiled, staring up at her hair. "It is quite . . . impressive. If she had stacked it any higher, you would have appeared taller than I."

"Ahh, but that is not her concern. Her concern is a hairstyle that is at least one and a half times as tall as my face. And given that I have an oval face . . ."

He laughed under his breath. " 'Twould have been something to see, but I still would have been the most fortunate man on the ballroom floor."

"How you flatter, Captain McKintrick," she chided with a smile, flinging open her fan to ease the sudden heat on her cheeks.

"How easy it is to do so when in your company, Mrs. McKintrick." He drew her closer to drop tiny delicious kisses along her neck.

She squirmed away. "There shall be dancing tonight, before any other shenanigans."

He sighed heavily. "If you insist." He took her arm in his, and they were walking toward the door when he whispered, "Do you have it?"

"I do," she returned.

His grin widened as they swept down the stairs and into the flow of guests streaming through the front doors. At the ballroom entrance, a servant took each group's invitation and read aloud their names before they entered the grand hall. If Santiago was present, her identity would again be affirmed. But he would not dare to approach her or Ian, would he?

She prayed that he would not.

An hour later, she realized she should have prayed that Lieutenant Ainsley would stay away as well.

"Captain and Mrs. McKintrick," he said, greeting them both. "The city appears to agree with you."

"Indeed," Ian said.

" 'Tis due to my cousin's warm hospitality," she said, "and the welcome relief of wider quarters than the ship's cabin."

"And you, m'lady, seem quite invested in this city," Ainsley said with a smile that did not reach his gray eyes. "What with your charity work in the mornings and balls to attend in the evenings."

She blinked. What was she to say to that? "I am happy to abide here for a time," she finally managed. "With Mrs. Harrington as our hostess, it has provided many opportunities to get to know the city and her people." She forced a bright smile. "Would we to tarry for a month, I wager I would be quite worn out."

"Quite. Tell me, Captain," Ainsley said, "do

you find any fault with my asking your bride to dance?"

Ian paused, clearly wishing he could find a plausible rationale with which to refuse Ainsley the pleasure. "No fault at all," he finally said, each word leaving his mouth as if pried from it. "So long as 'tis only the one. I'm a jealous sort of husband, you see. I aim to be my wife's primary escort this eve."

"Understood, Captain." Ainsley offered his arm, and Verity forced another smile. Together they joined the lines of men and women preparing to dance. Once the music began, they came together in long lines, drew apart, came together again, then parted as couples in circles of twelve. " 'Tis an honor to dance with the great-granddaughter of a fine British officer," the lieutenant said.

"And for me, to dance with a loyal servant of the Crown," she replied demurely. She made it a point not to glance down at her stays. With the dancing and arm movements, she could swear that Roberta's letter was gradually riding upward. Was it visible even now? Beads of sweat began to form on her upper lip even though the room was not overly warm.

They parted and circled with the others for a few measures—a blessed relief—but then came back together just as she confirmed that a bit of white paper was indeed peeking from her neckline. " 'Tis a grand room for a ball, is it not?"

she asked the lieutenant, encouraging him to look up and about.

"A fine home, worthy of a Loyalist," he agreed. An instant later, he was taking her hands in his and, after a few steps, lifting both and leading her to his other side.

Verity's mouth went dry as she felt the letter rise higher. Against her tanned skin, how could he miss it?

"Do you know many of the people in this hall, Lieutenant?"

Again he looked about the room. "A good number of them, yes."

"It must be an assurance to be surrounded by the familiar, even when so far from one's home."

"New York is my home now, Mrs. McKintrick," he said and turned to face her as they circled again. "Just as Nevis was once yours. Do you plan to return, by the way?"

"As oft as our business allows, I hope." What would he do if he learned they had fled from the island in the middle of the night? That Ian was likely a wanted man, after attacking Angus Shubert? The letter now almost felt hot against her skin—which was madness, she knew. How could parchment be hot?

They reached the end of the measure and spun away from each other, and as they did so, she had no choice but to casually reach up and tuck it back down in her stays, praying that if anyone watched, they would assume she had stashed a kerchief there and nothing more. But as she remembered to adopt the expression of none but a lady entirely enjoying herself, she caught his eye.

Santiago.

He stood beside a young lady, saying something that made her laugh, but his eyes were on her the whole while. He had not missed her move, hiding the paper again. Now her face burned.

"Your color is quite high," the lieutenant said, slightly frowning. "Perhaps I ought to fetch you some punch?"

"That would be welcome," she said, softening her eyes in what she hoped would appear as disappointment over the early end to their dance. "I confess I have become far more accustomed to island breezes than what the city affords."

"I imagine so," he said, ushering her over to the table as if fearing she might faint at any moment. A servant handed him a crystal goblet full of a golden red punch. She took a grateful drink of it and then blinked in surprise. " 'Tis quite strong."

"We in New York do our best to keep our friends in the Indies employed," the lieutenant said.

"Yes. I see," she said, looking about for Ian. Surely he had seen them exit the dance floor.

He looked up at her hair. "You look quite comely this eve, Mrs. McKintrick."

"You are most kind."

"Did you purchase that hat somewhere nearby? My sister has requested I bring something back from America the next time I visit her."

"Oh, this? It is from a haberdashery Mrs. Harrington recommended."

"A fine recommendation, it appears. My sister would adore such a creation. Might I ask, is the shop in this part of the city?"

"I do not quite remember," she hedged.

"What is its name?"

"Charlotte's . . . owned by a Mr. Mosely."

"The one in Hanover Square," he sniffed. It was then that Verity knew the lieutenant was already quite aware where she had purchased the hat. Had he ordered someone to follow her? And if so, had they spotted Ian too?

"Indeed." She took a sip of her punch and looked about the ballroom. Where was Ian?

Her heart began to race. What if he had not only seen Ian in the Dock Ward but followed her to the Fly Market workhouse? Seen her pass off the eggs? But then, had he not examined those eggs to his own satisfaction?

"I am surprised that ladies of station still shop in Hanover Square. It is surrounded by those who refuse to swear fealty to the Crown. Hardly the sort who deserve Loyalist business."

She gave him a quizzical look. "Why, Lieutenant, are you accusing Mr. Mosely of being a rebel? Certainly someone of his fine taste would not err so egregiously. And should we not support a Loyalist's business, even if he is surrounded by rebels? Why abandon him now?"

"You might be surprised at who rebels against the Crown, Mrs. McKintrick," he said, taking a sip of his own punch at long last. His gray eyes searched hers and then flicked down to her neckline—not in the curiously male manner of most, but more like Brutus, reviewing where he had last seen a tasty mouse.

That was when she knew for certain. Ainsley had suspected them all along, and now he knew she carried something on her person that she preferred not be found.

She forced a smile. "I beg your pardon, Lieutenant Ainsley, but I must go and see my husband. I promised him the next dance, and now that I am quite recovered, I must do my duty."

He lifted his crystal goblet. "Cheers, Mrs. McKintrick."

He did not offer to escort her back to her husband's side, a common courtesy. Another gesture meant to throw her? With some awkward hesitation, she turned from him and began making her way through the crowd. Casually glancing over her shoulder, she saw Ainsley following her. He was determined not to let her out of his sight.

Ian was beside her then, taking her elbow.

"Keep your sea legs, lass," he said quietly. "The storm is intensifying, but all is not lost."

"Are you certain?" she asked wanly. "Ainsley continues to watch me. Shall we continue this conversation on the dance floor?"

"Indeed."

Thankfully, the instrumentalists had just begun an allemande. Ian swept her out onto the floor in a dance only meant for couples. But whilst he appeared to be looking down at her with love and whispering intimate words, she could see his eyes dart over her left shoulder, then her right. "I have reason to suspect, lass, that more men than Ainsley keep keen watch on us."

"That is grim news," she said with a pretend smile. "And I fear he glimpsed Roberta's letter peeking from my stays."

"Do ye still have the letter on your person?"

"I do. I have not yet seen the blonde. Might she have been intercepted?"

"Perhaps. And yet it is not the appointed time. We must find a way to hide or destroy it."

"In the fire?" she asked, striving to appear as nothing more than a woman enjoying herself at a party.

"Not with Ainsley watching your every move."

"There is something more, Ian. Something I ought to have told you before."

"Aye. Get on with it, lass."

"Captain Santiago. He is here too."

She felt both of Ian's hands stiffen, at her back and beneath her right hand.

"And how is it that ye know who he is?" he asked, his tone betraying a hint of his fury, though he managed to maintain his genteel mask.

She paused. "I saw him earlier. At Charlotte's. He came into the shop with two young women. We did not speak, but he discovered my identity. As I did his. He watches us as well."

Ian was silent for several measures, sweeping her about the floor with a calm authority. Finally he spoke. "And Santiago is where now?"

They turned in the circle of the dance, and all the while her eyes surveyed the crowd. "He nears Roberta. Dark hair, dark beard, silver coat and breeches."

They continued their turn, twice, thrice, and Verity could feel it the moment Ian spotted him. It was she who led then, forcing him to bring his foot down, carry through. "Be at ease, love. Be at ease."

But he gripped her now with greater intensity.

"We do not yet know why he is here, but he is clearly aiding the English," she whispered, leaning back and pretending to laugh, as if he'd just said something witty.

"Which makes no sense. I shall address him before Major Rye and demand justice for my brother's life."

"First, take pause and think, for the English

know of Santiago and his history. 'Twas they who told you of his attack upon Duncan, yes?"

His eyes swept over hers, back and forth. "Indeed."

"Well, if they know of his transgressions, how is it he could find himself here in our company, his ship now crowned by the Union Jack?"

Again those keen blue eyes she so loved came in contact with hers as he pondered what she said. "Given that the Spanish and French are now allies, and yet the French are more amenable to the rebels' cause than the Spanish . . . perhaps he spies on the French."

"There 'tis at last," she said. "That *must* be it."

Ian could not contain his sigh. "Then it would matter not to Rye if I were to tell him. He already knows the man killed my brother. And he is willing to look past it, because Santiago works for him now."

"Or others. Perhaps the major knows nothing."

They continued to dance, each striving to be naught but one of a hundred swept away by the beautiful music.

"Why tell me now, Verity? That he is present?" he asked after they separated and came together again.

Her hand arched above his head as the dazzling chandelier—holding a hundred or more candles—appeared behind him. "I fear Santiago and Ainsley both glimpsed the note I carry."

His eyes stilled over hers. "Truly?"

"Truly," she said, forcing another smile.

His brows lifted as he led her forward in the next step and then backward. "If we are discovered, so are Roberta and Albert."

"Yes," she said.

"I must warn them straightaway." Ian spun her in his arms and then back again as the song ended. "And you must dispose of that note."

"I shall. But now?"

"Now," he said, bowing to her. "Ask for the tea, see if the girl emerges."

"But Ian," she said, gripping his arm, "you do not intend to engage Captain Santiago, do you?"

His eyes scanned the crowd and settled, then quickly narrowed. "I intend that he at least know who I am and that someday, somehow, I shall demand satisfaction for how he wronged me and my kin."

"You shall only draw attention to yourself," she whispered, stubbornly holding on to his hands when he tried to pull away.

"Aye, and what would be the wrong in that?" He glanced at her. "If all eyes are on me, they shall not be on you."

She frowned. Surely this was not an ideal plan . . .

"Trust me, my love," he said, leaning close and then drawing back with a grin. "I shall not murder him this very night. Much as I'd like to."

Chapter Thirty-Seven

Verity turned away from her husband, hoping he would make it to Albert or Roberta, that he would not eviscerate Captain Santiago on the Harringtons' grand ballroom floor. For now, however, she had to concentrate on escaping Ainsley's eye. He remained stubbornly on her flank, not five paces off, not seeming to care that she knew he was following her. With him watching, she could not go to the kitchen and ask for tea, not when there was a punch bowl set out in all four corners of the ballroom. 'Twould be too obvious. If she went out of doors, could she find someplace to dispose of the letter? But it was pouring rain. Not a single other guest was outside. What would she tell anyone who discovered her there?

It was then that Verity glimpsed her, hovering about twenty paces away. Soaking wet in a hooded cape, peeking around one of the fat columns of the portico outside. And staring at her with those startling blue eyes and blond tendrils about her cheeks. She must have failed to find a reason to enter the kitchen but was now offering Verity this one chance. The girl eased back to her hiding place behind the column.

A large group of men and women who had stood near the portico door moved off, apparently headed to the dance floor. They surrounded her and separated her from Ainsley. For the moment Verity was alone, and she saw her opportunity.

She opened the glass door without pausing, glad that it slid open and closed on well-oiled hinges, all the while wondering if she was making a fatal mistake. She prayed Ainsley's view was still blocked as she pulled the letter from her stays and approached the column. She couldn't see the girl. Was she behind it? It was certainly wide enough—

"Mrs. McKintrick!" Ainsley called, his voice high and tight.

She paused beside the column, burying the letter in the folds of her skirts and turning halfway around. "Why, Lieutenant! I was still quite warm in there. I thought I might catch a bit of this delicious cool air, born by the rain."

Three fingers tapped at her lower back, still hidden from Ainsley's view. *The girl! Please, God, let her stay hidden.*

It was their only chance, she decided. If she held on to the letter, it would only be a matter of a few moments before Ainsley demanded she be searched and it be discovered.

The girl slipped it from her fingers, and immediately Verity stepped forward toward the lieutenant, hoping to keep him from getting any closer to the column. "Do you like the rain as well as I, Lieutenant Ainsley?" she asked with a sigh, gazing out toward the sculpted gardens. "It reminds me a bit of Nevis. It is so marvelous, how the rains wash through, leaving everything looking brighter. Though the air is far more sultry on-island than here in New York."

"Yes," he sniffed. "So I hear."

"Well, I am quite cooled now," she said. "If you shall excuse me."

But as she moved toward the door, Ainsley reached out and gripped her arm.

"Lieutenant?" she said in alarm.

"Come with me, if you please, Mrs. McKintrick," he growled, rushing her past the glass door to the side wall, out of view of the others inside.

"What are you doing?" she shrieked.

"Obtaining evidence." He pinned her against the wall and roughly reached up and dipped his hand into the top of her stays.

She screamed. In outrage, for certain. But then realizing it was a perfect way to escape him, she screamed again. "Help! *Help!*"

His face reddened as he struggled to hold on to her, madly trying to reach into her stays again, a man desperate to prove what he thought was true.

The door opened.

"See here!" cried a man, hastening over to them.

"Lieutenant Ainsley!" shouted another.

Together, they pried him off her. "What goes on here?"

Verity was crying and lifted a trembling hand to her mouth.

"She is a spy! She has a note on her person, destined for the enemy!" Ainsley rushed to explain, struggling against their grip on him. Others began pouring out of the hall.

"What a terrible accusation!" Verity said, nervous tears flowing down her cheeks. "This man accosted me!"

More men arrived, some women, all surrounding them.

"She has a note in her stays!" Ainsley said in disgust. "If she is innocent, she shall take no issue in undressing before three ladies in the privacy of her chambers and so prove it."

"A far better idea than manhandling the woman, do you not think?" said a stately gentleman.

"I feared she would run off!"

"In this rain? Are you mad?"

"This is war, sir. And spies will go to great lengths to . . ."

He paused, spotting Ian coming through the door. Verity cried out and hastened over to her husband, sheltering under his arm. "Oh, Ian. Lieutenant Ainsley accosted me! He was most inappropriate. He seemed to think I had an ill-begotten note in my stays!"

"What is this?" Ian asked, turning to the man even as he gently placed Verity behind him. "You dared to abuse my *wife?*"

The other men let go of Ainsley and the lieutenant stood as tall as he could, fists clenching and unclenching. "I have reason to believe that you and your wife are working for the enemy." He looked beyond Ian to the other soldiers present. "Surround them!"

Ian leaned closer to Ainsley as the soldiers obeyed. "You manhandle my wife and then *dare* to question my *allegiance* to the Crown?" He didn't give the man further warning but instead pulled back and brought a powerful fist across Ainsley's jaw.

The lieutenant careened backward. If it weren't for the two men who had pried him away from Verity, Ainsley might have fallen onto his back in the wet gravel beyond the portico. He righted himself, seething mad, cradling his jaw.

Red-faced, he strode directly back to Ian. "Ever since you arrived in New York, the rebels have gained intelligence that only Mr. Harrington and a few other civilians knew about. I believe that either Mr. Harrington is cooperating with you, or you have stolen into his study and found private documents."

"Of all the insults!" Verity cried. "Albert is my cousin!"

"If you and your husband are *innocent,*" he

went on, annunciating each syllable of the word, "then do as I suggested. Agree to three Loyalist women searching you in the privacy of your chambers."

"Fine," Verity said, edging between Ainsley and Ian before her husband advanced on him again. "But know that you shall have a very serious mark on your record because of this." She folded her arms. "Name the women you would trust for such an important task."

Ainsley's gray eyes narrowed over her confidence. For the first time, he looked as though he feared she'd rid herself of the note. He scanned the gardens, the side of the building, even the ground where she had stood.

"Lieutenant?" Major Rye said. "What has transpired here?"

Ainsley stiffened, and his neck reddened again. "These two were seen near the Dock Ward three days past, Major. A known environs of rebel spies."

"I visited a *haberdashery* in Hanover Square that Mrs. Harrington suggested," Verity said derisively, shaking her head as if she were greatly upset. "For the very hat you see atop my head now. Do I appear a spy, Major?" she asked him, hands outstretched in outrage.

"Then I discovered Mrs. Harrington and Mrs. McKintrick making their way through a checkpoint into a rebel district," Ainsley continued.

"To aid the poor," she said, growing righteous in her indignation.

"So it seems," Ainsley said. "Two days ago we suffered a robbery of ammunitions at the harbor," the lieutenant pressed on. "Only five people knew of that shipment, one of which was Mr. Harrington."

"And four others," the major clarified. "These are serious charges, Lieutenant."

"I understand, Major. Just last night we raided a known ammunitions stash, only to find the Sons of Liberty had narrowly escaped. And again, that was knowledge Mr. Harrington was privy to."

"Among others," the major allowed, motioning for him to go on.

"But if we find the note that was on Mrs. McKintrick's person when she was on the dance floor, I believe we shall learn a great deal about the McKintricks' loyalties . . . as well as the Harringtons'. The haberdashery might not have been their only drop point. Perhaps they passed a missive over to rebel cohorts at the workhouse."

"Did you see that transpire, Lieutenant?" the major asked.

"No, but I very much suspect that I shall be vindicated for my rough manners if you simply have this woman searched for the letter I glimpsed in her stays." He stared hard at Verity.

The major reluctantly turned to Verity. "I beg your pardon, Mrs. McKintrick. But these are perilous times and we cannot be too cautious. While I regret that the lieutenant's accusations might well be ill placed, I fear the only way to clear your husband's good name, as well as your own and our fine hosts, is to do as he asks. Would you be so kind as to retreat to the privacy of your quarters and allow my wife and two others to observe?"

"Major, this is *most* inappropriate," Ian said.

"I am quite aware, Captain McKintrick." To his credit, his face was flaming red now too. "And yet I have been informed that when you last weighed anchor here, you refused to hoist the Union Jack. That fact gives me pause, Captain."

Ian clamped his lips shut for a moment. "That was in a moment of crisis," he said. "I have since thought better of my ways, as well as married a fine Nevisian woman, loyal to the Crown."

"Still, sir, we must see this through," the major said. "No matter how improper the circumstances might be. Lives are at stake."

Cheeks burning, Verity lifted her chin high and faced him. "And when my innocence is proven, do I have your word that Lieutenant Ainsley shall never approach me or mine again?"

"You can be most certain of it, my dear. If he is wrong about this—" the major paused to send a scornful look in the younger officer's direction— "he shall be reassigned to the most regretful post I can find."

"Very well," she said, stepping toward the door. "I shall go to my quarters."

"Wait!" sputtered Ainsley. "She must be attended at all times!"

"Cease your vitriol, Lieutenant," hissed the major. "You have done quite enough. Leave it to my wife and her friends to make certain that Mrs. McKintrick is no *spy.*"

Verity continued on, but she noted that the major's wife and her friends were directly on her heels. The music continued, with a few on the dance floor still, but most of the party's attention was directed at them, wondering what was transpiring. As much as she longed to do so, she dared not look back to the portico. Was the girl in the cape still hovering beyond the portico column? How daring she was! And clearly in as much mortal danger as Verity herself.

She smiled to herself as she climbed the stairs. The missive they'd passed off near the haberdashery resulted in another shipment of armaments, hopefully now in the hands of the Continental Army. And information on the eggs, she assumed, had spared the capture of other ammunition that the Sons of Liberty had stashed. That gratified her. If only they had been able to keep up this charade for longer . . .

Perhaps there would be other ways to aid the cause in the days to come. But what exactly had she just passed off to the blonde outside behind the column? Whatever it was, she hoped it was well worth the humiliation she now suffered.

They turned down the hall and, five doors down, into the room she shared with Ian, the ladies directly behind her. Two of them whispered excitedly, no doubt thinking of the stories they might tell in the days ahead. Mrs. Rye appeared beleaguered by the task before her. *This shall not be so bad,* she thought. *I shall pretend that they are my sisters, not strangers.* But as Verity turned to shut the door behind them, she saw there were four soldiers in dress uniform, fully armed, following them as well. They took positions in pairs on either side of the bedroom door. And at the end of the hall stood Major Rye and Ian, as well as Lieutenant Ainsley. The Harringtons were present too, doing their best to look indignant rather than frightened. Four more soldiers surrounded them.

She closed the door and turned to face the women. "Please, ladies. Surround me. I want you each to attest to the fact that I have nothing on my person and had no opportunity to throw anything in the fire."

The women did as she asked, one giggling nervously.

"Now, if one of you will kindly unlace me?"

In short order she was undressed to her stays and petticoat.

One woman searched her waistband and every

inch of her hem. The other took a quick peek down her stays. All while Major Rye's pretty wife looked on, arms crossed. When they were through, she sighed and shook her head. "You must forgive us this egregious intrusion, Mrs. McKintrick," she said. "Understand that we owe you a debt of service, given your willingness to endure this violation of your privacy."

"Thank you, Mrs. Rye," Verity said, curtseying in her stays and petticoat.

They waited until she was behind the dressing screen before filing out of the room. Between the slats of the screen, Verity witnessed the pacing Lieutenant Ainsley, the word being shared between the major and his wife, and then Ian's approach, quietly closing the door behind him.

He met her behind the screen, taking her in his arms. "You marvelous girl," he said, pulling her closer and stroking her cheek, her neck, her shoulder before looking into her eyes again. "You marvelous, wonderful girl. Not only did ye manage to pass off the letter, but ye had our tormentor removed."

She laughed, then reached up to cradle his face and kiss him. "Yes." But then she pulled back. "Yet, Ian . . . what became of your exchange with Santiago?"

"I told him that if I did not have a wife to consider, I would be challenging him to a duel.

That somehow, someway, my brother's death would be avenged. And then I became aware that you had need of me, outside."

She frowned. "Why do you think that he did not step forward to say that he himself saw a note peeking from my bodice? Might it have been a means of making amends?"

"I do not know," Ian said, running a hand through his hair. " 'Twould be a start. But it does not settle our score. Or he intends to use it against you later."

She grimaced at the thought. "Did you get to Roberta or Albert? Tell them we think it is too dangerous to remain? Will they find a way to get to the *Inverness* this night?"

"I did. Once you are all safely aboard the ship, I shall bring an end to Santiago and then we shall make our escape."

He tried to step past her, but she grabbed his arm. "Ian, you told him yourself that if you did not have a wife to consider, you would challenge him to a duel."

"Aye."

She rested a gentle hand on his chest. "If you go after him and you are caught, where does that leave me? I helped you escape Nevis. I am quite certain I would not be as successful here in New York."

"But Santiago's testimony—"

"Santiago cannot hurt me if I am far from him,"

she said, stepping back into her gown. "From all of them. We have done what we could here, husband. And I know you wish to see Santiago punished for what he did. But, Ian . . . what if instead you simply inform the French that they may well have a Spanish enemy spying upon them? Allow *them* to see justice served, as well as protect your own?"

He sighed heavily, paced away and back, rubbing his face, thinking.

She did not press the matter further. 'Twould take a bit of time for him to think clearly again. "Lace me up?" she said.

He eased her toward him and kissed her temple, then reached for the laces. "Do you think Roberta and Albert will come?" he asked, looking up and around the fine room.

"I hope so. Do you mind?"

"Nay. 'Tis wise, lass. Despite Major Rye's defense of them, Ainsley has introduced potential suspicion. Best for them to leave now on account of the wee one."

Little Francis. What would become of the babe if his parents were discovered? If they were found guilty and hanged? The thought of it made Verity feel sick to her stomach. *We would take him,* she thought fiercely. And yet if Roberta and Albert were indeed found guilty, there would be many after their necks as well.

Thoughts of the little chubby boy landing in

an orphanage, as his parents were led away in chains, chilled her.

"What of the *Inverness*? Is she ready to sail? The crew?"

"If McKay has done as I ordered him, the crew will be close at hand, and she will be loaded with ample supplies and ready for the journey back to the Indies." Ian knew she had heard the same rumors he had.

"Dried fish? Flour?"

"Aye, lass. We shall see the Double T provisioned, one way or another."

"Oh, Ian," she said, embracing him and kissing him twice, then once again for good measure. She had not realized how it burdened her so, the threat against those they loved and cared for.

"They shall make it through the harvest." He ran his fingers along her hairline. "After that . . ."

"After that 'tis all in God's hands," she finished.

He paused, took her hands in his, and looked into her eyes. "Verity, I . . ." He ducked his head, then looked at her again. This time, regret drew down the corners of his eyes. "I know that ye want nothing more than to return to your sisters, lass. But I cannot take ye. Not with Shubert about."

"I know," she said.

"But I shall get ye as close as I can. Send word to Gray. He can come for the supplies. On Statia, if necessary. Or Martinique."

She lifted a hand to his cheek. "You do not think my sisters will come with him?" She laughed lightly. "There shall be a Banning reunion yet."

"They would risk that? Coming to Statia from Nevis?"

"I doubt they shall be the only planters trying to secure provisions from any source they can find. Regardless, they shall find the rationale to come to me. I am confident of that."

"Good, then," he said, lifting her hands to his lips. "Pack what you must. And then we shall steal away, looking for where the Lord wishes for us to pick up our sword next."

"Or our stays and baskets of eggs," she said saucily.

He laughed. "Oh, Verity, how I love ye." He bent to kiss her, softly, then deeper, searchingly.

She pried his warm hands from her waist. "Remember that ardor for when we are again alone on the *Inverness*, Captain."

"Aye. You may count on it."

CHAPTER THIRTY-EIGHT

Her words rang in Ian's head as he pulled on an oilskin slicker and led Verity down the servants' staircase. He still felt the constant pull to give in to his anger, to mete out his own form of justice when it came to Santiago. But Verity had been right; his responsibility was to her first. Their lives would be best served by leaving justice in God's hands—and in the hands of the French. What became of his enemy would be up to them.

But oh, how he itched to borrow Albert's pistols and meet the Spaniard in the gardens at dawn! Back and forth went his mind. Only his heart—Verity—kept him centered on the task at hand. He would not have his wife, his beautiful, wonderful, daring wife meeting him in the same New York jail where they had first met. Worse yet would be to have a hangman's noose tightened about his neck as she looked on.

Her words as they left Nevis for the last time came back to him. *"I do not care to lose my new husband to the gallows. My heart could not take that. You wish to protect me? Protect my heart."*

No, he would see her to safety. Protect her heart by choosing to protect his life above seeing

Santiago face justice. That was his highest duty. That was where the greater honor would be found. Duncan was gone. Verity was here beside him. And she was right—there might be another way to make the Spanish privateer pay . . .

He paused at a tiny service window in the servants' hall that ran along one part of the ballroom. Now in the early hours of the morning, the party was winding down, only the most stalwart—and drunken—guests still in attendance. Albert was saying farewell to a couple, but Roberta was not in sight. He hoped she would have the good sense to gather up their son, her husband, and quickly follow them to the wharf. Taking the time to pack a trunk would only attract unwelcome attention. "Come," he said to Verity.

They moved into the kitchen, where three exhausted cooks glanced up at them in confusion. Ian reached for a loaf of leftover bread and raised it for them to see. "A late-night snack for the missus and me," he explained cheerfully.

"We did so much dancing, I awoke and found myself fairly famished," Verity added.

All three cooks continued to blink wearily at them as they passed by. None bothered to ask where they were going.

"Too much of the punch, if you ask me," said one of them as Ian and Verity disappeared down the hall.

"That rain shall sober them up in short order," said another.

They exited the house from the back, and Ian was glad for the rain. In tandem with the dark of the early morning hour, it would make it terribly difficult for anyone to spot them. They hurried down toward the stables but didn't run, for to run would make it seem as if they were fleeing.

All the grooms and stableboys were out in front of the mansion, helping guests into their carriages. Verity and Ian hitched two of the Harringtons' horses to an older carriage, which they would use to get to the harbor. The Harringtons would bring their finest horses and their new carriage come dawn. It had been her idea not only to utilize the horses and carriages to make their escape, but also take them aboard the *Inverness*. Wherever they landed, the horses and carriages could be used or sold, and they would serve as provision for Albert and Roberta in beginning anew. As would Roberta's diamond and pearl necklace.

Verity stroked the nearest gelding's cheek after tying him to the post. Being so near such a fine horse made her think of the geldings Duncan had purchased and Ian had brought to her. Were they well? Were Ket and Gray able to care for them? Feed them? During the war to come, what would happen to horses on islands in which their masters struggled to feed their children and slaves?

"Ready?" Ian said.

"I wish we could wait for them. All of us go together."

"Nay. We shall be less conspicuous on our own. And this way we can be certain the *Inverness* is set to sail at first light when they arrive."

"Very well," she said, accepting his hand up and into the carriage. There would be no servant to drive them; Ian would see to the task himself.

Thankfully, the dreadful weather had forced most of the soldiers indoors. No one wished to be out in the drenching rain, with a whipping wind that more than hinted at autumn's approach. And given the hour and inclement weather, those soldiers on duty would be more apt to let them pass.

It was only when they reached the wharf that they came across a blockade, where two visibly shivering soldiers stood stalwartly at the entrance to the pier. "Who goes there?" called one as Ian pulled the carriage to a stop. Two others rushed out of a small warming hut near Verity's window, hurriedly donning their tricorns.

" 'Tis I, Captain McKintrick, of the *Inverness* at the end of this pier, and my wife. We arrive late, a party at the Harringtons' home keeping us. We hope to gain a portion of the night's slumber before we head out come daybreak."

"Indeed." The man who inquired stepped forward. "Papers, please, Captain."

Ian pulled out a leather-wrapped scroll. "Mind you review them in the hut where they shall be kept dry, Lieutenant."

"Very good, sir," he said stiffly, going to do as Ian suggested. "Search the carriage," he said over his shoulder to the soaked soldiers. "Be certain that there is none but Mrs. McKintrick inside. Nor any contraband cargo anywhere on the carriage."

Ian heaved a sigh, wanting to scream at the soldier's slow pace. Common courtesy would demand that the man move with haste! Did he not notice the pouring rain? Or perhaps he relished the opportunity to get a bit of warmth in the hut, a respite from this weather? Regardless, it was nothing less than what he expected to encounter. He simply did not believe his heart would cease its mad galloping beat until Verity was safely aboard the *Inverness* and Michael was ready to cast off and haul sail.

At last the man returned. "You may proceed, Captain," he said, offering the leather-wrapped scroll back to him.

"Thank you. Good eve, gentlemen."

"Good eve, sir."

Ian flicked the reins, and they moved on to the *Inverness*. Two men on watch straightened and then called out to others when they saw him.

"Bring out the wide cargo gangplank, sailor," Ian directed. "We aim to bring these fine mounts and carriage with us."

"Aye, aye, Cap'n," said the man.

Soon Michael appeared on the deck, even as the men began shoving out the gangplank over which they would lead the horses in.

"Good to see you, Captain," Michael said, leaning over the rail with a grin.

"And I you, McKay," he returned, water pouring from his tricorn. " 'Tis a lovely night to consider setting sail, no?"

McKay looked up, rain splashing his face, then back to them. "None finer. All is in order, Cap'n. We can heave anchor and sail just as soon as you order to do so, no matter the weather."

"Good man," Ian said with relief. "But we shall await three others before departing. They are due to arrive at first light."

"Aye. Who shall be our guests this time?"

"Albert and Roberta Harrington, and their young son."

"Oh?" Michael said. "The city not to their liking any longer?"

"Something like that," he said, sharing a smile with his first mate.

Ian went to the carriage, opened the door, and assisted Verity down onto the deck. Once they were aboard, Ian looked down the length of the pier. Everything in him wanted to cut loose and head to open sea. Negotiating patrols on open water would be one thing. If they had to fight their way out of the crowded harbor and past the Narrows of Sandy Hook, 'twould be quite another. He could not set sail until sunrise without arousing some suspicion. But as soon as there was a bit of light to the east, he wanted to call the men to action.

"Make haste, Harrington," he muttered. "Secure your wife and child and make haste."

Ian would not come inside their cabin, no matter how much Verity pleaded. Instead, he remained on deck, pacing. And given that it was her cousin's family who kept them tied to the pier, she stubbornly remained awake, though in the warm and dry protection of the cabin. Three in the morning became four, four became five, and to the east the first vestiges of sunrise appeared as a rust-colored glow. The rain had finally stopped, so she decided to join Ian on deck to pace the ship with her husband.

She knew they had to go. Now. For the tenth time she gazed down the pier. The crew had breakfasted early and were all about the masts and deck at their stations, ready to follow their captain's orders, well aware that there was a chance they might be pursued. *Albert, Roberta, where are you?* she wondered, wringing her hands.

Had they been waylaid? Changed their minds? Were Ian and she endangering themselves by waiting a minute longer?

"How much longer shall we wait?" she asked Ian. She shivered, wet right through despite her oilskin cape. "We told the soldiers last night we intended to set sail at first light."

"Give them just a wee bit longer, lass. I promised them until sunrise."

She scanned the wharf again, biting her bottom lip. All along it she could see the drowsy movements of those beginning their day—lifting awnings, moving crates, fetching firewood. A few on horseback . . . but no carriages within view.

And then they came around a corner, the fine carriage and pair of geldings immediately recognizable.

"There!" she said excitedly.

"Aye!" he said. "Prepare to make way!" he cried.

"Prepare to make way!" Michael echoed. But it was more of a reminder than a true order, for the crew was more than ready. All eyes moved to the end of the pier, where the redcoats stopped the carriage and the dreadfully slow soldier asked for Albert's papers.

"Come now, man," Ian grunted. "Let them pass!"

As if in defiance, the small figure in the

distance casually strolled to the warming hut and disappeared inside. Was he truly questioning the identity of a city alderman?

Verity willed him to return to the carriage and gesture them onward. "Please, Lord. Go before them, beside them, behind them . . ." she prayed under her breath. "Please, Lord!"

She fought tears when the man finally emerged again, and the redcoats separated. Albert flicked the reins. Finally, the carriage was coming their way.

"At the ready, men!" called Ian. "As soon as that carriage is aboard, we shall be under way!"

"Aye, Cap'n!" cried one after another, from the forecastle to the mizzenmast.

As the Harringtons reached the side of the *Inverness*, Albert hopped onto the pier and rushed to help Roberta—holding a sleeping Francis—down from the carriage. She hurried up the gangplank and embraced Verity. Then Albert prepared to lead his team aboard the ship.

"We told the guards that we had secured passage with you," Roberta said.

"If word reaches any of the officers at your party that you are leaving the city, they shall suspect . . ."

"With what your wife passed off to the girl last night," Albert said, "we shall only have until midmorn before 'tis determined I am the mole."

He gripped the rail and looked down the pier,

clearly worried that they were being pursued.

Ian glanced over his shoulder. "Michael, the ropes."

"Aye, Cap'n."

"Just as soon as the last wheels enter—"

"Aye, Cap'n!"

Verity said, "I shall show Roberta to their cabin and go to the horses and get them settled." She hurried down the steep stairs into the hold, knowing the crew assigned to the stables could well do it themselves but aware she had to do something or she'd either scream or begin crying. Down in the hold she opened a cabin door for Roberta.

"May I come with you?" asked the woman, carefully setting her baby on a cot and covering him with a blanket. "I am far too nervous to find rest yet. And Francis is dead asleep."

"Of course," Verity replied, then led her to the stables. The men inside were already shutting the two new horses in the small corral and hauling in the loading plank. In minutes they were heaving the hold door shut.

"How did you manage it?" she asked Roberta quietly as she moved to reassure one nervous gelding with long, gentle strokes to his cheek.

"With our staff we claimed the baby was sick and we had to seek out a doctor. Without a bag or trunk, they did not question our urgent departure."

"What kept you so long?"

"The last guests," she said. "It was only when Albert offered Mr. Tucker and Mr. and Mrs. Hanneman accommodations for what remained of the night that they finally retired. If he hadn't, I believe we would still be sitting there in the parlor, making conversation with them."

The men uncinched the remaining harnesses and straps from the geldings and gave them fresh hay before they all climbed back up the stairs to the deck. With a thrill, Verity saw that the first sails had unfurled, and they were already slowly moving out past the next ship. *Breathe into those sails, Lord. Cover us. Help us escape this harbor!*

It took a while to ease a ship this size into motion, but she continued to gain speed. After Ian had negotiated his way through the anchored ships and reached wider water, he called for more sails.

Verity peered up toward the Union Jack, merrily dancing in the wind. At the moment, she was glad for it, as the flag would cause any patrolling ships to allow them passage. But she knew there would come a day when Ian would strike it and raise a Continental flag, firmly declaring himself, come what may.

She glanced back to the harbor, now covered in the morning's golden light, several other ships dropping sail, men moving on skiffs between, more people along the wharf. She did not mind leaving the city behind. No, give her the swaying palms of the islands, the methodic turning of mill blades, the green-blue of the sea, the leaping of dolphins. She shivered as Ian approached her.

"We're safely away. Into the cabin with ye, lass, and into warmer clothes. Ye shall catch your death in that ball gown."

"Not yet. I want to remain here, until I cannot see it any longer," she said through chattering teeth. She knew it was half nerves, half her damp clothing. "I need to know that no one follows us."

" 'Twill take some time," he said. "But if anyone gives chase, it will be some hours, I wager."

Finally clear of the last ships, he called for still more sails—but not all, he explained, because it would appear as if they were running, not gradually setting to sea as was customary. "Let us not make those who see us wonder, eh?"

CHAPTER THIRTY-NINE

It took Verity a full day out of New York to cease her trembling, another day to settle into the reassuring rise and fall of the ship on the waves. Yet many ships had been spotted along the coast of America, nine out of ten of them British. It seemed the Royal Navy intended to do all it could to keep the rebels in check.

But Albert did not wish to sail to the Indies as Verity and Ian urged him to. Instead, he was eager to reach Philadelphia, where the Second Continental Congress was meeting. He intended to offer his services to the cause there, either by accepting a command or by helping strategize in winning the war.

And yet they could not get the Harringtons back to land along the coasts of New Jersey or Delaware, so thick was the Brits' presence. They feared that some might know of the suspicions about Albert Harrington and capture him. Farther south, as they sailed along the coast of Maryland and British vessels became more scarce, Ian had to decide—was it best to strike the Union Jack? Who was he more likely to see in these waters, the Brits or rebel privateers?

" 'Tis now or never to fly our true colors," Albert said to him. He turned to Roberta, who handed him a paper-wrapped cloth. "Here. I have it on good authority that General Washington aims to fly these on the six schooners he is outfitting now."

Ian unwrapped it and let the cloth fall open. On the flag was an embroidered, towering pine tree, and the words *An Appeal to Heaven* beneath it. "Is this how the general aims to win this war?" he asked Albert, eyes wide.

"It cannot hurt, having the Almighty on one's side," Albert returned with a smile. "Since the Brits outlawed the stripes, 'tis a way of declaring yourself and yet not breaking the law, right? And when you take us to shore," he said, nodding toward the coast, "it might keep any minutemen from shooting the hats from our heads."

Ian laughed. He looked at McKay. "Are cannons ready, should we have need of them?"

"Ever since we left New York, Cap'n," Michael answered.

"Good man. So be it. Strike the Union Jack."

"Strike the Union Jack!" called Michael.

Solemnly, many gathered to watch the flag come down. Most doffed their hats in respect, including Ian and Albert. Regardless of where their loyalties now lay, the country of their birth deserved that much. It brought a tear to Verity's eye. Even though she had helped the rebels, it was not until that very moment that she felt the final tearing of separation. But Albert was right—it was time to declare themselves. To make it known as to which side they truly belonged, and for whom they would fight. No longer in the shadows but in the full light of day.

"Hoist the tree!" Ian called gravely.

"Hoist the tree!" Michael repeated.

This time, every man's hat was held to his chest, each watching as the flag fluttered and then spread in the wind.

An appeal to heaven. On six schooners, besides the *Inverness*. But only seven ships . . . against the multitude they had left behind in New York. Likely there were other privateers who even now were hoisting the stripes or the coiled snake favored by the Massachusetts Minutemen.

Yes, Lord, Verity prayed, *please hear our call. Help us. We are small, so small. But with you, we are mighty.*

Albert was able to give them directions to a shielded cove near the Chesapeake and the town of Applewood, which was known to be held by the rebels—and ignored for the moment by the Brits. Albert's knowledge proved true. They spotted a pair of British vessels over the course of the afternoon, and each seemed to ignore the *Inverness* with her green-tree flag at the mast, perhaps due to a more pressing mission or electing to save their firepower for a different front.

"If only we always knew what our enemy was thinking," Verity said to Albert when they had tensely watched the last schooner pass, all the while wondering if puffs of smoke would erupt from her cannon portholes, the early warning sign of cannon balls on their way to destroy the *Inverness*'s deck and masts.

"Alas, I do not think the British shall welcome me again into their inner sanctum," said Albert, giving Verity a wink. "But there are others who yet tarry behind enemy lines."

Verity looped her arm through his. They had spent summers together at Hartwick, though not since they were children. It felt strange, befriending Albert again as an adult. And yet it felt right too, somehow. Familiar. "Did you mind it very much, leaving behind the council seat? The mansion? The staff?"

"Truthfully, my dear, I did not give it a thought. Only your question just now made me consider all that was forfeited." He looked over the whitecaps before them. "Perhaps if I had married a lesser girl . . ."

"But you did not," Verity said. "I adore your Roberta."

"As do I," he said. He shook his head as if in wonderment. "From the very start, 'twas as if the Lord entwined our minds, as well as our hearts."

Verity glanced over at Ian, standing at the wheel, twenty paces away. The wind caught his shirt, opening a small window to expose smooth, tanned skin and muscle. But it was his eyes— which, sensing her gaze, turned upon her—that sent a shiver of delight down her spine. "I know of what you speak, Cousin," she said. "The Lord brought me love once, and I lost him. But then He brought another . . ."

Ian's expression turned quizzical, clearly aware that she spoke of him, and she grinned.

"Go to him," Albert said, nudging her. "Make him willing to endure the dangers these family ties have brought him."

"Ian McKintrick?" she said with a laugh. "I think the rebel was already in him before he ever caught wind of a proper rebellion."

Three days after the storm on Nevis, the roads were at last passable. Gray and Philip rode for town, eager to see if any ships and supplies had arrived, while the others returned to the fields.

Selah could not help herself. It had rained all through the next day, and then little Madeleine had a wee cold and she'd spent the following day helping Keturah pace the floors with the suffering child. Now this morning she was ever so curious, wondering if that odd Mr. Reed was still about or if, with the roads passable again, he was on his way to another plantation.

She asked Abe to saddle her horse and then rode out to the middle field, where they were working. She heard them singing before she reached them, their voices rising together in that field beneath the green Nevis Peak . . . " 'Rock of Ages, cleft for me, let me hide myself in Thee. Let the water and the blood, from Thy riven side which flowed, be of sin the double cure, cleanse me from its guilt and power.' "

She had not heard the hymn since before the night of the storm. It was sung to a familiar tune in England but never with these lyrics. She'd been humming the tune for days after hearing Mr. Reed teaching it to them. Now, listening to her friends sing together, with all their varied accents, in their imperfection it was somehow more than perfect. A shiver ran down her neck. 'Twas as if she were hearing from heaven itself. *People of so many nations, praising God as though with one voice . . .*

And Mr. Reed was in the midst of them, singing and swinging a hoe, weeding. Matthew glimpsed her and made his way over, his boots covered in mud. "Miss Selah?"

"Good morning, Matthew. So . . . that Mr. Reed. He remained with you through the storm?"

"Through it all," Matthew said, shifting his hat back on his head to wipe his forehead of sweat.

"Does he expect us to pay him for his toil?" she asked.

"No, Miss Selah. Says he's paying for the bread he ate and for more time with his friends."

"What do the others think of him?"

Matthew let a slow grin spread across his face, and he tilted his head. "Well now, I don' think they know what to think of Mr. Reed. But he's rather difficult not to like, Miss Selah. The man is . . ." He paused, shook his head. "Different."

As if he sensed they were talking about him, the lanky man straightened and looked their way. In spite of herself, Selah smiled. His lopsided grin and lifted hand were impossible to greet in any other fashion.

"You should come to the meetinghouse tonight, Miss Selah. Listen to how the man talks to our people."

"I think I shall, Matthew, thank you."

He did not have to ask twice. Selah had regretted not staying with them the other night to observe the man. Now she'd finally have the opportunity.

Gray had managed to secure two hogsheads of dried cornmeal that morning in Charlestown, and the first corn on the garden stalks were just getting big enough to pick. All afternoon Selah worked with Sansa and Mitilda to prepare four large pots of corn-and-squash chowder and pans of corn bread. Together they carried it up to the meetinghouse as the field workers started to gather for the evening meal. It was their pattern to stop work about four in the afternoon, walk back to clean up, rest a bit, and then come together again around six in the evening. This, too, had caused other planters consternation, as most tended to work their slaves from sunup to sundown. But that mattered not to Gray and Keturah. More and more, they were committed to running the Double T as the Lord guided them, not how their neighbors insisted they do so.

Selah found that such decisions brought her heart a measure of peace. She saw firsthand how weary they all were, even if they quit the fields several hours before their neighbors. Laboring in the fields or the house on the Double T was not what she wanted for all of them, but at least they were better cared for here than elsewhere. Here, they had a measure of respect. Dignity. Protection. Other plantations were apt to work their slaves to death, especially with the supply shortages of late. She'd seen plenty of other slaves around town who looked like living skeletons. Gray and Ket had settled on a course that not only kept their people alive, it was leading them to the hope of a better life than they might have ever wished for. If they could just make it through . . .

Already more than twenty freed men and women had come to live at the Double T and work for a wage. The majority of others were on a seven-year track to earn their emancipation as well. The few who were not—the churlish Frederick, who physically challenged Matthew nearly every day, the lazy Bonita, who refused to do more than pretend to work—were examples of the kind of people Gray and Ket had decided not to bring to the Double T again. "I shall not beat them into submission, as others urge me. But neither of us aids the other," Gray said one night to Ket, weary face in his hands after talking to his overseer. Even Matthew did not know what to do with them.

"There are others," Selah had said. "Others who need us. Want us. And we want them." And it was true. Word had spread across the island about the Double T. There was a reason Mr. Reed heard he should come here—to her home first—when he began to talk to the black folk. 'Twas because there was not a slave on Nevis who did not yearn to be at the Double T themselves. Already a young freed couple, Betty and Homer, had made their way over from St. Kitts to work on their plantation, drawn by the stories alone.

Being a slave in the West Indies was nigh unto a sentence leading to certain death. Planters in the Carolinas routinely threatened their own slaves that they would sell them to another in the Indies if they did not cooperate. Yet here on the Double T, Selah had witnessed something new among both the slaves and freed people.

The courage, the teensiest bit of courage, to dream.

It was with that thought that Selah entered the meetinghouse, smiling in delight, waiting for everyone to clap and shout their approval as they brought in their supper. She could hear folks murmuring and talking among themselves as she climbed the stairs, already gathering together. But as she rounded the corner, she saw that they hovered around the young Mr. Reed, who was holding a worn Bible in his hand and reaching out to talk to the little ones and old people alike.

Some in back spied them and hurried to help relieve their burdens, lifting the heavy pots of soup and carrying them to the table at the side of the room. But the majority were too captivated by Mr. Reed to even notice their arrival.

"Here was a girl—a girl!" Mr. Reed went on, reaching down to tap the chin of an adolescent, "who had been taken from her home and made little more than a slave in the house of a king."

Men and women groaned and shook their heads. The children seemed to lean closer to the preacher. *What is this?* Selah thought. *Just what is he preaching about?*

"In that time, no one approached the king unless he or she was summoned. To do so could very well mean certain death."

"Mmm, mmm," said one man.

"Yessir, she knew what was right," said a woman.

"But her uncle," Mr. Reed said, drawing himself upward, waiting until all were silent, "knew that Esther was the only one who might possibly save them all. For it had been set in motion by their enemies . . . this plan to kill every Jew in every part of the empire. And that empire, my friends, was vast. Think of all the different lands you came from. It was the same for the Jews—conquered and spread to many nations. Thousands upon thousands were condemned to die."

He glanced at his Bible, but Selah could see that he did not need to refer to Scripture to tell this story; he'd clearly told it many times before. "Now Esther was very afraid," he said soberly. "She knew that if she dared to enter the king's rooms, she could be killed in minutes. Had not the king put his previous queen to death for displeasing him?"

"Yessir, yes he did," said a man.

"That Queen Vashti was done cold in her grave," said another.

"Yes, she was." Mr. Reed set down his Bible and rolled up his shirtsleeves, exposing his tanned skin. Earned by working alongside these people. What kind of person did that? Verity wondered. Worked the fields without compensation?

Well, I have done so, she admitted. But then this land was partly hers. Her home. Why would Mr. Reed go to such lengths?

"The king was not a righteous man. Not a good man. But he had a tender place in his heart for Esther." He paused and looked around the room. "And the good Lord who loved her, who loved her people, knew that. And mind, that is the same Lord who loves each of us . . . you, and you, and you . . ."

Mr. Reed bent to gently touch several in the circle before him. And there was something in the gesture that made Selah's breath catch. This was not a sermon like anything she had ever experienced at St. Philip's or back at home at the parish church near Hartwick, where the priest wearily climbed to his perch on high to lecture the people. No, this man was with them. One with them.

He straightened and looked over the gathering. "The Lord who loves you, and you, and even you," he said, pointing at a man who stood with his arms crossed. "You and you and you," he went on. Finally, he glimpsed her, and that slow lopsided grin teased at the corners of his mouth. "And you too, Miss Banning." He dragged his eyes away from her. "The good Lord who loved them all, who loves us all, urged Esther to do the most frightening thing possible for a woman with little power. To go to the king, unbidden, and find

530

a way to plead for her people. And do you know what she did?"

"No sir," said several.

"What did she do?" asked another.

"She and her servants fasted for three days and three nights and prayed, prayed with everything in them. I wager she was asking for protection. For favor. But do you know what she said, once she was decided?" he cried.

He turned back and picked up his Bible again. " 'If I die, then I die,' " he finished in a whisper.

At that moment, Selah doubted she'd ever heard the meeting hall this quiet. Perhaps only when all were in the fields. Even the babies seemed enraptured by this man, as even she was.

His wide, somber eyes remained on the people before him. "That, my friends, was faith. Trust, that she was in that place, at that moment, for a special reason. Just as we are all here today on the Double T." He shook his head slowly. "I doubt that your mothers and fathers, those who cradled you in their arms and sang you to sleep and taught you to hunt or cook . . . nay, none of them ever dreamed of your future and hoped you would end up here."

He seemed to remember himself then, and Selah's presence among them. "I beg your pardon, Miss Banning. I mean no offense to you or the Covingtons . . ."

"No," she said, in little more than a whisper.

She cleared her throat. "I do not take offense." For he clearly had not meant to lead these people toward any sort of insurrection. He was simply lost in the story. As they all were.

He continued to shake his head, his wide eyes shifting back and forth, thinking. Then that infectious smile emerged again. "I can tell you that my mother and father never hoped and dreamed I would be here, far from home, a penniless preacher. And I would bet that Miss Selah's mother and father never hoped and dreamed she would be here as well, a place where few ladies come to live and make their home."

He looked upon her, a steady stare, silently asking if he was right.

In spite of herself, she found herself nodding her head, knowing that everyone was watching, and yet in that moment she was capable of nothing but utter honesty. Matching his own.

"And yet here we are, friends," Mr. Reed said. "All of us. Brought here from Africa and England. Seen by God. Known by Him. Brought together by Him here on the Double T. 'For such a time as this.' The question is . . . how might we make the most of it?"

CHAPTER FORTY

"Sail, ho!" cried Talisker from up in the crow's nest of the *Inverness.*

Eight days out of Maryland, en route to the Indies, Ian frowned. He reached for his spyglass and searched the horizon. There were not many vessels who tacked back against the tides and trade winds on their way to the Indies. Most carried on from North America to England, Ireland, France.

"Can you make out a flag, Talisker?" he called.

The man studied the horizon. "No, Cap'n! Too far, but I think she's closing."

Closing. Giving chase? Or simply making better time than they?

"Keep an eye on her! I want a report in an hour!"

"Aye, Cap'n!"

Ian began pacing the deck, unable to stop staring at the tiny vessel trailing them, glad that Verity was belowdecks with the horses, then seeing to a bath in their cabin and working on journal entries. Three hours later, when she emerged on deck, Ian grimaced as Talisker called down his hourly report. "She's a Spanish vessel, Cap'n, but flyin' the Union Jack too! Looks to me like the *Juliana*!"

Verity's head whipped around to where Ian and Michael and three other sailors stared. "It is him? He follows us?"

"Follows. Or chases," Ian said grimly. "Could be that he was tasked with capturing us." He held back on saying the rest: *or killing us.*

He began pacing again, cursing himself for not killing the man when he had the chance. Now here, on the open sea, in a smaller vessel, there was no way for them to outrun him. And given the greater size of his ship, he'd likely have twice the number of men in a fight . . .

He ran a hand through his hair. *And now there is Verity. What am I to do, Lord? How can I keep her safe out here?*

She moved to stand beside him, taking his hand, her very touch becalming. He pulled her closer in an embrace, not caring who saw. "Verity . . ." he said, not able to speak another word.

She looked up at him, seeming to understand all he felt, all he was thinking with but the utterance of her name. She laid a hand on his chest. "Ian."

And in her eyes, in her tone, he could hear the rest of her unspoken words too. If they must, they would stand and face Santiago together; they would live or die together.

"When they draw closer, you must hide, my love," he said. "Will you do that for me? Until the fight is over?"

She frowned. He could see that she longed to fight beside him but knew such was foolhardy. Reluctantly, she nodded. "I shall be in the stables below." A small smile teased at her lips. "With my sgian dubh in hand."

"That's my lass." With one more hug, he released her and started shouting orders. "Prepare for engagement, men! Ready the cannons! Don pistol and dagger!"

Verity fled to the hold when the *Juliana* was but three hundred feet behind them and closing fast. The ship had twenty-four guns to the *Inverness*'s twelve. Likely twice as many men. She had wanted to beg Ian to consider negotiating with Santiago, but she knew that the Spanish privateer had not chased them across the Atlantic to negotiate. He was here to bring them down. Either on British orders or to preserve his cover among the French. Once the McKintricks and Harringtons had fled, it would not have taken the British long to determine they were indeed the rebel spies, the ones responsible for several key losses of late, and declare them enemies of the Crown.

No, Captain Alejandro Santiago was not here to negotiate. He aimed to see the *Inverness* and her crew destroyed, sent to the bottom of the ocean.

And yet, down in the stables, brushing one horse after another to busy her trembling hands, there was no cannon fire. She could hear men shouting above on the deck. The beat of running feet, back and forth. More shouting. The customary groans and cracks of the timbers of the ship made her jump, certain each one was a cannon ball bursting through. Even so, none came. Was the *Juliana* not directly beside them? She dared to steal toward a small porthole, high on the side of the ship, and peer through it.

She gasped and backed up. Santiago's ship was but twenty feet off the port side. She forced herself to step forward and peek out again. She could just make out a portion of a man's hand, swinging a rope in a wide circle with a giant iron claw at the end. Ian screamed orders above, his voice too muffled to make out the words. Then she heard a clang, then another. Gunfire, shot after shot. More clanging, scratching, dragging. She backed up and under the neck of the closest gelding.

They were being boarded.

Not obliterated by cannon balls, but boarded.

For what purpose? To commandeer her? Capture the *Inverness*?

She put a hand to her mouth. Would Santiago kill Ian just as he had killed Duncan? Tears sprang to her eyes. Then anger welled up and made her heart begin to pound. She clutched at her dirk—the very knife Duncan had left with her—and longed to run up the steep stairs to stand beside Ian.

But she knew such a move would prove more a danger to him than a boon. He would fret more over her safety than his own, and it would distract him from the fight. No, her fight would come—she was certain of it. For now, she needed to remain hidden.

Men continued to yell, cry out, and fall on the deck above her. She backed up to the tiny hayloft and, seeing no other option, climbed up and into it, covering herself with hay, her face to the boards that lined the stables. From here, she could see through a narrow crack to a small portion of the stables.

She began to pray.

A man screamed, others cried in outrage. More fell to the deck in scuffles . . . from the sound of it, on all sides now. But the commotion was waning, it seemed. The action slowing. Fewer fighting? Some men raced down to the hold, upsetting the horses, who whinnied and pranced back and forth. Brutus was screeching, despite his covering, which usually helped him ignore all until he again saw the light.

The men in the hold were speaking Spanish. Searching. For what? For goods? Treasure?

"Mrs. McKintrick," Captain Santiago called,

his voice soothing, gentle. "Please show your-self." He was in the stables. "We have searched the captain's quarters, but I hear you are quite the horsewoman. I wager you are here among them. Come out. I shall not harm you."

What was she to do? It would be only a matter of time until they found her. By the sound of it, there were now ten or more men in the hold, searching. And Santiago was terribly close.

"I am here," she said, rising, dirk in hand.

He blinked in surprise as she rose, shaking off the straw, knowing much still clung to her but ignoring it.

"Have you killed my husband?"

"Not yet," he said. "I do not wish to, but he fights on. His tenacity made me realize that you must be somewhere about too."

"What do you want?"

"Come." He gestured her outward. "Let us speak of this in a more civilized manner."

She hesitated.

His handsome face became stony. "Drop that dagger and come now." He snapped his fingers twice at his shoulder, and a man rushed over. Santiago whispered something in his ear. The man went to another. One stepped over to the gelding nearest Verity and brought a sword under the skittish horse's neck. The other man lifted Brutus's cage.

Santiago looked back to Verity. "Come or I

shall have them kill your falcon. Then one horse at a time as you watch."

He had found her weakness that easily, she thought forlornly.

She dropped her dirk.

Ian, bloody and bruised, fought on beside McKay as they had always done. But there were so many . . .

He brought down a slender man and jerked his head around, thinking he had seen Santiago again.

And he had.

But what the privateer held brought him up short.

Verity. Her beautiful eyes full of sorrow, Santiago's long, curved knife beneath her throat.

The man's eyes were purely on Ian as they neared. "I have seen murder in many a man's eye. 'Tis in yours, Captain McKintrick. I assume you still wish to avenge your brother's death?"

"More than ever. If you did not have a dagger to my wife's throat, I would surely have a dagger to yours."

Santiago considered that. "As I tried to first tell you, I only wish to talk."

Ian let out a humorless laugh and looked around. "You forcibly boarded my ship and have killed three of my men, wounded more."

"We have sustained our own losses," Santiago

returned. "But there is negotiation to be done this night."

"Tell your men to stand down. Release my wife. Then I shall consider *negotiation*," Ian sneered, hands clenching.

Again, Santiago considered him. Finally, he looked over his shoulder and shouted, "Stand down! Men of the *Juliana*! Stand down!" All around them, the Spanish crew took a step back from their adversaries. Santiago shifted his arms around Verity. "Now do the same, Captain."

Gritting his teeth, Ian called, "Men of the *Inverness*, stand down!" Any of his men still warily lifting their weapons immediately obeyed.

With that, Santiago released Verity, and she stumbled into Ian's arms, turning to face the privateer.

Santiago lifted his arms. "Now, may we go and—"

"Here. We shall have this out here," Ian said.

Santiago stared at him, nonplussed. "I never wished for your brother to die. I made too much from him," he said with a soft laugh. "But then he came after me. Boarded *my* ship. Killed five of *my* men. I was not in those waters as a privateer. I had another task at hand, on behalf of the British, despite my Spanish flag. Had he not overtaken us, I would have passed to his starboard side with nothing but a courteous bow." He made a circular motion with his hand.

Ian stared hard at him. Could it be true? It made sense that Duncan had sought retribution when he ran across Santiago again. Seized the moment to make wrongs done to him right. Retribution. Was that not what he, too, sought? And yet had that been Duncan's downfall?

Sorrow crept into the man's dark eyes. "I was on my knees, hands on my head. To my mind, McKintrick—your brother—had bested me. 'Twas his turn to have the upper hand. His turn to empty my hold as an English prize. I'd already lost five men. I did not intend to lose more. As I said, my privateering had been set aside in favor of my new mission. I had a larger task before me, one that promised a greater bounty should I be successful."

Ian's breaths came short and fast as he thought of that fateful night. "And then?"

"And then my mate turned and stabbed your brother," Santiago said with regret. "He'd managed to secure a dagger and, as your brother walked by, succeeded in a death stroke. Your brother's men immediately went after my mate. He died shortly before your brother breathed his last."

While this was not what Duncan's surviving crew reported, there was something in Santiago's manner that made Ian believe him. Had they collectively lied in order to preserve their pride?

Ian swallowed hard. "Did he . . . did my

brother say anything? Before he died, did he say anything?"

Santiago shook his head. "Nay. But he died with dignity. Many of his men wept as he passed. He was well loved."

"Indeed," Ian growled, moving his head back and forth as he often did when working something through in his mind. "She loved him." He gestured to Verity.

Santiago looked swiftly to Verity and then back to Ian. "Her? *Your* wife?"

"She was once my brother Duncan's intended."

"Then I owe you my deepest apologies too, madame," Santiago said. He dropped to one knee, hand on his heart. "As I said, I did not intend for your Duncan to die. I ask your forgiveness that one of my crew ended—"

He stopped abruptly. For in three rapid steps, Ian had savagely drawn a handful of Santiago's hair back and had his sgian dubh to the man's throat.

"Ian!" Verity screamed. "Stop!"

Ian was trembling with rage, concentrating only on Santiago. " 'Tis a pretty story. A pretty apology. Did you truly think 'twould be that simple?"

"Captain," Michael tried, looking around at Santiago's crew, all with weapons in hand again.

But Ian was looking upon Santiago and no one else.

Verity stepped forward, lifting a hand toward her husband but not daring to touch him. "Ian, this man did not kill your brother. 'Twas not him who stole Duncan from us."

"But it was *his* man who did so," he seethed.

"Not on his order," she insisted.

"As God as my witness," Santiago croaked out.

"As God as his witness," she repeated. She took another step closer to him. "I believe him, Ian. Do you not? Deep within, does it not resonate as truth?"

Ian paused. He believed the man, much as he did not wish to do so. He had long dreamed of retribution as the solution.

"You must leave this in God's hands now, Ian. He will see that justice is done, in this life or the next, for whoever was truly responsible."

Ian heaved a great sigh, then stepped away from Santiago. Verity rushed to his side, and he again put a heavy, weary arm about her.

The man let his head drop in relief and then slowly got to his feet and faced them. They shared a long look.

"There is more," Santiago said. "I was sent by the English to capture you. I have done so. But I shall release you if you swear to me that your vendetta ends here. If you shall no longer hold your brother's death against me, then I shall release you and your crew."

"And if I do not?" Ian said wearily.

"Then I shall commandeer this ship, put you all in chains, and take you back to New York, where they shall likely hang the lot of you."

Ian looked down at Verity, and she up at him.

" 'Tis over, is it not?" she asked. "This is not the retribution you sought, but it is a reprieve. Is it not enough? To live on, together, to fight another day?"

Ian paused. What would Duncan have him do? Had he regretted his decisions in those last moments as he lay on deck, dying of his wounds? Thinking of Verity? Ian? Marjorie?

What had a thirst for revenge against Santiago cost him?

Everything.

His present. His future.

"Aye, lass," Ian said at last. " 'Tis enough. 'Tis more than enough."

Ian released her and took one step toward Santiago. "I accept your conditions. On the streets of New York, you need not fear me. But on a new field of battle, do not expect me to spare you."

"Nor I you, *Capitán*," Santiago returned with a genteel tilt of his head and a slight grin. "No doubt you shall soon inform the French of my alliance with the British. That shall leave me with little to do but hunt American privateers. Shall you be considered such?"

"I wager I am one now," Ian allowed, glancing up toward the flag at his mast.

"Then until the next time, Capitán," Santiago said. "*Adiós*."

CHAPTER FORTY-ONE

Keturah and Selah were almost to Charlestown when they spied Mr. Reed ambling along the road, one hand clinging to a rough wooden cross necklace, his somber, lovely baritone frightening birds from the trees to flight as he gestured at the end of each verse. He did not stop singing as Gideon pulled up alongside him.

" 'Love so amazing, so divine. Demands my soul, my life, my all,' " his song coming to an end. He tipped his head toward them at last and reached out to pat the nearest gelding's rump.

"Well done, Mr. Reed," Keturah said with a magnanimous grin. "Your voice is well matched to the beauty of this island."

"You are too kind, Mrs. Covington."

"Not really. I seldom offer idle compliments."

"She does not," Selah affirmed with a small smile. "Would you care for a ride to town?"

"That would be most lovely," he said, climbing onto the seat facing them. "I am off to post some letters home."

"Pity, that," Keturah said as Gideon flicked the reins. "We would have gladly posted them for you."

"I do not mind a walk on this island at all. Look at it!" he said, gesturing to the sea. "That turquoise green. The sway of the palms. The chattering of the monkeys above us." He waved his arms about them. " 'Tis a bit of Eden itself."

"You seem to have a heart for the hymns of Isaac Watts," Selah said.

"An astute observation, Miss Banning. Do you like to sing?"

"Yes, but not as well as you."

"She does play the harpsichord," Keturah put in.

"Again, not as well as I ought."

"Ah, well, it is all sweet to the Savior's ear when one is singing or playing for Him. The point is to be earnest about it. That is what my grandfather always said."

"A point you have clearly taken to heart," Keturah said, with a small grin meant for Selah to catch. They were not laughing at Mr. Reed, 'twas only that they did not quite know what to make of him yet.

"Indeed," he said. "I must ask, though, why might a proper Church of England lady know of Isaac Watts?"

Selah shifted in her seat. It was an understandable question, for in most churches the only singing was likely that of the Psalms. "Your teaching of his other hymn, 'Rock of Ages,' set me to asking about."

"Ahh, I see." Mr. Reed nodded. "Watts does that to a person. His hymns get under one's skin. 'Tis part of the charm of them. Do you know why he writes them?"

"I do not," Selah admitted.

" 'Tis not that he doesn't care for the treasured Psalms. 'Tis because he feels that it restricts a Christian from celebrating all the beauty illuminated in the New Testament as well."

They entered Charlestown. But even as they passed the silversmith, the milliner, the fishmonger, Selah kept thinking about his words. Had she felt that same thing when at service? A longing for something of a New Testament variety in their singing? It rang as truth to her.

Gideon pulled up beside the tiny building where the islanders came to send letters via ships heading out of Charlestown. "You wished to post something, Mr. Reed?"

"Indeed. Thank you for the ride." He clambered down, brushed off his breeches, and straightened his shirt. "To where do you ladies venture?"

"We are picking up new dresses from the tailor and checking on our sister's shop while she is away," Keturah answered. "Would you like to ride back with us?"

"If it is no trouble. But I am well accustomed to walking too. If you do not see me on your way home, please do not tarry on my account."

"Very well, Mr. Reed." She nodded to Gideon,

who snapped the reins, and they were off again.

Selah did not bother to go into the tailor's with Ket, electing instead to wait in the carriage. Keturah cast her a curious look, shrugged, then handed her a parasol so she would not bake in the heat.

Rather than opening it, Selah turned her face up to the sun, thinking about Mr. Reed's seeming delight in everything around him. Every person. Every turn in the road. Every opportunity, whether to post a letter or hoe a trench or dig into a bowl of chowder. Never had she met a man so confounding and yet so . . . so exuberant.

Soon Keturah returned, catching her daydreaming. "Selah, really," she hissed, looking about.

Belatedly, Selah saw that she had drawn the attention of some men passing by. She'd thought Gideon had something caught in his throat, but he had been trying to get her attention. She swallowed hard and resettled herself on the hot bench. "Ready?" she said to Ket. When her sister nodded, she said to Gideon, "To Verity's," then relaxed as they left behind the curious stares of the men.

"Does he have you in such a state?" Keturah asked quietly.

"Whatever do you mean?"

"This Mr. Reed. Is it he who has set you to daydreaming?"

Selah frowned and shifted again in her seat, glad to see Banning's Bridlery coming into view. "Not at all. I only have Verity in mind."

"Mmmhmm," Ket said doubtfully.

"What?" Selah asked, irritated. "Truly!"

"Mmmhmmm," she repeated.

Gideon pulled the carriage to a stop and hopped out to assist the two sisters down. Ket pulled a key from a ribbon at her waist, and they entered the dark, dusty, empty store.

"Do you think she is all right?" Selah asked quietly.

"Knowing Verity, she is more than all right," Ket replied, looking a bit forlorn. "Hopefully she is married by now, if not that very night Ian took her away from us."

Selah walked about the room, remembering it full of saddles and reins and riding hats and more. Of little Abe and his excitement over his "first job as a man" for Miss Verity. Of Trisa and dear, dear Terence . . . She swallowed hard, remembering Angus Shubert. How he had so cruelly taken a man's life, and once again he had escaped punishment. She could only be glad that over the last two months they had run across the man but a couple of times in town. And each time he had all but ignored them.

Which was fine by her. Fine by all of the Covingtons and Bannings. Better to be ignored by Councilman Shubert than targeted and harassed, was it not? Or was the man merely biding his time, finding a way to seek retribution?

Selah turned toward her sister. "Can she . . . Ket, do you believe . . . Might they ever return home?" she asked.

Keturah moved toward her, rested a hand on her shoulder, and ran it down to her elbow. "I hope so. But, Selah, things shall have to change before they will be welcome here again."

Selah met Ket's eyes. "I know."

"In the meantime, we can rest in the fact that she has Ian, who shall look after her. And I would bet she longs for us as much as we long for her. Someday, someway, we shall be reunited."

"Do you believe that?" Selah asked. "Truly?"

"Truly. I have to. Anything else is—" her voice cracked, and she lifted a knuckle to rest beneath her nose—"unthinkable."

Selah nodded and pressed into her arms. The sisters clung together for several long moments. "Someday," Selah repeated. "Someway."

Two weeks after their encounter with Santiago, Verity spent the morning with Ian climbing to the top of the peak on tiny Saba. It was nowhere near the height of Nevis Peak, but it was high enough. Pressing through the palms, she stepped closer to the edge of a cliff. It was here she needed to be. Here that she could look out and see the outline of St. Kitts, and beyond it in the distance, Nevis.

Ian put his hands on her shoulders, and they stood there in silence for a time. She leaned back against his chest, the aching need to see her sisters, Gray, her niece, Philip—all of them—overwhelming her. "Do you think they shall come?"

"I do not know, love," he said softly, wrapping an arm across her upper chest. "I have sent word to them. I do not know if they will risk it. Nor if they should."

She nodded. It was hot, dreadfully hot, and their clothes clung to them. But still, Verity wanted nothing but this. Her husband's touch. And to be this close to home.

"You asked me, with Santiago, if it was enough. The reprieve we were granted. In that moment, I realized that the day was enough. Another day with you, Verity. Another day to see where God might lead us next. Might our being this close to Nevis and yet not seeing your family, only knowing they are there, if we receive word of their well-being . . ." He paused. "Might that be enough? For now?"

Tears slipped down her cheeks at the thought. Of being so close . . . right here, with Nevis in plain sight, and yet possibly not seeing her dear family for a long while still.

She turned in his arms and lifted a hand to his cheek. Glanced out at the glittering water, the Caribbean on one side, the Atlantic on the other.

Far below, the *Inverness* was moored in a little harbor, bobbing on the waves. She could almost feel Nevis behind her like a living, breathing physical force. Part of her past. Part of her present.

But this force in her arms, her husband, was part of her present too. And she knew that he was her future as well.

" 'Tis enough," she said. Then she cast him a small smile. "And yet my sisters shall come. They shall overcome Gray's objections and find a way here, perhaps under cover of darkness. I would wager a gold florin on it."

Ian laughed, leaning back with the force of it. "Ah, Mrs. McKintrick, I would never place a bet against ye if it involved your sisters."

"Wise man," she said, tipping her head up for a kiss.

"Wiser by the day." He pressed his lips to hers. "I married you, did I not? It has only gotten better from there." And then he kissed her again, as if he were trying to make her forget about her sisters altogether.

And yet not succeeding entirely.

They shall come to me, she thought again as they made their way back down the trail. *They shall come.*

HISTORICAL NOTES

In the interest of making it easier on the modern reader, I changed the title of "provost general" to "sheriff" on Nevis—essentially the same role.

Although this novel takes place during the spring and summer of 1775, exports were officially shut down for Americans in December 1775 when the Prohibitory Act was passed in retribution for rebel actions. I imagined there was a gradual "narrowing funnel" in the months before that (giving Ainsley cause to deny Ian permission to export), but that is not based on anything I definitively found in research, only a fictional device.

Smuggling was prevalent in the region before and after the Declaration of Independence. Control of New York Harbor repeatedly switched sides. The Royal Navy controlled entry to the harbor, while the Sons of Liberty controlled the docks. Conditions were tense, war already on the swell, but no formal declaration had been made as the tidal wave rose. Both sides prepared for war, and yet there was still a significant effort to avoid it. As an example, in June of 1775, both General Washington and the new British governor, William Tryon, arrived in New York on the same day. To avoid conflict, Tryon wisely waited until Washington had arrived safely at his inn before landing. My historian consultants agreed it was plausible that with a Loyalist cousin in the city, the McKintricks might have gained access for trade, even *after* the Prohibitory Act was passed. Therefore, we figured it was feasible during the timeline of the novel.

While editing, I discovered it is a Hollywood myth that nautical captains have the power to conduct marriage ceremonies. Indeed, today they need to get a license to do so. But in the eighteenth century, in many parts of the world, marriage was based on "mutual consent," and no one really took issue with this unless one party later claimed fraud. And captains had the authority to be both judge and jury in those days, as well as to execute physical punishment and incarceration if necessary. With those things in mind, I kept the wedding scene as written.

ACKNOWLEDGMENTS

Many thanks to my Bethany editorial team, Raela Schoenherr, Luke Hinrichs, and Kate Deppe, as well as to their fantastic marketing/PR team, including Noelle Chew and Amy Green. Michael Bauer from Akerbeltz Translations helped me with the Gaelic, Chip MacGregor helped me with the French. Lt. Colonel John Roche gave me early historical feedback when I was just starting to think through *Verity*'s plot, and the amazing Revolutionary War historian Karen Quinones gave me comprehensive and detailed feedback later on to help me make this novel as historically accurate as possible (while still exercising some fictional license). If you're into history or want to know more about spies during the Revolutionary War, Karen offers wonderful walking tours in New York (PatriotToursNYC.com). It was a highlight of my trip!

ABOUT THE AUTHOR

Lisa T. Bergren is the acclaimed author of *Keturah*, Book One in THE SUGAR BARON'S DAUGHTERS series. Lisa has published more than fifty books with combined sales exceeding three million copies. A recipient of the RT Lifetime Achievement Award, she's also the author of the Christy Award-winning *Waterfall*, RITA-finalist *Firestorm*, bestselling *God Gave Us You*, as well as several historical series such as HOMEWARD and GRAND TOUR. Lisa lives in Colorado with her husband and three big kids—one of whom just got married—and a fluffy white Terrier who makes her walk once in a while rather than just sit around and write. To learn more, visit www.lisatbergren.com.

| Books are produced in the United States using U.S.-based materials | Books are printed using a revolutionary new process called THINKtech™ that lowers energy usage by 70% and increases overall quality | Books are durable and flexible because of Smyth-sewing | Paper is sourced using environmentally responsible foresting methods and the paper is acid-free |

Center Point Large Print

600 Brooks Road / PO Box 1
Thorndike, ME 04986-0001 USA

(207) 568-3717

US & Canada:
1 800 929-9108
www.centerpointlargeprint.com